BLIND SWITCH

Michael Sova

Dedication:

This is for Michael and Samantha. You continually amaze me with your wealth of talents and abilities, and you make me proud every day of my life. Thank you for taking after your mother. That was a wise choice.

-1-

He squinted into the darkness, trying to determine if the tiny point of light he'd just noticed was from a passing ship, a distant island, or a faint star sitting low on the horizon. It was of no consequence, and Scott Fisher finally turned his attention back to the Selfie Stick he'd positioned on the balcony railing. His smart phone camera app was ready for business, but he had no intention of taking any pictures, certainly not of himself. It was for surveillance purposes only, and with the tool fully extended, he had a clear view into the adjoining cabin.

So far, his assignment had gone off without a hitch. He'd spent the better part of a week biding his time, casually monitoring his target, relaxing, keeping a low profile—something he always did as a matter of course—and enjoying the sunshine, hot days, and dozens upon dozens of scantily clad women. There'd been some beautiful scenery for sure. That was a nice perk but he was anxious to be done. He believed he was minutes away from completing the mission and couldn't imagine anything stopping him now.

Fisher knew he still couldn't drop his guard. Even with the screen dimmed to the lowest brightness setting, the phone's display stood out in sharp contrast to the nighttime sky. If the target glanced towards his open balcony door at the wrong moment.... He probably still wouldn't realize what was about to happen but he could become curious and that might make him more alert. It wouldn't save him. It could, however, present complications. Fisher wanted to avoid that if possible. He slid the Selfie Stick a few inches to the side where it and the phone could no longer be seen.

He popped a chocolate-covered strawberry into his mouth and propped his feet on a small plastic end table. He was looking forward to the next couple days when he had no responsibilities at all. Well, there'd be a few small tasks to complete but he'd really just be going through the motions. He'd no longer have anything or anyone to fear. And once he was home? He supposed he'd have to figure out what to do with the fifty thousand dollars he was being paid. Fisher had half of it already, and he'd deposited the money in three different banks. That was probably overly cautious but why take chances? And when he had the rest? He'd bank some, pay off a few debts, and maybe use the remainder to book another cruise, strictly for pleasure next time. Those bikini babes could be a lot more entertaining if he had more freedom of movement. He had a sudden vision of a long-haired redhead he'd seen earlier that day. She'd given him the eye, her enormous breasts barely contained by a tiny leopard print top.

Fisher quickly stood and leaned against the railing, shaking his head to clear the image. The distraction was nice but this was not the time or place. He could fantasize all he wanted once the job was over. Until then, he owed it to the client to remain vigilant. He sat and again used his phone to check on his neighbor. Nothing had changed.

Since departing from New York Harbor, Martin Reginald had been the picture of predictability, especially when it came to his evening routine. He ate early, attended a show, visited the Pioneer Lounge where he stayed long enough to consume two rum and Cokes, and then returned to his room. He typically drank and dined alone, and always left the lounge at about the same time regardless.

His daytime practices were a bit more varied. That actually worked out well because it meant no one would expect to see him at a particular place or time. He didn't seem to have any real friends onboard either, just the types of casual acquaintances people make when traveling. Fisher was told that would be the case but it was still good to have verification. When, the following day, Reginald didn't show up for breakfast, or to walk laps around the deck, or to hit golf balls into a net, no one was likely to raise the alarm. Nothing could be done about that anyway. Fisher would do what he could to make everything appear natural and normal. Beyond that, it was really out of his hands. He'd be in the clear, and that was what mattered.

Once back in his cabin each night, Martin Reginald was about as interesting as drying paint. He always changed into the same pair of red plaid pajama pants. He'd then stretch out on the small couch with a paperback copy of *Mississippi Blood* by Greg Iles and read until eleven o'clock. Then, like he had a timer set, he'd close his book, spend a couple minutes in the bathroom, and then get into bed and turn off the lights. He conveniently kept the curtains open all the time, and that made it ridiculously easy to keep tabs on him.

It was ten to eleven now, and Fisher knew it would soon be time to make his move. He was glad he'd be doing it under the cover of darkness. It wasn't that he was afraid of being spotted. The private balconies were completely secluded. He knew that, if he'd wanted to, he could prance around naked in broad daylight and no one would be the wiser. Maybe he'd do a little victory dance to celebrate when the time was right. For now, though, he had to try to ignore his increasing heart rate and concentrate on his work.

Only about 8 inches separated his balcony from Reginald's. However, he was on the tenth floor; and while traversing those few inches, he'd be hanging what he estimated was about a hundred feet above the water. He wasn't afraid of heights, at least not in a clinical sense, but glancing over the railing did make his feet tingle. The trick was to not look down. Thankfully, he couldn't see as much at night anyway and that made what he was about to do somewhat easier to stomach.

Fisher worked his hands into a pair of black nylon gloves. He wasn't concerned with leaving fingerprints but wanted to make damn sure he had a good grip in those few critical moments. He stood and flexed his fingers, noticing the faint sounds of big band music floating up from one of the lounges a floor or two below. He paused to listen. The song might have been *Take the "A" Train* but he couldn't tell for sure, not over the low, steady thrum of the big diesel engines. Otherwise, the night was nearly silent.

It was strange. Between the guests and the crew, there had to be close to five thousand people aboard the Explorer, the newest ship in the Island cruise line. In addition to the numerous bars, lounges and night clubs, there were three pools, a giant waterslide, a bowling alley, a movie theater, a casino, a luxury spa, a fitness center, and ten different restaurants, buffets and snack bars. There were activities and various forms of entertainment all around him. Yet, right then, he felt like he was almost alone in the world. The only other person that mattered was Martin Reginald, and he wouldn't matter much longer.

Fisher again extended the Selfie Stick. This, he knew, was the riskiest part of the operation. He had to be ready to move as soon as Reginald did, and that meant watching him closely for the final few minutes. The scene was unchanged, Reginald facing the balcony doors with his book open in front of him. It would have been nice if, just this once, he'd turned the other way. Chances were good the bright reading light over his head would make it difficult to distinguish much of anything outside. That included smart phone display screens, but Fisher did not like leaving things to happenstance. He stared intently, tensed to yank the phone away if Reginald's eyes so much as flickered his way.

As he looked on, Reginald flipped a page, yawned and scratched his crotch. *Beautiful,* Fisher thought, thankful his target was reading a mystery novel and not soft porn or something else that might inspire him to do more than scratch. Honestly, though, such indulgences would have been shocking coming from someone so incredibly dull.

Fisher hadn't really known what to expect but he'd expected something. After all, the guy was famous. He might not be internationally renowned but definitely had a strong following in America. All his books were immediate bestsellers. Passengers aboard the Island Explorer had been mixing and mingling with an honest to goodness celebrity and none of them had a clue. Maybe that was for the better. It wouldn't do Reginald's reputation any good if word got out he was a drip. He'd soon be making headlines for another reason anyway, and as a result, Fisher bet his sales would skyrocket. Too bad his next novel would never see the light of day.

Checking the time once more, he inspected the drawstring bag at his feet to make sure it held everything he would need. Reginald continued to read, and Scott Fisher continued to try to shake the strange feeling he'd had for days that something about the scene was... wrong.

Authors, he understood, weren't as recognizable as some other public figures. And when Reginald traveled under the name of Martin R. Worth, as he was doing now, it seemed he was as inconspicuous as any other sunscreen slathered tourist. Fisher could appreciate that. There was a good deal to be said for anonymity, and he knew from long experience it was difficult to remain focused on a particular task if you were always worried about being recognized, or worse, approached. Curiously, though, that was the very thing that had been bothering him about Reginald.

As was customary, he'd received a complete dossier on the man weeks before the assignment began. It contained photos, a detailed biography, and information about his personal habits. That was how Fisher had learned about the annual *working vacations*. Reginald always went on a cruise, always traveled alone and always, at least according to the reports, used the time to work on his next novel. It all sounded reasonable enough. However, they'd be back in New York Harbor in just over two and a half days and, up to that point, the guy had barely worked at all. He had a Macbook computer with him. He'd only taken it out of its carrying bag twice and didn't use it for more than a few minutes either time. Why?

Fisher had a couple theories. He'd certainly been given bad information before. Maybe that was the case with Reginald. Or, with all the pressure that came from success, maybe he was just burned out and wanted to do nothing more than relax and drink his rum and Coke. Fisher didn't know but thought the whole thing smelled funny

Not my problem, he decided, getting to his feet. He couldn't dwell on it anymore anyway. Martin Reginald had closed his book and was headed for the john. Time for Fisher to make his move.

-2-

"Wow. You guys seem like you're in a good mood tonight. Everyone enjoy Nassau?"

While the audience applauded, Freddie Franco took a long sip of what looked like bottled water but was actually straight vodka. He savored the burn as he waited for the noise to subside.

"Beautiful, right? I love the Bahamas so much I come back every week."

That got a chuckle, which was all the joke was worth.

"And how about the Island Explorer? Have you enjoyed your time aboard?"

That got a good reaction but he stopped and made a face like the crowd hadn't responded.

"You guys sound tired all of a sudden. What's wrong? You haven't been getting enough to eat?"

Big laugh there because they all knew the ship was a floating feed trough. Most of the audience had just come from dinner and, as soon as the show was over, many of them would head straight for the colossal chocolate extravaganza buffet. Freddie's eyes fell on the two women seated front and center. They both wore brightly colored sun dresses that could have passed for hot air balloons. He pitied the fool that got between them and their chocolate, not that he really had much to say.

As a performer, he didn't have the same access to the never-ending food supply as the paying customers. Still, after nine weeks at sea, he'd put on enough extra pounds that he was really starting to feel it. Freddie had never been much for gyms and fitness centers but knew he had to at least start walking more or he'd turn into a fat slob. He was already pale-skinned, short and balding. He didn't need a weight problem too.

"Yeah," he said, taking another quick sip and then screwing the cap back on the bottle. "Cruises are awesome. It's nice to get away from home and be pampered for a little while. And, you got the great weather, the fresh air, the open sea; and let's not forget about the casino. Anyone hit it big yet?"

Right on cue, there was an enthusiastic shriek from the darkest corner of the room. To Freddie, it sounded contrived, which it was. The cruise director, a sickeningly bubbly blonde named China, had worked it out ahead of time because she thought it would be good for business. The shrieker was another cruise line employee. There was little chance anyone would recognize her because she spent most of her time in the laundry room. She'd already exited the lounge anyway.

"Hey, that's great," Freddie said, "I hope you all hit the jackpot before we get back to New York the day after tomorrow. And if any of you ladies want to hit the jackpot tonight, just come see me after the show." He waggled his eyebrows suggestively to a chorus of cheers, whistles and laughter.

"Relax guys," he went on. "I'm a happily married man. In fact, my wife and I just celebrated our thirteenth anniversary."

That was total bullshit. He wasn't married and never had been. However, Island had strict rules about what they called *fraternizing* with the guests. To be blunt, he'd get canned if he was caught messing around with the passengers. Some women did make advances, quite a few actually, and that's why he always threw in the line about the anniversary. It helped create a little more distance. And just because the customers were hands off, that didn't mean he couldn't be "hands on" with the staff. He'd spent a couple minutes with laundry girl before he went on stage. There might have been a little spark there. If he played his cards right, maybe she'd treat him to a private spin cycle later on.

"Are there a lot of married people here tonight?"

Applause.

"How about happily married?"

Applause mixed with hoots and laughter.

"It's tough," Freddie said. "I read that three out of every five marriages end in divorce. That's sad. I mean, you've really got to feel for those other two couples. 'Til death do us part? No thanks. Not unless one of us is gonna die young.

"I'm kidding. Marriage is great. You just have to learn how to communicate. When you hit a rough patch you gotta work through it. It's worth it in the end. And you know what? It just so happens that I found the key to the perfect marriage. Anyone want to know what it is?

"Yeah?

"Okay. I'm going to let you in on my secret. If you do this, I can pretty much guarantee your marriage will last forever. It's simple too. Spend forty weeks a year on a cruise ship and leave the spouse at home."

The audience roared. Freddie knew his punch line was predictable and not especially witty but the alcohol was flowing and the 18 plus crowd was eager to be entertained. He was only too happy to oblige. He uncapped his bottle, raised it in a toast, and took a swig, reveling in the rush that always came with one of his really strong performances.

It began the moment he stepped onto the darkened stage, the theme song from "Peter Gunn" thumping through the speakers. He positioned himself with his back to the crowd, clouds of fog swirling around him as the music faded and the spotlight came on. This was the only part of the show that was truly choreographed and Freddie made the most of it. He hunched his shoulders, giving the audience a good look at his silver spangled, high collared, black leather jacket. And as the applause subsided, he started mimicking the movements of Andrew Dice Clay in his classic entrance. Freddie jerked his head to one side then the other, and then reached all the way over his head to scratch his neck. That was supposed to be the giveaway; and when much of the crowd started laughing he knew they'd clued in to what he was doing. He went through the motions of lighting a cigarette, his body language deliberate, quick and aggressive.

Thanks to the careful placement of the spotlight, he knew he could only be seen from the waist up, until he spun around and all the lights came on, revealing his pink bathing trunks, Hello Kitty sunglasses and Tweety Bird t-shirt. His *cigarette* lighter was actually a Scooby-Doo Pez dispenser. Freddie popped a Pez and tossed the dispenser into the crowd. The final piece of his ensemble was a pair of bright orange, over-sized swim fins. He couldn't walk on stage with the swim fins on, not without looking like a moron, so he positioned them ahead of time and that helped him know exactly where to stand. It all went off like clockwork. Everyone laughed, pointed and cheered. Freddie gave them a minute. Then, in his best Jersey accent, he grabbed the mic and said, "So what the fuck are you lookin' at?" With that, he was off and rolling.

He removed his jacket and kicked the swim fins to the side, but Freddie kept the cartoon shades on for a while, knowing how ridiculous they looked on a middle-aged man, especially one built like him.

Starting with his opening line, the energy in the room had been palpable and he wanted to ride that wave every second he could. He went through his standard forty-five minute routine, spending a good part of it making fun of his fictitious wife. He did some observational humor as well, and a little crowd interaction before finally returning to the subject of the cruise ship.

"Cruises are awesome," he said. "Especially with Island. And you know what I like best? This is gonna sound weird so bear with me.

Better than the food, the sun, the scenery and all the rest, I love that there are no birds."

Confused chuckle.

"That probably sounds nuts but I'm dead serious. Think about it. We were at sea all day. Anyone see any birds anywhere? You don't have to check with your neighbor. The answer is no. You're still looking at me like I'm off my rocker so let me explain. I know we got a bunch of people here from New York City."

Enthusiastic applause.

"Yeah. I'm from New York too, but I live out in the country. Let me tell you. It's a totally different ballgame. I'm talking rolling hills, open pastures, dairy farms: the whole deal. And you know what those things all have in common? They're quiet. Don't get me wrong. I love the Big Apple but it's noisy. The city that never sleeps? Sure. Because it's too fucking loud."

Freddie stalked from one end of the stage to the other. Nearly everyone was laughing or at least smiling, but he could tell they weren't quite following him yet. That was fine. In fact, it's exactly what he wanted. A big part of what made a joke funny was that element of surprise; that and timing. That's why the setup was crucial.

"When I'm home," he went on, "there's nothing I like better than listening to that stillness. No traffic or blaring music or construction or any of that shit. I love to lie in bed in the morning and just soak it in. But here's what happens. As soon as the sun starts to rise--and keep in mind, I work nights, I don't do fucking sunrises--but as soon as the sun starts to come up, this little damn bird sets up shop in a tree right outside my bedroom window. I always know the second he gets there because he announces it to the world. Then he keeps announcing it every five seconds for the next three freaking hours.

"**HELLO! HELLO! HELLO! HELLO!**"

Freddie flapped his arms and bobbed his head up and down. "I don't know if that's what he's saying. Maybe he's telling me I'm an asshole. I just know it's annoying and it never stops. I swear I'm not making this up either. It's every time I'm home and it seems like it's been going on for years. It can't be the same bird. I don't think they live that long so I figure it's some sort of family tradition they keep passing down from generation to generation. I can picture the mama bird up in the nest, teaching her little bird brats the ways of the world. *Okay, kids. This is how you fly. This is how you catch a worm. This is how you annoy the hell out of the jackass that lives in the house over there."*

Freddie paused. Out of the corner of his eye, he saw the two cows in the front row. They were laughing so hard they both looked ready to piss themselves. It wasn't an attractive sight but at least he knew he was hitting the mark.

"It's crazy," he said. "And it happens every damn morning. You ever wonder what idea birds are trying to convey when they chirp or peep or caw or whatever the fuck it is they're doing? I know one thing. They're not very good at it because they never get their point across the first time. They keep going and going. It doesn't even matter if there are any other birds around. I don't get it. It reminds me of this girl I used to date. We were together for three years. She talked constantly and never said one fucking thing of consequence.

"Sure. Go ahead and laugh. It wasn't your life she was destroying. But," he raised a finger, "I bet you know exactly the type of person I'm talking about. If you didn't actually date her you probably worked with her at some point because she's standard equipment in any office setting. You usually find her at the reception desk or maybe in human resources. She's always the first one there in the morning, and she's so bright and cheerful and inquisitive that you just want to grab her tongue, yank it all the way out of her mouth and staple it to her forehead."

Freddie picked up his bottle, saw that it was empty and tossed it aside. An attractive brunette sitting at one of the tables near the stage noticed and held out her glass to him. He was tempted to take it, but the main reason he refused her offer with a smile and a shake of the head was because that sort of impromptu interaction could send his whole routine off course and he was nearing the end.

"I used to have a desk job," he said, picking up the pace of his delivery. "It was a long time ago. I got out because I couldn't stand it anymore. I sold home security systems and I spend eight hours a day in a little cubical about the size of a fucking microwave oven. I had a chair, a phone, a desk, and a computer. That was it, unless you count Brandi, the human resources person from hell. My ex-girlfriend was bad but Brandi was about a million times worse. She was a cross between a stalker and one of those greeters at fucking Disney World or somewhere. You know what I mean? It was like she was friendly but so in your face about it that it totally creeps you out. She had one of those little tiny voices too. It's sort of cute at first but, after like five minutes, you just want to step on her neck and crush her larynx.

"I see you guys nodding. You never met Brandi before; at least I hope not, but you know who I'm talking about. Every office has one.

She never calls in sick. She pops up everywhere you try to go, and she inserts herself into the middle of every conversation. Here's a typical day right here.

"You take the fire stairs all the way to the fifteenth floor in hopes you can sneak in the back and make it to your desk before she realizes you're there. You wait just outside the door and you listen. Then, when you don't hear anything, you ease it open."

Freddie goes through the motions, tip-toeing up an imaginary staircase and then cupping a hand to one ear.

"This is the moment of truth. Still hearing nothing, you think the coast is clear so you poke your head through. Everything looks good so you take a breath, step into the hall. And she's on you like a raging case of hemorrhoids.

"Good morning, Freddie. I see you took the stairs again. I don't know how you do it. I wish I had that much energy. It's all I can do to drag myself out of bed. Hey, did you hear about Jan? She's taking a different job? Can you believe it? We've shared an office for-EVER! Why would she want to leave? Do you think we should have a going away party? We need to at least have a cake, right? I'm happy to arrange it. Will you chip in? Of course you will. Do you like cake? How silly of me. Everybody likes cake. What's your favorite flavor? I absolutely adore red velvet. I went out for dessert over the weekend and had this scrumptious red velvet cake with this amazing raspberry filling. Oh my god. It was to die for. We definitely need to do that. I wonder if that place delivers. I doubt it. Do you know any good bakeries nearby? I should ask Tina. She got married last fall and I think she got her cake from that place over on Wilson. I heard it was really good. I didn't get to try it because I wasn't invited. I know Tina wanted to invite me but weddings are so expensive these days. Can you believe it? Anyway, you've got to draw the line somewhere. I totally understand. Have you ever been married, Freddie? I know you were dating that one girl. She was so sweet. What was her name again? You are still together, right? You really should settle down and tie that big old knot. It's no fun going through life alone. Do you know what I mean? I can't wait until my wedding. I've got the church and reception hall all picked out. All I need to do now is pick that perfect Mr. Right to come along and make an honest woman out of me."

While Freddie was talking, his voice high-pitched and breathless, he went to the edge of the stage, grabbed a chair and dragged it to the middle. He then mimicked fashioning a noose which he looped over his head. He climbed onto the chair, crossed himself and jumped.

"I wish," he said, pushing the chair off to the side once more, "I was exaggerating but that's exactly the kind of crap I had to listen to every day. I couldn't avoid her. She'd be flapping her gums and all I'd want to do was run to my office and slam the door, except I couldn't do that because I worked in a cubical! I had no door and nowhere to hide. My co-workers were no help either. They'd hear us coming--correction--they'd hear her coming, and they'd all pick up their phones and act like they were busy.

"Don't get me wrong," he said, holding up a hand. "I didn't blame them. I'd rather throw myself on a landmine then listen to one more of her endless, worthless and totally fucking pointless stories."

Freddie paused and made a face like he'd just had a horrible thought. "I probably should have asked this before but is there anyone from the human resources department with us tonight?" He had several responses ready if the answer was yes but his question elicited nothing but hoots and more laughter.

"That's good," he said. "So no one will be offended when I tell you how I finally killed the bitch."

A pale-skinned man at a nearby table laughed so hard he started choking on his drink.

"You okay, buddy?" Freddie asked. "I've already got one death on my conscience. I don't need another one.

"Of course I'm kidding. To the best of my knowledge, Brandi is still alive and well and driving everyone around her nuts. Thankfully, it's no longer my problem. I got fired."

Chorus of sympathetic noises.

"Don't give me that shit. It was all for the best. I wasn't doing my work anyway. The boss would come in and I'd be sitting there at my tiny little desk, staring into space. I'm sure she thought I was on drugs or something but I was busy planning the perfect murder. I would have gone through with it too. I didn't even care about getting caught. A life sentence in a maximum security prison would be a day at a nude beach compared to five more minutes trapped in an office with her. They'd drag me away in handcuffs and my co-workers would all be jealous because I was the one getting out. I'm serious. And I'll tell you the one thing that stopped me from grabbing my ornamental letter opener and using it to cut her head off. I was petrified I'd hack my way through that last bit of bone and gristle, kick her head down the hall and then watch it bounce off every step of the fire stairs from the fifteenth floor all the way down to the fucking basement. And she'd never stop talking!

"*Did I do something to upset you, Freddie?* BOUNCE!

"*I don't understand why you found it necessary to cut my head off.* BOUNCE!

"*Does this trail of blood and spinal fluid make my butt look big?* BOUNCE!"

Freddie clamped his hands over his ears. "That's what I was afraid would happen and that's why I never acted on my evil impulses. I can't help wondering if somebody did, though. They killed her. She was reincarnated and she came back as that bird that's outside my window every fucking morning. That, my friends, is why I spend forty weeks a year on a cruise ship. No birds and no HR department.

"I gotta get outta here. You guys have been awesome. Have a great night and enjoy the rest of your time aboard the Island Explorer. Thank you."

Freddie bowed, waved, and left the stage to enthusiastic applause. Normally, he'd head right for the bar at the back of the lounge. There were always people there eager to meet him, shake his hand, and buy him a drink. As an employee, he didn't have to pay as much for his beverages as the regular cruise passengers but the prices were still exorbitant and it was nice to let someone else pick up the tab once in a while. Sometimes, though, the alcohol went down a lot easier in solitude. As Lonesome George famously sang, "You know when I drink alone, I prefer to be by myself."

Freddie's routine was a lot more autobiographical than most people would probably guess. They took him at his word when he said he was married but assumed the rest of the story was fiction. In reality, he'd only changed a few minor details. He sold insurance instead of home security systems, and the horrible HR person was actually a customer service representative named Brenda. She wasn't as bad as he'd let on either. In truth, he'd fallen for her hard, and quit his job once he realized his feelings were not nor would they ever be returned. That was ancient history by now but the pain of rejection was still as fresh as ever. Turning Brenda into Brandi and making her the butt of so many jokes was meant to be a form of therapy. He figured it would help him get over her once and for all. Instead, each telling of the story picked at that old wound until it was raw and bleeding. It was fine when the lights were on and the audience laughed and cheered. But once the stage was dark and quiet, the performance rush left him faster than a callous woman can break your heart.

The best thing, Freddie knew, was to come up with some new material and an entirely different routine. That was the only way to put the past behind him. He'd been meaning to do it but never seemed to have the mental energy it required. He wasn't about to tackle it tonight either, nor would he seek out the lovely laundry girl. She probably wasn't interested anyway and he was no longer in the mood. He'd return to his cabin, retrieve another bottle of 'water' from his private stash, and then find a deck chair and some out of the way place where he could sit and contemplate his sad excuse for a life.

-3-

Traversing the few inches to the adjoining balcony proved even easier than Fisher anticipated, the entire process taking less than ten seconds. He still wished he could have utilized the connecting door but it was dead-bolted from both sides. He was no stranger to locks or lock picks. If he put his mind to it, he knew he could have dealt with both barriers in short order. Two things stood in his way. The first was practicality. There was no way he could pick a lock and keep an eye on his neighbor at the same time. That wasn't a big deal because he wouldn't have to actually open the door until he was damn sure Reginald wasn't around. However, Fisher had also been instructed that he was not to leave a trail. He could use picks but he wasn't an expert. He might leave scratches or other telltale signs. Depending on the quality and intensity of the investigation—and there would be an investigation soon enough—something like that could come back to bite him in the ass. He couldn't take that chance or he too might end up as shark food.

The high railing was the only real problem. For obvious reasons, the cruise line didn't want people climbing up or hanging over. Fisher had to do both. He looked at the plastic end table but doubted it was sturdy enough to support his two hundred pound frame. Smashed furniture wasn't a good idea if he wanted to continue to fly under the radar. So, he grabbed the railing with both hands and boosted himself up high enough that he was able to lock his elbows. He was sure Reginald was still in the bathroom but he leaned out and peered around just to be safe. The room was empty, the reading lamp still on, as was one of the wall mounted lights over the bed. It was now or never.

Fisher swung his right leg over so he was straddling the railing and facing the narrow dividing wall. He paused to balance himself; then, clutching the wall with one hand and the railing with the other, he swung his leg again. He now had his right leg on Reginald's side, his left leg on his own, the dividing wall in his face and a hundred foot fall at his back. Against his better judgment, he couldn't resist the urge to glance down. The water looked peaceful, swirls of white and blue foam sliding away silently into the night. It didn't look like too far of a drop either. That illusion would change in an instant if he lost his grip and plunged to his almost certain death. Even in daylight, he knew the chance of safely recovering a passenger who'd fallen from the tenth floor was slim at best. And in the dark with no one around to call for help? He'd have better odds of winning the Power Ball jackpot. Fisher was actually counting on that. His job, after all, was to make Martin Reginald disappear.

Exposed as he now was, he could feel the ocean breeze plucking at his thin jacket. He'd tucked the drawstring bag inside and, for a moment, thought it might fall out the bottom. He couldn't free one of his hands to grab it so he pressed himself even tighter against the wall, smashing his crotch in the process. Fisher swore, shifted his weight and slid safely onto Reginald's balcony. He was still breathing normally so his nuts seemed blessedly undamaged. Thank goodness for small favors.

He stepped forward and pushed the sliding glass door smoothly aside. He had a Slim Jim in his bag but would have been surprised if he'd needed it. Why lock a door when the only access point is a private tenth floor balcony? *I'm about to show you*, Fisher thought, moving quickly and silently toward the closed bathroom door.

Martin Reginald dropped a piece of dental floss into the trash can and squeezed Aquafresh onto his toothbrush. He started on his lower teeth, studying his reflection in the small mirror over the sink. He noticed recently that he'd started to gray at the temples. He wasn't dismayed by that. He actually thought it made him look more serious and literary, especially when paired with the prescription-less eye glasses he always wore on one of his book tours. Thankfully, with the exception of a few telephone interviews, his promotional schedule had been fairly light of late. That would change in a big way a few months down the road when the next book was released.

Reginald sighed and spit a blob of bluish goo into the sink. He enjoyed the spotlight and the ego boost a book tour provided. It also became a grind after a while; and each media tour seemed a little longer and more grueling than the last. On the plus side, his fame, such as it was, had opened some doors. It was odd, though. He'd receive hundreds of flattering emails and tweets following his interview with Terry Gross on NPR's *Fresh Air,* yet he could stroll down 5th Avenue or pretty much any other major thoroughfare any day of the week without anyone showing a spark of recognition. There were exceptions of course. The week before, he'd been cornered in a Starbuck's by a trio of adoring NYU students. For the most part, though, he was anonymously famous—a name without a face. In some ways, that was kind of the point of the whole thing. Being too recognized, too scrutinized would inevitably lead to problems.

Despite the precautions, Reginald suspected it would still come to a head sooner or later. It almost had to. And when that day came? He might lose a fat paycheck but wasn't risking all that much otherwise. It could be a different story for the movers and shakers at Tower Brothers Publishing. Then again, they'd probably dealt with similar situations before and had a contingency plan already in place. That, no doubt, was why Reginald had been given such specific instructions on how to handle himself. It seemed unnecessary to the point of paranoia. They were protecting their investment. He got that, but what difference would it really make if the truth came out? Why all the secrecy? Reginald had asked those questions on several occasions but never received a satisfactory answer. He knew he had a good thing going but also knew there were no guarantees and absolutely nothing to be gained from rocking the boat so he'd eventually let it drop.

On that proverbial note, he was glad the cruise was nearly at an end. He certainly enjoyed the annual trips. He just would have liked them better if he were able to be more himself. He would have preferred to spend more time at the bar, more time in the casino, and a whole lot less time worrying about keeping up appearances. He hadn't been recognized once, at least not as far as he knew, so again, what was the big deal?

Ours is not to question why, he thought, still studying his reflection. He had his part to play, and as long as he did so the gravy train should keep chugging along. All things considered, he could do a lot worse.

The first seven or eight Martin Reginald novels had been straight-up thrillers, mainstream and predictable. They all featured the same protagonist, a retired cop with a vigilante streak. He went after rapists, sadists, serial killers, pedophiles, one necrophiliac rodeo clown, and all manner of other deviants, and with no legal code to bind him, he was free to dole out the satisfying brand of fictional justice the bad guys deserved and fans of the genre both expected and adored.

In terms of true "literature," those early books were neither groundbreaking nor memorable. However, they were written with a style and flare that helped separate them from the pack. Even so, the series had sort of run its course. The last couple novels sold just as many units but the enthusiasm level seemed to have tailed off. The Tower Brothers brain trust recognized that and decided it was time to take Martin Reginald's career in a new direction. He was skeptical at first, but now believed he might be on the verge of something momentous.

Unlike prior releases, the newer books dealt with real issues. In *Deepwater Deception,* the first book in a new Martin Reginald trilogy, an explosion aboard an oil rig leads to a fire and a catastrophic spill that lasts five months and dumps over two hundred million gallons of crude oil into the Gulf of Mexico, the largest accidental marine spill since the advent of the petroleum industry.

By now, going on a decade after the fact, most people were at least casually aware of the details surrounding the BP Deepwater Horizon disaster of 2010. It was a huge story that remained in the headlines far beyond the average news cycle. Once the gusher was finally capped, a full eighty-seven days after it started spewing toxins into the marine ecosystem, media coverage shifted to the lengthy cleanup, the dead and dying wildlife, the impact on local economies, and the billions upon billions of dollars in legislation.

No one would be interested in a retelling of such a familiar tale, so *Deepwater Deception* took that story and gave it a devious twist. The entire event, according to the novel, was an act of sabotage. The poorly trained and barely qualified safety inspector who missed so many obvious signs of pending disaster was being paid by the same person responsible for the defective cement used on the well. In essence, the calamity that killed eleven people and destroyed or severely damaged untold numbers of lives, businesses, and property was not only malicious but manufactured.

At the novel's conclusion, the finger points firmly at Olivia Gerhart, the top executive at NOS, or Natural Oil Solutions, a rapidly growing green energy provider and one of the largest international competitors to British Petroleum and every other oil company. But could a staunch environmentalist really mastermind such a malevolent scheme? That's how it appeared. Then, in *Deepwater Denial*, the second book in the series, the investigation takes a startling turn and begins focusing more on Charles Briggs, an unscrupulous real estate developer with serious political aspirations.

Following a sluggish start, *Deepwater Deception* gained some traction and climbed to No. 14 on the *New York Times* bestseller's list. *Deepwater Denial* was currently No. 7 with indications it could go higher. And already, more than six months in advance of the anticipated release date, there was some serious industry buzz surrounding *The Well from Hell*, the final installment in the series, and speculation it could debut at No. 1. That would be a first for Reginald but he tried not to think about it. He knew how strong the first two books were and, based on that, believed the third might have true blockbuster potential. He felt stirrings of pride in spite of himself.

Reginald rinsed his mouth, spit, then capped his toothbrush and placed it on the small vanity. He caught his reflection again and saw that he was smiling. It was stupid really. With so many different people involved: agents, publicists, marketers, graphic designers, publishers, editors, researchers and the like, he sometimes felt like he was little more than a single cog in one giant mother of a machine. Still, whether he deserved the credit or not, he was the face of the franchise and he figured he may as well enjoy the ride for however long it lasted. He squared his shoulders, gazed into the mirror with the most literary expression he could muster, and then broke into a goofy grin before turning and reaching for the light switch.

Scott Fisher had already turned the rest of the room's lights off so, even if he hadn't been paying close attention, he still would have noticed when the thin strip of light under the bathroom door suddenly winked out. Of course he had been paying attention. He'd been poised and ready for the past five minutes. He'd heard Reginald gargling, spitting and, at one point, it sounded like he might have been talking to himself. Fisher had already decided authors were loopy so that didn't really come as much of a surprise.

He'd noted that the bathroom door opened inward which meant Fisher couldn't hide behind it. That would have been his preference because it would make it so easy for him to make his move without any risk of being seen. The layout of Reginald's cabin didn't allow for that at all.

Like any standard hotel room, the bathroom faced a plain wall in a narrow hallway. Reginald could go left into the room's interior, or right where he'd face the main cabin door. In his pajamas and ready for bed, he'd obviously head left. Fisher's first thought was to position himself on the opposite side, between the bathroom and the door to the hall. Reginald probably wouldn't even glance that way. However, even at eleven o'clock at night, the hallway was well lit and some light did filter in around the door frame. Fisher doubted it was enough for him to cast any noticeable shadows, especially with Reginald emerging from a brightly lit bathroom. Still, he didn't think he should risk it. This had to be quick and quiet, and that meant he needed the element of surprise.

Wherever he stood, Fisher knew he'd be more exposed than he liked. The only real hiding spot was the closet, but like nearly everything else in the room, it was a little smaller than normal and he doubted he could have fit inside even if he'd tried. He never considered it anyway. Judging from his own cabin, he already knew the closet doors were tough to open. Fisher assumed they were designed that way intentionally due to the possibility of rough seas and the need to keep everything as secure as possible.

The closet was also around the corner from the bathroom and only about eighteen inches from the edge of the queen-size bed. That made for tight quarters to say the least. He imagined what it would be like to try to extricate himself from there and decided he may as well just wear a bell around his neck to announce his arrival.

Having no better options, he waited directly in front of the bathroom door. The target would see him right away, or so Fisher assumed, but he didn't plan on giving Reginald time to think let alone react. He'd grab his wrist and yank him forward. In that same motion, he'd get an arm around his neck, bring him to the floor, and the syringe tucked into Fisher's waistband would do the rest. He'd managed similar takedowns half a dozen times before and never had a problem.

This time, however, the plan had to be modified slightly when Reginald turned the bathroom light off before pulling the door open. Fisher hadn't considered that and it gave him pause. His eyes had already adjusted to the room's dimness but he still couldn't see for shit and he knew Reginald wouldn't be able to see much of anything. For a moment, he wasn't sure what to do. If he didn't hit Reginald just right, the asshole might fall backwards, slam into the bathroom door and send it crashing into the wall. Fisher doubted the sound would carry far but it might cause someone in a nearby cabin to come investigate. That wouldn't do.

He took a step to the side, giving Reginald space to move into the room. Except… he didn't. Fisher couldn't see much but he could sense Reginald frozen in the bathroom doorway, no doubt wondering what the hell was going on. His room hadn't been dark when he went into the bathroom so why was it dark now? Was there a power outage? Had he turned the lights off himself without being aware of the act? Had something somehow come unplugged?

Reginald was weighing the various scenarios. That's what anyone would do in that situation and had to be the reason he still hadn't moved. Fisher wished he could see the expression on his face but all he could really make out was an indistinct mass against a pitch-black background. If Reginald were smart, if he had one shred of common sense, he'd retreat into the bathroom and close and lock the door.

What the fuck could Fisher do then? It wasn't like his target would sit there quietly while he went to work with his set of picks. But whatever the guy was thinking, Reginald must not have felt threatened because he reached back into the bathroom and hit the wall switch.

The room was instantly filled with bright, florescent light, as was a small area right in front of the door. That's right where Fisher had been standing a few moments before. He'd moved but not far enough. His left shoe and the lower part of that leg were now brightly illuminated. Reginald stared at them dumbly and then his gaze slowly lifted. He had time to take in the black shoes, black pants, black jacket and black gloves. A question formed on his lips. That's when one of the shoes shot up and caught him squarely in the nuts. His mouth hanging open, Reginald crumpled to the floor as Scott Fisher moved in.

-4-

Freddie exited the showroom through a rear door, hoping he'd be able to avoid the hoards of people making their way to the casino, one of the bars or lounges, or the flab fest at the chocolate buffet. He'd put on a great performance. He knew that, from the looks on their faces and the slight tingling feeling that still hadn't entirely left his body. If he needed further reassurance, he'd learned earlier that day that, if he chose to, he could renew his contract with Island for an additional three months. He had the option of remaining aboard the Explorer or he could transfer to one of the cruise line's other ships. The brand new Island Destiny departed from San Diego and spent a week and a half touring the Hawaiian Islands. That was enticing. He'd never been to Hawaii and was starting to think the change of scenery might do him good.

The more Freddie thought about it the more he'd come to believe that a big part of his struggle to get over Brenda was due to the simple fact that he had to return to her hometown each and every Saturday morning. Hell, he could practically see her apartment from the port. He often caught himself gazing off in that direction, wishing, wondering and generally making himself miserable. He'd gained some great comedic material turning Brenda into Brandi but was it really worth the price he was still paying? She didn't love him and made it abundantly clear she never would. That ship had sailed, and he figured it might be high time he use one of Island's many ships to get away and get on with his life. If not Hawaii, there were plenty of other places he could go. What about Alaska, Florida, or the Mexican Riviera? What about South America or Europe? He knew he'd never get rich performing two or three times a week in front of a few hundred people, but a little distance might help him make a break from his past. On the other hand, Freddie still owned a home in New York and he wasn't about to walk away from that solely because one cold-hearted bitch broke his heart.

He needed time to consider all his options, but felt like a shakeup was definitely in order. He was just afraid of doing something so rash and drastic he'd end up regretting it. As much appeal as a remote destination like Alaska seemed to have at the moment, could spending the next three months staring at icebergs really improve his disposition? He doubted it. But sadly, just then, he couldn't envision finding happiness or even contentment anywhere else either; and that was the problem.

Freddie was in a funk. He knew it, and that was the main reason he was in no mood to shake hands or sign autographs, and why the prospect of a quick tumble with a cute little tart from the laundry room didn't even lift his spirits. He wanted nothing more than to return to his tiny impersonal cabin, refill his 'water' bottle,, and then find a nice secluded spot to sit, sip and contemplate his future.

He kept his head down, skirting noisy hallways and stairwells, and all the places passengers typically gathered that time of night. His destination was the seventh floor deck on the starboard side of the ship. People played shuffleboard there during the day. At night, though, in the shadow of one of the suspended life boats, Freddie could recline against the wall, look out at the blackness of the Atlantic and be nearly invisible. Even if someone walked past, which almost never happened, he knew they probably wouldn't see him unless he spoke up. He'd learned that his first week aboard.

He'd been strolling along, going over his act in his head and minding his own business when this disembodied voice had floated out of the darkness and said, "Beautiful night, huh?"

Freddie was so surprised he'd practically jumped out of his skin. "Shit!" he said, one hand flying to his chest. He turned around and was just able to make out a pair of flip-flopped feet poking out of the shadows.

"Sorry," a man said. "Thought you knew I was here."

Once he'd recovered enough to carry on a conversation, Freddie learned the speaker, a nice guy as it turned out, was a widower and claims adjuster from Viking, Minnesota who was on the cruise to commemorate what would have been his thirty-fifth wedding anniversary. Freddie talked with him for a good half hour. Ever since then, he'd returned to that same spot whenever he needed a little solitude after one of his shows.

Freddie spent a few minutes leaning against the railing and staring down into the water. As always, he found it mesmerizing. There was something almost hypnotic about the constantly shifting patterns of foam cast off by the ship's massive hull.

The Island Explorer was nearly a thousand feet long, over a hundred feet wide and weighed in at over one hundred thousand tons. Freddie had flunked physics twice and didn't understand water displacement ratios or anything like that. Regardless of the shape, he couldn't get his head around the idea that something so insanely big and heavy could float. But what was even more stunning was what he'd been told about fuel consumption.

The Explorer was one of the larger vessels in the Island line. At its regular cruising speed of twenty-three knots, it burned something like twelve hundred gallons of fuel per hour. When Freddie heard that, sitting in a lounge and talking to a couple bartenders, he'd grabbed a pen and a cocktail napkin and done the math. He stared at the final figure, unsure if he should be more impressed or disgusted. What was the carbon footprint for something that used almost thirty thousand gallons of fuel per day? Some cars got fifty plus miles per gallon. With the big cruise ships it was more like fifty plus gallons per foot. How much did all that fuel weigh and how did they even store it all? Freddie knew he could find out easily enough but decided he really didn't want to. Sometimes ignorance was better.

He dug a coin from his pocket and pinched it between thumb and forefinger. He paused, arm extended out over the railing, and then let the coin drop. He tried to track it all the way down but lost sight of it long before it reached the waves. There was no splash and no sound. It was there and then gone never to be seen again. What if he followed that same path? Who would know or care? How long would it take before anyone even realized he was missing?

Pathetic, Freddie thought, taking a step backward. He'd hit a rough patch no doubt; but even in his worst moments, he'd never considered suicide, not seriously anyway. He saw that as the coward's way out. He may not have a ton going for him but he never thought of himself as a coward and couldn't stomach the idea of being remembered that way. He'd get over Brenda and be fine. It was a simple matter of extracting his head from his hiney. Tonight, though, he sort of liked it up there. With help from his beverage of choice, he wanted to spend a while savoring his sorrow and thinking about how she'd torn his heart out bit by bit. And in the morning, he vowed to cast her memory aside just like he'd done with that coin. Too bad he couldn't also sink her ass to the bottom of the ocean.

"Here's to you," he said, lifting his bottle and taking a long sip. "You put me through hell but I'm comin' out the other side."

Freddie grabbed one of the big plastic lounge chairs and dragged it to the darkest corner of the deck. He wasn't allowed to use the chairs in the day time, not when there were paying customers who might want them. They did too. On a sunny day at sea, lounge chairs would be sardined around the swimming pools so tightly it was hard to walk from one side of the deck to the other. Freddie was only too happy to avoid that scene. But once the sun went down and the indoor entertainment heated up, the exposed deck spaces lost a lot of their appeal. That was fine with him. Even keeping his distance, he'd had more than his fill of pale skin, body piercings, tattoos and testosterone. What he wanted now was a little peace and quiet.

What he didn't want was to wake up with a hangover so he promised himself he'd limit his vodka intake. However, less than an hour later, his bottle was nearly empty.

Well, fuck it, he thought, tipping it up and sucking out every last drop. *I've done my last show. I got no other obligations before we get back to port. Who cares if I spend the whole time sloshed?*

But Freddie cared, for a couple reasons. First and foremost, he needed his job. Island had what they called an employee conduct contract. Everyone signed, and it basically gave the cruise line liberty to fire his ass if they thought he stepped out of line. Drugs and alcohol were number one on the hit parade. Point of fact, the main reason he'd gotten the job was because the last comedian to work the ship was a little too fond of a certain white powder.

He'd heard there were other issues too and Freddie doubted a little casual drinking was likely to get him into trouble. However, he also thought he should try to keep a clear head so he could hopefully figure out the next phase of his life. He might not stay aboard the Explorer but wanted to remain with the company, at least until something better came along.

Freddie cocked his arm back, planning on tossing the bottle into the sea. That, he believed, would lessen the temptation to return to his cabin for a refill. He was about to let fly when he remembered something he'd seen on the Discovery Channel about a giant garbage patch floating around in the Pacific Ocean. It was supposedly larger than the entire state of Texas. Did all marine waste eventually end up there or did every ocean have its own version of Trash Island? Freddie couldn't even guess at that but knew he didn't want to play any part in contributing to anything so disgusting. He leaned over to set the bottle on the ground, almost toppling out of his chair in the process.

"Damn," he said, realizing he had perhaps gone beyond the clear head stage already. That was okay. No reason he couldn't delay any life-altering decisions until the morning. He was plenty comfortable at the moment and thought it might be nice to just tip back, close his eyes and enjoy the ocean air.

Freddie's lids were at about half mast when he saw or maybe sensed a shadow pass in front of him. He opened his eyes and looked to the right and left. The deck was as empty and quiet as it had been. He listened but couldn't hear any fading footsteps. He then glanced upward. The life boat was still there, secured so tightly it didn't even sway with the wind or the motion of the ship. Whatever caused the shadow it hadn't been that.

He struggled into a sitting position and then got unsteadily to his feet. He had the impression that, whatever he'd seen, it was moving vertically not horizontally. He didn't like the implication and shook his head as if doing so might reorganize his thoughts into a more acceptable pattern. Had he imagined it?

No, Freddie decided. He might not be a hundred percent lucid but he felt sure he'd seen something.

After a moment's hesitation, he crossed to the railing and looked down. Freddie didn't know what he expected to see but was mildly surprised when he saw nothing at all; nothing out of the ordinary anyway. The ship continued to plow forward, carving a path through the waves and sending a cascade of spray and foam off to the side.

He watched for a few seconds and was about to turn away when he caught something out of the corner of his eye. He snapped his head to the right, towards the stern of the ship.

Nothing.

"What the hell?" he muttered, starting to wonder if his mind and the vodka had teamed up to mess with him. Like before, though, he was sure he had seen something. And just then, he saw it again—a splash of color where there shouldn't have been one. Freddie blinked and then it was gone. He watched a moment longer but then returned to his chair, thinking someone's partying had gotten out of hand and they'd tossed a piece of clothing overboard. Would it eventually end up on Trash Island? Freddie thought about that as he drifted off to sleep. He later roused himself enough to go back to his room. By then, the shadow and that sudden flash of color were already forgotten.

-5-

I woke to the low, nearly inaudible hum of the ceiling fan and a gentle breeze across the right side of my face. I wish I could say I'd been roused by a sudden sense of impending doom. Let's get real, though. I had to pee—my reward for having that third glass of chardonnay with dinner.

I turned to peer at the clock but, as usual, had to shift my entire body until my eyes were a few inches from the greenish display. Even then, I had to squint to make out the numbers. 3:11. That was good. It meant I could sleep another four hours, plus a snooze button or two, before I'd have to finally drag my fanny into the shower and get ready to face the day.

Anxious to return to dreamland, I rolled out of bed, trying to move as few body parts as possible. I shuffled the short distance to the bathroom, keeping my eyes closed and automatically trailing one hand along the wall so I didn't stray off course. My mission accomplished, I reversed direction, fell back into bed and had almost managed to drift off when my iPhone buzzed.

I suppose there might have been a twinge of foreboding then but I can't say for sure because I was too annoyed. Barring a death in the family, and I really had no family to speak of, there was no good reason to contact anyone at that time of night, or morning.

Because the phone had buzzed instead of rung, I knew it was an incoming text which, by nature, wasn't as important as a call. Most likely, the sender assumed his or her message wouldn't be seen for hours. With that in mind, I thought about ignoring the thing, but then the phone buzzed again and I knew it would buzz a few more times before finally falling silent for good. I'd be wide awake by then. Heck, I was wide awake already.

With a groan of resignation, I flung an arm out and plucked the phone off the night stand. I still didn't need any lights. Everything on the night stand, nearly every item in my apartment, was in its assigned spot. My keys were on the shelf by the door. My sunglasses were on the kitchen counter to the left of the tissue box. The TV remote was on the back right corner of the coffee table. My purses were on hooks in the back of the closet: black, then blue, then brown, tan, and red. Yes, I know that's alphabetical order. And no, I'm not OCD. I just can't see. I have to stay organized or I'd never be able to find anything. Or, I might inadvertently grab the wrong item and head off to a date wearing black pants to match my blue purse and shoes. In case you're wondering, I've made that mistake before. So, a place for everything and everything in its place.

I unlocked the phone and a faintly robotic female voice said," You have one new notification."

I ran a finger across the screen until I located the appropriate app. The same voice said, "Messages. Double tap to open."

I followed that prompt and the voice informed me I had an unread message from Vicki Goldstein. A text from her wasn't unheard of but somewhat out of the ordinary. She generally preferred to have her underlings handle all the business communications. There was a chance her note was of a more personal nature but, given that our relationship was in that indefinable range between friends and professional acquaintances, I couldn't think of one reason she'd reach out to me at such an ungodly hour.

Curiosity gradually replacing annoyance, I held the phone close enough to my face so I could make out the various text boxes but the print was still too small for me to read: even with inverted colors, bold text, zoom, and the other accessibility settings designed for the visually impaired.

To physically *read* a text, I'd have to increase the font size so large that a single letter would occupy most of the screen. The iPhone didn't give me that option and it would have been too cumbersome anyway. Thank goodness for whoever came up with the Voice-Over tool. With that activated, and it always was, all I had to do was touch a finger to a portion of the screen and I'd be told everything I couldn't see. It worked for texts, emails, apps, the web browser, and pretty much everything else. About the only thing Voice-Over couldn't do was describe photos or images but the technology on that was advancing all the time.

Vicki's text was the most recent so her name was at the top of the list of senders. I tapped it twice and that opened up our minimal texting history. Everything was innocuous and over a month old. We had a good relationship but it was a business relationship. When there was no business we usually didn't talk. If we did, it was typically phone or email. In fact, I couldn't recall one occasion when Vicki texted me without me texting her first.

Strange, I thought, moving the phone an inch closer to my face.

Vicki's new text was at the bottom of the screen and looked like it was only a couple of words. I touched a finger to it and what I heard brought me up short.

"*Martin is gone.* 3:17AM."

The time stamp was not part of the text but Voice-Over's attempt at being helpful. At the moment, I didn't much care about the time because the text was so bizarre. Of course Martin was gone. They'd sent him off on one of those cruises. Vicki knew that and she was certainly aware I knew it too so why did she feel the need, at three in the morning no less, to send me a status update?

I touched the message again.

"*Martin is gone.* 3:17AM."

Vicki had to mean something more than what those three words suggested. I'd known the woman for years and there was no way she'd take the time or trouble to tell me what I obviously already knew. She often didn't share information I needed until I started rattling cages and then it usually came from someone else. I squinted at the clock again, still wondering why the vice president of Tower Brothers Publishing would do something so out of character as to contact me personally.

"*Martin is gone.* 3:17AM."

I then had a chilling realization. It was Sunday. Vicki did not work on Sundays and wouldn't without good cause. And unless I'd mixed up my dates, I was about ninety-nine percent sure Martin should be home by now. The cruise was Saturday to Saturday and should have docked sometime the previous morning. So, when she said he was gone....

I might have said a bad word then. *He can't be gone,* I rationalized. People didn't disappear from cruise ships. Vicki must have meant something else. Maybe he wanted out of his contract. Maybe he'd taken another job. But the tightening in my gut told me that, whatever was happening, it wasn't that simple.

I grabbed my phone again, held it for a moment while I stared at nothing, then I sighed and depressed the home button. A second later, I got the double beep that told me Siri was listening. I said, "Send a text to Vicki."

Siri's response came a couple seconds later. "What do you want to say to Vicki Goldstein?" followed by that same double beep.

"What do you mean he's gone?" I said, and then had to repeat myself because Siri converted my question to "What do you mean has gun?" I spoke slowly and deliberately, over-emphasizing each vowel sound, and she finally got it right.

"Ready to send it?" she asked.

"Yes."

"Okay. Consider it done."

"Thanks a bunch," I muttered, figuring Siri's programmed politeness was Apple's way of compensating for her lousy hearing. On the other hand, flawed as it might be, without things like speech to text technology, smart phones would do me no good. I really shouldn't complain, but I knew I would the next time she converted something I said into a garbled mess. There were other ways I could send text messages. That, believe it or not, was the most reliable.

The phone buzzed and I navigated to Vicki's new message.

"He didn't get off the boat. I'll call you."

I barely had time for that to register when *Sex Type Thing* by "Stone Temple Pilots" started playing way too loud. That was my ringtone and a holdover from my last boyfriend, a part time actor, musician, and poet, and full time loser. He was a huge STP fan. I wasn't and I knew I should make a change. I just hadn't gotten around to it yet. .

"Hello?" I said, my voice cracking between the first and second syllable.

Silence—and then, "Alex? Is that you?"

"It's me," I said, swallowing against the dryness in my throat as I worked myself into a sitting position.

"Are you sick? You sound funny."

I croaked out a laugh. "I'm pretty sure I always sound this way at three in the morning. So what's up?"

This time, Vicki's silence was even longer. "Oh shit!" she finally said, and I heard a smack that must have been hand against forehead. "I am so sorry."

"What on earth for?"

"I'm in London," she explained. "It's twenty after eight here. I was so worked up, I never thought about the time difference. Go back to sleep. I'll call you again in a few hours. I'm really sorry"

"Wait!" I said, afraid she'd already hung up. "Tell me what's going on. What's happened with Martin?"

"Are you sure?" Vicki asked. "We can talk about it later."

"You're kidding, right? I couldn't go back to sleep now if you loaded me with tranquilizers."

"Damn, Alex. I'm sorry."

"Stop saying that. It's fine. Just tell me."

"Okay. So the cruise was this past week."

"Right. And it was supposed to return yesterday morning."

"It did. The..." she paused like she was searching for something. "The Island Explorer docked right on schedule. Passengers began disembarking just after nine o'clock and the ship was empty by eleven."

"But?"

"But Martin never got off."

"What does that mean?" It was a stupid question but I didn't know what else to ask.

"At this point," Vicki said, "I honestly don't know."

"Could he have gotten off the ship somewhere and not got back on?"

"I doubt it," Vicki replied. "Have you ever been on a cruise?"

"No!" I tried to sound miffed. "You always send Martin instead."

Yes, he was traveling on the company dime as he did every year. The trips were part of his contract. I'm sure I could get the same perk if I wanted. I didn't.

"I've cruised a few times," Vicki said. "You get an ID card when you check in and you need it each time you get on or off the boat. That's how they track the passengers."

"Is the system foolproof?"

"I can't answer that but the representative we've been in contact with is sure they didn't leave him in the Bahamas or somewhere."

"Okay," I said, running a hand through tangled hair. "So he goes missing and you're only hearing about it now? That doesn't seem right."

"Remember," Vicki said. "He travels under a different name. It was a while before he was properly identified. That happened sometime yesterday evening. It's the weekend, though, and like I said, I'm in London....

She trailed off then and, for a while, neither of us said a word. I fell back onto my pillow, wishing I had an answer to at least one of the two pressing questions now crashing around inside my skull. First and foremost, I wanted to know what happened to the guy.

I'd known Martin for—some quick finger counting—around a decade and a half. He was nice and about as interesting as a store brand graham cracker; not the cinnamon kind either. However, he was enthusiastic about his work, possessed natural charm, and could effortlessly work a single interviewer or an entire room full of people. In that regard, he was like a politician but without that invisible yet omnipresent layer of slime. He also seemed to think the sun shone out of my bellybutton and, if it came to it, I knew I'd really miss him.

That brought me to question two. What if he truly was gone? What if he'd—I tried to imagine the likeliest scenario—gotten drunk and fallen overboard? He surely wouldn't be the first to do that. I could see it happening too because he did have a clumsy streak. That was probably one of the things that made him so automatically likeable. What would I do—what would **we** do—if he never turned up? I couldn't even begin to get my head around that, mostly because it all seemed so ridiculous. Of course he'd turn up. Whatever happened, there had to be an innocent, reasonable explanation. Twenty-four hours from now we'd all be laughing about it and all of our plans would move forward as scheduled.

"I assume they searched the ship?" I asked, gripping the phone so tightly the edge of the hard case was cutting into my palm.

"Of course," Vicki said. "I'm told they train their staff for those types of situations."

"So people go missing all the time? What sort of cruise line are we dealing with?" I was getting a little hysterical and Vicki must have sensed it.

"Usually," she explained, "they're looking for a missing child or an elderly person that got confused and wandered off. Those things do happen."

"I know," I snapped, even though I'd never given it a second's thought. "So they searched and found nothing. What happens next?"

"I'm not sure yet. It's been difficult getting information. We spoke to someone from the cruise line at first and he answered some of our questions. But when it comes to personal details, they will only deal with the emergency contact."

"And who is that?"

"His mother. She lives in Georgia. She's been helpful but she's obviously upset too. We don't want to pressure her. It's also the middle of the night there."

"Yeah, here too."

Vicki ignored that. "I hate it that I'm in London. I'm only getting up to speed on all of this now."

"Who are you talking to?"

"Nobody yet. Well, no one but you; but I've got a whole string of emails and texts I've been reading through."

"Any clues?" I asked, the word sounding strange even as I said it.

I heard Vicki sigh and take a sip of something. I imagined her clutching a mug of tea in one hand while massaging her temples with the other. Of course, if she were doing both of those things, she wouldn't be able to hold the phone and it didn't sound like she had me on the speaker. My mental images apparently weren't any better than what I could actually see.

"All we know right now," said Vicki, "is that there are no signs of foul play. Those are their words, not mine."

"Okay. So we're assuming what exactly?"

"I don't know. This is not what I expected to wake up to today."

Me neither, I thought, also thinking I should start turning off my text notifications before I go to bed. "Is there anything I can do to help?"

"For now, just keep doing what you do. We're kind of in a holding pattern until people on your side of the pond start waking up."

"And then?"

"Shit, Lex. Let's pray this is a misunderstanding and it will work itself out."

"Do you believe that?"

"No," Vicki said without hesitation. "I think we're at the brink of a real crap storm; but there's nothing we can do until we have some more answers. Do yourself a favor and try to get some sleep. I'll check in with you later."

-6-

"So where do we stand?" Vicki asked, striding into the room and taking her seat at the end of the table.

"And good morning to you too," someone muttered from a few chairs to my left. I couldn't tell who it was but Vicki answered the question for me.

"Peter? Was there something you wanted to say?"

Peter Ireland. He had, according to what I'd been told, been a vice president at Tower Brothers once upon a time. He'd left to open his own publishing company and returned when it folded a few years later. He was working his way back up the corporate ladder but the large chip on his shoulder was apparently slowing him down. That was the popular version of the story anyway and I'd never heard anything to make me think otherwise.

"Um, no," he said, leather creaking as he shifted in his seat. "I was... just saying good morning."

"Oh. Well that's very nice; and good morning to you too. I'm so happy you were able to join us today."

Vicki's tone was friendly but I doubt anyone missed the undertone of sarcasm. I couldn't help wondering, not for the first time either, if she and Peter had a history that went beyond publishing. That, I knew, was none of my business. I couldn't even get my own love life sorted out, so rather than worry about theirs, I turned my attention to more important matters and tried to figure out who else was seated around the table.

Vicki's assistant, a twig of a thing named Jess, was in her normal spot to Vicki's right. She had big hair and wore jangly bracelets that made her easy to identify. I appreciated that. I usually did better with women anyway and hair style had a lot to do with it.

I wasn't sure who was on Vicki's left. I noted a patterned shirt, plus longish brown or dirty blonde hair without much body. Maybe eye glasses too but I couldn't swear to that. Either way, I didn't have enough information to draw any conclusions and I knew I'd have to wait until the person spoke or was spoken to before I could fit any more pieces into that puzzle.

As always, I'd been one of the first to arrive and I automatically selected a seat so the row of big windows overlooking Central Park was at my back. I had no doubt the view was gorgeous, especially on such a bright sunny day; however, one of the things that makes my *disability* such a nuisance is extreme sensitivity to light. Had I sat facing the windows the rest of the room would have been in shadow for as long as the meeting lasted, effectively limiting my vision even more than normal. I have a hard enough time making out much detail even in ideal conditions so I've picked up a few tricks and learned to adapt as best I can. It's still a pain but that's how it goes.

Bob something-or-other was one of the guys from legal and he was right across the table from me. I would have known that even if I hadn't seen him lumber into the room. He was around six feet tall, a good hundred pounds overweight and couldn't uncap his pen without getting out of breath. Based on his level of wheezing, keeping himself upright seemed to be about all his body could handle. I was actually thankful I couldn't see him better because the sounds he was making were repulsive enough. I imagine heavy jowls, sunken eyes, a rumpled, ill-fitting suit, and a food-stained tie. Oh, and body odor. With any luck, I'd never get close enough to him for visual or olfactory verification.

I had the uncomfortable feeling Bob had been staring at me, but since I couldn't really tell, I turned my attention elsewhere. The men to his immediate left and right must have also been from the Tower Brothers legal department. They wore suits, which helped me identify gender, but that also set them apart because everyone else typically dressed more casually.

I wore jeans and a light knit top, and even that was more formal than my usual professional attire of shorts and t-shirt. There were times I never even bothered changing out of my pajamas.

Yes. Working so far behind the scenes does have its perks. With no current love interests, I'd gotten into the habit of only showering about four days a week. But, I showered today and even took the time to shave my legs. It was a sacrifice but one I was willing to make for the cause. I just hoped I wouldn't have to attend too many more of these meetings. I much preferred staying in my apartment or at least keeping closer to home. I had my favorite pub, restaurant, deli, and grocery store, and necessity had made me a fan of familiar surroundings. Don't sell me short. I can get around fine, but I like it better when I don't have to.

There were three or four more people in attendance that I hadn't yet identified but that would have to wait because Vicki was ready to get under way.

"Now that we've taken care of all the pleasantries," she said, a hand on the stack of papers Jess had placed in front of her, "What's the latest? Peter? Would you care to start us off?"

"Of course," he said, clearing his throat. "We're making progress. Martin's mother has given the various authorities permission to speak to us directly and that has really sped up the flow of information."

"That's good. So what do we know?"

"Well, that's still a little tough to quantify. Based on what has been established from Island's passenger records, Martin Reginald, or Martin Worth as far as they are concerned, was still on that ship as of 7:43 on the morning of last Saturday, September 24th."

"And we know that because?"

"He used his ID card at the..."

I heard Peter poking at the screen of his tablet.

"Sunrise Grill."

"That's a restaurant I assume?"

"Yes," he said. "The curious thing is he ate breakfast at one of the buffets every other day. Well, either he ate at a buffet or he didn't eat at all."

"How do we know that?"

The speaker was the tallish woman seated right next to me. She'd been one of the last to arrive and I was fairly sure I hadn't met her before. Her thin, rather nasally voice confirmed that suspicion. I was no good with faces, obviously, but I could pick out a voice anywhere.

"I can answer that one," Vicki said. "The cruise lines are all pretty much the same. You need your card to eat at one of the restaurants, grills or even room service." She paused briefly. "I should clarify that. "In my experience, there's no actual scanning of cards with room service but it's connected to your cabin number so there would be a record of the transaction. With the buffets, though, it's different. You just walk up and grab a tray. No one even knows you're there unless you order an alcoholic beverage or something of that sort."

"That's correct," Peter went on. "So we know Martin was on the ship that Saturday morning. We just don't know what happened to him in the couple hours that followed. He didn't get off the boat; not with the other passengers anyway, and he never claimed his luggage."

"Those card readers must make mistakes sometimes," my neighbor said.

"Actually, Morgan, Alex mentioned that same thing when we first talked about this."

Morgan. Morgan. Morgan? I did a quick check of my mental rolodex. The name didn't ring any immediate bells but then I had it. *Morgan Kaplan.* I didn't know her exact title but was pretty sure she was on the public relations side of things. It made sense for her to be there, especially if the whole thing went sideways.

"No system is perfect," Vicki said. "I don't know how likely it is that an error was made in this case but we should at least consider the possibility."

"Okay," Peter said with what I thought was a note of disapproval. "Then if we go back to the night before, he purchased a Cuba Libre at around quarter of ten and a second one about twenty minutes later."

"I'm sorry," Morgan said. "A what?"

"Rum and Coke, but that doesn't matter. The point is he frequented one of the bars. Can we assume those records are correct?"

Vicki let out an almost but not quite inaudible sigh. "I'm sure everything you have reported is correct. Given the uncertainty of the situation and all the unanswered questions, I just think it's important that we keep an open mind."

"Of course," Peter said after a moment. He poked at his tablet some more. "Even without the digital records from his passenger ID card, there are numerous indications he was still aboard the Island Explorer as of early Saturday morning. Vicki, did you get the email I sent you yesterday afternoon?"

"Yes," she said. "Thank you. I went ahead and made copies for everyone."

Jess immediately scooped up the stack of papers in front of her and began passing them around the table.

"Alex," Vicki said. "I forwarded Peter's email to you. You can look it over at your convenience." She knew printed material wouldn't do me any good but I had computer software that would either magnify text so much I could read it or, better yet, the speech synthesizer tool would read it to me.

"Thanks," I said, with that omnipresent bit of self consciousness that came anytime special arrangements were made for my benefit. "I actually saw it before I came in today. It doesn't make any sense."

"I have to agree. As the rest of you can see," Vicki picked up one of the papers. "What you have there is a fairly detailed summary of Martin's movements for the seventy-two hours prior to his... disappearance. God, I hate using that word. Anyway, we've got all the transactions that were tracked by his ID card but also what's been uncovered from questioning members of the cruise staff. What stands out to me is that nothing stands out. It all looks like normal behavior. He ate. He drank. He slept, showered, ordered room service, etc."

"Hold on," Peter said. "We have no proof that he showered."

I figured he was just trying to lighten the mood and I appreciated that because scrutinizing what may prove to be Martin's last movements on this earth was starting to creep me out.

"You're right," Vicki said. "We can't prove he slept either. But, we know housekeeping made his bed every morning, turned it down at night, and cleaned the bathroom and replaced what appeared to be soiled towels twice a day. We also know he packed his belongings and left his bags outside his room that Friday night as every passenger is instructed to do."

"Why is that?" asked one of the suits from legal.

"I assume it makes it easier in the morning if passengers aren't filling stairwells and elevators with their luggage. The cruise staff transports baggage while guests are asleep"

Bob spoke up for the first time. "So are we all convinced Martin was still on that boat when it pulled into New York Harbor?" He had his head turned toward Peter but Vicki was the one who answered.

"I don't know how we could come to any other conclusion."

"So, what? He jumped into the East River or something?"

"No way," Peter said. "It was broad daylight. He would have been seen, if not by a cruise passenger than by somebody else. That's a pretty busy waterway. They also had search teams out there for three days straight. They didn't find anything."

"Then where does that leave us?" I asked, a sudden quaver in my voice. Martin and I weren't exactly close. I mean, we were friends but few of our interactions went beyond our professional relationship. I still liked the guy and, whatever happened to him, it didn't seem like it could be good.

"I wish I knew," said Vicki, and I noticed that her voice didn't sound all that strong either. "For now, I think we should focus on damage control. As much as I hate to even think it, we have to be prepared in the event Martin doesn't come back.

"Wait a second." Peter drummed his fingers on the table top. "Damage control? Aren't we getting a little dramatic here? It wasn't like the guy was busted for drug trafficking or peddling child porn."

I figured Vicki had to at least be rolling her eyes at that but she seemed to keep her cool.

"It doesn't matter how we label it. We need a strategy moving forward. As I'm sure you're all aware, the Martin Reginald novels are, by far, the Tower Brothers' top sellers. That brand is the flagship for the company. If we're faced with the need to divert from what we've been doing it's going to require a delicate and well-worded explanation. If we botch it, we may all be in damage control mode. The easiest way to avoid that might be to shut the whole thing down but I don't think any of us really wants to do that."

I felt several pairs of eyes on me. I had no idea what to say so I picked up my phone and stared fixedly at a screen I could barely see. I didn't want to, as Vicki put it, shut the whole thing down. But if Martin truly was gone, I wasn't sure what choice we'd have. I could keep writing. I would keep writing. I had to. But he was the front man for the Martin Reginald machine and I didn't see how we could possibly spin a web that would allow us to go on without him.

"Any suggestions?" Vicki asked as if she'd read my mind.

I thought this would be a good time for Ms. PR to chime in again but she evidently had nothing to offer. Bob leaned over to whisper something to one of his cohorts. The comment elicited a chuckle. Whatever was said, though, it plainly wasn't meant for the rest of the group.

"Nothing?" Vicki asked, and I could tell that she too was at a loss.

"Well," said Peter. "We do have one thing working in our favor."

"And what's that?"

"We don't have to make any snap decisions. We still have some time because no one knows yet what's happened."

We don't even know what's happened, I thought, but kept that to myself.

"What I mean is, because Martin keeps such a low profile, the media hasn't yet learned that he's missing."

"They damn sure know Martin Worth is missing," Vicki said. "That's been all over the news for days."

"Right. But until someone puts those pieces together, we can deal with this at our own pace."

"Maybe," Vicki admitted. "We may also be on borrowed time already. No one has made the connection but, before now, there's never been a reason to give Martin Worth much scrutiny. That has obviously changed. Really, what is our best case scenario here?"

"That Martin walks in that door right now," Peter said.

I instinctively glanced that way but the conference room door remained stubbornly closed.

"Obviously, we all hope and pray for a positive resolution," Vicki said, suddenly sounding very tired. "Barring that, the latest promotional tour resumes…"

"November 18th." Jess said, bracelets jangling.

"Okay. That gives us a little over a month and a half. Even if we had the luxury, and I highly doubt we will, I don't think it would be prudent to try to sit on the information that long. We'll have to address it and we need to determine the best way to do that.

"Point taken." Peter picked up his tablet but then put it down again. "We can hopefully get some definitive answers before we have to make any kind of a public statement. We want to protect our own interests; Martin's too, and I think it would be foolish to try to get out in front of this now when there is still so much we don't know."

"Sure. That makes se—"

Vicki stopped when someone knocked on the door and then opened it and stuck their head in.

"What is it, Jake?" she snapped. "We're in the middle of a meeting and I gave instructions we were not to be interrupted."

"I know. I… um… I'm sorry," he said and swallowed. "They told me it was important."

"That what was important?"

"This," he said, holding a slip of paper out in front of him like he expected someone to come take it; except he was still in the doorway and no one was within ten feet of him.

"Well bring it here!" Vicki said, actually snapping her fingers.

"Right." Jake took one step forward but then stumbled and the paper slipped from his fingers and fluttered to the floor. "Sorry," he muttered.

Vicki didn't reply. She simply waited while Jake, after a few fits and starts, mastered the gross motor skills necessary to retrieve the message, deliver it to the table and then hurriedly exit the room.

I felt bad for the kid. He sounded like he couldn't have been any more than eighteen. I guessed he was an intern or temp. He was clearly out of his depth and I wondered if he'd bother showing up for work the following morning.

"Tough to find good help," Bob said, laughing at his own joke.

Peter started to say something in reply but then stopped short. "Vicki? Is something wrong?"

Everyone turned toward that end of the table.

"There's been a development," she said and my stomach sank. I didn't yet know what was coming but it was clear from Vicki's somber tone that she wasn't preparing to announce our Christmas bonuses.

"This is a report from the Broward County Sheriff's Office. They've got the body of a middle-aged male that was retrieved by a couple fishermen; caught up in their net apparently."

"Wait," Peter said. "Broward County? Isn't that…?"

"Florida," Vicki finished. "Fort Lauderdale to be specific."

"And have they…?" I began but then my voice caught in my throat.

"There's been no formal identification," Vicki said, thankfully completing my train of thought. "I don't have much detail here but circumstances have evidently made visual identification difficult."

I didn't even want to think about what that meant.

"There are, however, reasons to believe that it's Martin."

"That can't be," Peter said. "We have proof he was still on the ship Saturday morning. If the ship was in New York, and we know it was, how would he have ended up in Florida?"

"I'm sure I don't know," Vicki said. "But I think we'd better try to figure it out in a hurry."

-7-

Freddie Franco paced back and forth, wiped his hands on his khaki shorts, and then ran one hand over the ever-expanding bald spot on the top of his head. His nervousness was irrational. It wasn't like he had anything to hide. On the other hand, he'd never been interviewed by the police and didn't know what to expect. He'd been summoned, though, and felt like he had no choice but to oblige. He told himself it was fine. He'd answer their questions; they'd realize he had nothing to offer and send him on his way. No problem. Why, then, was his stomach tied in knots? Freddie glanced at the door and wondered if he had time for a quick trip to the head to relieve some of that pressure.

"Mr. Franco?"

Shit! Too late.

A uniformed policeman with a clipboard stood in the now open doorway of the Crystal Lounge. He beckoned Freddie with a look and a nod.

Over the past few weeks, Freddie had become very familiar with the Crystal, and not just because the regular bartender had a generous pour. He'd struck up a casual friendship with Kevin Brando, one of Island's onboard performers. The guy played piano and sang and was really pretty good, even if Freddie would have preferred not to hear "Sweet Caroline,""Piano Man" and American Pie" every fucking night. Still, when he wasn't performing himself, he'd gotten into the habit of catching Kevin's show and he knew that was one thing about Island he would miss.

The lounge looked different in broad daylight; nowhere near as intimate and welcoming. Freddie knew that was due in part to the covered piano, empty bar, and complete lack of fun-seeking cruise passengers. In their place were several of what Freddie assumed had to be plain clothes detectives. They sat one to a table, and the tables were spaced just far enough apart so private conversations could not be overheard. Most detectives were busy with various members of the cruise staff but one sat alone. She looked up and met Freddie's eye, and he headed warily her way.

"Good afternoon," she said, gesturing for him to sit down. "I'm Detective Lynch. Please call me Megan. I'd like to thank you for taking time to speak with me today."

"Sure," Freddie said, shaking a slender hand as he sunk into one of the cushy, barrel-style chairs. The low seats with high wrap-around backs made him feel instantly awkward because he didn't know what to do with his hands. Resting them in his lap seemed weird; but if he tried to use what passed for arm rests he ended up with his elbows almost as high as his shoulders. He finally settled on crossing his legs, placing his hands on one knee and trying not to feel like a schmuck.

"Your name is Freddie Franco?" the detective asked, clearly at ease. He couldn't help noticing she was rather easy on the eyes too: shoulder length strawberry blonde hair, big brown eyes and a lovely smile. He doubted she was any more than five and a half feet tall, although it was tough to judge sitting down.

"It's, um, actually John," he replied.

She raised an eyebrow. "John Franco? Like the ball player?"

"You don't look old enough to remember him," Freddie said and immediately regretted it. It sounded like a cheap pick up line. *She thinks I'm flirting with her. Well,* he thought, *there's no chance of that.* Cute as she was, he couldn't imagine dating a cop. He figured he was off women for a while anyway, but she didn't know that and probably thought he was a letch.

"Thanks," she said, apparently taking his comment at face value. "But you can't call yourself a Mets fan if you don't know who John Franco is."

"That's true," said Freddie, responding to her casual tone and beginning to feel more relaxed. "And based in New York and all, I thought it made good professional sense to go with something else."

"So Freddie Franco is what, just a stage name?"

"It started out that way. I know it's cheesy but it's got some flare and seems to work well for what I do. I've been Freddie so long now that it's really all I go by."

"I understand. And you're a comedian?"

"Yeah. That's one of the nicer things I've been called."

Detective Lynch smiled. "And you said you're based in New York. Do you live in the city then?"

Freddie shook his head. "I spend a lot of time here because of the cruise gig. More than I'd like really, but I actually live upstate; a little town I'm sure you've never heard of."

"Try me."

"It's a place called Canastota. It's about twenty minutes east of—"

“Syracuse,” she finished. “I know Canastota. Home of the International Boxing Hall of Fame.”

“So you like boxing too?”

“Not even a little bit; but I am familiar with that area. I transferred here from the Oswego Police Department.

“Small world,” Freddie said. He’d never done much more than fill his gas tank in Oswego but he had spent plenty of time fishing in Pulaski, Sandy Creek, Mexico, and some of the other nearby towns. “That’s a beautiful part of the state.”

“Oh yeah; but there’s a lot to be said for concrete and skyscrapers too.”

“You don’t like it here?”

“I wouldn’t say that. It just takes some getting used to.”

“Well, I don’t have to be used to it much longer. This is my last cruise on this ship. I’ll spend a month at home and then head to Florida right before the weather here gets cold.”

“Do you have another job lined up?”

“I’m staying with Island,” Freddie said. “I’ll just be on a different ship and sailing out of Miami instead of New York, unless I change my mind sometime between now and then.”

“Sounds like a nice way to spend the winter.”

“It’s great. You should try it sometime.”

Damn! That sounded like a come on too. Probably thinks I’m lonely and desperate, which I am, but that’s none of her business.

“I’ll consider it,” she said noncommittally. “But speaking of time, I’m told we need to be out of here by one o’clock so we’d better get busy. I’m going to take notes on our conversation but I’d like to record it too if that’s okay.”

“Sure thing,” Freddie said, watching and feeling awkward all over again as she placed a small digital recorder on the table between them.

“You have already been interviewed by the Island Cruise security staff. Is that correct?”

“Yeah,” Freddie said. “But there wasn’t a whole lot to it. At that time, I think they were looking for an accomplice or something. From what I heard everyone thought the guy was still on the ship when we got back to New York. I guess they assumed he found a way to get off without following the normal protocol. You couldn’t do that without some inside help.”

“Why would anyone go to the trouble?”

Freddie shrugged. "I got no idea; but he wouldn't be the first guy who tried to disappear for a while."

"So this sort of thing has happened before?"

"No!" Freddie said, shaking his head. "I mean, not that I'm aware of." He didn't want her to get the impression he was criticizing his employer. That could be bad for job security. "I just meant people do some strange things for all sorts of fu— messed up reasons."

"So you believed his disappearance was deliberate."

"Well sure. It made sense, right? I heard he was a pretty quiet guy, kept to himself and all that. No reason to think anything bad happened to him. At worst, we figured he got drunk and fell overboard. That kind of thing does happen from time to time."

"And who's we?"

"Huh?" Freddie asked.

"You said we thought."

"Oh. Just some of the other people that work on the ship. They all had their theories, you know?"

"And what about you? Do you have a theory?"

Freddie grinned. "I got enough of my own problems. I don't have time to worry about anyone else's."

"All right," Detective Lynch said, underlining something she'd just written before flipping to the next page in her yellow legal pad. "Let's move on then. Please tell me if you had any personal contact with Mr. Worth."

"I didn't know him if that's what you mean. I probably saw him around the ship here and there but I don't have any specific recollections of that. We definitely never talked."

"And do you remember where you were and what you were doing the night of Thursday, September 22nd?" "

"Was that when he went into the drink?" Freddie knew that must sound callous but thinking about it in those terms made the stark reality of the situation seem less real. Someone had been killed on a ship he was working and he was still having a hard time getting his head around that. And if the stories he'd heard were true about someone using the poor bastard's passenger ID card to buy cocktails, access his cabin and so forth, there was no way the death was accidental. He hadn't gotten tipsy and fallen over the railing. He'd been murdered and by one hell of a cool customer too.

"This is an ongoing investigation and there are certain details I can not divulge. However, based on when and where the body was found, that is our best estimate at this time."

"So... what? You're asking me for an alibi?"

The detective stared at him and her frustration was plain. "I wouldn't put it that way," she said, capping and uncapping her pen. "Over the past seventy-two hours, between passengers and crew, we have interviewed over five hundred people. Given recent developments we will probably have to interview some of them again plus as many others as we can track down. So far, no one has reported seeing or hearing anything of consequence. That strikes me as unusual to say the least. There were about three thousand passengers and another eight hundred or so crewmembers on board. Cruise ships are big but they're not that big. The laws of probability suggest someone had to see something even if they didn't realize it at the time. All I want you to do is tell me what you remember from that night. Be as specific as you can. It might prove helpful."

She didn't sound any more optimistic than Freddie felt but he figured it couldn't hurt to give it a shot. Until they set sail again in a few hours, he really didn't have anything better to do anyway.

"You've got to understand," he said, blowing out his cheeks. "I don't really deal with the passengers. I do my shows but I'm not supposed to *interact* with them. You know what I'm saying?""

"Of course. Just do your best and tell me whatever you can."

"All right. Don't expect much, though. For me, one week is just like the rest. It all sort of runs together."

The detective nodded but otherwise didn't respond.

"Okay," Freddie said. "Well it was a Thursday so I would have had a show that night; my final one of the week. I perform three times on each cruise. The first one is in the main showroom and it's family friendly. The other two are R rated I guess you could say. Those shows are in one of the lounges and they start later in the evening."

"So that Thursday?"

"It was one of the adult shows. I went on at nine and finished about an hour later."

"And then?"

"Yeah. That's where we get into kind of a gray area. It's like I was saying. I've done this so many times. One cruise is just like the next. Nothing stands out."

"What is your normal routine once you finish a show?"

"I might hang around for a drink and to sign autographs. If I'm not in the mood for that I usually have a drink or two on my own and then turn in."

"And that Thursday night?"

"I don't know," Freddie said with a shrug. "I guess I did one or the other. I honestly can't remember."

"That's fine," Megan said, making a note. "We'll go at it another way. Think about the show itself. Did anything out of the ordinary take place? Is there anything you can recall?"

Freddie was about to say no and then he had a sudden vision of those two brightly clad plus-size women seated right near the stage. Had that been that night? *Yes!* He was sure of it, and then some other details started coming back to him.

"It was one of my better performances," he said, gazing up at one of the big, ornate chandeliers that gave the Crystal Lounge its name. "The crowd was really enthusiastic and just into it, ya know?"

"Go on."

"Okay, so when the show was over, I was pretty pumped but still not up for the whole meet and greet thing."

"Why was that?"

"It's draining," Freddie said after a pause. "But more than that, I had a lot of stuff on my mind. I've been dealing with some personal issues I guess you could say."

"Would you care to elaborate?" Megan inquired, making another note.

Freddie shook his head. "It isn't relevant. Not related to the cruise in any way. I only bring it up because that was the first night I really started thinking about my situation and trying to figure out what to do about it."

"Did you make any decisions?"

"Again, not relevant. But, like I told you before, this will be my last week on this ship. I'm thinking the change of scenery will do me good."

"I hope you're right," the detective said, and Freddie could tell she would have liked to press him for more details.

Occupational hazard, he supposed. *She asks people questions all day long. Gotta be second nature by now.*

"So getting back to that night," Megan said, studying him over the top of her legal pad. "If you didn't meet anyone after your show what did you do?"

"Actually," he chuckled, "I got drunk. Wait. That came out wrong. I wasn't plastered or anything. I was just mellow."

"And where did you do this *mellowing*? Were you in your cabin?"

"No," Freddie answered. "I would be normally. Island is pretty strict in terms of employee conduct. They don't want us doing anything unseemly in the public eye."

"That makes sense."

"Of course," said Freddie. "I'm not complaining."

"Then if you weren't in your room,.." Megan prompted.

"I was on the seventh floor deck. There's a place there that's real secluded and private at night. It's a great spot to sit and think."

"And what happened then?"

"Well, nothing. I kind of dozed off for a while and then I got up and went back to my room."

"That's it?" Megan asked, disappointed. "You didn't see or hear anything?"

Freddie thought back. He remembered sitting in the shadows, steadily draining his bottle while he contemplated Alaska, icebergs, floating garbage heaps, Brenda, and the evil nature of women. In hindsight, he realized he may have been a bit more inebriated than he'd let on. *Oh well.* He remembered standing at the railing, dropping the coin and having that fleeting impulse to follow it down. And then....

"Hold on!" Freddie said, snapping his fingers. "I did see something, or I might have anyway. It was right before I returned to my cabin. I'd been lying on one of the deck chairs, half asleep and my eyes half open. All of a sudden, I saw something cross in front of me. Well, I didn't see it exactly. I guess I sort of sensed it."

"What does that mean?" Megan asked with a frown.

"I don't know. Nothing maybe." Freddie looked toward the large windows that lined one wall. "At first I thought someone had walked or run past but there was nobody around. I then wondered if my eyes were playing tricks on me. I didn't think so because... well, I wasn't a hundred percent sober at that point but I didn't feel impaired either.

"I thought about it for a second, and then got up and went over to the railing. I don't know what I was looking for. I guess I figured something must have flown by and fallen into the water. It could have been a towel, clothing or a piece of furniture. A lot of alcohol gets consumed on cruise ships and people do dumb shit."

"But you didn't think it was a person."

"Oh God, no. That never even crossed my mind. People fall in or even jump once in a while but even the drunk ones yell on the way down. I never heard a sound."

"And what did you see?"

Freddie gave a shrug. "I wish I could tell you. It was dark. There's water swirling all over the place and the deck I was on is a long way up."

The detective gazed at him but didn't reply.

"A flash of color," Freddie said finally. "That was it. It was there and then gone. I couldn't make out any detail."

"What color?"

Freddie shook his head helplessly. "I don't even know that; not that I could swear to anyway. With the lighting and the distance and everything…." He shrugged and fell silent.

"Okay. I have one final question and I want you to think carefully before you respond. Whatever you saw, do you think it's at least possible it could have been a person?"

Freddie closed his eyes and tried to put himself back in the moment. He'd certainly stood on that section of deck and looked over that particular railing enough times that it wasn't difficult to recreate the scene. As always, the ship's lights had given everything below a bluish almost luminescent cast. Beyond that, had he observed anything more than what he'd already said? Freddie bit his lower lip as he concentrated. He remembered gazing overboard and, at first, seeing nothing. But then?

He'd been about to turn away when he'd caught something from the corner of his eye. Freddie pressed fingers against his temples as if that might bring the memory into better focus. He'd been standing at about mid-ship and the object had been nearly at the stern when he'd finally seen it. He thought he had an impression of red but also thought it hadn't been a single solid color. There were stripes, or some sort of pattern anyway. What did that suggest? It could have still been an article of clothing. And, Freddie supposed, that clothing might have still been in use. Had he seen anything that could have been flesh? He shivered involuntarily and then opened his eyes, looked at the detective and nodded.

-8-

"So what do ya got?" asked Captain Weiserman, leading Megan Lynch into his office and taking a seat behind a plain metal desk.

Megan placed her faux-leather laptop bag in one of the visitor's chairs, sat down in the other and looked across at her boss.

His first name was Gerald, but pretty much everyone at the 6th Precinct referred to him as Wigs. She wasn't sure why. It definitely had nothing to do with his hairdo. The guy was bald as a baby's butt, and it was the sort of bald that made you think he'd been that way his whole life.

Not for the first time, Megan considered asking him about it, something she should have done when she first joined the NYPD. After nearly six months on the job, though, it felt like that window of opportunity had closed. She was still curious but bit her tongue, reached into her bag and pulled out her pages of notes. They amounted to fuck all, or that's how Tana French would put it. Lately, Megan had developed a fondness for French's Dublin Murder Squad novels. The Irish were so much more articulate, especially when it came to cussing.

"We still don't have much to go on," she said, crossing her ankles and tucking her feet under her chair. "I personally interviewed nineteen different members of the cruise staff today. All told, we've spoken to over two hundred stewards, bartenders, waiters, waitresses, concierges, sommeliers, performers, food service workers, hospitality workers, blackjack dealers, masseuses, etcetera, etcetera. Basically, we've talked to, or tried talking to, anyone who might have come in contact with our vic."

"And?" Wigs asked, tenting his fingers under a prominent chin.

"And it seems like the guy just vanished. I mean, we know where he ended up. We're just not having much luck determining how exactly he got there."

"I just spoke to someone with the Coast Guard, a Lieutenant..." Weiserman rifled through a stack of papers on his desk. "Ah, here it is. Lieutenant Susan Vrabel. She told me that based on when and where the body was found, ocean currents and all that, he most likely went in the water sometime between twelve o'clock on the afternoon of September 22nd—"

"That would be the Thursday."

"Right. So sometime between then and eight o'clock the following morning."

"We're assuming he was already dead?"

"I think that's reasonable. His wrists and ankles were bound, so even if he had been alive, I doubt he would've stayed that way for long. The Broward County ME is conducting the autopsy. We'll know more once we have a specific time of death."

"Sure," Megan said. "But what we have now already matches our working timeline. What blows me away is that no one saw a thing. Well, I've got one guy who thinks he maybe, possibly, just might have seen something he couldn't identify. Put it this way. No DA will be using him on the witness stand."

"It's still a lead."

"We'll see. For now, though, I think we can safely narrow that lieutenant's timetable by a good twelve hours."

"How do you figure?" Wigs asked, looking at her as if he already knew.

"It's what I just said," Megan replied. "No one saw anything. That means there's about a ninety-nine percent chance this did not happen during daylight. It isn't fully dark until around eight. The sun is up again by six-thirty or seven. That's the maximum time period I think we should be focusing on, but I'd bet my badge the dirty deed was done either late that night or in the wee hours of the morning."

"I tend to agree with you," Wigs said, adjusting the cuffs on his starched white dress shirt. He then moved to his navy blue, pin stripped tie, fingering the Windsor knot thoughtfully. "It would definitely help if this wasn't such a jurisdictional nightmare."

"At least the cruise line has been cooperative."

"They're probably worrying about being sued by the family. But you're right. Everyone has been cooperative. It's just tough to get organized when everything is so spread out. You've got the Coast Guard doing their thing. Broward County is involved because that's where the body was recovered. We're involved because we have the easiest access to the cruise employees and passengers. This shouldn't be our problem at all but I feel like we're the ones leading the investigation. I don't like that. Too many people to point fingers if it all goes to shit."

"Look on the bright side," Megan said. "At least we know he's not floating around somewhere in the East River. That takes a little heat off."

"I'm not so sure about that, and I'm not making any assumptions until that body has been positively identified."

"Tomorrow," Megan said.

"Yeah. That's what they tell me. It's a formality really but it will still be nice to have it confirmed."

Wigs checked his watch. "Five past three," he muttered. "I never made it to lunch today. I'm gonna grab some coffee and a snack. Can I get you anything?"

Megan shook her head and he hurried out of the room.

He was back a few minutes later, holding a bag of Ritz Bitz in one hand and balancing a Styrofoam coffee cup and a can of Diet Coke in the other. "Maybe you'll want this later," he said, placing the soda on the desk and sinking into his chair.

"Thanks," said Megan, touched that he not only was willing to wait on her but that he evidently knew she preferred Diet Coke to coffee, tea, or anything else the vending machine had to offer. She sensed he was fond of her, in a professional manner only. He had pictures of his wife and kids all over his office. He also had Megan by a good twenty years. Still, the positive working relationship she'd felt from day one made her transition to life in the city that much easier.

"So you're saying what?" Wigs asked, tearing the crackers open and popping one into his mouth. He tipped the bag Megan's way but she again shook her head. "That he died around midnight say?"

"Give or take. And I think that's when he actually went over. It is possible he was killed earlier."

"Right," Wigs nodded. "And that has to do with that witness you mentioned?"

"Potentially. Like I said, he isn't sure he saw anything. However, he was on the deck three floors down from Mr. Worth's state room. I mean directly below too. It's a straight line. So if anything or anyone had dropped from that balcony, he was in position to see it."

"And what time would that have been?"

Megan frowned. "It's impossible to say with any accuracy. As I indicated in my report, Mr. Franco had been dipping his bill."

"He was drunk then."

"Let's just say his senses were dulled."

"Beautiful." Wigs blew on his coffee and took a sip. "Does he at least have a best guess?"

"Yes. He thinks it was around 1AM."

"And do you think that information is credible?"

Megan hesitated. "I think it's possible, and under the circumstances, that may be all we need."

"How so?"

"The way I see it, if Mr. Franco really did see the vic go over, there's an extremely high probability Worth came from his own balcony."

"Explain," Wigs said, popping a few more crackers into his mouth and then brushing crumbs off his fingers.

"I got a good look at that ship from the pier and I also went inside for the balcony view. The seventh floor has a lot of open deck space for sunbathing, exercise, and recreation. Mr. Franco took me to the spot he said he was sitting. The floors directly above that consist of state rooms and some areas not accessible to the general public. Basically, there's nowhere else Worth could have come from except for his balcony."

"Or one of the others nearby."

"That's true," Megan conceded. "But we know from security footage that he entered his cabin at two minutes past ten that same night."

"I assume you've looked at other security footage as well?" Wigs' desk phone chirped. He glanced at it, frowned, and then gestured for Megan to continue.

"That's where this gets strange. I believe Worth was dead long before breakfast time Friday morning. However, although no one claims to have seen him, security video has him entering and exiting his room on Friday."

"Are you sure it was him?"

Megan paused and bit her lip. "That's difficult to say. The body type was similar and the clothing did match some of the stuff we found in Worth's luggage."

"But?"

It was Megan's turn to frown. "He had this wide-brimmed hat on both times and it made it practically impossible to get a good look at his face. If I didn't know better, I'd think he knew where the cameras were positioned and how best to avoid them."

Wigs dropped the empty cracker bag on his desk and sat back and laced his fingers behind his head. "So you think we're dealing with a professional."

"I think it's a possibility we have to consider."

"Pardon me for saying so but you don't sound convinced."

"I'm not!" Megan said, a bit louder than she meant to. "It could be a coincidence. The first time he was looking down at a brochure or something. The video doesn't show much more than the top of his head."

"Which is covered by a hat."

"Right. And the second time it looked like he was adjusting the settings on his watch."

"Was it Worth's watch?"

"Yes. I already confirmed that with Broward County."

"So he was dead, presumably, but still strolling around the Island Explorer?"

"That's obviously not possible but it's damn sure how it looks."

"Or how it was made to look," Wigs mused, fingers again drifting back to his tie knot. "And how did he enter the room? Was he using a key card?"

"No question," Megan said. "But here's something else. I scanned security video from earlier in the week and Worth never wore that hat before, not that I saw anyway. It wasn't in his belongings either."

"Could have gone overboard with him."

"It could have."

"But you don't think that's what happened." Wigs stared at her, his expression giving away nothing. "You've got a theory," he said. "So lay it out and we'll see if it holds water."

Megan smiled wryly. "Probably not the best metaphor under the circumstances."

"Excuse my insensitivity." Wigs waved a hand, indicating that she should get on with it.

Megan didn't feel ready to do that. She believed she was on the right track but also knew they still had a whole lot of unanswered questions. She'd rather do some more digging before sharing her thoughts but her captain apparently wasn't inclined to give her that option.

"Okay," she began, swallowing her misgivings and trying to concentrate on making a solid argument. "Based on the evidence we've gathered, surveillance video and otherwise, I believe Martin Worth was killed late that Thursday night or Friday morning and the person responsible spent the next thirty-six hours going to great lengths to make it look like he was still alive and following his normal routine. He used his keycard, his room, his bed and bathroom, and even wore some of his clothes."

"Why?"

Megan blinked. "Pardon me, Sir, but I think it's too early to speculate on motive."

Wigs looked at her, something playing at the corner of his mouth. "I'm not sure I agree with that but I think you misunderstood my question. I'm not asking why Mr. Worth was killed. I want to know why you think the perp bothered with all the rest of it. Why not just knock him off, dump the body and call it a day? If he really did the sort of thing you're suggesting, he ran the risk of leaving signs of his activities."

"That's true," Megan said. "But he was also long gone before anyone realized a crime had been committed. He probably figured the trade off was worth it."

"Okay," Wigs said, nodding slowly. "Go on."

Megan looked at the wall to her left and a framed eight by ten of Wigs with an attractive, smartly dressed woman and a couple teenage boys. The younger of the two, maybe thirteen, was mugging for the camera. Megan could see the Twin Towers just visible in the background so knew the picture was more than fifteen years old. Wigs—*Did his wife call him that too?*—was just as bald then as now. She glanced at other photos, Weiserman with various politicians, dignitaries and low level celebrities, and noticed that he hadn't changed much over the years. He was a few pounds heavier, a little paler maybe but that was about it. He still looked good for his age. In fact, had it not been for the 1977 Hofstra University diploma, hanging right next to a certificate she couldn't make out except for the distinctive NYPD seal, she would have guessed he was closer to fifty than sixty. She wondered if his wife had aged as gracefully. Her eyes again flitted to the family photo before she turned and focused on her boss.

"I don't think we're talking about a crime of passion or a random act of violence," said Megan. "This was a hit and it was planned with excessive care."

"Why do you think so?" Wigs asked.

"It's a lot of what I've already said. We can rehash it all but it boils down to a well thought out, well executed scheme. He committed murder in close proximity to a few thousand people and no one knew anything about it. That's almost impressive."

"So we're dealing with a pro."

"I think so." Megan picked up her Coke, popped the top and took a long sip. "I also think he made a mistake and that's how we're gonna track him down."

-9-

I exited the cab, crossed the sidewalk and, for the second time in as many days, entered Tower Brothers Publishing. Vicki met me at the door and led me past the main conference room and into her spacious corner office.

"Can I get you anything?" she asked, her tone suggesting she'd rather not waste the time.

I shook my head and she directed me to a small seating area on one side of the room. There were soft leather arm chairs, a kidney-shaped table of dark wood and glass, and a throw rug in earth tones and a pattern I couldn't make out. It looked vaguely Native American but I wouldn't have bet my royalty check on that.

"So," Vicki said, sitting and gesturing for me to do the same. "We meet again."

That didn't seem to require a response so I gave none.

She knew trips to the office were not on my list of favorite things to do. In fact, from the time I'd signed my first contract, I averaged maybe two visits per year. On those infrequent occasions we had business that couldn't be handled by phone or email, Vicki and Jess, her bejangled assistant, typically met me at a coffee shop, restaurant, or my own apartment.

One of the things I liked about her from day one, one of the reasons I'd signed with Tower Brothers in the first place, was that Vicki Goldstein seemed to understand that familiar surroundings were simply easier for me and she went out of her way to accommodate whenever possible. I appreciated that, probably more than she knew, and it was why I didn't even consider objecting when she texted earlier that morning and told me I needed to come in.

"We have a decision to make," she said, the small talk obviously over.

The first thing that struck me was her choice of pronoun. Maybe she wanted to give the impression *WE* were all in this together. I suppose we were to an extent, but when you got right down to it, the next course of action was up to me and me alone.

"What are our choices?" I asked, going along with her at least for the time being.

The truth was I didn't know yet what I wanted to do. Martin's death had thrown me for a serious loop, in part because I genuinely liked him but also because he made my professional career so much more manageable and lucrative. I wasn't exactly rolling in the dough but I was comfortable and stable, and I don't know if that would have been the case had he not played his role so perfectly. It was possible some of my fears, my insecurities were unfounded. I didn't know, and in all honesty I never wanted to find out. However, depending on what happened moving forward, I knew I might no longer have a choice.

In case you've been wondering, I have a condition called Best disease which is really a huge misnomer because it totally sucks. Most people have never heard of that particular disorder so think of it like macular degeneration. The symptomology is similar enough. I have a whole lot of blind spots. As a result, my central vision is shot to hell so I see everything peripherally. That includes objects right in front of my face. I know that sounds weird. It's no picnic either. Everyone's peripheral vision is lousy; you just don't notice it unless that's all you've got to work with.

I get this question all the time so I'll save you the trouble. No. My vision is not blurry or cloudy. I suppose it might be but I can't see well enough to tell. Really, everything just lacks detail. Hand me a newspaper and I could distinguish the headlines, photos and columns of print. However, the whole thing could be written in Chinese and I wouldn't know the difference. Your nose could fall clean off, and unless we were getting ready to kiss, I probably wouldn't notice that either. Still, I'm able to get around well enough that most people would never know there's a problem. I know. You're confused, right? Well, I've explained it as best I can so how about we just move on?

I think it's time I properly introduce myself, or should I say re-introduce myself? My name is Alex Rhodes. As far as the general public knows I'm a freelance journalist and I mostly write fluff pieces for various online publications. It isn't glamorous work but does allow me to stay behind the scenes while earning enough to cover the rent on my New York apartment. I also have one source of, well, let's call it "supplemental income." I am the real author of every Martin Reginald novel.

Surprised you, right? And now you're wondering why I don't publicly take the credit for my most notable accomplishments. I'll let you in on a trade secret. The vast majority of fiction authors are introverts. Why else would we willingly spend so much time alone?

I was shy even when I was a kid with normal sight. Yes. I could see fine once upon a time. That all changed about when most of my friends were getting driver's permits. It was a major downer but what are you gonna do? I'll tell you what I did. I took the walls I'd already started building around myself and fortified them until I had a fortress complete with parapets, armed guards, and a lava-filled moat stocked with ill-tempered crocodiles. I'm speaking figuratively but I think you get the point. I withdrew; and although I didn't become a recluse, I did make every effort to remove myself from any potentially uncomfortable situations.

I know. I'm making myself sound like a freak, but do keep in mind I have a tendency towards hyperbole. Call it trade craft. But whatever you might be thinking to the contrary, I am not dysfunctional—not even a little bit. Unless we're talking about my sex life and we're absolutely not doing that. I'm self-conscious for sure, and when the federal government slapped me with the legally blind label, that took my already private nature and multiplied it by a thousand.

Freelance writing seemed like the perfect solution. I could work on my terms and in my own space, and stay out of the public eye. The job just didn't occupy enough of my time. I filled the void by starting a novel which I finished in about six months. On a whim, I sent out a few queries. I expected nothing and was stunned when three different publishers expressed interest. That's when things started to get complicated.

"You know what the options are," Vicki said, smoothing her skirt over her knees. "We can come clean or pull the plug on the whole thing."

Again with the 'we.' And she made it sound so easy too. Of course, for all Vicki knew, it was a simple matter of managing the situation to minimize losses. To be clear, I don't mean to imply that her only worry was Tower Brothers and their bottom line. She wasn't like that. Besides, there were things in play of which she had no knowledge, or did she? When Vicki said we could come clean, was that an indication she'd figured out what was really going on and an invitation for me to fess up?

No way, I decided. I'd been as tightlipped as a clam with lockjaw and there was really no one else that could have shared my secret. I wasn't even sure how much of it was fact and how much was fiction, but I'm getting ahead of myself.

I knew I should try to look at things from Vicki's point of view. We were friends, sort of. Even so, her job came first. In her position, it had to; and if she had the slightest inkling of what might really be happening, this little pow-wow would be a lot less informal and probably include Big

Bob and every other member of the legal department. We had the office to ourselves, and that told me she had no objectives beyond balancing my best interests with those of the company.

I was coming to realize I'd inadvertently, or perhaps carelessly, put her, and by extension the rest of Tower Brothers Publishing, in an extremely difficult spot. I also had to somehow come to grips with the fact that I was the reason Martin was dead. I mean, I didn't *know* that but it seemed like the likeliest scenario. Why else would he have been murdered?

As yet, there'd been no official ruling of homicide but I knew that would come. I was equally sure I was to blame. In my defense, I swear on my great grandmother's grave I never imagined anything like this would happen. Of course that's no excuse. Hindsight is as unforgiving as old age and I understood now that the risk should have been obvious. It was all harmless enough in the beginning; but when the situation changed, I should have taken a serious look at what I was doing and the possible implications. I hadn't done that and would have to live with the consequences.

"I think we should pull the plug," I said, staring at my fingernails and feeling like a coward. I knew I couldn't run from my problems. But at that moment, nothing would have made me happier than to figuratively close the book on Martin Reginald and devote the rest of my days to freelance assignments of no real significance. It wouldn't be a rewarding career move but at least no one else would get hurt. I also thought I deserved to serve some form of penance.

"You don't mean that," said Vicki, seemingly sensing my lack of conviction.

"Then what do I mean?"

"Good question. Why don't you tell me?"

I blew out a breath. "I don't know," I said, looking at Vicki but, as usual, not being able to read her expression. I really hated that. "I don't even want to be having this conversation because nothing good can come out of it."

"I agree that that's how it feels right now. We are all dealing with a tragic loss; but there's something we have to keep in mind."

"What?" I asked, voice cracking as my emotions started to get the better of me. I had to bite the inside of my cheek to stop from crying. The tears had come and I knew they would again. I just couldn't deal with that right now.

"This isn't just about us," Vicki explained. "Martin was our friend and colleague but he had millions of fans too. It would be a disservice to them and to his memory if we just called a halt to everything."

"But isn't it up to me?"

"Of course," Vicki said. "I can't force you to continue and I wouldn't try. I just don't want you to make any rash decisions."

"But you think I should "come clean," as you put it."

Vicki sighed. "Again, Alex, I can't tell you what to do, but I feel like I've come to know you pretty well over the years. You're passionate about your work. You're also two novels into a blockbuster series. Will you be able to rest easy if the final chapters of that story are never told?"

I'd actually been thinking a lot about that and it wasn't just because I take pride in my writing. I felt like I had unfinished business, perhaps more now than ever. It was of course possible the investigation would show that Martin's death was an unfortunate accident, completely unrelated to anything I'd done, but I didn't believe that for a second. He had been murdered and that suggested one of two things. It either ended the immediate threat or had been meant as a warning. Regardless, if I went public, there was an excellent chance I would become the new target. I supposed I might have been misinterpreting the situation but wasn't sure I really wanted to roll the dice on that one.

"The final manuscript is almost done," I said, looking for an out. "We could claim Martin wrote it before he...."

"Is that what you want?" Vicki asked, doing me the favor of not making me finish the sentence.

I shrugged, feeling helpless and trapped. "And now we're right back where we started. I don't know what I want. I'm sorry but that hasn't changed in the last few minutes."

Vicki stood, went to a sideboard and I heard the tinkle of ice cubes. "Would you like some water?" she asked, filling a glass.

"Not unless you've got the fountain of wisdom over there."

"Does Poland Spring Water count?'

"I'm not sure Poles are known for their brains."

"Then I guess you're on your own," Vicki said, returning to her chair.

"I was afraid you'd say that."

She sipped from her glass and then placed it on the table. "What are you afraid of, Alex?"

You mean besides potentially drawing the attention of a cold blooded killer? But I knew that wasn't what she meant. I was still tempted to spill my guts right then and there. How would she react if I told her the fiction

I'd been peddling for Tower Brothers was, well… not? No chance I was going down that road. For one thing, I had no proof. And for another, there was no one in the world that could or would validate my claim.

I'd never been able to verify any of the information I'd been given. True or not, though, it was one hell of a tale and far too juicy to keep to myself. I probably should have at least tried doing a little more research before kicking the hornets' nest. Instead, I merely changed some names and dates and, because the details I had were sketchy at best, drew my own conclusions and filled in the gaps with what I assumed was total bullshit. That's what fiction writers do. We call it literary license. However, if someone was killed because of what I'd written, I must have hit a little too close to the mark.

"I can't do the things Martin did," I said, considering Vicki's last question and how best to respond. "That's why we hired him."

"That's true; and I know it can be difficult for you when it comes to travel and such. I understand that."

"The travel is only part of it."

"Yes," Vicki said. "I realize there are other concerns. However, circumstances are different now and I wonder if it's time to reevaluate."

Circumstances are different? Is she really not aware that my condition is degenerative, and if anything has gotten marginally worse in the years I'd known her? I couldn't see any better and never would. Given that seemingly obvious fact, I couldn't imagine what there was to reevaluate. With nothing to offer, I gazed at Vicki and waited for her to continue.

"When you came to Tower," she said, "we made certain accommodations because we believed in your first book and the potential it exhibited."

"I know that and I'm grateful."

Vicki waved that off. "At the time, it never occurred to me that something like a promo tour would be logistically problematic. I didn't know how we'd get around that, and then you suggested having Martin represent your books. I didn't understand why you wanted to be what amounted to a ghost writer but I really couldn't argue, especially when you agreed to pay part of his salary out of your own royalties."

Vicki picked up her glass and took another sip. "I've come across some unusual arrangements in the publishing industry but nothing like that. You had no interest in the fame, and the promise of fortune didn't seem to be much of a motivator either."

"I thought that's what I had to do to break in. I couldn't give you all of what you wanted so I decided to find someone who could."

"It was shrewd," said Vicki, "especially from a business standpoint. This business has changed so drastically over the past decade and a half. It's riskier than ever to take on new authors. We all believed in you but we could only invest so much. You understand that, right?"

I nodded, wondering where she was going with this. The way I saw it they'd always supported me a hundred percent and made a lot of concessions along the way.

"You gave us what amounted to a safety net and we took advantage of that."

I shrugged. "I think it worked out well for everyone involved." *Everyone except for Martin.*

"The point is," Vicki said, "you have more than proven your worth to the company. You're successful, established, and famous, or you would be if you let the word out."

"What does that have to do with anything?" I asked, not liking the direction the conversation had taken.

"Plenty," Vicki replied. "You are one of our most valuable commodities. I shouldn't be telling you this but you've got leverage now. You can call your shots. Demand a personal assistant and I'm sure you'll get it. I'll even give you Jess if that's who you want. She can take you to book signings, promotional events, interviews, writing conferences, and all the rest. You wouldn't have anything to worry about."

I so wished that were true but my eyesight created a slew of other difficulties Vicki plainly hadn't envisioned—pardon the pun. I couldn't properly look a fan in the eye or even see well enough to legibly sign my own name let alone inscribe a book to someone. I didn't feel like getting into any of that now and didn't see the need because what Vicki wanted simply wasn't going to happen. Bottom line, my 20/2,000 vision made me vulnerable and that trumped all other concerns. Martin was dead because of what I had written. I believed that and felt guilty as hell but still wasn't about to step into the spotlight. Call me chicken shit if you want but I knew that sacrificing myself wouldn't miraculously bring him back.

"We had an agreement." I didn't mean to be confrontational but had to make Vicki understand where I was coming from. "I said I didn't want my name or face attached to my novels and everyone here signed off on that. Are you gonna go back on your word?"

"Well, n-no," Vicki stammered; "not against your wishes, but we have to do something. Do you really want us to shut the whole thing down?"

Now it was my turn to hesitate. I knew Tower Brothers couldn't keep releasing Martin Reginald novels, not while the world believed the creator was dead. There was, however, one more book at minimum I felt compelled to complete. I could no longer use his name and would not under any circumstances use my own. Where did that leave me? And then I thought of a possible solution.

"Okay," I said. "So what if we pay tribute to him by continuing the Martin Reginald brand? We just credit someone else for the writing. It's been done before."

"You mean like Tom Clancy and Robert Ludlum?"

"Yeah, along with Vince Flynn, Robert B. Parker, Dick Francis, and Michael Palmer; probably a few others too. They all authored incredibly popular series, franchises really."

"And those series continued even after their authors passed away."

"Right! So I'm not proposing anything unprecedented.'

Vicki looked at me. "These circumstances are different. For one thing, they actually wrote their own books. They didn't have a ghost writer behind the scenes."

"Well that just means our transition will be easier because the quality of the work will not change. We just need to find the right person to step into Martin's shoes." But even as I said it, I realized my plan had an unavoidable flaw.

"With all the examples you gave," Vicki said, talking to herself as much as to me, "I believe unit sales did drop off at least initially. I'll have to look into that; but maybe, if we spin this the right way, there won't be a significant decline. I'd obviously rather give you the public acknowledgement you deserve. However, if you're saying that's not an option, I wonder if we could somehow...."

She kept going but I'd already tuned out. I realized I could not, as I'd so cavalierly put it, find someone to *fill Martin's shoes* or they may well end up the same way he did. *Here. Try these on. They're made of cement. Now if you'd mind taking a brief stroll off this short pier.*

"I've got to go!" I said, getting to my feet so quickly that I lost my balance, slammed my leg into the table and knocked Vicki's glass over in the process. It thankfully didn't break.

"Are you all right?" she asked, also getting to her feet and clearly surprised by my sudden action.

"Oh. Yeah. I'm really sorry about that." I reached down and rather clumsily righted the glass. "Do you have something I can wipe this up with?"

"It's a little water," Vicki said. "Don't worry about it. Is there something wrong, Alex?"

"No. I just... I've got to think about all of this. I'll give you a call later. I'm sorry." With that, I rushed from the room.

-10-

Mikhail Vasilek caught the bartender's eye and raised a finger. She nodded as she continued dumping light and dark rum, grenadine and an assortment of fruit juices into a large shaker. She then began to shake which Mikhail watched with interest because of the way certain parts of her body responded to the exercise. He'd never gone in for dark skin and cornrows. Still, he couldn't deny that she was built like a brick shit house, whatever that meant. It was one of those quintessentially American expressions he'd often heard but never understood. What was attractive about a shit house regardless of its construction?

Crude, he thought. *Always crude, but also charming in an indefinable way.* He again wondered how Americans managed to be simultaneously offensive and likeable. He'd lived and worked in the States for half his life and had decided he'd never figure that one out. The best he could do was to try and fit in, and that had never been much of a problem no matter where he went.

The bartender, who'd said her name was Jade, placed three tall, pastel-colored glasses on a tray, filled them, and garnished each with an umbrella and fruit skewer. Mikhail made a face. What was the point of drinking if there was so much garbage in the glass you couldn't taste the alcohol? It was revolting.

Jade rang a bell and a young server, equally dark skinned and cornrowed, came and thankfully swept the tray away. Of course, as much as Mikhail would never consider ordering such a concoction, he was glad when others did so he could admire Jade's preparation. She tried to make a production out of his vodka neat, but working with just one bottle, there was only so much a person, even a brick shit house person could do.

She placed the glass in front of him and gave him a grin. "No papaya juice for you, yah?"

He looked at her and tried to decide if she was making fun. It didn't seem like it so he smiled in return, took a sip and then swiveled on his stool to gaze out at a stretch of white sand beach, palm trees, and water so incredibly blue and clear it didn't seem real.

Nothing had seemed real for the past five days but that, he knew, was because life at the all-inclusive Jamaican resort was so profoundly different from his normal daily existence. The whole concept of a vacation was foreign to him and, as much as he enjoyed the freedom and relaxation, the experience was unsettling too. The next time his bank balance ballooned he figured he'd do something else with the money and definitely stay closer to home, wherever that happened to be at the time. He didn't have any jobs lined up right then but knew that would change soon enough. That was the beauty of his line of work. There were always people with problems they needed someone like him to solve.

He'd no sooner had the thought when his phone vibrated in the back pocket of his tan slacks. He checked the display and his eyes darkened when he recognized the incoming number. There was, Mikhail believed, no reason for that individual to call him. Their business was concluded. He'd completed his assigned task exactly as requested and been paid for that service. End of story. Any further contact was a direct violation of the rules he laid out explicitly to every perspective client. It had never been a problem before and he didn't appreciate it that this one client, his most recent, didn't seem to get it.

Mikhail looked at the phone again and considered letting the call roll over to voicemail but then decided he'd be better served by dealing with the issue head on and avoiding any further confusion.

"Yes?" he said, scanning the beach as he slid from his stool and moved far enough from the waterfront cabana that the Bob Marley music bleeding from ceiling-mounted speakers could no longer be heard. He actually liked reggae, Marley in particular, but didn't think it sounded professional and he wanted to set the proper tone for what he knew would be a brief conversation.

"Fisher? Is that you?"

Hell no. He'd ceased being Scott Fisher the moment he'd stepped off the Island Explorer for the last time. The passport, driver's license, credit cards and everything else associated with that identity had long since been destroyed.

Mikhail had a few other identities that he kept and used for both work and travel. With the bigger jobs, though, he'd developed a practice of creating a new identity, using it once, and then retiring it permanently upon completion. It was, perhaps, a bit more cloak and dagger than was necessary but he placed an exceedingly high value on self-preservation, so to him, it was worth the extra trouble.

"Why do you call me?" he asked, his irritation allowing a bit of his old Russian accent to creep into his voice. "We had a business arrangement and that business is over. There is no further need for communication. Please forget my number; forget we ever spoke and refrain from calling again. Goodbye." He started to end the call but didn't move quickly enough.

"Hey. Hold on there, Sport. You did good work and all but our business isn't done."

"Excuse me?" Mikhail said, his lip curling as he brought the phone back to his ear. He didn't appreciate being called Sport. The name was demeaning and juvenile but he chose to let that go in favor of more important matters. "You requested a service. That service was rendered and I was duly compensated. There is nothing else we--"

"You got the wrong guy."

"Excuse me?" he said again. Mikhail's first thought was that the man was yanking his chain, another expression that didn't seem to make sense. Did it refer to bondage? If so, where was the humor in that? But the caller didn't sound like he was joking.

"I am sure I did precisely as promised. You have the laptop and the photos. That was the agreement. What further proof do you require?"

"None. We're just gonna need you to do a little... well, we'll call it cleanup."

Cleanup? His hand tightened around the phone. It seemed like the quality of his work was being called into question and he had no tolerance for that.

Per instructions, he had eliminated the target. He was sure of it and would have been even if he hadn't stood right there on the balcony and watched Mr. Martin Reginald, or Martin Worth if you prefer, disappear beneath the waves. He believed, hell, he knew, his plan had been executed to perfection. Why, then, did he have a sudden pain in the pit of his stomach?

He glanced back toward the bar cabana. Jade was looking his way but he couldn't tell if she was really focused on him or not. He still moved further down the beach, walking until he came to a stack of ocean kayaks in a tubular metal rack along with a pile of brightly-colored life jackets and paddles. There was a small booth nearby too but it was unmanned and no one appeared interested in kayaks at that time of day. It was approaching the dinner hour and he knew many guests would be busy showering and trading their swimwear for more formal attire.

"Perhaps you could explain," he said, using the toe of one sandal to pry a large pinkish shell out of the sand.

"Happy to, Sport. Like I said; you got the wrong dude."

Mikhail bristled at the repeated use of the nickname as well as the condescending tone. Who did the clown think he was talking to?

He had, of course, never actually met the person at the other end of the line. Over the years, he'd developed a strict no face-to-face policy with all his clients. That was so they could never identify him by anything more than his voice and whatever bogus name he was using for the job.

Each new transaction started with a third party contact, one Mikhail trusted unequivocally. Sam, or so he called himself, would lay all the groundwork and explain the rules to the *punter*, the odd term he used for any perspective client. Once everything was agreed upon and the initial deposit made, Mikhail would receive an encrypted email with instructions and contact information. Sam would then take his generous commission and that ended his involvement. He wouldn't even know what identity Mikhail would assume for the assignment. The system was simple and secure and had always worked perfectly, at least until now.

Mikhail had rarely bothered with burner phones or frequent number changes because in the dozens of jobs he'd done, no one had ever broken the rules and called him after the fact. He still should have been more cautious and was suddenly regretting that oversight.

"I assure you, I did exactly as—"

"Oh, it ain't your fault," the caller said, cutting him off. "I believe we had some bad intel, you might say. I'm sure you can straighten it out and we'll of course make it worth your while."

Mikhail did a slow five count as he stared out at the water. Although he'd never laid his eyes on Clayton Babbit III, he thought he knew the type well enough to construct a fairly accurate mental image. He pictured a large man with the cocky self-assuredness that so often came with the territory. He also would have bet on ruddy, weathered skin, a square jaw, boots—no doubt propped on the corner of his desk—blue jeans, thick belt, checkered shirt, a low-brimmed cowboy hat, a thin smile that rarely reached his eyes, and stained teeth from too many cigars. There was, Mikhail readily admitted, some stereotyping based on the unmistakable southern twang but he figured he was close enough.

"There is nothing I need to *straighten out*," he said, turning and beginning to slowly make his way back to the cabana. "I no longer work for you. If you wish to negotiate a new deal you must follow the proper channels. Until that happens, I would ask you to refrain from any further contact. Thank you."

Mikhail knew there would be no more contact. For reasons of security and privacy, he had never done more than one job for anyone and wasn't about to start making exceptions for an arrogant redneck blowhard, especially one that called him Sport. Clayton Babbit III could call Sam if he wanted to but that was as far as it would go. Mikhail allowed himself a small smile, his thumb hovering over the End button. Then, he heard something that froze him in his tracks.

"You'll work for me as long as I want," Babbit said, his voice calm but unmistakably menacing. "I ain't goin' through no channels either. You got that, Sport? Or should I call you Mikhail?"

The sound of his own name, his real name, was like a hard shot to the stomach. No one knew his real identity—well, excluding those who were supposed to know and that was a very, very short list. He'd never used his name professionally in any capacity. It likewise wasn't connected to any of his residences or assorted business dealings. He never traveled with it either. Sam of course knew the truth but he'd pull out his own fingernails before volunteering the information. Mikhail would have bet his life on that, so how had Babbit found out?

His eyes burned as he thought about what he'd do to whoever had betrayed him. He'd start digging and he wouldn't stop until he learned who was responsible for the deceit. That person would come to regret their lapse in judgment. Mikhail wanted to get on their trail immediately but, at the moment, he had a more pressing concern.

"How do you know my name?" he asked, weighing the value of playing dumb and deciding it would have been a waste of time.

Babbit chuckled as if they were old pals. "Oh, I know all sorts of things, Mi-kha-il Va-si-lek," each prolonged syllable like a sharp jab to the chest. "Take my word on that. I advise you don't test me either. I'm not looking to cause you any trouble. Help me clear up this problem we've got and you can carry on like we never even met."

"And if I refuse?"

Clayton Babbit III paused and then chuckled again. "I wouldn't recommend it."

"Is that a threat?"

"Call it a promise, Sport. And I always keep my promises."

Hardly able to feel his own legs, Mikhail returned to the bar, downed his drink in a single gulp and raised his finger for another. Jade had been filling wooden bowls from a large bag of plantain chips but she immediately stopped and walked over.

"Another vodka?"

He nodded. "Make it a double."

She looked at him and he thought she wanted to comment but something in his expression must have made her reconsider. Without flourish, she grabbed a bottle of Smirnoff and his glass and filled it to the brim.

"On the house, yah?" She smiled and raised an eyebrow. "I think you could use it."

He started to say "Spasibo," but caught himself in time and said a simple thank you instead.

Jade moved off and Mikhail wondered what in the world had gotten into him. *Spasibo*? Why didn't he just start spouting Russian all over the place so he could tip everyone off to his real identity? Better yet, he could hang a big *I'm a killer* sign around his neck. That would be a good conversation starter.

Shaking his head, he hoisted his glass and took a swig. His hand wasn't trembling but he was shaken nonetheless. He couldn't believe he'd been discovered. And the fact that his elaborate security had been breached by a guy like Babbit made him feel incompetent. This was unfamiliar territory and he didn't know how to proceed. He would, of course, make some changes in terms of how he went about his business. That, however, would have to wait because he was now a puppet and Babbit was the one pulling the strings.

He despised the very idea of being forced into doing someone else's bidding. He called his own shots. That's the way it had been and the way he always thought it would remain. Suddenly, though, he saw that he had no choice but to at least play along until he found some way to turn the tables.

He unfortunately didn't know how much Babbit knew about him or what the self-serving son of a bitch would do with that information if pressed. But, as Babbit clearly understood, Mikhail Vasilek was in no position to test him. He had too much at stake. What he needed was some leverage of his own and, given enough time, he had no doubt he'd get it. If Clayton Babbit III was the sort to hire a professional hit man to do his dirty work, he must have closets overflowing with skeletons and Mikhail was determined to find them.

He still didn't understand what exactly had gone wrong aboard the Island Explorer. Babbit said he'd killed the wrong person but that, Mikhail now knew, wasn't really the case. Martin Reginald was the intended target and he was definitely dead. Somehow, though, it turned out he was not who Babbit thought he was. Mikhail didn't know or care how such a monumental error had been made. It wasn't his problem, but he did zero in on one simple yet critical fact. Babbit had not yet identified who the next target would be. That meant Mikhail had an indeterminant amount of time for his own investigation. He would use it wisely. With a nod and a stiff smile, he threw some bills on the bar and headed to his room to pack.

-11-

I was still in a funk as I rode the elevator to the nineteenth floor and, moments later, let myself into my apartment. Without any conscious thought I deposited my keys in their designated spot, dropped my purse on the kitchen counter, walked into my tiny living room, and collapsed onto the couch. I considered a glass of wine, but with my current state of mind, I feared I might not stop once I got started. Thinking that might not be such a bad thing, I stretched out full length, wedged a throw pillow behind my head, kicked off one shoe, and I was working on the other when the muffled sounds of "Sex Type Thing" began to play.

"Leave me alone!" I said, already deciding I wasn't going to answer even if my phone hadn't been somewhere at the bottom of my purse which was a good fifteen feet away. Retrieving it was out of the question. I knew it was Vicki anyway and I had nothing more to say to her right then. A tiny voice in my head suggested someone else could be calling but a second voice told the first one to shut up and go to hell as I obviously wasn't in the mood to speak to anyone. I was thankful the two voices sorted it all out so I didn't have to get involved.

After what seemed like an unusually long time, my phone finally realized I wasn't interested and blessedly stopped ringing. I sighed, folded my arms over my chest, and tried to relax. I even contemplated napping as a means to clear my head, but following prolonged periods of alternately staring at the ceiling or staring at the inside of my eyelids, I groaned and sat up.

"Alexa, what time is it?" I asked, and the Amazon Echo device sitting on the end table informed me it was five thirty-seven. That came as a surprise, but I honestly didn't know if I thought it should be earlier or later. It seemed my funk had not yet dissipated. That, I knew, was because of everything now weighing on my mind. The internal clutter of negative emotions was preventing me from catching a few much needed Z's and had me feeling both indecisive and so tense I felt ready to climb the walls.

Giving into the inevitable, I uncorked a bottle of pinot noir, filled a glass, and took a healthy swig. It was medicine as much as anything else. Without the sedative effects of a good red wine, I knew I'd be up half the night. I also knew that, denied sufficient rest, the dangerous combination of stress and exhaustion would turn me into a basket case.

I really hated the way my brain worked sometimes. When I was dealing with writer's block, a not uncommon occurrence, I might sit for hours on end, fingers poised over the computer keys while I waited in helpless anticipation for my muse to make an appearance. As often as not, he acted like I was Typhoid Mary and wouldn't come anywhere near. I'd always thought of my muse as male. That was surely because he was as reliable as the weather and a royal pain in my ass to boot.

He had a twisted sense of humor too. After pointedly ignoring me all day, Monty—that was the name I'd come up with for the cantankerous little twit—would suddenly swing into action at around two in the morning and proceed to bombard me with a flurry of totally random and unwelcome thoughts. It always happened the same way. I'd wake up intent on doing nothing more than flipping my pillow and finding a more comfortable position. Next thing I knew I'd be thinking about my list of household chores, the Buy One Get One sale at Dollar General, Syrian refugees, my expanding waistline, Internet trolls, the broken hinge on the bathroom vanity, the New York Rangers, drone strikes, cupcakes, string theory, and, invariably, whatever writing project or projects I had in the works. Of course, by the time I got around to that, I'd be wide awake and epically pissed off.

Because that sort of thing happened on a frustratingly regular basis, I'd actually tried adjusting my work schedule and doing my writing in the middle of the night. That was another perk to being mostly self-employed. I could call my own shots. Unfortunately, *see also predictably*, my new nocturnal strategy worked about as well as you would expect. I was even less productive than before with the added bonus of being dead tired all the time. Think PMS with a side of diarrhea. Lovely, right?

At various times, I've experimented with meditation, yoga, dietary changes, and a variety of vitamin supplements in hopes I could retrain my scatterbrain to work a normal nine to five. None of it did any good. Alcohol consumption was the only thing that made a noticeable difference and even that was hit or miss. I didn't want to come to depend on that anyway, and I am now resigned to the possibility and perhaps likelihood that I will forever remain at the mercy of my messed-up mind, my temperamental muse, and all the other odd forces that seem to conspire against me.

Setting my glass aside, I stood, walked to the window, and then returned to the couch and sat down again right where I'd been before.

My stomach growled and I considered having some food delivered or, God forbid, actually getting up and making a meal. I likewise thought about cleaning the bathroom, doing laundry, balancing my checkbook, playing some music, or listening to the next chapter in the Robert Crais novel I'd started a few nights before.

It all seemed more trouble than it was worth so I grabbed the remote, powered on the television and clicked through the channels until I found an old episode of "Home Improvement." Tim the Tool *Man* Taylor was building the perfect man's bathroom complete with a multi-head shower, full-body dryer, a fridge, a lot of stainless steel, and a lazy bowl reclining toilet. I watched, or more accurately listened, for a few minutes but the program failed to capture my interest. I knew why, too. It was the same reason I'd bolted from Vicki's office a couple hours before. I was facing a major, potentially life-altering decision and I didn't feel like I was up to the challenge.

Was I really to blame for the death of another human being? It didn't seem possible. Hell, it still didn't seem real. I obviously wasn't the one who'd pushed Martin off the deck of a cruise ship, or whatever had actually happened to him, but it was a reasonable enough assumption that he'd still be alive if not for the role he'd been playing on my behalf. My books, my 'fiction,' had angered or scared someone enough to resort to murder. I was pretty sure I knew who. But until a few days ago, I hadn't had an inkling that person truly existed, let alone could be so dangerous.

That was only part of the problem. Vicki Goldstein, the individual most responsible for my success, could be up to her neck in a shit storm of my making and she had no idea. I had to tell her but I didn't know what possible good it could do. My entire literary career was a secret. Even if I was inclined to reveal my identity, I couldn't convincingly do so without Tower Brothers confirming my claim. That would expose Vicki and her company to who knew what and might catapult me directly into the eye of a hurricane. I didn't like my odds on that one and, until I had a better idea of where things stood, a personal sacrifice seemed pointless at best.

On legs I didn't entirely trust, I got up and moved to the bedroom. I wanted to slip under the covers and curl into a fetal position but I instead opened the closet, dropped to my knees, and placed my finger into the scanner of my small floor safe. There was a beep and then I heard the lock disengage. After a bit of rummaging, I withdrew a single well-worn envelope. I stared at it for a long moment but then had to close my eyes against a fresh tide of emotion.

I wished with every fiber of my being that the blasted thing had never come into my possession, or that I'd followed my instincts and dropped it in the trash after the first time I'd reviewed the contents. Nothing I could do about that now. I'd gone ahead blindly, as it were, and that led to a huge boost in book sales and popularity, for Martin anyway. He was gone now but I would continue receiving my royalty checks. The size of those checks would probably increase following the news of his death, as would my feelings of regret and remorse.

Still clutching the envelope, I went into my converted bedroom of an office where I turned on my desk lamp and computer. I sat, my chair emitting a low, squeaky moan as I swiveled back and forth. I was so accustomed to the noise it usually didn't register. Now, though, it sounded louder, more persistent and somehow accusatory. It seemed to say, "You. **You. YOU!**"

I was a habitual swiveler but, after a few seconds of that, I couldn't take it anymore. I choked back a sob and then bent over and depressed the lever at the base of the chair that would keep the fucking thing from moving. The sudden silence felt oppressive but still better than the alternative.

There was no real reason for me to reread the letter. I practically knew it by heart. But with nothing more proactive to do, I opened the envelope, removed two sheets of plain stationary and spread them out in front of me, using an index finger to smooth the creases. I then dug in a lower desk drawer until I located the little electronic device I refer to as my eyeball.

The real name, in case you're wondering, is the Acrobat HD Ultra, and it's a camera roughly the size of a computer mouse. It attaches to a movable arm and I can plug it into any television or monitor. The camera magnifies whatever it's pointed at and projects it onto the screen. I primarily use it for reading letters, bills, and other printed material, and on rare occasions—emphasis on rare—it assists with makeup application. Take it from me. You haven't lived until you've seen your own pores magnified a few hundred times. Yikes!

You're probably thinking my little visual aid sounds pretty cool. I consider it a necessary evil and that's it. Sure, the thing does make my life easier. It just isn't much fun shelling out a couple thousand dollars so I can do the things most people are able to do simply by opening their peepers. I'm not complaining. Okay, I guess I am. The technology is amazing. I'll give you that. But it's not a comfortable, practical, or easy way to read and I avoid it whenever possible. If you ever feel the need to get in touch with me for whatever reason, do me a favor and send me an email. Better yet, just call.

Dear Alex, I began reading, squinting at the computer screen while I deftly guided the paper under the camera's eye.

Using the Acrobat, or any similar device, is an acquired skill because that particular type of deft does not come naturally. You're basically looking at one thing while doing something else. And it's not like the entire document, or whatever you happened to be reading, is magnified all at once. Depending on how bad your eyesight is, you might only get a word or two at a time. You have to keep moving the paper accordingly, word by word and line by line. It requires a smooth, steady hand because one wrong twitch and you're suddenly half way down the page.

Of course, the real challenge is when you've got to rely on that sort of setup for handwriting. It's second nature to me now but still doesn't feel normal. There's really nothing I can even compare it to. Despite countless hours of practice, my penmanship is still chicken scratch. It's legible, barely, and that's as good as it's ever gonna get. It can get worse, though.

When I don't have a camera at my disposal, my writing resembles something you might get from an intoxicated preschooler. It's embarrassing. And believe it or not, that was one of my biggest motivators behind my decision to find someone else to represent me on my books. It wasn't supposed to be a high-risk job. My only objective was in avoiding uncomfortable situations. That was it, or that's all it had been, but I was second guessing all of that now.

I adjusted the camera's brightness and continued to read.

It was so nice to see you last July. I still can't believe it's been SO long. Where does the time go? You seem to be doing really well for yourself. I think that's great! And how long before we start hearing wedding bells? That guy you were with looked like a real catch and I could tell he was totally into you. I hope you two are still going strong.

Going strong wasn't exactly how I'd put it. Our *relationship,* such as it was, had been more or less on the rocks even before a friend treated me to an evening of margaritas and then convinced me to attend our twenty-year high school reunion. I'd successfully avoided the five, the ten and the fifteen, and I'd planned on keeping that streak alive but then.... *Stupid tequila.*

Anyway, I'd gone to the reunion and dragged Brooks—yes, his name really was Brooks—along, for moral support I guess. We kept our fake smiles on all evening and then departed in separate cabs. I hadn't seen him since and that was extremely okay with me. The guy shaved his legs, drank wine coolers, and listened to Nickelback. Talk about a trifecta. We were doomed from the start. Apparently, though, someone saw something we hadn't. Either that or, and this was a lot more likely, Deb was just making small talk until she got to the real reason she'd written to me.

Debbie Royal was one of dozens of people I'd been friendly enough with in high school but hadn't thought about at all after graduation. Had she not come up and introduced herself, I doubt I ever would have recognized her. Then again, I'm not so good with faces.

You mentioned that you are a freelance writer. I'm sorry but I don't remember the details.

That was because I hadn't offered any. Most of my assignments are on the dull side, technical writing and the like, and really not worth talking about. On those infrequent occasions when anyone asks, I tend to keep my responses short and as vague as possible.

You must know a lot of fascinating people and have all sorts of connections. That's got to be so exciting.

That might be true of some writers but not me, all safely tucked away in my self-dug bunker.

I have a little problem and it occurred to me that, in your line of work, you might be able to help. I apologize if it's inappropriate to ask but I don't know where else to turn.

Her problem, as it turned out, wasn't little at all. Deb's brother Bryan, according to her letter, was an engineer aboard the Deepwater Horizon drilling rig. She either didn't know or didn't say what his specific responsibilities were. She did, however, claim he'd told her about some serious safety concerns. That wasn't exactly enlightening.

Following the April 20, 2010 blowout, explosion, and fire that cost eleven workers their lives, the only real surprise was that the disaster hadn't happened sooner. The various safety-related shortcuts the company had taken were, by now, well documented. One thing I hadn't known was that many employees had been aware of potentially serious problems but hadn't reported them over fears they would lose their jobs. I'd done a quick Google search and determined that part of Bryan's story was not only disturbing but accurate. The rest of his claims were more difficult to prove, not that I'd put as much effort into that as I knew I should have.

Bryan had supposedly told his sister on two separate occasions about suspicions that a third party, an outside party, was responsible for equipment tampering that, in his opinion, could prove catastrophic. He got that part right. He never used the word "sabotage," or Deb hadn't anyway, but that was how it sounded to me. Unfortunately, the conversations had taken place over the phone so there was nothing in writing. All I had was Deb's letter and that could not be considered evidence even in the loosest definition of the word.

There's a world of difference between freelance writing and true journalism. I've done my share of op-ed pieces but that's as close as I ever get to reporting hard news. The point is I lack both the training and the resources to properly vet a story. I couldn't even go to the source because Bryan was dead. No, he was not one of the eleven. He'd died two days later in what was officially ruled an accident. Deb hadn't given any specifics.

Using my left hand to hold my right one steady, I slid the paper along and re-read Deb's final paragraph.

I wish I had paid more attention but, well, Bryan has always been fanciful. It's not that I didn't believe him. I just figured he was exaggerating. I do remember one name. It was Clayton Babbage III. Something like that anyway. He lives in Louisiana and Bryan said he was the one behind it all. I just wish I'd taken him more seriously. Had I told the authorities what he told me, maybe something would have been done and those poor workers would still be alive. Maybe he'd be alive too. I know I could still go to the police. But you being a writer and all, I figure you're the perfect person to bring this whole thing to light. You can find that Babbage guy, expose him and bring him to justice. I'm happy to help any way I can.

I took a shuddering breath, folded the letter and slipped it back into the envelope. Despite all my efforts, I had failed to locate a Clayton Babbage III, in Louisiana or anywhere else. I had, however, found a Clayton Babbit III. He was the owner and president of Sand-Sational, a successful yet somewhat controversial beach nourishment business that mainly operated in the Gulf Coast region. He appeared to have numerous other business interests too. I didn't know if he was the right person and had no good way to find out. I couldn't even ask my former classmate for more information.

A day after posting the letter to me, Debora Lynn Royal, age thirty nine, stepped in front of a city bus and was pronounced dead at the scene. According to the police report, it was dark and rainy and there were no witnesses. In his statement, the bus driver said, "It was like she came out of nowhere."

So far as I'd been able to determine, there was no indication she'd been pushed or any hint of foul play. Now, though, I had to wonder if her death was something more than it had initially appeared. And what about her brother? What sort of *accident* had befallen him? I started typing his name into my search engine but then decided I wasn't mentally prepared for whatever results I might find. I powered the computer off, refilled my wine glass, returned to the sofa, and for the first time in decades, cried myself to sleep.

-12-

"Go fuck a sea horse!" Babbit shouted, but only after he'd slammed down the phone in disgust.

"Problem?"

Clayton Babbit III sat back and propped his freshly polished cowboy boots on the edge of his desk and glared at Louie, his fulltime technical advisor, sometime informal legal counsel, and near constant source of aggravation. "What was your first clue?" he asked through a haze of bluish cigar smoke.

Louie angled his tall, thin frame out of his chair, crossed to the window and opened it wide.

"Make yourself at home," Babbit muttered, stogie poking out of the right side of his mouth.

Louie didn't respond to that or return to his seat, instead leaning against the wall and folding his arms over his chest. "So what's wrong?" he asked, gesturing with his chin towards the telephone.

"Same shit, different day."

"Care to elaborate?"

Babbit glowered. He wasn't in the mood to answer Louie's questions. On the other hand, he couldn't very well keep the man in the dark; not when there were possible legal repercussions someone, namely Louie, might have to deal with.

Babbit had always been a big believer in covering his own ass, and at times that meant divulging more information than he might have otherwise been inclined to. The key, he'd learned long ago, was to always control the information and only dole it out to serve a specific purpose or achieve the maximum effect. To put that another way, he never volunteered anything unless he had a hell of a good reason.

Babbit reflected on his recent conversation with Mikhail Vasilek, the former Scott Fisher. It had gone almost exactly as anticipated. At first, the guy was dismissive, confrontational, and understandably uncooperative. How quickly he'd changed his tune once he was addressed by his real name. It was like Babbit had dropped a grenade right down the poor bastard's shorts. BANG! Vasilek was suddenly so scared Babbit would have sworn he could hear him sweating right down the phone line. The message had been delivered with maximum efficiency and Mikhail Vasilek would do Babbit's bidding, at least in the short term.

In truth, Clayton Babbit had not gone looking for dirt on the man. He'd just gotten lucky. Not long after beginning negotiations for the Reginald hit with someone named Sam, an email meant for Vasilek had gone to Babbit instead. It had been encrypted, but Louie worked his computer mumbo-mojo and managed to crack the code.

The content of the email had been largely insignificant, something about a job in Baltimore he'd turned down; but Louie's efforts yielded a name and Babbit was sure he'd be able to use it someday. He just hadn't imagined that day would come so soon. He had informed Vasilek he knew other things about him too. That had been something of an exaggeration. Actually, it was an outright lie but Babbit knew Vasilek was in no position to call his bluff. If only the rest of his problems could be solved so easily.

"You know that Skyward project I was telling you about?"

Louie bit a knuckle thoughtfully. "The hotel, right?"

"More than that," Babbit replied.

The Grand Skyward was an entire resort complex—four high end hotels on the same premises. Skyward Seclusion offered bungalow-style lodging and catered to adults only. The Skyward Splendor took a similar approach but in a more family-friendly format. Skyward Escape was a standard high rise which made the accommodations more economical. And Skyward Envy was the crown jewel—villa-style lodging, each unit boasting a private pool, butler service, complimentary spa treatments, greens fees, and eye-popping nightly rates. The complex was also all-inclusive, which meant restaurants, bars, nightclubs, boutiques, a water park, a recreation center, a casino, a theatre, an adjoining pro-level golf course, and numerous other amenities.

Babbit couldn't even guess at the total size of the property and grounds. What he knew for sure was that the Grand Skyward, in addition to everything else, sat on almost three quarters of a mile of pristine and private white sand beach—over 225,000 square feet of pure Gulf Coast paradise. That's how it was described in the brochure anyway. However, a season of uncharacteristically strong storms pounded that section of the Louisiana coastline and left the waterfront portion of the Skyward looking a lot less grand than its name would suggest. It all happened during a two billion dollar renovation project and the Grand Skyward was now just weeks away from the heavily publicized grand reopening. The owners wanted everything to be just right so they'd called Sand-Sational, one of Babbit's many business interests, and paid an astronomical fee to have their beach restored ASAP. It was now up to Babbit to earn that money, and all of a sudden, it was proving frustratingly difficult.

He'd purchased Sand-Sational on a whim in the fall of 2005. At the time, he had no plans to branch into beach nourishment, or what's often referred to as renourishment or refurbishment. He hadn't even known that was a thing until he sat down at a poker table in Pensacola and struck up a conversation with a talkative and clearly intoxicated captain of a barge, one of three barges owned by the man's brother-in-law. They had, according to the captain, just delivered a large shipment of sand to an area of beach especially susceptible to erosion.

"Hold on," Babbit had said. "You gotta be shittin' me. Why would someone pay for something they know is going to wash away again anyway?"

"Don't know," the man said, throwing back a double shot of bourbon. "But it happens all the time and it's good money too."

Babbit was mystified. He'd grown up in Wrightsville Beach, a small community just east of Wilmington, North Carolina, and he knew how quickly a strong storm surge could ravage a coastline and the surrounding areas. He'd lived through hurricanes, tropical storms, and the devastating floods that so often followed. In fact, it was the flooding in the aftermath of Hurricane Fran that finally forced his family to relocate.

Babbit's father, recently retired from the banking industry, had purchased three vacation homes to be used as rental properties. He believed it to be a terrific investment. That was in the spring of 1996. Fran made landfall early that September and dumped nearly a foot and a half of rain in the region. Two of the Babbit homes were badly damaged. The third was leveled and swept out to sea. As was so often the case, the "comprehensive" insurance policy included some loopholes and other disqualifiers, and in the end only covered about fifty percent of the loss. Rebuilding was out of the question, and it became necessary to sell the family home to pay off the mortgages on the rentals and avoid personal bankruptcy. Clayton Babbit II died of a heart attack three months later.

What happened to him was tragic but not uncommon. Homes and businesses get wiped out all the time. It's the risk you take. Where his dad screwed up was putting so many eggs in such a fragile basket. It might have worked out great and probably would have under normal circumstances. Instead, he was the victim of bad luck and bad timing, and the basket broke. Would he have made the same decisions had he known how it would turn out? Of course not, and that was why Babbit couldn't fathom why anyone would willingly and with foresight pay one red cent to restore a fucking beach. To him, that didn't seem much different than opening a ski resort in Miami or somewhere equally unsuitable and trucking in a mountain of snow. It might look great for a while but there was no way to avoid the inevitable. Sand might last a little longer but it too would disappear sooner or later so what in hell was the point?

However, over the next few hours, he purchased several rounds of drinks, pocketed eight hundred dollars playing Texas Hold 'Em and got a full rundown on the Sand-Sational operation. The business model was ridiculously simple. Take sand from one place and dump it somewhere else. The demand would always be there so, as long as you had the supply, it was a fool-proof proposition. That was the theory and it had proved true for a while. Then, Sand-Sational inadvertently sucked thousands of pounds of sand from a manatee sanctuary. No animals were harmed or even inconvenienced so far as anyone knew. Nevertheless, the company ended up at odds with the Florida Department of Environmental Protection.

"You don't mess with the DEP," the captain said, draining his glass again.

"So what happened?" Babbit asked.

The captain shrugged. "I don't rightly know but our business dried up in a hurry. No one wanted anything to do with us anymore. I guess that's what you get for crossing the government."

"They sandbagged you, huh?"

"Poor choice of words but that's about the size of it. This is the first job we've had in the past month and we had to call in a lot of favors to get it."

"So what are you gonna do?"

"That ain't up to me, but if you're in the market for some barges, I think I know where you can get a good price."

Babbit asked a few more questions but he thought that was the end of it until the following morning when the Sand-Sational owner tracked him down at his hotel and presented him with an offer he flat out couldn't refuse. He bought the company and, in order to circumvent the Florida DEP, moved the operation to Louisiana. Business was good from the start and then Babbit orchestrated a deal that literally paid millions. For a period of about two years, beach restoration was generating more revenue than all his other businesses combined. Things had changed, though, and various environmental agencies were crawling up his ass on what seemed like a daily basis and making his life hell. He was about ready to sell his barges, dredging equipment, and all the rest to the first sucker that came along.

"It's political bullshit," Babbit said, stubbing out his cigar in a lead crystal ashtray.

"How so?" Louie returned to his chair but he left the office window open.

"Skyward gave us that contract because I promised I'd get the job done in time. I wasn't blowing smoke either. It isn't easy to fill an order that large, especially on short notice, but I have a source. This "gentleman" I occasionally do business with owns his own island. It's about three miles off the coast."

"And?"

"And he wants to remove a large area of sand beach to put in a pier or break-wall or some shit."

"Okay," Louie said, but didn't sound like he was making the connection.

"You understand what I'm saying?" Babbit asked. "I need sand and this guy's got a beach he doesn't want. It's perfect."

"Yeah. I get that. So what's the problem?"

Babbit shook his head. "If you ask me, there shouldn't be one. It's his island. He ought to be able to do what he wants."

"But?"

"But that island, along with a couple neighboring islands, is apparently the natural habitat for some useless turtle that's on the endangered species list. This is there nesting time and they, of course, nest in the fucking sand."

"So you can't take it."

"Oh, I can take it. I just need to wait a month."

"Which is too late for the Skyward job."

Babbit stared at him. "And that's why I pay you the big bucks. You have an amazing grasp of the obvious. Now get on the phone and find me some fucking sand or I'll feed your skinny ass through the shredder and spread you on the beach instead."

-13-

I opened my eyes at about quarter past one with a stiff neck and no clue where I was. I blinked and stared and, for a time, couldn't put any of it together. Everything looked strange and I couldn't make sense of it. Why was there so much street light coming through the window and why did it seem like the window was in the wrong place altogether? I started to roll over, felt myself falling, and had a moment of simultaneous panic and clarity right before I hit the floor.

"Shit," I swore as my elbow smacked against the sofa leg.

Bleary-eyed and irritated, I got up and stumbled into the bedroom where I peeled off yesterday's clothes, fell into bed, and pulled the comforter over my head. I had this crazy fantasy of somehow salvaging a decent night sleep. I should have known better. I tossed and turned for the next few hours, and when I did occasionally manage to drift off, I dreamt of having insomnia.

Yeah. I do that sometimes and it's every bit as frustrating as it sounds. I finally gave up rather than woke up, possibly muttering some unladylike words as I freed myself from a tangle of sheets and blankets. I didn't even bother checking the time because it was still full dark out and that was proof enough that it was too damn early.

In the kitchen, I brewed a pot of coffee, went to the trouble of filling a mug and adding French vanilla creamer, and then I sat there and gazed at it until it got cold. By then, I could detect a hint of daylight out and I decided I should at least attempt to do something productive.

I started by showering, washing, and conditioning my hair twice so I had an excuse to remain there under the spray as long as I could. I was, I acknowledged, intentionally delaying the tasks that were, well, let's say less desirable. It was really just one task and, no matter how much I might want to, I couldn't put it off forever. That was the one decision I had made while lying in bed not sleeping. I had to take that bull by the horns, even if it meant I might be setting myself up for a Pamplona-style gouging.

To prove I was up to the challenge, I dressed in jeans, boots and a bright red shirt. *Olé,* I thought, and then I spent the next ninety minutes pacing my apartment and trying to talk myself out of what I knew I had to do. I was unsuccessful, which I think is to my credit, and at eight o'clock sharp, I grabbed my keys and phone and headed for the door.

"Is Vicki in?" I asked, entering Tower Brothers Publishing and removing my sunglasses as I approached the reception desk.

"Hey, Alex. Good morning. I didn't know you were coming in today."

"I'm full of surprises. How are you, Tammy?"

"Same old," the receptionist replied.

A short, round woman, she'd been manning that same desk as long as I'd been with Tower. We'd always been friendly but our conversations rarely extended much beyond the weather.

"Is she in then?" I asked, starting to move past.

"I think so. Is she expecting you?"

Only if she's clairvoyant. I had thought about contacting Vicki ahead of time. I'd even pulled out my phone and gone as far as opening the messaging app once or twice on the way over. In the end, though, I hadn't texted, emailed, or called because I was afraid I might still chicken out and go home. I hadn't exactly passed the point of no return but, now that the Rubicon was in sight, I was anxious to dive in and get it over with.

I was about to tell Tammy that Vicki would certainly want to see me whether she was expecting me or not when I heard a nearby door open, and a moment later, the woman herself entered the lobby.

"Tammy, could you ple—" she began but stopped mid-word. "Alex?" Vicki turned her attention to me. "This is something of a surprise. After yesterday I...."

She kind of trailed off there but we both understood what hadn't been said. I'd run out like a maniac and neither of us thought I'd be back so soon.

"Do you have a few minutes?" I asked, already taking a step towards her office.

"Of course," she said. "Follow me."

I picked up on the note of optimism in her voice and knew what it meant. She believed I was there because I'd come to my senses and decided to not only continue my literary career but, at long last, take credit for my work.

Be careful what you wish for, I thought sullenly. Vicki may well get what she wanted but at what cost? The whole company was still reeling over Martin's death. I'd inadvertently given Vicki a glimmer of hope and I was about to pop that balloon in a serious way.

"Ms. Goldstein?" Tammy's voice trailed us down the hall. "Did you need me for something?"

“Later,” Vicki said, waving a hand as she opened the door and ushered me into her office.

-14-

Detective Megan Lynch unrolled a poster-sized photo displaying a full bow to stern view of the starboard side of the Island Explorer. She studied it, concentrating mostly on the tenth floor. She then nodded to herself, re-rolled the photo, and slid that and some other pictures and drawings into a long cardboard tube. She sat for a time, tapping polished fingernails against the tube as she searched for holes in her theory. Finding none, she finally stood and went in search of Captain Weiserman.

"Can I show you something?" she asked, poking her head inside his open office door.

"One sec," he mouthed, and she saw he had a phone receiver wedged between his neck and shoulder.

"Sorry," she mouthed in reply, backing away and retreating a few steps down the hall.

As she waited, looking at the big bulletin board and the collection of outdated postings about chicken barbecues, a Lion's Club fundraiser, a food drive, and someone trying to sell a twenty-year-old Toyota Corolla, Megan thought about her decision to leave the small lakeside town of Oswego in favor of the glamour of the NYPD. She hadn't really been unhappy. She was well respected and knew she was good at her job, but she also had felt under-utilized.

It wasn't like Oswego was crime-free, but much of her work had gotten too routine: burglary, larceny, bar fights, DUIs, drugs, and domestic violence; and money was the common denominator throughout all of it. People did dumb things when they had expensive addictions or simply didn't have enough to eat. She'd seen it more times than she could count. And with the exception of one case involving a local race car driver and attempted murder, very little of what she dealt with was memorable, challenging,, or even interesting.

After months of soul searching, she'd traded in title and tenure for a tiny apartment, a slight bump in salary, and the expectation of more excitement or at least more variety. She wasn't regretting her decision. But all of a sudden, Megan found herself wondering if she'd maybe bitten off more than she could chew. *A professional assassin?* That's what she thought they were dealing with and her head was spinning.

"Come on in," Captain Weiserman called. "Sorry to keep you waiting."

"And I'm sorry for interrupting," she said, returning to stand in the doorway. "I didn't realize you were on the phone."

He made a disgusted sound. "It was the Broward County ME again. Remember that jurisdictional pissing contest I mentioned before?"

Megan nodded and took another step into the room.

"It's worse than I feared. Our Mr. Worth—we now have a positive ID by the way—was discovered just off the Florida coast but there's apparently a decent chance he actually went overboard in international waters."

"And that makes a difference?"

"Not to me, but I'm not the one calling the shots. And get this. I learned this morning that the Island Explorer—the entire Island cruise line as a matter of fact—is registered in Malta. We've been instructed that we have to keep the International Relations Unit, that's a division of the Maltese Police Force in case you didn't know, apprised of *any and all significant developments*."

"What constitutes a significant development?"

"Hell if I know." Captain Weiserman ran a hand over his bald head. "Malta's got to be five thousand miles from where the crime took place. Why would any of it be significant to them?"

"Liability?" Megan offered

"Maybe so. It definitely isn't practicality. Different jurisdictions with different sets of rules. It's ridiculous. And trying to follow all the proper protocols, I feel like I have to jump through half a dozen hoops before I can get anything done."

"Has your hoop-hopping been helpful?"

"That's cute," he said, giving her a look. "I didn't realize you were such a wise ass. But to answer your question, I don't honestly know."

"So what's the latest?"

The captain shook his head. "You're gonna love this one. There's suddenly a lot of pressure to determine a specific cause of death. The condition of the body is making that predictably difficult and it's slowing everything else down."

"Where's the pressure coming from?"

"Not sure," he said with a shrug. "And I don't see why it matters anyway. We know we're dealing with a homicide, but up to this point we have no suspects and no hint of a motive. That should be our focus. We can worry about the rest of it later.

"Actually," Megan said. "That's kind of why I'm here. I've got something I'd like to show you."

"Am I gonna like it?'

"I hope so," she said. "I think it supports a theory I've been kicking around."

"That sounds a lot better than nothing. Come in, sit down and show me what you've got."

Megan looked at his desk and the stacks of papers, file folders, and other assorted detritus. "It might be easier to do it in the conference room"

"I see how you are," he said, glancing at his cluttered desktop and then his watch. "But I've got a better idea. Let's go find a nice big booth somewhere and grab some lunch. I'm buying."

Half an hour later, Megan was picking her way through a garden salad with light vinaigrette dressing and a Diet Coke while trying not to drool over Captain Weiserman's New York style Reuben and fries. She wasn't really watching her weight but had been making a concerted effort to eat healthier, and for the most part it sucked. She knew she'd pass no fewer than five pizzerias on her way home that night and was already doubting her ability to run that savory gauntlet without giving into the temptation of at least one hot, fresh garlic knot. Annoyed, she stabbed a cucumber slice and ran it around the inside of her bowl in search of some actual flavor.

"You want some fries?" Weiserman asked, gesturing at his plate.

Shit, Megan thought. *Was I staring?* She shook her head and popped the cucumber into her mouth.

"I don't know how you can eat like that," he said. "I wouldn't be able to make it through the day."

"Oh, it's not so bad," said Megan, wondering if her words sounded as hollow and empty as her stomach felt.

"If you say so." He picked up his napkin and wiped grease from his mouth and hands. "I've got to get back soon, so if you're finished we should probably get down to business."

"Sure." Megan slid all the dishes to the edge of the table and then removed the large photo from the cardboard tube she'd placed on the seat beside her. "This," she said, turning the photo his way and using his unused fork as a pointer, "was Martin Worth's cabin."

Captain Weiserman nodded.

"And here," Megan continued, moving the fork down three floors, "is where Mr. Franco says he was the night we believe Worth most likely went overboard."

"This Mr. Franco is the witness?"

"Yes. He is a performer employed by Island Cruise Lines."

"And as I recall, he says he may have heard or seen something but he was alone and possibly intoxicated at the time."

"It's not a great testimonial," Megan acknowledged. "I realize that. But, he's all we've got right now and his story does match my working timeline."

"Okay," Weiserman said. "Of course, in addition to not knowing the cause of death, we don't yet have an exact time of death either. That could be the key to this whole thing."

"I think you're right, and I think it's why our perpetrator tried so hard to make it look like Worth was still on that ship."

"He did a damn good job of it."

"Agreed. But in doing so he may have given us an opening."

The captain shifted in his seat and draped an arm along the back of the booth. He regarded Megan with interest. "So spill it," he said. "What's on your mind?"

Megan reached for her legal pad automatically but she'd memorized all the pertinent facts. Her line of reasoning required a small leap of faith. She acknowledged that but also knew in her gut she was on the right track. "Do you notice anything about his cabin?" she asked, nodding at the photo.

He leaned forward and looked. "Long drop to the water."

"Ninety plus feet give or take. Anything else?"

"Well, it's somewhat isolated. Is that what you wanted me to say?"

That elicited a small smile. "I think it's a significant detail."

"Why?" Wigs asked, but Megan thought he already knew.

"See this?" She pointed at a glass-fronted room just to the left of Martin Worth's cabin. "That's what they call their reading room. It isn't very big but you've still got a twenty-five foot stretch with no hand or foot holds. Those aren't regular windows either. They don't open. I don't see any way his balcony could have been accessed from that direction."

"Who says his balcony was accessed from anywhere?'

"And look here," Megan continued, ignoring his question and jabbing her fork at the eleventh floor. That area is all open deck space. Although it would be easy enough for some brave soul to find a rope and lower himself down, you have a restaurant here." She indicated an area just to the left. "And that's where they do all the late-night buffets. I'm told a lot of people take their plates of food and go outside. I doubt anyone would be able to hop that railing without being seen."

"How late is the restaurant open?"

"They stop serving at 1AM."

"So it could have happened after that."

"It could have," Megan conceded, "but I don't believe it. It's too improbable."

"Okay. Then what do you believe?"

Megan took a breath. "We have to make a couple assumptions. The first is that Martin Worth really was dumped overboard sometime between late Thursday night and early Friday morning."

"I think the evidence supports that," Captain Weiserman allowed. "No one reported seeing him after he left the lounge sometime after ten o'clock Thursday night. All we have from that point forward is the paper trail of his movements which we know now is bogus. He wasn't ordering room service breakfast and bobbing in the Atlantic at the same time."

"Actually," Megan said. "I was a little confused by the room service thing but only because I've never cruised before."

"Well I have. They don't bring breakfast orders into your room. They don't even knock on the door. The tray is left outside at the designated time and it's there when you're ready."

"Yeah. I know that now. So our perp used Worth's room phone to order juice, coffee, Danish, and a fruit plate, and by doing so, he left a convenient and misleading record of that transaction."

"He's a cold son of a bitch no doubt. Damn clever too. But you've—"

"Can I get you anything else?" their server asked, stopping at the end of their table, a tray of drinks balanced in one hand."

"We're good," Captain Weiserman said, never taking his eyes off Megan. "We'll take the check now."

"You got it," she replied, moving away as he dug for his wallet.

"You mentioned a couple assumptions," he said. "What was the other one?"

"It has to do with Freddie Franco." Megan looked down at her pad without seeing anything she'd written there. "Although he was under the influence, I think he saw exactly what he told me."

"Why do you say that?"

Megan felt like she was out on a limb but didn't see anything in her boss's face or hear anything in his tone to make her think he wasn't prepared to give her the benefit of the doubt."

"Well," she said, emboldened, "it just fits. To me, the strangest thing about this whole incident is the lack of reliable witnesses. At first, that was driving me crazy but I think now that it might be a clue."

"How so?"

"We're talking about a cruise ship full of passengers and crew. How many private places are there, really? I mean the ones that would be accessible to the guests. How many places could you kill a person, or bring a person that was already dead, and dump him overboard without running a huge risk of being spotted?"

"So you believe he was dropped from his own balcony?"

"I do," Megan said. "It's really the only thing that makes sense. That's why I think Mr. Franco's story is believable and should be given proper credence."

"Fine," Captain Weiserman said. "Then what would that tell us?"

Megan gave a thin smile. "I've scanned every second of that security video. With the exception of housekeeping, the only other person who ever entered Worth's cabin through the front door was Worth himself, or someone who could have easily been mistaken for him. And before you ask, none of that nonsense with the big hat or him always looking down happened until after Worth had presumably gone for his eternal swim. "

"So?"

"So I'm willing to bet our killer gained access to Worth's cabin through the balcony, and I'm equally sure there's just one guy that could have pulled that off."

"And that's the main theory you want to work?"

"Yes," Megan said immediately.

"Then run with it. Get some help, though. I'll bring Zanetti up to speed and send him your way."

-15-

This time I accepted Vicki's offer of water. I sat in the same chair I'd briefly occupied the day before, and while she played hostess, the last act of kindness I was likely to receive from her for quite a while, I busied myself by wringing my hands and biting down on the inside of my cheek. The woman was going to kill me. That's all there was to it. Of course, given her lofty position in the world of literature, the killing would be figurative and I knew I deserved much worse. I supposed Vicki might feel the same way by the time I got to the end of my story.

"So what's up?" she asked, handing me a glass and then sitting down. "Have you made a decision?" Her tone was more subdued than it had been moments before and I supposed she'd gauged from my demeanor that my sudden presence there was not to proclaim the imminent arrival of rainbows and butterflies.

"There's, uh, something I need to talk to you about. I'm afraid you're not going to like it." I took a sip of water but what I really wanted to do was hold the cool glass up against the side of my head. I didn't think that would look suitably professional so I held it in my lap instead. That wasn't as comforting but at least it gave my hands something to do.

"I've got a meeting in about twenty minutes. I can reschedule if necessary."

"Well, if it isn't too much trouble...."

Vicki was silent for several seconds and I knew my response surprised her. She opened her mouth to say something but then stood and crossed to her desk and I heard her push a button on her phone.

"Hey, Jess. It's me. Do me a favor. I'd like you to clear my calendar for the next two hours.

"I know," Vicki went on after a pause. "I'm just not gonna be able to do it today. Call him with my apologies and try to set something up for early next week. I'll go to him if that's what I need to do.

"No. That's it for now. I'm here with Alex and I don't know how long we'll be. I don't want to be disturbed so please tell Tammy to put all my calls through to you.

"Right. I'll let you know. Thanks.

"O—kay," Vicki said, cradling the receiver and returning to her seat. "I'm all yours. Can I assume this has to do with your books?"

I almost laughed at that. *No, Vicki. I heard I could save fifteen percent on my car insurance and I thought we could discuss that.*

"It, um, it does," I said. "I think—"

"You're quitting." Vicki didn't ask the question but delivered the statement with all the solemnity of a guilty verdict in a murder trial. "I had a feeling when you dashed out of here yesterday. Listen, Alex. I know Martin's death has hit us all hard; you more than anyone. You still need to keep things in perspective. You're too good to—"

"I'm not quitting," I said, with more conviction than I felt but Vicki still rambled on a while longer before my words sunk in.

"Wait," she said, halting mid plea. "What did you say?"

"That I'm not quitting. At least, I don't think so."

"Well that's great!" She actually clapped. "Alex, I'm so relieved. I was afraid you'd make a snap decision and end up regretting it."

And how do you know I haven't done that already?

"I appreciate your support," I said, gripping my water glass so tightly I thought it might crack. "Really, I do. You've always been so fantastic to me. I can't thank you enough."

I sort of faltered there, having no earthly idea how I should continue. Vicki put her trust in me which meant Tower Brothers had too. How was I supposed to tell her that, because of my carelessness and laziness, I had in all likelihood unleashed a killer and paved the way for a world-class defamatory lawsuit against her employer?

She was ebullient yet I wanted to sink into the floor and disappear, or at least bolt from the office like I'd done the day before. I knew I had to explain what happened or I'd never be able to live with myself. I owed that much to Martin and to Vicki too. I just couldn't find the words to begin.

"What is it?" Vicki asked, surprising me by reaching over and taking my hand. "This is a good thing, for your career I mean. Why do you look so troubled?"

I stared at her and, for once, I was grateful I couldn't read her expression. "It's… m—my fault," I stammered, and then completely lost it, breaking down in a wave of shuttering sobs.

"I'm sorry," I kept saying anytime I caught my breath enough to speak.

Vicki didn't answer, or if she did I couldn't hear her over my own pathetic blubbering. She did let go of my hand long enough to retrieve a box of tissues from somewhere. I accepted them gratefully and used a handful to dab at my eyes and nose. I felt like an asshole and knew I was making a fool of myself, but I couldn't seem to pull it together. To her credit, Vicki didn't ask any questions or offer any inanities about how everything would be all right. She simply sat and waited. The tears finally stopped coming and, in time, my breath more or less returned to normal too.

"I'm sorry," I said again. "That was stupid. I... I shouldn't have come in today."

Vicki took my sodden wad of tissues and dropped them into a trash can. "It seems to me that you believe you have a pretty compelling reason for being here. Of course, we're not gonna get anywhere unless you tell me what it is."

"You're right." I picked up the water glass which had somehow ended up on the table. I drained the contents and put the glass down again.

"Would you like more?" Vicki asked and I couldn't hear any trace of the impatience I knew she must be feeling.

I'd showed up unannounced, thrown her morning schedule completely out of whack, cried like a baby, and still hadn't given her any idea why I was there. I wanted to tell her but still didn't know how or where to start.

"You said it was your fault," Vicki prompted, apparently sensing my uncertainty. "Any chance you were referring to Martin?"

That brought me up short and my surprise must have shown.

"I'll take that as a yes,"

"How did you know?" I asked, wondering what else she might have figured out.

"No offense, Alex, but you don't hide your emotions well. Of course we were all upset when we learned Martin was dead. He's part of the Tower Brothers family. But your reaction was different. I know you worked with him more closely than the rest of us: prepping him for promo tours, coaching him on characters, plot points, subtext, etcetera. Still, I could see how badly you were shaken and I thought there must be something more going on. Is that true?"

I nodded.

"Were you two involved? I know that's none of my business. I just want—"

"It's not that," I said, cutting her off. "We were friends. There was nothing more to it."

"Then why—"

"I'm the reason he was killed," I blurted

Vicki drew in a sharp breath. "How can you even think that?" She sounded concerned but also confused. "You had nothing to do with it."

“I had everything to do with it. I made him a celebrity and that made him a target too. I didn’t mean to but that’s what happened.”

“You’re serious?” Vicki asked, her voice going up a full octave. She’d transitioned from confusion to utter mystification and I didn’t get it. The connection was so obvious. How in the world was she missing it?

“I wrote the books but it’s Martin Reginald’s name on the cover. Don’t you see?”

“Sure,” Vicki said, a hand on her forehead. “I understand that, but why do you think it matters? I mean, people don’t go after fiction authors. I’ve never even heard of anything like that. Besides, even if someone was after him for some unfathomable reason, how would they find him on a cruise ship where he’s traveling inconspicuously under his real name and not his pen name? We don’t disseminate that information. You know that.”

I started to reply but stopped as abruptly as if I’d been bitch-slapped. *Why would someone go after a fiction author?* I was pretty sure I knew not only the why but the who. I’d been about to lay that all out, but it was Vicki’s other question that had me reeling.

How would they find him on a cruise ship? How indeed? And more to the point, how could they have identified him in the first place? Martin Reginald hadn’t booked a relaxing vacation aboard the Island Explorer. Martin Worth had. Sure, they were one and the same, but that wasn’t common knowledge. You weren’t going to find it on a dust jacket, on Wikipedia, on the Tower Brothers website, or on any of the numerous social media platforms. I knew that because I checked constantly so I could be sure his secret, our secret, remained safe.

Martin, I knew from my many conversations with him on the subject, held dual citizenship for the United States and Canada. He had two passports too. That in itself was unremarkable. But he also held what amounted to two legal forms of ID. His American passport, driver’s license, credit cards, social security card, and his birth certificate all said Martin Reginald with no middle name or initial. His Canadian passport, however, listed him as Martin R. Worth.

I wasn’t exactly sure how or why he’d obtained two different passports. It apparently had something to do with his parents, an ugly divorce, and a legal name change somewhere down the line. I was also unclear as to why he was able to use both passports. He tried to explain the various loopholes and wide expanses of gray area when it came to dual citizenship. None of it made any sense to me and the Google searches I’d done hadn’t provided much clarification. It wasn’t my problem anyway. Martin was Reginald about ninety-eight percent of the time and Worth on those infrequent occasions when he wanted to protect his privacy. That had come in especially handy once he'd started representing my books for Tower Brothers Publishing.

How would they find him on a cruise ship?" I asked myself again, wondering for the first time if I had somehow misread the sinister tea leaves. Could his death have been either accidental or random? Could Martin Worth have been the intended victim after all? I considered that. Maybe I didn't know him as well as I'd thought. Maybe his passport story was a bunch of hooey and was actually a cover for something more nefarious. He could have been a drug smuggler, a child trafficker, an organ harvester, or the capo de tuti capi of the Canadian mafia, assuming there was such a thing.

Right, and he spent the bulk of his time schlepping my books because his doctor told him to get some exercise. Martin had no secrets, at least none that were likely to put him on a killer's radar. He was a kind, gentle man and was now the subject of a homicide investigation because of what I'd done, and that brought me back to that same question once again. *How did they find him*?

It doesn't matter, I told myself, giving a mental head shake to get the gears turning again.

Except it did. I knew that. But right then, the "how" was far less important than the "why." That's what I was there to talk about. I'd told Vicki it was my fault, but as yet I'd failed to hit any of my other bullet points. Time to get focused.

"Please understand," I began, squeezing my knees together and clasping my hands in my lap. "I never dreamed anything like this could happen. I swear."

"What are you saying?" Vicki asked. "You can't keep beating yourself up about something you had nothing to do with."

"I wish that were true," I said, hanging my head. I felt the tears coming again but this time I managed to hold them back. "I put Martin in a vulnerable position. He didn't know it, and honestly, I didn't either. I should have, though, and I think that's why he's dead."

"Alex, you're not making sense. You can't—"

I stopped her with a raised hand. "Just hear me out," I said.

We stared at each other for what felt like a full minute and then I took a breath and told her the whole story.

I started with the letter from Debbie Royal, my old high school friend, and everything she'd told me about her brother and his claims about the

Deepwater Horizon drilling rig, specifically the numerous safety violations, the prevailing fear that workers would lose their jobs if they raised the alarm, and finally, his assertion that the entire disaster had been an act of sabotage. Vicki was already familiar with that storyline because it had all been outlined in detail in Deep Water Deception," the first book in my trilogy. The only new information I'd provided was the surely unwelcome revelation that my blockbuster plot was potentially neither original nor fictional. At one point, she grabbed her tablet and started typing notes and I gave her a photo copy of Deb's letter so she'd have a record of that too.

"Were you able to confirm any of this?" she asked, her tone so businesslike I couldn't get a read on what she was thinking.

"No," I said, "but it wasn't for lack of trying. Deb's brother died days after the Deepwater explosion. His death was ruled an accident but I wonder now if there was more to it."

"And why's that?"

"Because Debbie Royal was killed not long after that letter was posted to me. She stepped in front of a city bus. It was dark, rainy, and there wasn't anyone else around, at least not according to the bus driver."

"You think she was murdered?"

"I think there is a distinct possibility."

"It could have been suicide," Vicki said. "She'd just lost her brother after all."

"You're right. And honestly, that was my first thought. Now, though," I gave a shrug.

"You're reconsidering because of what happened to Martin."

"Give the woman a cigar," I said without humor. "The two people I could have spoken to were dead and that left me with what I believed was nothing more than a fanciful or grossly-exaggerated story. You saw that well gushing oil into the Gulf. The world saw it and the devastating impacts that it had on the environment. It was inconceivable to me that anyone could have done that deliberately."

"You didn't believe your friend?"

"I suppose I didn't believe her brother. I'd never met him so it wasn't hard to come to that conclusion."

"I assume you researched the story anyway."

"As much as I could. Needless to say, there wasn't a lot of information available. I found nothing that would either refute or validate what I'd been told."

"I see." Vicki continued to type and it seemed like she was using a lot more force than necessary. It was also possible her keystrokes were being amplified by the blood rushing in my ears. I felt like I was on the verge of a panic attack and I hadn't even gotten to the really bad part. We were on the threshold, though. I thought Vicki must have sensed that too because she hesitated before asking her next question.

"So this Clayton Babbage," she finally said, referring to Deb's letter. "Is he a real person?"

"Yes and no," I replied, realizing I sounded evasive. "What I mean is I couldn't locate him but I did find a Clayton Babbit III and he seemed to fit what little I knew about him."

Vicki put her tablet aside. "Okay. I think I understand. I could spin the wheel again but I'm going to try to solve the puzzle. Stop me if I'm wrong.

"You were given a story that was too good not to tell. You took the few facts you had and... well, let's just say embellished the rest. You obviously couldn't identify this Clayton Babbit as the real culprit so you called him Charles Briggs instead. Wasn't that the name you used?"

She didn't give me a chance to reply.

"Do me a favor and at least change the initials next time. Whether there will be a next time remains to be seen because you impetuously wrote two books which we then published with the promise of a third to follow. In the interim, you, me, and everyone at Tower Brothers Publishing might be sued for libel, slander, defamation, assassination of character, and who knows what else? Is that about the size of it?"

I thought she'd summed it up horrifyingly well but there was something that in her justifiable anger she'd overlooked. Legal action might be the least of our problems because there was potentially still a killer on the loose.

-16-

"Have a nice day," the flight attendant said, her frozen smile stating plainly that she didn't care one way or the other.

"Thank you," Mikhail Vasilek replied, giving her a polite nod as he moved past. He started down the gangway and that's when his cell phone began to buzz.

Damn, he thought. *Was he tracking my flight so he'd know the second it touched down?*

He picked up his pace, putting some distance between himself and the other passengers. Vasilek didn't know yet what Babbit wanted but he was sure that's who was calling and that no one else needed to be listening in on their conversation. He shifted his brown leather carry-on from his right hand to his left and then retrieved his phone from the inside pocket of his sport coat. He answered on the fifth buzz.

"Yes?" he said, exiting the gangway, turning right and following the signs for baggage claim.

"Bout time," Babbit boomed. "Were you chatting up the stewardess or what?"

"What do you want?" Vasilek snapped.

"Hey, settle down there Mi-kha-il."

"Please do not call me that. As far as our business is concerned my name is Scott Fisher."

"Sure thing, Sport. As long as you understand that I know who you are and what you do. Cross me and you'll regret it."

Vasilek didn't reply to that. In his experience, regret was often a two-way street. Babbit may know enough to take him down but he wouldn't do so without suffering some consequences of his own. Vasilek would make sure of that. He was back in the States now and learning everything he could about Clayton Babbit III was priority number one.

"Okay," Babbit said. "I've booked you a suite at the Grand Hyatt so I don't want to hear any bitching about the accommodations."

"I'm sure it will be fine."

"It better be, Sport. And the room is in your name, as in Mikhail Vasilek. I didn't realize you'd be so uptight about that. I suppose I can change it if you want."

"Not necessary," Vasilek said. He was annoyed but also relieved because he no longer possessed any credit cards, license, or other documentation identifying him as Scott Fisher. He had other identities he could use but didn't want to divulge that information, definitely not to Babbit. For once, conducting business under his real name was probably his best and safest course of action, at least for the time being.

"There's a package waiting for you. It contains enough cash to cover any expenses you're likely to incur. "

Incur? Where had the redneck learned a word like that? "And what will I be doing?" Vasilek asked, stepping onto a moving sidewalk and making his way past a young couple and their three whining children. They'd spotted an ice cream stand and were pleading their case to little avail.

"You'll be following orders," Babbit said. "I say jump and you're on the next rocket to the fucking moon."

"Of course," Vasilek replied dryly. "But perhaps you could provide more detail."

"You got it, Sport, but I don't have time to explain everything now. Here's what you do. Catch a cab to the hotel. Check in and take the package straight to your room. Don't open it at the desk, in the bar, or anywhere you can be seen."

Vasilek didn't like Babbit's condescension or the implication that he might do something so blatantly stupid but he bit his tongue.

"Along with the cash," Babbit continued, "I left an encryption key for an email drop box. It's the one we used before. I assume you still have that information?"

"It's tattooed on the back of my hand."

"Funny," Babbit said, and then covered the phone and muttered something that might have been asshole. "There's an email there and it should answer your questions. It will then be up to you to determine how to proceed."

"If it's up to me I'll get on the plane and head back to Jamaica. I liked it there"

"I wouldn't recommend that. In fact, it would be foolish to try to go anywhere before our problem has been resolved."

"It's not my problem," Vasilek retorted. "It's yours. I did the job I was hired for."

"Yeah. You said that, and it doesn't matter because there is still a job to be done. You are mine until that happens. Is that clear comrade?"

Vasilek started to respond but then thought better of it and ended the call. He needed to keep a cool head and that meant not letting his emotions get the better of him. He assumed Babbit would call him right back but instead his phone chirped indicating an incoming text.

"Go get that package. I'll call you tonight. Welcome to New York."

Vasilek read and then deleted the message. Babbit had his agenda and that was fine, but he had his own way of doing things too and that would be made evident soon enough. *A rocket to the moon? I don't think so*¸ Vasilek mused. *I've got my own mode of transportation and a different destination in mind.*

Unfortunately, Vasilek knew he had to appear to go along with the program until he'd acquired the information and leverage necessary to extricate himself from whatever Babbit was up to. That didn't mean he had to do exactly as he was told. There was, Vasilek believed, only one reason Babbit would have booked him into a luxury hotel and it wasn't because he was such a great guy. The master wanted to keep tabs on the puppet. Maybe he had a Hyatt employee—perhaps a member of the security staff—already on his payroll. Maybe his room had been prepared ahead of time with some custom audio or video surveillance equipment. Maybe Babbit just wanted to show off by throwing money around. Whatever the case, it wasn't going to work out as he'd planned.

Vasilek reached the baggage claim area and, after a surprisingly brief wait, retrieved his single, black, nondescript suitcase. He then headed outside, and still following the Babbit playbook, hopped into the first cab he saw. He was in the spacious lobby of the Grand Hyatt Hotel less than half an hour later. And half an hour after that, his package in hand, Vasilek checked himself into a ground floor room at the Days Inn.

He still used his real name because he didn't care if Babbit located him or not. In fact, he kind of hoped the jerk would try. How long would it take him to call the more than seven hundred hotels in the New York City area? Maybe he should have chosen one a little later in the alphabet to keep Babbit's fingers walking as long as possible.

Smiling, Vasilek used a key card and let himself into his room. Wrung out from the trip but also wired, he tossed his suitcase and carry-on onto the bed and then liberated a bottle of Smirnoff from the mini bar. The vodka wasn't chilled or his preferred brand but he'd make do. He unscrewed the cap, emptied the bottle into a glass and took a sip as he studied the 'package' Babbit had left for him.

It was plain white cardboard and smaller than he'd expected, roughly the same size as a standard business envelope and not much thicker. It didn't have a lot of weight to it either. An encryption code could be written on a business card or Post-it but the money? It seemed Mr. Babbit had not been quite as generous as he'd let on. The little package definitely wasn't bulging with cash. Vasilek held it up to his ear and shook and he could both hear and feel something solid slide from one end to the other. Curious, he grasped the self-adhesive flap and tugged it open.

He peered inside and then tipped three items into his hand. The first was a Sand-Sational business card identifying Mr. Clayton Babbit III as President and CEO. In addition to the toll free office phone number listed, Babbit or one of his flunkies had added two more numbers labeled *home* and *cell.* Vasilek flipped the card over and, in that same handwriting, he saw a string of 14 seemingly random characters he knew he'd need to access the email drop box. Next, he fingered a thin stack of fifty dollar bills secured with a paperclip. They totaled a whopping five hundred bucks.

I won't be retiring on that, he thought and then looked at the final item. It was apparently the rest of his cash reserve in the form of an American Express debit card.

"Clever," he said aloud, fingering the embossed numbers. The card might have a balance of fifty dollars or five thousand. He'd have to use it to find out, and Babbit would be able to track him each and every time it was swiped.

He could, he knew, go back to the Hyatt and withdraw the maximum amount from the closest ATM he could find. Hadn't there been one in the lobby? Vasilek thought so, but because he knew he wouldn't be staying, he hadn't paid especially close attention. He could check it out if need be. Or he might employ some counter-surveillance measures and intentionally use Babbit's AmEx in strange, out of the way places to throw him off the scent. Maybe he'd find a porn shop in China Town and spend a thousand dollars on sex toys just for the hell of it. That was tempting but Vasilek decided he'd better read the email before he made any real moves. He ordered some dinner from room service and then fired up his tablet computer.

Martin Reginald, so it appeared, was exactly who they thought he was at least in the sense that the man the now nonexistent Scott Fisher had killed was the same one whose name and picture appeared on every Martin Reginald novel. He was traveling under the name of Martin Worth at the time of his unexpected demise. Vasilek had of course known that already and it was information that had apparently been gleaned months before through a hack of the Tower Brothers Publishing computer system and some data mining from their personnel records. Babbit, or more likely someone working for him, had not only learned Worth would be a passenger on the Island Explorer but also managed to book Scott Fisher in the adjoining cabin. That was slick and took some real know-how.

Vasilek had always been pretty good with computers and had even conducted some low level hacks. He knew he'd never be able to pull off anything like that, though. Given what he now knew, maybe using his own name on the hotel registration form hadn't been such a brilliant idea after all. Underestimating Babbit wouldn't be wise either. Vasilek considered that and finally decided he should be safe enough as long as Babbit still believed he was working for him. Almost on cue, his phone buzzed and Clayton Babbit's name appeared in the display.

"Just where the fuck are you?" he demanded as soon as Vasilek answered.

"I'm in my room," which wasn't technically a lie.

"Well you're not at the Hyatt."

"How do you know this?" Vasilek asked even though it was obvious.

"I called and they told me you never checked in."

"You are keeping tabs on me then?"

"Yes," Babbit said, unashamed. "Sorry, but I don't trust guys that kill people for a living."

"That's funny because I don't trust anyone that would hire a killer."

Babbit was silent for a beat and then he barked out a laugh. "I guess we know where we stand then. And I guess I don't care where you're staying as long as I can reach you when I need to."

"My phone is always on," Vasilek said, thinking Babbit would start searching for him as soon as their call was over.

"Good enough," he said in a friendly tone Vasilek wasn't buying. "I assume you got the package?"

"Yes. I was just reading your email."

"And what do you think?"

"I don't know yet but I do have some questions."

"Such as?"

Vasilek hesitated. When he was hired for a job he never asked why a particular person was being targeted because it was none of his business and because he didn't want to be given any information that might make his task more difficult to complete. He sometimes made assumptions, though, and he thought he needed to know if the one he'd made in this case was correct.

"Martin Reginald was an author," he began. "Was he eliminated because of something he wrote?"

This time it was Babbit's turn to hesitate, but not for long. "Let's just say there's a story I'd rather not be made public."

Vasilek didn't understand what sort of threat a fiction author could pose but he had the confirmation he wanted so he didn't press. "But now you're convinced he didn't write the books?" he asked instead.

"I'm almost sure of it."

"How?"

"You ask a lot of questions," Babbit retorted. "Why do you care?"

"Normally I wouldn't, but you're telling me you had the wrong person killed and I'd like to make sure that doesn't happen again."

"A hit man with a conscience. That's a new one."

"No," Vasilek said honestly. "I just don't want to be called in to clean up another mess. I'm done after this and I mean it."

"You're done when I say so but I get your point. You remember that computer you took from Reginald's room?"

"Of course."

"Did you look at it before you sent it to me?"

"I was instructed not to."

"That's great, Sport, but that's not what I asked."

"I did as you said, and no, I didn't look."

"Huh," Babbit said. "I think I believe you. Now let me ask you a question. Did you ever see him use that thing?"

"Actually, no," Vasilek replied. He remembered thinking how strange it was that the writer had the computer with him but never seemed to spend any time actually writing. "I only saw him turn it on once or twice and never for very long."

"Wish I'd known that before you dumped him in the drink. I got that computer and figured it would be loaded with manuscripts, notes, research materials, and whatever else writers use. You know what I found instead?"

Vasilek didn't think a response was expected so he gave none.

"Bupkis. You know what that means, Sport?"

"I think I can guess."

"I didn't find one damn thing of use to me," Babbit said as if he hadn't heard. "There was a word processing program but it hadn't been accessed in weeks. He sent a couple of emails to his mother and that was all."

"Maybe he had a work computer somewhere else?" Vasilek offered.

"Right. And maybe he wrote everything long hand on legal pads. We looked into that and got nowhere. That's when I had my associate take a closer look at the publisher's payroll records. Martin Reginald wasn't earning much for a big shot author. It looked like he was receiving an annual salary with no bonuses, royalties, or anything else. I don't know how those things normally work but that didn't seem right to me. We dug a little deeper and that's when we found Alex Rhodes. You don't need to know anything more than that. The address is in the email. Find him and take him out!"

-17-

Detective Megan Lynch sat at her desk, nibbling a thumbnail as she stared at the blank legal pad in front of her. Her pen was armed and ready but she couldn't think of one damn thing worth writing down. Exasperated, she shot a glance at her computer and cursed it for its stubbornness and lack of cooperation.

Prior to leaving the diner, she not only had told Wigs how she thought the crime aboard the Island Explorer had been committed but also gave him the identity of who she believed was the most likely perpetrator. She'd studied all the available information and would have bet her badge that one Scott Fisher, former occupant of cabin 1016, had accessed cabin 1015 via the tenth floor balcony on at least one occasion, probably many more, and for reasons as yet undetermined, murdered Martin Worth. She'd tried but couldn't come up with any other even remotely plausible scenarios. Megan fully expected an argument but hadn't gotten one. The captain hadn't attempted to poke holes in her theory either. He'd simply instructed her to find some *solid and non-circumstantial evidence* and get back to him then.

She started with her own records and quickly verified what she'd already known. Fisher had not been among the dozens of Explorer passengers she'd interviewed personally. According to the file, none of Megan's colleagues had interviewed him either. That wasn't necessarily significant. Despite their best efforts, they'd only managed to speak to about fifteen percent of the cruise passengers. They focused on the ones from New York and New Jersey because they were the most readily at hand but there'd also been guests from eleven other states plus Canada, France, Germany, England, Ireland, Russia and the Netherlands. Department resources were limited and it wasn't practical or feasible to try to track down everyone just for the sake of asking a few basic questions. Of course, now that Scott Fisher was officially a person of interest, Megan had a lot more leeway as to what she could and would do in order to find him.

According to his Island registration form, Fisher lived in a twenty-fifth floor apartment on 183rd Street in the Bronx. She plugged that address into Google Maps and what actually came up was a small kosher deli that definitely did not double as a place of residence. Megan made a note to arrange for a drive-by just to be sure but she was already getting a bad feeling.

She looked for a phone number and found one with a 347 area code. She hadn't been in the City long enough to have memorized which area codes were connected to the various boroughs but Megan was sure 347 was a local exchange.

As much as she wanted her initial contact with Fisher to be face to face, she decided to call just to see who or what she'd get. There was a beep and a click, and then a recorded message that the number she'd dialed was *no longer in service.* She'd follow up with the phone company which would probably turn out to be one of the cellular providers. Megan knew there was little chance her inquiries would yield a thing. Odds were good the phone had either never belonged to Fisher or it had been purchased in cash from one of the big box stores. That trail would lead nowhere.

She scrolled further down the registration form and found a section for emergency contacts. There was no name listed bit it did show a phone number with the same ten digits she'd just tried.

"Fuck me," she said, sitting back and blowing a strand of hair out of her eyes.

"You say something, Lynch?"

She started because she hadn't realized she'd spoken out loud. "Yeah," Megan said to the detective in the adjoining cubical. "I was telling you to mind your own business for a change."

Paul Zanetti poked his head around the corner. "I was but my antenna goes up whenever a good looking woman starts talking about sex."

"I've heard about your antenna. Must be tough to pick up anything with hardware so small."

"Screw you," he said.

"In your dreams, Zanetti."

He grinned at her. "That's true but who told you?"

Megan fluttered her eyelashes. "Sometimes a girl can just tell."

He stared as if trying to figure out if she was serious but then he shifted his gaze to her computer. "Any luck?"

"Only if you count a fake phone number and address."

"But that's a lead, right? No one falsifies personal records without cause."

"You're too optimistic. Haven't you ever given bogus info to someone so you wouldn't end up on some junk mail list?"

"I suppose, but this guy was going on a cruise," Zanetti argued, using a hand to loosen the knot on his tie. "You wouldn't fake that information unless you were trying to hide something."

"You're probably right, but probably isn't good enough. I have to prove he's hiding something and then find out what. I was about to check DMV records to see if that gets me anywhere"

"May the force be with you."

"That'd be good. I wouldn't mind a little supernatural intervention."

Zanetti snorted. "You may need it. I mean, Scott Fisher? Could he have come up with a more generic name?"

"I know. I'm thinking I may get one or two hits in the greater New York City area."

"More like one or two dozen... if you're lucky. Let me know if you want help."

"Thanks," Megan said, turning back to her desk as Detective Zanetti disappeared behind his cubical wall. She appreciated his offer but knew he had his own haystacks to sift and wouldn't even think about pulling him away unless she had something to go on. That certainly wasn't the case yet.

She started with DMV which, all told, yielded twenty-seven different Scott Fishers or S. Fishers in and around New York City. The only one that really attracted her attention lived in Brooklyn and had nineteen outstanding parking tickets. He plainly had no respect for the law. Unfortunately, he was also a sixty-six-year-old black man and that effectively ruled him out as the possible killer. The guy Megan was after was decades younger and several shades paler.

She'd examined the Explorer's surveillance video until she thought she knew every relevant frame and time stamp by heart. Martin Worth entered his own cabin at two minutes past ten on the Thursday night in question and for the next thirty-four hours, until the ship docked in New York Harbor Saturday morning, she hadn't seen one thing she deemed conclusive because she never again got a good look at the person entering or exiting cabin 1016. He always seemed to be looking away from the camera.

Scott Fisher, on the other hand, went in and out of cabin 1015 plenty, his face normally in full view. It was impossible to draw any conclusions from that. He was acting like any other cruise passenger which was, of course, exactly the point. Worth and Fisher were of similar enough age, size, and build, so if one wanted to impersonate the other or at least appear as the other, it wouldn't be much of a stretch.

"You over there, Zanetti?" Megan called.

She got no response, looked around the corner and saw that his desk chair was empty and his computer had been turned off. She wondered about that but then realized it was nearly six o'clock. *Where the hell did the day go?*

"I should get out of here," she said to herself but was reluctant to leave while she still felt so unproductive.

Megan brought up the picture of Scott Fisher that had been taken for the Island Explorer onboard ID card and compared that to the same picture of Martin Worth. The two didn't look alike but they didn't look unalike either. They were early middle-aged, somewhere between thirty-four and forty-five, and both were Caucasian men with shortish, brownish hair and bland features. That could have been coincidence. Countless people fit that same general description. It was also possible Fisher had used makeup or some other means to alter his appearance. She had no way of knowing—yet, but felt determined to keep digging until she came up with something concrete.

Her resolve lasted another hour but she finally gave in to hunger pangs and a headache that started behind her eyes and was now creeping down to her neck and shoulders. She was familiar with the symptoms and knew it wasn't anything some food and rest wouldn't cure. Maybe she'd even treat herself to a glass of red wine. She thought she'd earned that much.

Megan was halfway down the hall when she stopped, noticing the light from around Captain Weiserman's partially open office door. She thought about pizza and garlic knots and then sighed, turned, and walked that way.

"Knock knock," she said, tapping gently on the door frame.

"Detective," Weiserman said, looking up from a stack of paperwork. "What are you still doing here?"

"I could ask you the same thing."

"You could, but I'm the one with the captain's bars, so I don't have to tell you. Come in and take a load off," he said, smiling and waving towards a chair."

"I don't want to interrupt."

"Please," he said. "I implore you to. This," he picked up the sheaf of papers and dropped them with a thud, "is our department budget. I would rather perform my own vasectomy than look at this crap for one more minute."

"I guess it's a good thing I stopped by then." Megan placed her purse on the floor and sat.

"And what about that?" Captain Weiserman asked. "The whistle blew a long time ago. Why you still hanging around this place?"

"I have a hard time leaving when the job isn't done."

"You better get over that unless you plan on moving in. Can I assume from your demeanor and the late hour that you have not reeled in Fisher yet?"

Megan gave him a look. "Are bad puns supposed to put me in a better mood?"

"You're too defensive. I hope you don't think I was trying to bait you."

Megan groaned. "I could tell you what I think but I'd probably get fired."

"Fair enough," Weiserman said. "So tell me what's happening"

"In a nutshell, nothing. I'm still working the same theory. I think this Scott Fisher character is our perp. I think he killed Martin Worth and spent the next day and a half making it look like he was still alive. There's a chance he altered his appearance so he could pass himself off as Worth more easily. I'm also convinced he sometimes dressed in Worth's clothes as part of the charade."

"Why?" Captain Weiserman asked, placing his hands flat on the desktop. "Why go to all that trouble when Worth was already dead?"

Megan didn't hesitate. "Because he's the only one that could have killed him. Fisher knew we'd figure that out and that was the reason for the smoke screen. He wanted to slow us down."

"Okay, but you're onto him now, so what's the problem?"

"The problem," Megan said, shoulders slumping, "is that I'm no longer sure Scott Fisher exists."

Wigs raised his eyebrows. "Pardon me?"

She sighed and told him about the false phone number and address, and getting nowhere with DMV records. "I plugged his name into every database I could think of including NCIC. If this guy's been operating for any length of time, I figured the National Crime Information Center would know something about him."

"No luck?"

"Oh, there are plenty of Scott Fishers in the system. One was arrested for tax evasion. Another was convicted on several counts of fraud and racketeering and spent five years in the pen. There's a D. Scott Fisher, first name DuJuan, wanted in connection with a drug smuggling ring. And finally, I found a Scott Fisher who, in August of last year, was brought up on charges of kidnapping and reckless endangerment."

"That sounds promising."

"I thought so too. He's thirty-six, Caucasian, and fits the description well enough if you can look past the world's ugliest goatee."

"Is he local?"

"Maryland."

"That's local enough, but something tells me you've already ruled him out."

"Two reasons," Megan said. "First, the kid he napped was his own. He didn't think his visitation rights were sufficient, so took matters into his own hands. No one was harmed and the charges were eventually dropped."

"He could still be unstable. What's the other reason?"

"He lost both legs in Afghanistan and has been wheelchair bound ever since. I think he'd have a hard time negotiating balcony railings."

"That's conclusive."

Megan smiled wryly. "I thought so too and now I don't know where to turn."

"Credit card records?"

"All I've got is the MasterCard he used to pay for the cruise. The history only goes back three months and every purchase was made online."

"Anything interesting?"

"So far I've got the retailers but not the actual merchandise. There are lots of ways to spend five or six hundred bucks at Amazon or Wal-Mart. I'll keep working on it but I'm not expecting much. This guy knows what he's doing."

"So what's your next trick?" Weiserman asked.

Megan made a face. "Forensics didn't give us anything. Why do cruise ships have to be so sterile anyway? Did you know they even spray down the outside each week? Even if he had left fingerprints, which I doubt, they were long gone before we got there. It's one dead-end after another. I even Googled the name Scott Fisher on the off-chance that would get me somewhere. Seventy-eight million hits if you can believe that. Most of the more prominent ones were related to some mountain man."

"You mean like Deliverance?" Captain Weiserman asked.

"I can't speak to his sexual preferences but he was a renowned climber known mostly for ascending high peaks without the use of supplemental air."

"Huh. I didn't know that was a thing. Any chance he killed people in his free time?"

"It's possible but he died in 1996."

"So you're saying he's got an alibi."

"And then some." Megan picked up her purse and got ready to leave. "I'm at a loss. I've got a totally generic name and not much else."

"You check with the State Department? He must have a passport."

"And probably as fake as everything else. I put in a call and I should hear something tomorrow. In the meantime, I'd like to look more into Martin Worth to see what I can learn about him. He must have been killed for a reason. If I can figure that out it might give me a new line of investigation."

"Speaking of," Weiserman said, shoving the budget aside and pawing through the papers underneath. "We have official IDs on the deceased. Came in a little while ago but I thought you were already gone."

"What?" Megan asked, thinking he either misspoke or she misheard. "Did you say IDs? As in plural? I thought we were dealing with a single homicide."

"We are. The victim held dual citizenship, U.S. and Canada, and used a different name for each."

"That's legal?"

"Apparently so. It doesn't happen often but it's not unheard of."

"So... who are we talking about then?" Megan asked, starting to think their murder victim might be as phony as his supposed killer.

Captain Weiserman adjusted his reading glasses. "Dental records have identified the deceased as Mr. Martin R. Worth of Ottawa, Canada. He has likewise been identified as Martin Reginald, no middle initial, of Manhattan."

"I'm sorry," Megan said, "but I don't understand. How can one person have two legal names? Even if there was a way to do it, why would you bother unless.... Wait! Did you say Martin Reginald?"

"Yeah, why? He removed his glasses and stared at her. "Does the name mean something to you?"

She began digging through her bowling bag-sized purse. "It can't be," she muttered, pulling out her notebook, her checkbook and a daily planner. "Where the hell is it?" She checked the outside zipper pocket and finally found her iPad Mini."

"What are you doing?"

"One sec!" She opened the Kindle app and her library of books. Megan hadn't read it yet but there it was, sandwiched between *Cold Wind* by C.J. Box and *Doctor Sleep* by Stephen King. *Deepwater Denial* by Martin Reginald. She stared at the title, and then realized what she should have already known. Ebooks have no back cover so no author photo was readily visible.

"Shit!"

"What?" Wigs asked. "What's wrong?"

Megan held up a finger and then brought up her web browser and the Amazon site. A few quick clicks and she found the Martin Reginald author page. His picture was front and center.

"Here," she proclaimed, tilting the screen so Weiserman could see it. "This is our man!"

-18-

Thinking the distraction would do me good, I turned on my computer and made a not so valiant attempt at getting some actual work done. Somehow, though, I seemed to lack the minimal level of concentration required to complete my groundbreaking article on *5 Ways to Stay Trim and Fit Without Diet or Exercise*. I get it. It's not Pulitzer material but I can't help it if there's a large market for drivel and I'm not a bad person just because I sometimes contribute. This time, however, I wasn't up to the challenge. I kept the document open and minimized while I played one game of spider solitaire after another. That was about the limit in terms of my mental capacity.

What, you might ask, had me so rattled? Nothing really, except that Vicki Goldstein, at that very moment, was meeting with Bob and other members of the Tower Brothers legal department and they were collectively deciding my fate.

I knew coming clean with Vicki was the right thing to do. From that standpoint, my conscience was clear. I still felt like there was a grand piano-sized anvil suspended just over my head and ready to come crashing down. Yes, that tolling bell you hear is undoubtedly my own tremulous heartbeat. Am I mixing metaphors? Sorry, but I often do that in moments of stress.

At first, I was relieved when Vicki told me I didn't have to be present for the discussion. I don't know if that decision was more for her sake or my own but I was more than happy to get the hell out of there.

"You know how Bob is," she'd said.

I really didn't but I let her go on.

"His glass isn't half empty. It's cracked and leaking. He will immediately put things in the worst possible context.

Is there a best context? I wondered. I appreciated Vicki for not coming right out and saying so but I figured we both knew I'd really screwed the pooch on this one.

"I've been working with him for a lot of years," she said. "I know how to handle him. I will present the facts as I understand them and he'll have a conniption right there on my office floor. There's no reason you should be here for that."

"Thanks," I said. "To tell you the truth, the guy gives me the willies."

"Join the club."

So Vicki set up a meeting with Bob and his cohorts and promised she'd let me know as soon as there was some news. Having nothing else to do, I reluctantly returned to my apartment where I spent the remainder of the afternoon bouncing off the walls. I checked my phone about a thousand times, all the while feeling like the jury was out and the longer they deliberated the worse it was going to be for me. Martin already received the death sentence. Was I looking at life without parole? I wasn't sure I deserved anything better but I was dying to hear one way or the other.

The call finally came around six o'clock and Vicki told me she'd be right over.

Great, I thought. *An executioner that makes house calls.*

I tried to put a positive spin on it but couldn't help wondering why she was coming to me instead of the other way around. Sure, we'd always been friendly if not actual friends, so maybe I should interpret her pending visit as a form of reassurance. It was just as likely she was eager to put as much distance as possible between me and Tower Brothers Publishing.

I considered chilling some wine and preparing a tray of appetizers, but not knowing how the conversation would go, I decided that might prove awkward.

I'm very sorry but we're nullifying your contract and suing you for everything you're worth.

Oh. Crab puff?

By the time the intercom finally announced her arrival I'd concluded I was about to be drawn and quartered, tarred and feathered, and strapped to that life-sucking torture machine from *The Princess Bride.*

"It's bad isn't it?" I asked before Vicki made it all the way through the door.

She looked at me and briefly placed a hand on my arm as she moved past. "Maybe not as bad as you think. Come sit down and I'll tell you about it."

With that, she walked into the living room and settled herself at one end of the sofa. I would have preferred to stand and pace but I gritted my teeth, figuratively anyway, and followed her lead.

It was only then that I noticed she was still in the dark slacks and sweater I'd seen her in earlier that day. She looked like the consummate professional and smelled good too—a hint of something light and floral.

I, on the other hand, looked like I was dressed for a teenage slumber party. The tan slacks and salmon blouse I'd worn that morning were now in an untidy pile on my bedroom floor. My new wardrobe consisted of fuzzy blue socks, Snoopy lounge pants, and a faded pink T-shirt. I'd been so distracted I'd somehow forgotten to change back into normal clothes.

Beautiful, I thought, thankful I'd at least kept my bra on. I surreptitiously checked my shirt front for evidence of the chocolate ice cream I'd had for lunch. No obvious stains, so I had that going for me anyway. I still felt like a loser and I didn't even want to consider what Vicki must be thinking.

"So," I began but immediately trailed off because I had no idea what to say.

"Are you all right?" she asked, perhaps realizing just how close I was to completely coming apart.

"I'm fine," I said a little too quickly. I suddenly didn't seem to know what to do with my hands so I sat on them to keep them still. "Really. I'm good. It's just been a long day."

"Okay," Vicki replied, sounding unconvinced. "But I gathered when I got here that you were expecting bad news."

I didn't trust myself to speak so I didn't, instead digging my fingernails into the bottoms of both legs.

How could I have been so careless and stupid? What was I thinking? I'm never gonna get another publishing contract as long as I live. I probably won't even be able to sell my fluff pieces anymore. I'll be another one of those self-published saps that keeps writing books no one buys, reads, or gives a crap about.

I thought I could deal with all of that. What was tearing me up inside was the idea that the third book in the *Deepwater* series would never be released, meaning Martin would have died for nothing. How could I ever choke down such an impossibly bitter pill?

"I want to put your mind at ease," Vicki continued, and it took me a moment to realize she wasn't responding to my own scattered thoughts.

"As you know, I met with legal today. Bob was apoplectic to be perfectly blunt. I got the impression he wanted to go all *Lord of the Flies* on you and mount your head on a pole."

I tried to swallow but my throat was too dry. "Am I missing something?" I rasped, "because that doesn't sound reassuring."

"That was his initial reaction and I was prepared for it. I let him rant for a while, but once we got past his tirade and started looking at things more rationally, it became increasingly evident that we probably don't have much to worry about, at least from a legal standpoint.

"How can you say that?" I asked, more surprised than anything. "Martin was killed because of my books. He had to be. And that tells me my account of sabotage aboard that drilling rig was accurate enough that someone got scared. I don't know if that Clayton Babbit guy I found was the actual killer but it seems like he must be involved somehow."

"I expect that's true."

"Then how—" I stopped there because none of it made any sense. Hadn't she just said I was right? Don't bother answering that. I might be blind but I'm not deaf and I'd damn well heard Vicki agree with my assessment not ten seconds earlier. How, then, could she sound so calm and poised? Why wasn't she tearing her hair out and mine too as she contemplated the potential legal and financial ramifications of what I'd done? It could be a public relations nightmare too. I didn't know what percentage of consumers knew or cared who published the books they purchased but a rash of bad publicity certainly wouldn't do Tower Brothers any good. Couldn't she see that?"

"I must admit," Vicki said. "When you spilled your guts this morning, I saw my career flash before my eyes. A major lawsuit wouldn't bankrupt Tower Brothers, most likely, but it would cause a big shake up, and you and I would both end up on the street. I have no delusions about that. On the surface this looks really, really bad."

"I know. I'm so sorry. I wish I'd never—"

"Stop," Vicki insisted. "We've been through this and I know how remorseful you are. You don't have to keep apologizing."

"Then what can I do? I fucked up, Vicki."

"You're right," she said with a level of candor I had to admire. "But as I indicated when I got here, it might not be the end of the world."

"Please explain that because it sure feels like it to me."

"Of course." She laced her fingers together and rested her hands on one knee. "Let's, for the sake of argument, say that everything you wrote in your books is true."

"That's seems like a stretch. I didn't have much in the way of solid information, so I drew a lot of my own conclusions."

"That's okay," Vicki said. "For right now, we're taking the Bob Whetton approach and casting everything in the worst light."

"So if I understand you," I said, still confused, "We are assuming Clayton Babbit III and my Charles Briggs character are in fact one and the same, and that person was ultimately responsible for the explosion aboard that drilling rig and everything that followed?"

"Yes. Now spin it forward and try to imagine that you are Clayton Babbit III. You've either read the books or someone else has and brought them to your attention."

"He really didn't come up much in book one. Well, actually," I amended. "He was still a primary character but there were few indications of anything nefarious unless you already knew where the storyline was headed."

"You were just laying the groundwork."

"Pretty much."

"That's what I thought," Vicki said. "But it's been a while since I've read either one of them and you're obviously more familiar with the plot structure and the key events and characters."

"Okay," I said. "But what's your point?"

"Just this. You're Clayton Babbit, right? You are the mastermind behind a horrifying scheme that killed eleven people and caused an environmental catastrophe. Your motive was simple greed because you knew your company would earn millions restoring the beaches you deliberately destroyed."

"Geez. Put it that way and I sound like a real asshole."

"Not only that but you're seriously pissed off." Vicki stood and walked to the window. The blinds were drawn and I knew there wasn't much to see out there anyway. She fingered one of the dust collector knick-knacks I keep on the window sill and then turned to face me. "You thought you'd gotten away with it and you and your company were in the clear."

"Then," I said, beginning to follow her train of thought. "These novels come out and they appear to be telling my story."

"Exactly!" She returned to the sofa and sat down beside me. "All the names have been changed and many of the details are wrong, presumably, but there are still enough particulars that you have legitimate cause for concern. It's being billed as mainstream fiction but what happens if or when people start connecting the dots? More significantly, you don't know who this Martin Reginald person is, how he came by his information, what he ultimately plans on doing with it, and why he seemingly has this axe to grind with you."

"Shit," I said. "I never thought about it like that."

"I think you need to. Put yourself in his shoes again. Your brilliant plan might be on the verge of blowing up in your face. What are you going to do?"

My head was spinning because I suddenly realized why Vicki was so convinced Tower Brothers Publishing had little to fear. Babbit couldn't sue anyone or threaten legal action on the QT. Any such moves would generate publicity and that was the last thing he wanted. It was good news for Tower but bad for Martin, obviously, and I suddenly wasn't liking my own prospects all that much either.

"Be right back," I said, leaping up and heading for the kitchen.

"Where are you going?" Vicki asked.

"I thought we could use some refreshments. I've got white wine, whiskey, and Percocet. Which would you like?"

"Uh, the wine would be fine. Are you okay, Alex?"

"No," I said, retrieving a water glass, pouring in two fingers of Jameson and then adding a couple fingers more. Vicki was standing in the doorway by then.

"You sure that's a good idea?" she asked, and this time I didn't need to read her expression to know what she was thinking.

I must have been quite a sight—a basket case in fuzzy socks and Snoopy pants. Right then, though, I didn't care. All I wanted was a few hours of alcohol-induced oblivion.

"Cheers," I said, raising my glass and taking a lumberjack-sized slug.

At this juncture, I think there's one more thing you should probably know about me. I'm not a whiskey drinker. That same bottle of Jameson had been in my apartment so long I don't even remember how it got there. A real aficionado would have pronounced the liquor *smoooooth*. To me, it was like swallowing a mouthful of burning, broken glass. I experienced roughly the same sensation when Mr. Jameson promptly reversed course. Thankfully, I was right next to the sink and that saved me from liquidating my assets all over the kitchen floor.

"That's disgusting!" I wheezed once I'd finally caught my breath enough to form words.

"And that's why I chose the wine. Can I get you some?"

"I think I'd prefer a piece of gum. Will you excuse me for a minute?"

I went to brush my teeth and then rejoined Vicki in the living room. She sipped her chardonnay while I nursed a diet soda on ice.

"Feeling better?" she asked.

"Yes and no," I said, one hand pressed to my forehead. "There's no longer a need to call 911 but I still feel like a jerk. I've made such a mess of this and I don't know what I should do."

"And I don't know what to tell you. When we first discussed it I said I thought you should make your identity known and release the third novel under your own name. That was before I fully understood what was going on."

"Yeah, well, I don't think I had a real firm grasp on things either."

"You knew why Martin had been killed."

"I thought I did but it still didn't seem real. Like, I knew what it could mean for me but I still felt disconnected if that makes any sense."

"Sure it does. You had a theory and now we seem to be getting close to proving it."

"I don't want to prove it!" I said, closing my eyes and thumping my head against the back of the sofa. "If I'm right it means there's a murderer on the loose and he could come after me next."

"He doesn't even know who you are."

Vicki's words were meant to be comforting but I could hear the worry in her voice.

"Actually," I said, "we have no way of determining what he knows."

"Don't blow things out of proportion. There's never been a hint that anyone other than Martin Reginald authored those books."

"Okay, but there's also never been a hint that Martin Reginald sometimes traveled under the name of Martin Worth. Someone figured it out and also learned he'd be on that ship. How do you explain that?"

"I can't," Vicki admitted after a pause.

"My point exactly. Tower might not have anything to worry about but I do. Call me a coward but I don't want to end up like Martin did."

"That's not gonna happen," Vicki said. "We won't let it."

"That's very nice but I don't know if there's anything Tower Brothers can do."

"Sure there is. We can go to the police."

"And say what?"

I'd been paying close attention to the news and there'd been no reports that the murder victim from the Island Explorer was actually a bestselling author. That told me the police did not yet have that information. I couldn't tell them why I believed I was in danger without also explaining my connection to Martins Worth and Reginald. They would, of course, want to know why I, and why Tower Brothers, had not come forward sooner. In the end, everything would be out in the open which would potentially make me even more vulnerable than I already felt. I didn't want to go there unless there was really no choice.

I was about to share that with Vicki when her cell phone rang. She glanced at the screen and made a sound of annoyance.

"Pardon me," she said. "I should take this.

"Yes, Peter. What is it?"

I assumed the Peter in question was Peter Ireland, her outspoken underling, and it didn't sound like Vicki made any attempt to hide her impatience.

"You just spoke to who?

"I don't know anyone by that name and I'm kind of in the middle of something right now. Can we discuss this in the morning?"

I could hear an agitated response from the other end of the line but I wasn't close enough to make out anything that was being said. Vicki mouthed something to me that I completely missed. As you might guess, I'm about as good at lip reading as I am at playing I Spy.

"No," Vicki said into the phone. "I wasn't trying to keep you in the dark. You know as much as I do.

"Right.

"Yes, nine o'clock should be fine. We'll see you then.

"Okay, good night, Peter. And thank you for calling."

She clicked off and looked at me. "The plot thickens," Vicki said, picking up her wine glass. "You got any of that Percocet left?"

"What's wrong?" I asked, "or don't I want to know."

"Oh, I'd say you need to know. Peter called because he'd just spoken with Detective Lynch of the NYPD's 6th Precinct." She stood and moved toward the door. "It's safe to say the cat is now out of the bag."

"Meaning?"

"They know about Martin and they're rather anxious to speak to us about him."

"Us?"

"Tower Brothers," Vicki clarified. "Your name didn't come up and I doubt they know anything about you. Under the circumstances, though, I think you might want to tell them. If you agree, be at the office tomorrow morning."

-19-

Mikhail Vasilek walked toward the apartment building slowly, all the while scanning for security cameras and anyone who appeared to be taking a more than passing interest in what he was doing. He knew the cameras were there, some hidden and others in plain sight, but they were not much of a concern. In his utilitarian brown pants and matching shirt and ball cap, he was sure he looked as unremarkable as any other courrier going about his daily business. More important, he bore little resemblance to any image that had ever been captured of him. That was thanks to the tinted glasses, and full beard and mustache that masked his regular features.

Rather than approaching his destination directly, he made an extra lap around the block, constantly using store windows, windshields and other reflective surfaces to survey his surroundings. He made a brief stop at a bakery, paused in front of a news stand, and bent to tie his shoes. He saw nothing remarkable—no familiar faces or sudden, awkward or evasive moves.

Vasilek had been on medium to high alert from the time he left his hotel ninety minutes earlier and during every moment of his deliberately circuitous subway trip into upper Manhattan. He hadn't observed any watchers, but that didn't necessarily mean there were no eyes upon him.

He doubted Clayton Babbit had discovered where he was staying and figured there was a decent chance he hadn't bothered trying. There was no point really. Vasilek's new target was Alex Rhodes and the only information that he'd been given was an address. That meant he'd have to show up there sooner or later. If Babbit really wanted him he could just sit and wait.

Vasilek believed he was safe and would remain that way at least until Rhodes had been successfully eliminated; but after that? He'd been in the business long enough to understand killing the killer was sometimes part of the playbook and that was the main reason for his UPS-like attire. He'd look completely different for any and all subsequent visits. He could show up as an old lady one day and a cripple the next. Whatever Babbit might be planning, Mikhail Vasilek wasn't going to make it easy on him. He'd do the job and then disappear faster than a smoke ring on a windy day.

After a final look around, he made a show of consulting his clipboard and then headed for the apartment's main entrance. The building was fronted by a small, open courtyard, and once Vasilek mounted the half flight of brick steps, he had a full view of double glass doors and the foyer beyond. He could also see the doorman or security guard seated at a desk just inside. The guy saw him too but made no move to get up.

You're lucky I'm not here for you, Vasilek thought as he reached for the buzzer.

"Can I help you?" came the tinny voice.

"I have package," Vasilek replied in the thickest Eastern European accent he could manage. He held up a large envelope which contained nothing more than some junk mail he'd liberated from a garbage can at the post office down the block from his hotel.

He waited, the door latch clicked and he let himself inside.

"Good morning," Vasilek said, approaching the desk as he took in the elevator bank off to the left, emergency stairs beyond that, and a single, closed door behind the desk to the right.

Security? Could be. Or maintenance, an office or a bathroom. It didn't matter. He wasn't planning on making the hit anywhere near Rhodes' apartment but still liked to know what he was up against, just in case.

"It is nice day today," he added, coming a few steps closer.

"Not bad," the man replied, leaning back in his chair. "This is New York, though. Probably be raining by lunchtime. That's usually the way it goes."

"If you don't like the weather wait five minutes," Vasilek said, repeating a line he'd heard many times.

"Ain't it the truth," came the response and the guy smiled.

Vasilek smiled too, but not because he enjoyed small talk. In the past few seconds he'd seen enough to convince himself he was dealing with a desk jockey—a regular doorman and not someone involved in building security.

The first clue was the computer monitor. There was only one and it displayed a spreadsheet rather than surveillance video. In addition, the man's jacket had fallen open when he sat back and it was obvious he wore no holster or sidearm. It seemed doubtful he'd know how to use a handgun anyway. The guy's appearance and demeanor didn't fit the typical security guard mold. He carried about thirty extra pounds, was a couple weeks overdue for a haircut, and looked generally soft and unkempt.

Vasilek would have bet the lump's attitude towards his job was equally lackadaisical. In fact, if he put his mind to it he was sure he'd be able to talk his way right up to Rhodes' front door, even without the costume and props. There were possibilities there, but nothing he was willing to act on yet. This first sortie was strictly informational. He wanted to find out what Rhodes looked like and then he'd figure out how best to take him out.

"I have package for an Alex Rhodes," Vasilek said, consulting his clipboard once again.

"You can leave it with me and I'll see—"

"I'm sorry," Vasilek said, "but this requires signature. Is Mr. Rhodes in please?"

"Nope," he answered, hitching a thumb in his belt. "There's no Mr. Alex Rhodes in residence here. We do have a Ms. Rhodes but she left right before you showed up. If you'd like I can sign for that and I'll be sure she gets it. I do it all the time."

"Thank you," Vasilek said, "but that is not possible. I must have personal signature."

"Well, I can't help you with that."

"And you are quite sure there is no Mr. Rhodes here?"

"Positive. I've been working this desk for eight years and I know everyone in the building. Are you sure it's a Mr. you're looking for? The name Alex isn't gender specific."

"No," Vasilek said. "I suppose not. I will have to look into this and perhaps come back later. Do you know when Ms. Rhodes will return?"

"Couldn't even guess. She's usually kind of a homebody but she's been going out more often lately. Don't know why. Real nice lady but we don't get too personal, ya know?"

He stopped there as if realizing he'd gotten too personal already. He blinked and turned to his computer keyboard. "There anything else I can do for you today?"

The tone was dismissive and his body language made it clear he was done with the conversation. That was fine. Vasilek had learned everything he was likely to and he wanted to have another chat with Babbit before proceeding. He thanked the man for his assistance and hurried out of the building.

He walked for a while, avoiding the crush around Rockefeller Center and deciding to instead head towards Central Park. Despite the doorman's prediction, there were no signs of rain. He spotted a few high, wispy clouds against a sky that was otherwise blue and clear. That made him think of the resort in Jamaica and he wished he'd never left.

He also wished he'd never agreed to work for Clayton Babbit III. With any luck that relationship would *expire* in the very near future.

He moved past a small crowd of people surrounding a group of street performers doing a dance routine to a thumping bass beat. One of the dancers called to him to come join the throng but Vasilek waved, looked at the clipboard he was still holding, and increased his pace. Maybe they'd think he was late for a delivery. Maybe he didn't care what they thought one way or the other. He continued along until the performers were out of sight and the drum beats had faded away.

Retrieving his cell phone from his back pocket, he headed for a stone bench at the base of a towering oak tree. He checked the path in both directions, verified that he was alone and placed the call.

"You get him?" Babbit asked as a form of greeting.

"Not exactly," Vasilek replied. "There are complications."

"Complications?" Babbit echoed, harsh and accusatory. "And just what does that mean?"

"It means you again gave me bad information."

"What are you talkin' about, Sport?"

Vasilek hesitated. He was enjoying the upper hand and the feeling that, for once, he knew something Babbit didn't. He considered stringing the guy along for a while just because he could, but he loathed Clayton Babbit and the control the man held over him, and Vasilek was therefore anxious to conclude the conversation and the job as quickly as possible. He still couldn't help having some fun at Babbit's expense.

"You put me on the trail of a Mr. Alex Rhodes."

"Yeah? What of it?"

"No such person exists."

"Bullshit!" Babbit retorted. "We got the name and address from Tower Brothers' own records."

"That may be, but your information is flawed."

"Tell you what," Babbit said. "How 'bout you stop jerking me around and just say whatever it is you gotta say."

"Very well." Vasilek stood and began walking in the direction from which he'd come. "I visited the address you provided and learned that Alex is most likely short for Alexis, Alexa or maybe Alexandra."

"You're saying—"

"I'm saying you put out a contract on a woman."

This time, it was Babbit's turn to hesitate and the silence stretched out so long Vasilek thought he might have disconnected.

"Are you still there?"

"Yeah. Hold on there, Sport."

He covered the phone and Vasilek could hear him cursing at someone in the background. It was probably the person that had obtained the information about Rhodes yet somehow missed such an important detail. That wouldn't go over well and Vasilek almost pitied that poor son of a bitch, but not really.

"All right," Babbit said once he came back on the line. "Here's what we're gonna do. We obviously need to dig into this a little deeper. Give me a few hours. I'll try to come up with a photo and some other identifiers and I'll get back to you in a bit."

"And then what?" Vasilek asked.

"What do you mean? We go ahead as planned."

"But you don't care that this person is a woman?"

"I don't care if it's Florence fucking Nightingale. You copy?"

"Sure," Vasilek said and hung up.

Did he care that his target was female? He'd been wrestling with that question from the moment he left her apartment building and still didn't know how he felt. It wasn't like he had qualms. He could knife her without reservation and remain impassive as she bled out all over the sidewalk. That wasn't a concern. But In Vasilek's estimation, women were too trusting and not smart enough, strong enough, or cunning enough to present a challenge. It wasn't a fair fight and he did have a problem with that. He'd have to get over it if he ever wanted Clayton Babbit III off his back.

No time like the present, Vasilek thought, exiting Central Park. He could return to his hotel and wait for Babbit's call but why not go on a little fact-finding mission of his own? After all, he was only five blocks from the offices of Tower Brothers Publishing and it was such a nice day. He decided a brief detour was in order.

-20-

"So how do you want to play this?" Detective Paul Zanetti asked as he and Megan Lynch climbed the steps and entered the 5th Avenue building where Tower Brothers Publishing was located.

"I don't know yet," she replied, leading the way to the elevator and pressing the up arrow. "I have a hard time believing anyone here was directly involved in the murder. Martin Reginald is their top selling author. No one is going to kill their own golden goose."

"Do I hear a "but" in there somewhere?"

Megan was about to respond when the elevator doors slid open. She and Zanetti took a step back to allow three men to exit. They all wore dark suits and smug expressions, and walked like they knew their shit didn't stink.

"What's the difference between a lawyer and God?" Zanetti asked once the men were out of earshot.

Megan gave him a quizzical look.

"God doesn't think he's a lawyer."

"Pretty good," she said, stepping into the elevator. "You know what happens when you give a lawyer Viagra?"

"Sure." Zanetti stood on his tip-toes. "He gets taller. But seriously folks. You were about to say."

Megan pressed the button for the eighteenth floor. "I'm just wondering why no one from here contacted us. The cruise ship story was big news. It got even bigger when the disappearance became a homicide. The only name the news media had was Martin Worth, but Tower Brothers must have known it was their man."

"Why? It's not like we found out right away."

"I know," Megan admitted. "And that's why I'm not sure how to approach this. We'll start with basic questions and sort of see which way the wind is blowing."

"This is your show," Zanetti said as the elevator stopped and the doors opened. "You do the talking and I'll follow your lead."

"That's fine, but jump in if you think I'm missing something. I feel like I've been chasing shadows at every turn."

Megan had never had occasion to visit a publisher before and wasn't sure what to expect. The impression she got when she walked into the lobby was upscale dentist's waiting room: marble floor, over-sized furniture, decorative lamps, and a water cooler with fresh orange and lemon slices bobbing inside.

"Good morning," she said, approaching a round, middle-aged, matronly looking woman seated behind a large, curved reception desk. "I'm Detective Lynch and this is Detective Zanetti. We have an appointment with Vicki Goldstein. Is she in please?"

The woman stared for a moment and then seemed to come to her senses. "Oh, of course," she said, flustered. "She's expecting you. I'll just..." She picked up a telephone receiver, dropped it and picked it up again, nearly upsetting a mug of coffee in the process. "I'll just get her for you. One moment."

She pressed a few buttons while shifting her body so her back was half turned. "It's Tammy," she said quietly. "The *police* are here," her tone suggesting she was passing along confidential information.

Megan gave her partner a look. It had always intrigued her to observe how different people responded to the presence of law enforcement. The ones that acted the guiltiest were frequently those with nothing to hide.

"She'll be right with you," the woman said, replacing the receiver with a clunk and offering a thin smile that appeared to be causing her pain. "You're welcome to have a seat."

"Thank you," Megan said. But instead of taking chairs she and Zanetti strolled around the reception area, inspecting an array of book cover images blown up to movie poster size and hung in expensive looking frames. Some of the titles and authors Megan had heard of. Most she hadn't. However, it was clear Martin Reginald was the jewel in the Tower Brothers' crown. His name was everywhere. That brought her back to the same question that had been nagging her since the evening before. If anyone at Tower had known or even suspected something had happened to their most valuable asset, why hadn't they come forward?

A door down the hall opened, and Megan heard the click of heels punctuated by a curious jingling sound. She turned as a pretty, big-haired brunette entered the room.

"Ms. Goldstein?" Megan inquired, stepping forward and extending a hand. "I'm Detective Lynch and this is my partner, Detective Zanetti."

"Nice to meet you," she replied, her many bracelets emitting that same jingle as she shook their hands. "But I'm not Ms. Goldstein. My name is Jess and I'm her personal assistant. She's waiting for you down the hall if you would please follow me."

The conference room she led them to was like so many others: an oblong wooden table surrounded by the types of chairs found at any upscale office supply store. What surprised Megan was seeing how many of the chairs were occupied. It looked like a corporate tour de force, which she actually saw as a good thing. If Tower Brothers was engaged in a cover-up of any kind it seemed unlikely there'd be so many people in on the secret.

"Vicki," Jess said, addressing a dark-haired woman at the far end of the table. "These are detectives Lynch and... Zanetti?" She gave him a quick look. "I hope I got that right."

"You did," he replied. "You're one of the few."

She didn't seem to know how to respond to that so turned and walked to an empty seat just to the right of the woman Megan now knew was Vicki Goldstein.

"Ms. Goldstein," Megan said with a nod. "I appreciate you taking the time to meet with us this morning."

"It's no trouble," she said, rising. "I expect we have a lot to discuss. Let me begin with introductions." She started around the table. "You already met my assistant, Jess. This gentleman is Bob Whetton. He's the head of our legal department. Next to him is Peter Ireland, an agent and one of our senior editors. Over here is Morgan Kaplan. She leads our PR staff. And finally, Alex Rhodes, one of our authors."

A few things struck Megan. First, Bob Whetton was one of the least attractive men she'd ever met. It wasn't the body type or the bad suit, neither of which did him any favors. What really stood out was a sour expression that seemed to drip disapproval and negativity. She supposed it was possible she and Zanetti had arrived in the midst of a heated argument and that's what accounted for his scowl but she would have laid odds he looked much the same on Christmas morning.

There was something going on with Peter Ireland too. He was the one she'd spoken to on the phone the previous evening. He'd made it clear he needed to discuss the matter with higher-ups, but also gave the impression he handled most of the daily business at Tower Brothers. Megan did know anything about the hierarchy within a publishing house but Ireland's job titles and his spot at the table, mid-way down one side, suggested he may have over-inflated his importance. She didn't need to concern herself with any of that. It was obvious from the outset that Vicki Goldstein was running the show and it was to her that Megan would be directing most of her questions.

She settled into one of the empty chairs and considered the third person that had attracted her interest. Megan had requested this meeting because the man they now knew as Martin Reginald had been murdered. Under those circumstances, she could absolutely understand why legal and public relations representatives would be on hand. If Peter Ireland was Reginald's agent, his presence there made some sense too. But why another author? What was Alex Rhodes' role?

Megan studied the woman discretely and tried to figure out what about her seemed strange. She was pretty enough: somewhere in her mid to late thirties, maybe five and a half feet tall, average build, dirty blonde hair just past her shoulders, eyes somewhere between green and blue… and that's when Megan had it. There was something unsettling about her eyes. Rhodes appeared to be looking in her direction but not actually at her or Zanetti. Her gaze instead seemed fixed on something just above them and slightly off to the left. Megan felt compelled to turn and look but she knew there was nothing back there but a blank wall.

Is she stoned? she wondered, already sensing there had to be something else going on.

"I'd like to begin with an apology," Vicki Goldstein said, interrupting Megan's train of thought and attracting everyone's attention to that end of the table. "We possessed information that could be important to your investigation and I realize now we were not as forthcoming as we should have been. I take full responsibility for that and I'm very sorry. I can also assure you Tower Brothers Publishing will cooperate in any way we can."

"We appreciate that," Megan said, pulling out a legal pad and making a note of the time, date and location.

She'd picked up on how, by speaking first, Ms. Goldstein was no doubt hoping to control the flow of conversation. She was probably accustomed to that. This time, however, they'd be following a different set of rules and Megan thought it was necessary to set the proper tone right from the get-go.

"But perhaps you could explain something," she said, her face giving away nothing. "This sudden willingness to help—it's very nice but I think Detective Zanetti and I would both like to know what took so long."

"I'm sorry?" Vicki asked.

Megan stared at her. "Well, you say Tower Brothers wants to cooperate. I just want to know where you were when we were tracking down and questioning cruise staff and passengers, and begging the public for information. As far as they knew, as far as **we** knew, the murder victim had no special significance. He was just this side of a John Doe, except he wasn't. We were actually dealing with a homicide involving a world-famous author but we didn't know that until a check of dental records revealed a double hit. Were you aware Martin Reginald was traveling under another name and that he essentially held two identities?"

"I can answer that," Peter Ireland said, clearing his throat and adjusting heavily-starched shirt cuffs. "In short, yes. We did know Martin sometimes used the name Worth. He did it for anonymity. Writers aren't as recognizable as actors, pro athletes, or rock stars but they do still get noticed and it can infringe on their personal life. It's the price they pay for fame. It has its benefits but can get trying too."

"Are you speaking from experience?" Zanetti asked.

"Only in the sense that I've seen it happen. Authors deal with it in different ways. When Martin needed privacy he used a different last name and became someone else. We were aware of that. But," he made a palms up gesture. "I think I can speak for everyone here when I say we didn't know this other identity was real. We figured it was a sort of pseudonym. That's common in the trade."

"I'm sure that's true," Megan said. "But there's a big difference between a pen name and dual citizenship."

"Of course you're right," Vicki interjected. "But as Peter said, we never asked for specifics. It was Martin's decision and really none of our concern." She paused and then looked at Lynch and Zanetti in turn. "Was he doing anything illegal?"

"I already told you he wasn't," Bob Whetton said. "He did nothing wrong and that goes for Tower Brothers Publishing too. This is completely unnecessary and against my advice."

"Thank you, Bob," Ms. Goldstein said with a sigh. "You've made your opinion clear, but I was speaking to the detectives."

Megan made a brief notation and looked up. "From a legal standpoint Mr. Whetton is correct... to a degree. Martin Reginald committed no crime. However, as for the advisability of this meeting, I'm not going to make idle threats but you should be aware that you potentially wasted a great deal of our time and resources by withholding critical information. Continuing to do so would not be in your best interest.

Vicki Goldstein was ready to reply but her senior editor once again jumped in ahead of her.

"Please understand," Peter Ireland said, glancing toward the door as if to show he had other things to do. "There was no official identification of the body for the first several days. We didn't want to jump the gun I guess you could say. You saw all the accolades all over our lobby walls. Martin Reginald had... has a considerable fan base. Call it a business decision but we didn't think it would be prudent to break the news of his death until we were absolutely sure."

A business decision? Was that really the only consideration?

Megan looked at Ms Goldstein and, noticing her narrowed eyes and tight lips, decided she wasn't on board with everything her colleague had just said. She'd been quick to silence Bob Whetton too.

Interesting, Megan thought. They're all in the literary business but maybe not on the same page. She supposed she could use that, try to play one against the other, but why get in the middle of whatever interoffice politics might be going on? She just wanted answers and the quicker the better.

She leaned forward. "Detective Zanetti and I both understand why you wouldn't want to alarm Martin Reginald's fans prematurely or unnecessarily. However, confiding in the police is not the same as issuing a press release or addressing the media."

"Of course we understand that," Ms. Goldstein said. "And again, I would like to apologize on behalf of myself and Tower Brothers Publishing. It was never our intention to make your job more difficult. We were dealing with certain factors, and that may have prevented us from seeing the larger picture."

She might have elaborated further had Alex Rhodes not chosen that moment to speak up.

"It was my fault," she said quietly, looking down while poking at the iPhone she'd placed on the table in front of her.

"Alex?" Vicki Goldstein inquired, concern plain in her voice. ""Are you sure?"

"No," she said, and it looked to Megan like she was blinking back tears. "But I'm the reason we're all here, right? That's what you're trying very delicately not to say."

"Listen," Bob Whetton cut in, beginning to rise. "I can't advise—"

"No one's asking you to," Ms. Goldstein replied, not even glancing his way. "In fact, this would be a good time for you to go for coffee. Take Peter with you. I'll call if your presence is again required."

After a few awkward moments, they both filed out of the room, followed closely by the PR person who'd remained silent throughout and seemed only too happy to be making her exit.

-21-

"Before we go any further," Vicki said, sitting back and sounding a lot more relaxed. "Would anyone like anything? I should have asked that before. We've got coffee, tea, water, soft drinks…."

"I'm fine," the female detective said and the other one followed suit.

I thought Jess had introduced them as Lynch and Zanetti but I'm notoriously bad at remembering names and I also wasn't sure which was which. The woman seemed to be in charge which struck me as pretty cool. I might have wondered what the other guy was even doing there given how quiet he'd been but I'd read enough crime novels to know cops often worked in pairs.

"Well," Vicki said. "I could use some coffee. I wish I had a shot of Kahlua to go with it. It's been that kind of morning. Alex? Anything for you?"

"Something with bubbles and caffeine. Thanks."

I usually tried to avoid soda before lunchtime at the earliest but I'd woken up feeling kind of wonky--nerves I was sure--and I thought I could use the boost.

"And nothing for you two?" Vicki asked, again turning to the detectives. "It's no trouble."

They both declined.

"Jess, would you mind?"

With a jangle of bracelets she stood and left the room, leaving an awkward silence in her wake. I hoped they weren't all waiting for me to start the show. I was prepared to answer any questions they threw at me but I didn't want to launch into a lengthy litany unprompted.

"I'm sorry about Bob Whetton," Vicki finally said. "He's an alarmist and he's concerned we could be implicated if we volunteer too much. Peter Ireland feels much the same way."

"And they are right."

"Excuse me?" Vicki said, and I could tell that wasn't what she'd expected to hear.

The female cop propped her elbows on the table. "Detective Zanetti and I are investigating a murder."

Well, that was one mystery solved. If he was Zanetti then she must be Lynch. I'd try to keep that straight.

"Of your own admission," she continued, "you withheld information. There were perhaps extenuating circumstances but that doesn't change anything. Technically, Tower Brothers and its representatives could be considered accessories after the fact."

"But we're cooperating."

"You've said that but I'm reserving judgment."

"Until?"

"Until we hear what you have to say and why it took so long to say it."

"Perhaps I should call Mr. Whetton back in here."

"It's your decision," Detective Lynch said. "I just want to be clear on where things stand. We've made little progress with this investigation and, right now, I'm holding Tower Brothers Publishing responsible."

I thought Vicki would flip her lid at that but she seemed to take it in stride. "I understand your frustration," she said. "I hope your opinion of me and this company is more favorable by the time we're done here. Ask your questions and we will be as forthcoming as we're able."

"And did you want your attorney present?"

"Bob Whetton is not our attorney. He merely advises on legal matters. For the time being, I would prefer to proceed without him."

I didn't know about anyone else but that was welcome news to me. It wasn't because I didn't like him, which I didn't; I just didn't want to have to admit my myriad blunders to any more people than was necessary. I knew they'd all hear about it anyway. They just didn't need to hear it from me. And in Bob's case, I knew Vicki had already brought him up to speed anyway because she'd told me as much.

"Ms. Rhodes," Detective Lynch said, turning to face me. "You said this was your fault. Could you please elaborate?"

I stared at her and noticed how she shifted her head slightly to one side. I'd seen that same reaction more times than I could count and I knew what it meant. She wanted to know what I was looking at because I didn't appear to be looking at her.

That's another one of the charming idiosyncrasies of Best Disease. As I think I've mentioned, I have a lot of blind spots and most of them are centrally located. My eyes try to compensate by physically looking around the dead area. To the casual observer it appears I'm focused on something off to my right even though I'm actually looking straight ahead. It's got to be disconcerting for them and makes me about as self conscious as an elephant at an ivory convention.

I paused and tried to decide how and where to begin. There was so much to tell and I didn't know if I should start with the revelation that the Martin Reginald books might not be entirely fictional, or that I was actually the one who'd written them. I got a brief reprieve when Jess bustled back into the room, placed a mug of coffee in front of Vicki and handed me a Mountain Dew. She walked to her chair but then didn't seem to know what to do with herself.

"Should I stay?" she asked, sounding hesitant.

"Yes," Vicki replied. "Some staff will need to be briefed and I may leave that up to you. Better if you hear this first hand. You can also take notes for Alex if necessary."

Great, I thought, spinning the can in my hand and fingering the top until I located the pull tab. *Now they think I'm not only a freak but illiterate to boot. Awesome sauce. I'll tell them my story and they probably won't even believe me.*

"Ms. Rhodes," Detective Zanetti said. "If you don't mind me asking, is there something wrong with your eyesight?"

I breathed an internal sigh of relief. "I'd appreciate it if you'd call me Alex," I said, "and yes there is. I'm legally blind."

"But Ms. Goldstein…."

"Vicki," she corrected.

"But Vicki introduced you as one of Tower Brothers' authors. How…."

He trailed off there, obviously wanting to finish the question but not knowing how to do so without being offensive. By that point, he couldn't have offended me if he'd tried. I'm not sensitive about my lousy vision. It's who I am. I just get weirded out when I'm around people who don't realize or don't understand there's an issue. The detectives might be feeling awkward but I felt a thousand times better now that my large print cards were on the table.

"You want to know how I'm able to write, right?"

"If you don't mind," Detective Lynch said. "Can you type?"

"Yes. I learned in high school, mostly because my hand-writing got so bad when my vision went south. I used to be able to see fine. Now, I can't even make out the giant E on the eye chart unless I'm standing right in front of it."

"Was it an accident?'

"I got kicked in the head by one of Santa's reindeer," I said, automatically giving my favorite response to that question without taking time to consider that my audience was a couple of NYPD detectives who might not appreciate my twisted brand of humor.

"I'm sorry," I amended. "That's just something I say. There was no accident. It's a disease with a hereditary component. I drew the short straw."

The detective made a sympathetic noise and then asked the completely predictable follow up. "So how much can you see?"

I knew from countless failed attempts how futile it would be to try to give a detailed and understandable response so I didn't even bother.

"I get around okay," I said, opting for simplicity. "I just can't read normal size print and you should definitely pull me over if you ever see me behind the wheel of a car."

"But you don't wear glasses," she observed.

"Oddly, they wouldn't do me any good except for reading, and the print would still have to be large and very close to my face."

"Yet you're still able to write books? How do you manage?"

I could educate them on speech synthesizers, screen magnification software, and other types of low vision aids but I decided we'd delved deeply enough into that aspect of my personal life for now. I instead said something I knew would instantly change the direction of our conversation.

"I do freelance writing for several online publications. I am also the true author of every Martin Reginald novel."

I spent the next forty-five minutes explaining my decision behind using what amounted to a stand in, the unexpected arrival of the letter from my old high school friend, the disturbingly coincidental deaths of both her and her brother, and finally, the possible correlation between the Deepwater novels and what little I actually knew about Clayton Babbit III.

Detective Lynch stopped me a few times to request clarification on certain points. For the most part, though, I told my story uninterrupted while she appeared to write down every word I said. By my count, she filled five pages of her legal pad. Detective Zanetti took some notes too. Vicki and Jess just sat and listened. I had brought the letter from Deb, and once I'd described its contents Jess took it and left to make copies for everyone.

"That's quite a tale," Detective Lynch said when I eventually ran out of steam. "You've got enough there for your next few books."

Interesting thought. Were I duly inclined, I could write a true crime account of events that, at the time, I'd believed were mostly fictional. It would be pretty wild, and I could already feel Vicki's eyes on me because I knew a story like that had major blockbuster potential. The publicity alone would make it an instant bestseller. I could picture it on the big screen too, which would be a career first. I fleetingly wondered who should play me in the movie. *Kristin Bell as Alex Rhodes?* I liked the sound of that, and I knew it would never happen. Or if it did it would have to be written by someone else. I'd had enough of it already and I knew in my bones it was far from over.

"So this Clayton Babbit," Detective Lynch said, glancing at her note pad. "You believe he could be behind the Martin Reginald killing?"

I did, but it was one thing to share my theories with Vicki and quite another to face two trained detectives and accuse a total stranger of murder.

"I don't have any proof," I said weakly. "But it does seem to make sense."

"And you're basing that on the letter from…" she checked her notes again. "Ms. Royal as well as the research you were able to do on your own?"

"Research might be too strong of a word. I didn't have much to work from, and the only two people I could have asked were dead. I poked around and found a guy with a name similar to the one Deb gave me. Some of his business dealings were, well, let's say suspect and that was good enough for me."

"What do you mean by suspect?"

"One of his companies does beach restoration and they'd apparently raised the ire of the Florida Department of Environmental Protection some time back."

"How so?" Detective Zanetti asked.

I shrugged. "I want to say it had something to do with manatees but I don't really remember. And quite honestly, I didn't care. The story Deb told me was compelling enough but I didn't see it as anything more than a story."

"A damn good one too," Zanetti said.

"You read one of my books?"

"I think I've read them all. They're all good but the Deepwater novels are fantastic."

I actually blushed at that. I'd sold books in the millions but, due to circumstances of my own making, I'd rarely come in contact with my fan base and I wasn't sure how to handle it now.

"Thank you," I finally said, dropping my gaze to the table and wanting badly to change the subject. It seemed Detective Zanetti wasn't ready to go there.

"You'll still release the third one, right?"

I looked at Vicki but she, of course, couldn't respond because I hadn't yet told her my plans.

"I don't know," I said. "I suppose it depends on what happens."

"With what?" asked Detective Lynch.

I shrugged again. "This whole thing. I'm still having a hard time believing Martin was killed because of my books. And if he was, do I need to be worried about my own safety? I know Vicki wants me to take credit for my novels so the series and my career can continue. I've always had reservations about that. It's worse now because I think I could be putting myself at risk. On the other hand, I kind of feel like I owe him, if that even makes sense."

"Of course it does," Detective Lynch said. "It's a form of survivor's guilt. But there's something I don't understand. You based a fictional character on what you know about Clayton Babbit III. Is that correct?"

I nodded

"So your theory is that he was somehow made aware of that and didn't like it."

"That's basically it."

"Okay." The detective clicked her pen a few times but then put it down, only to scoop it up again seconds later. "If all that's true, why would he respond so violently and why now? Didn't those books come out a couple years ago? That's a long time to wait if his goal was revenge."

Detective Zanetti shifted in his seat and it looked like he wanted to say something but he remained silent.

"I must not have explained myself well," I said, realizing Detective Lynch and I were not on the same page. "I don't suppose you read *Deepwater Deception?"*

"No," she said, unapologetic. "I buy a lot more books than I ever get around to reading."

"It's the first book in the series and it did come out a little over two years ago. The premise is that the big BP drilling rig explosion of 2010 was an act of sabotage orchestrated so there would be a serious and immediate need for beach restoration. I'm sure you remember what it looked like once all that crude oil started washing ashore."

"Of course."

"Well, that first book was nothing more than a detailed red herring. I made it look like someone else was responsible and Clayton Babbit, or my Charles Briggs character, wasn't an obvious part of the equation. In other words, even if Babbit had seen the book there wasn't anything there to alarm him."

"That changed with *Deepwater Denial,"* Detective Zanetti said.

I smiled at him. "That's right. The whole focus shifted and Charles Briggs and his unspeakable motives moved more to the forefront."

"And that book's been out for how long?" Detective Lynch asked.

"About six months."

"That still seems like a considerable delay. Why wait to act?"

The smile died on my lips and my throat felt dry. I picked up the soda and took a long drink. "I don't believe his goal was revenge," I said, finding myself thinking about Martin in his final moments on earth. *Had he known what was coming? Did he, even for a second, understand why he was going to die? Was it terrifying and painful? Did he have the presence of mind to blame me?*

I gave a mental head shake and put the soda can down. "Martin was killed to keep him quiet. The most critical parts of the story have not yet been told and won't be until *The Well from Hell,* the final book in the trilogy is released."

"And that happens when?"

"We decided on an eighteen month schedule," Vicki said. "That's a little slower than the industry standard but it seems to have worked well for us so far."

"So the last book won't be out for a year?"

"That's correct."

Detective Lynch turned back to me. "And you're saying Mr. Reginald was murdered so the final book would never get published?"

I shuttered and took a breath. "That's what I believe. Yes."

She ran a finger along the bottom edge of her notepad. "Alex,' she said. "This may seem like an odd question but do you have any idea what Clayton Babbit looks like?"

"He's got gray hair," I said. "I know that from a photo I found on the bio page on some corporate website. That's about the best I can do. The picture was small and I can't really distinguish facial features anyway."

"Do you remember the website?"

"No, but it wasn't hard to find. I'm sure I can do it again if you need me to. Oh, and it said he was born in 1959."

"You're sure about that?"

"I'm positive because I intentionally made my Charles Briggs character a decade younger."

"So Babbit's in his late 50's now," Detective Zanetti mused. "Probably can't be our guy."

"I know," Detective Lynch replied, sounding disappointed. "For a second, I thought we might be onto something."

She bent over and retrieved a folder from somewhere beneath the table. She'd apparently come in with a bag or briefcase I had failed to notice. No big wonder there. Depending on which way I'm looking, an entire city bus can hide in one of my blind spots and that's no lie. I'm all about self-preservation, though, and I've learned to listen carefully before crossing the road. Otherwise, the results could be deadly, not to mention messy. That made me think of poor Deb Royal, and I was glad when Detective Lynch directed our attention to what she was holding.

"Does the name Scott Fisher mean anything to you?" she asked, opening the folder but not yet showing us what was inside.

"Not me," I said.

"Vicki?"

"I don't think so. We published a couple books for a Paul Fisher but his stuff didn't sell and we dropped him, geez, it's got to be ten or twelve years ago now. Why do you ask? Is this Scott Fisher a suspect?"

"He's a person of interest." She slid an eight by ten picture in front of us. "Does this man look familiar to any of you? I'm sorry the resolution isn't better. That's a blow-up of an ID photo."

Vicki and Jess both looked and agreed they'd never seen him.

"Alex?" Detective Lynch asked. "Can you...?"

I shook my head. "Pictures don't do me much good. Even if I could see it, I generally can't see people well enough to draw any solid comparisons. I'm sorry."

"It's okay," the detective said with a sigh. She returned the photo to the folder. "I doubt he looks much like that anyway."

"You mean it could be a disguise?" Vicki asked.

"It's possible he altered his appearance. All we know for sure is that he was using a false name."

"So Scott Fisher...."

"Never existed as far as we can tell. It's a name he was using aboard the cruise ship so we wanted to know if it meant anything to any of you."

"And you think that's the man behind Martin's murder?" Vicki asked, saying what I would have had I been able to form the words around the lump in my throat.

"As I said, he is a person of interest. I'm sorry but we cannot elaborate any further at this time."

"I understand," Vicki said, but was interrupted when Jess suddenly burst out laughing.

"I'm sorry," she said, hand flying to her mouth and causing her many bracelets to clink together. "It's just…." She tried to say more but broke down in a fresh round of laughter.

"Jess!" Vicki said, plainly annoyed and embarrassed. "I don't know what's gotten into you but you need to leave if you can't pull yourself together. There's nothing funny here."

"I know," she said, now using both hands to try to hide her face. "I know. It's just that…." She stopped again and took a few slow, shuddering breaths. She then straightened and used a corner of a shirt sleeve to dab at her eyes. "Alex has been writing books and using Martin Reginald, who's also Martin Worth, to represent her. In the Deepwater novels, Charles Briggs is apparently a fictional representation of some guy named Clayton Babbit III. No one's come right out and said it but we can probably assume Martin was killed by this Scott Fisher person, except that's not his real name either. "It's all horrible of course but… I don't know. It just struck me… funny. I apologize." She followed that up with another barely controlled giggle, and after a moment, Vicki and Detective Zanetti were chuckling too.

"It does sound kind of ridiculous," Detective Lynch admitted.

I agreed with her but might have also added the word hopeless. With so many things not as they seemed, what chance did the police really have of getting to the bottom of it all? My self-preservation instincts immediately spiked to DEFCON 5 as I thought about the possibility of a nameless, faceless killer hot on my trail, and the likelihood that I'd never see him coming.

-22-

Mikhail Vasilek lounged on a forest green, wrought iron park bench, his legs stretched out in front of him so passersby were forced to detour around his size eleven shoes. Although he wore the same pants as before, his work shirt had been replaced by an oversized, cream-colored t-shirt displaying a large guitar and the phrase *Go Acoustic!* His beard and nondescript cap were gone too, his face now mostly hidden by a wig of wavy, graying hair and a pair of John Lennon shades. He'd ditched his clipboard in the grimy bathroom stall where he completed his costume change, and now held a copy of *Rolling Stone Magazine*, open to a two page spread on Sir Ray Davies. Vasilek had never heard of the guy but noted that he sure was an ugly son of a bitch.

In case the need arose for an additional transformation, he still had a small, fanny-pack-type carrier secured beneath his shirt. It contained a second wig, some makeup, the ball cap--reversible so it could be brown or black--a checkered bandana, and an assortment of stick-on tattoos. It was overkill he knew, but he'd always believed it was preferable to be prepared rather than surprised.

Vasilek didn't know which set of windows belonged to Tower Brothers Publishing but, from his position, he had an unobstructed view of the building's main entrance. In truth, he didn't expect to see anything of note. There'd been people going in and out at a steady rate as long as he'd been sitting there which was now an hour plus. The majority of those people were women and, with no physical description to work from, any one of them could have been Alex Rhodes. However, Vasilek had a good memory for faces and he knew, if he saw someone now and then spotted that same woman again in the vicinity of Rhodes' apartment, his brain would make the connection instantly.

Of course, that sort of thing couldn't happen unless Alex Rhodes made an appearance. He had no idea how likely that was. Did authors make daily trips to the office? He sort of doubted it. But he also doubted it was business as usual now that Martin Reginald was dead. He figured everyone at Tower would be scrambling to come up with a new plan and it stood to reason that the real author of the books would be part of that equation. And hadn't that dumb ass doorman said she'd been going out more than usual? Where would she be headed if not to her employer? And until Babbit supplied him with more information, Vasilek had nothing better to do with his time.

He flipped a page in the magazine and, although he appeared to be looking down, his attention was focused on the couple that had just exited the building. The first person was a trim, striking, middle-aged woman in a lavender blouse and pale gray pant suit. She hurried toward a dark sedan parked in front of a hydrant and moved like she meant business. Her companion was a bit older, maybe late 40's, and wore his shirt and tie as if doing it under protest. The woman clutched a soft-sided briefcase and they both wore good quality black shoes with rubber soles and no heels.

Cops, Vasilek thought as he turned another page.

He had no interest in the new Q & A with pop star Demi Lovato, even if she was as hot as a five-alarm fire. Vasilek was, however, extremely intrigued by the apparent presence of law enforcement. He watched furtively as the two climbed into their car, a solid black Impala with bars between the front and rear seats, and a small dent in the right rear quarter panel. They had a brief conversation and then pulled an illegal U-turn and sped away, the man driving while the woman jabbed at a cell phone.

"Very interesting," Vasilek murmured, closing the magazine, folding it lengthwise and tapping it against his knees.

He knew the scene he'd just witnessed didn't necessarily mean anything. That the two were cops was not up for debate. To Vasilek, they couldn't have been more conspicuous had they dashed out in full swat gear and peeled away in a black and white with lights and sirens ablaze. What he could not be as sure about was what they'd been doing there in the first place. He considered the possibilities.

It was reasonable to assume and even expect that the revered NYPD would call on the publisher at some point. They were trying to solve a murder after all. But, in addition to Tower Brothers, the building Vasilek had spent a good part of his morning observing likewise housed the offices of attorneys, CPAs, financial advisors, and many other professions that stood largely for corruption and duplicity. For all he knew, the men and women in blue stopped by every other day as a matter of course. But even as he told himself that, he somehow knew the truth. They'd been there because of him and because of what he'd done. He felt it in his bones. He supposed he should have been frightened but realized he was oddly invigorated instead.

Mikhail Vasilek had been in the same line of work most of his adult life. Not all of the contracts involved hits but he'd eliminated more targets than he cared to remember. To date, he'd never been questioned by the police or, so far as he knew, even suspected of committing any crime. The reason was simple. He planned and prepared meticulously, and never left anything to chance. He created an identity for a particular job and abandoned that persona as soon as the job was complete. He therefore had never been around a police investigation but instead had to satisfy himself by imagining his pursuers encountering one dead end after another. What was the saying? *A wild goose chase?* Well, he'd given them a glimpse of the goose this time and that was all they were going to get. Still, it was thrilling to know they'd been that close, passing within a dozen feet of his park bench, and had no idea.

If pressed, Vasilek knew he could describe the two detectives down to his slightly frayed pant cuffs or the gold Claddagh ring she wore on a chain around her neck. What had they seen of him? Could they pick him out of a lineup? Had they noticed him at all?

No, he thought, standing up, tucking the magazine under an arm and strolling toward a sidewalk cart where he purchased a foot-long hot dog and a bottle of water. He returned to his bench, chewing, watching, and wondering what information the police might have gleaned from their visit. He had not seen them arrive which meant they'd been in the building quite a while. Why?

Very, very interesting, he thought, smiling behind the tiny paper napkin he used to wipe his lips.

Presumably, the Scott Fisher identity had been blown wide open. If the police knew Martin Worth Reginald had been murdered, procedure dictated their investigation would focus on motive and opportunity. However, since the world wasn't publically mourning the loss of a beloved author, Vasilek had to assume the news media had not yet learned the truth. That probably meant the cops had only just figured it out themselves. So, until recently, they had no clear motive which would have brought opportunity to the forefront.

Vasilek again considered his decision to impersonate Reginald during the critical thirty-six hours that followed the hit. None of that had been specified in Babbit's instructions. He just wanted Reginald dead and for Vasilek, or Fisher, to obtain the computer he'd thought was so important. Based on that, Vasilek could have simply thumped the guy and dropped him overboard and not spent the next day and a half entering and exiting his cabin, ordering room service, wearing his clothes and all the rest. In some respects, those actions had given investigators more to work with, but he hoped and believed the curious paper trail he'd left would beg more questions than it answered.

Worst case, how much could the cops really have on him? They had a bullshit name, a useless photo, possibly some equally useless security video, and whatever forensic evidence they'd gathered at the scene, which couldn't have amounted to much. Cabins were cleaned twice daily and a more thorough cleaning would come at the end of each cruise. Even if he had left behind a stray finger print or pubic hair, and even if it had been collected by some investigator's fine-tooth comb, it wouldn't do anyone any good because Scott Fisher never existed, and the cops had nothing on Mikhail Vasilek or any of the myriad identities he'd ever assumed. Had he been so inclined, he could have left blood and excrement all over the room and they would still be no closer to tracking him down.

And as for the ruse of pretending to be Martin Reginald, Vasilek believed that was a stroke of genius, perhaps one of his finest moments. The deception delayed the discovery of the passenger's disappearance until the ship was back in port. By then, of course, Scott Fisher had disappeared too.

Flipping through the magazine again, Vasilek wondered if he was giving the police too much credit. Maybe Fisher had never even made it onto their radar. But that was too much to hope for. With no clear motive for the murder, they'd have to double down on opportunity. That would inevitably lead them to the former occupant of cabin 1015.

The Island Explorer was a huge ship and, especially at night, there were plenty of secluded spots where a body could be dumped without anyone being the wiser. That limited opportunity to virtually everyone on board. However, if the cops knew Reginald was killed, which they did, they also knew he hadn't ordered room service breakfast the final morning of the cruise despite what records had surely indicated. They'd start putting the pieces together, and it wouldn't take long before the pool of suspects was narrowed to include only those people who knew Reginald personally and those who could have gained easy and repeated access to his room. In other words, they'd look at Island employees, those few passengers Reginald had any real contact with, and the ones whose cabins were in the closest proximity. How long would it take for them to identify Scott Fisher and note the curious resemblance between him and the murder victim? Vasilek was convinced that had already happened.

So what would pretty lady cop and partner do once they discovered their primary suspect was little more than a ghost? Vasilek wished he could have been privy to that conversation plus whatever discussions had just taken place in the publisher's office. Regardless, it was a fair bet everyone involved now knew Martin Worth and Reginald were actually the same guy. That, Vasilek supposed, would shift the investigation from opportunity to motive... which meant what exactly?

Sooner or later, the police would have to look at Reginald's books and at least consider the theory that he'd been killed to ensure his silence. With the true author of those books still alive and well, and talking presumably, they might reach that conclusion much faster than anticipated. That was interesting, but not overly concerning because there was nothing tangible to connect Vasilek either to Reginald or to Babbit. He could stroll into the police station and make a full confession and they'd still be hard pressed to find sufficient physical evidence to prove he was telling the truth.

Of course, confessing was not in his plans. He was going to off Alex Rhodes and then vanish, only re-emerging once he'd uncovered enough dirt on Clayton Babbit to eliminate any threat he might pose. The other option was to eliminate Babbit himself. That would be satisfying, but Vasilek hadn't decided if it was his best course of action. He'd take care of the immediate problem and then re-evaluate.

He checked the clock on his phone and discovered another twenty minutes had passed. Time to move on. He could return to his hotel, change his appearance again, and then stake out Rhodes' apartment in hopes he'd see a familiar face and something would click.

Vasilek stood and deposited his magazine, napkin and nearly full water bottle in a nearby trash can. He started down the block but then paused to watch a woman who'd just emerged from that same office building. At first, she didn't seem any more remarkable than anyone else he'd observed that day. She was in casual clothes, jeans and a mint green top, and she'd slipped on large, round-framed sunglasses as soon as she got outside. What he'd noticed of her face was attractive but not striking. Why, then, was he having a hard time pulling his eyes away?

He studied her and decided it was something about the way she walked. She started off quickly, but slowed as she approached a set of stone stairs, sort of sliding each foot forward as if testing for solid ground. She reached for the handrail too, which most young, healthy people wouldn't bother with. Maybe she wasn't healthy. She could have had something wrong with a foot or ankle. Except she'd seemed fine before and seemed to walk normally again once she descended.

Weird, Vasilek thought, as the woman lowered her sunglasses and shielded her eyes with a hand. *Now why'd she do that?* It was a nice day, more sun than clouds, but it didn't seem especially bright to him.

She stepped off the curb, looking down the whole time, and then the sunglasses went back on.

Vasilek was intrigued. He considered following her out of simple curiosity. Something about the woman was off kilter and he wanted to figure out what. So, when she began crossing to his side of the street, he wandered in her direction and timed his gait so he'd fall in right behind her. Then, someone called a name which made both of them turn to look.

"Alex!"

A second woman burst out of the building and rushed down the steps. The first two things Vasilek noticed were her big hair and the string of colorful bracelets that ran halfway up one arm. *What was the deal with that? Couldn't she decide which one to wear?*

"Alex," she called again. "Hold up. You forgot this."

As she approached, she held out a small item Vasilek saw was a cell phone.

"You left it on the table," the woman said.

The device changed hands and the women exchanged a few more words he couldn't make out over the clatter of a passing sanitation vehicle. That was fine because he'd already heard enough. The strange woman was Alex and very likely his new target.

Vasilek wouldn't act before receiving more info from Babbit, but following the woman was now a priority and it seemed the search for her was going to end a lot more easily than he'd imagined. Diligence would always get the job done in the end. Sometimes, though, a bit of plain, dumb luck couldn't be beat. His luck held when she headed for the subway stop instead of hailing a cab, and again when, as he was casually watching her from the opposite end of a subway car, his own cell phone buzzed.

"Yes?" Vasilek said

"Hey, Sport! I've found our girl."

"Me too," Vasilek replied, not even bothered by the nickname.

"What?"

"Never mind," he said. "What do you have for me?"

His phone buzzed again.

"I sent you a present. It's from the DMV so the quality isn't great but it should be good enough for your purposes. One thing. It's a New York State ID card and not an actual driver's license. She doesn't seem to have one of those. I don't know why."

"I do," Vasilek said, studying the thumbnail image and noticing how, although her head faced the camera, her eyes did not. He'd also seen her fumble her MetroCard into the reader and negotiate the escalator with caution as if it might pose a threat.

"I'm sitting twenty feet from her and I'm fairly sure our girl is blind. Consider the target eliminated."

He ended the call and fingered the thin, sharp blade that was always tucked inside his belt.

-23-

Give me some credit. I think I held it together pretty well while Vicki and I were being grilled by two of New York City's finest. I told my story, answered their questions, and didn't once start crying or sucking my thumb. But after they left, well, what can I say? I gave into my baser instincts and let the stress of the situation get the better of me. I sort of lost it, okay? But I think I was justified.

I had, by my careful calculations, exactly one day left of sanity. With some help from Vicki and Emily what's-her-name from PR, Peter Ireland was putting the finishing touches on a headline-grabbing press release and it was set to go out bright and early the following morning. No longer having much choice in the matter, Tower Brothers would officially announce that Martin Reginald, their prize possession and top-selling author, was fish food. I'm paraphrasing, of course, and also trying unsuccessfully to make light of a horrible situation.

Despite Peter's many objections, Vicki had not given me a deadline on my own professional future. I was grateful she was still in my corner, but I also knew there wasn't much sand left in that particular hour glass. In a perfect world, I wouldn't make any determinations until sometime after Scott Fisher and Clayton Babbit III were arrested, tried and convicted. Spoiler alert—this world ain't perfect, and I didn't have the luxury of waiting that long.

Once the big news was in the hands of the media, I'd have a limited window in which I could credibly acknowledge my unique role in the Martin Reginald literary machine. As much as I might wish to wait another six or eight months, no one would believe it at that point. Going public so long after the fact would seem like a well-contrived publicity stunt to promote the release of *The Well from Hell*, the final book in the series. It wasn't a now or never proposition but soon or never certainly seemed to apply.

So when was the right time? Good question. The pressure to make what I knew would be a life-altering decision was a major stressor, but not one I hadn't seen coming. After all, I'd sort of been preparing for it ever since I got Vicki's early morning text about Martin's bizarre disappearance. Even then, I'd known in my gut it wasn't going to end well. I think I'd also known that, no matter what, I would someday have to tell my secret. That was daunting but only in a distant, intangible sort of way. I mean, I knew it would happen but so far down the road it wasn't really a concern.

My security bubble of naiveté and self deception burst when Detective Megan Lynch told us about Scott Fisher. I kept my composure, barely, but that was a major shock to an already fragile system. All of a sudden, that reassuring distance and intangibility were gone.

The detective's bomb shell shook me to the core and I scurried for my burrow at the first opportunity. I'd been in such turmoil that I left Tower Brothers without my phone and didn't even notice. It may not seem so, but that is a really, really big deal. And before you start making assumptions I want to make one thing clear. I'm not addicted to technology as so many people are these days. I don't need to *stay connected.* I'm not forever checking my Twitter feed or tallying Facebook likes. I abhor social media and I closed my Facebook account years ago. No offense but I'm not interested in all those darling pictures of kittens, puppies, and baby's first bowel movement. There may be a sour grapes component too since I can't see the photos and videos everyone else is oohing and aahing about. I can't play all those stupidly popular app games either. I've never once angered a bird or crushed a candy, and the words I have with friends are typically in person.

Why, then, do I have a phone? It can't be for the sole purpose of making calls.

Quite true my dear Watson, but it's still a kind of lifeline for me. It contains my music and audio book libraries, both of which I consider necessities. Primarily, though, I've got some specialized accessibility apps without which I'd have a tough time getting around. There's a magnifier, a text, email and webpage reader, a color identifier, a paper currency identifier and a customizable audio GPS, to name just a few.

Unfortunately, when it comes to navigation, my single biggest issue is extreme light sensitivity. Believe it or not, there is no app for that. It's not that sunlight bothers me. I mean, it doesn't hurt or anything. For whatever reason, it just takes an inordinately long time for my pupils to dilate, or constrict, or whatever it is I ask of them. Even stepping from sun to shadow can be a problem especially if I'm not sure of my surroundings.

It's always the worst when I have to go from the bright sidewalk to, say, the dimness of a restaurant's interior, I'll be blind as a bat and it may take several minutes for my eyes to return to what, for me, passes as normal. In the interim, I might be bumping into tables, walking into walls or who knows what?

I wear sunglasses pretty much anytime I'm outdoors. They help ease the transition but are a stop gap measure at best. The only real solution is to avoid strange places, which I sometimes do at tremendous personal inconvenience. I'm no hermit, though. I'm not an invalid either and I refuse to lock myself away for the duration merely because I have a minor disability.

Okay, fine. I'm more of a homebody than most single women my age but I still get out on occasion and I find ways to deal with all the little hurdles life throws in my path. My favorites are those yellow-painted sections of curb. You've seen them, right? Have you noticed that the yellow sometimes indicates a slope for easy wheelchair access and other times it seems to signify nothing more than the presence of the curb itself? Could we get a better color coding system please? I mean, I appreciate the effort and everything but I usually can't tell the difference between a slope and a regular curb so I guess and end up either stubbing my toe or high stepping over something that isn't there. I don't know how foolish I look but I can imagine it and it's not a flattering sight. Pardon the pun.

I wish my pedestrian perils ended there but I'm only scratching the surface. I can't see street lights or street signs, or signage of any kind really. By the way, I'm convinced those damn folding sign boards they put in front of stores were designed just to mess with my head.

You may not realize this but New York City sidewalks are full of obstructions. I keep a running list and I have walked into or tripped over, in no particular order, fire hydrants, traffic cones, potholes, mailboxes, construction scaffolding, a violin case full of loose change, garbage bags, garbage cans, street signs, lamp posts, homeless people, crime scene tape, Jerry Seinfeld—I think—and one poor guy's seeing eye dog. Don't you love irony?

It seems my mental train has strayed rather far from the tracks. I apologize but it's been a rough day. In fact, by the time I escaped Tower Brothers and made it to the street, sans telefono, I was so rattled my nerves felt like they'd been worked over with the business end of a cheese grater.

Scott Fisher? Who in the hell was that?

I already told you I was no good with names but I was still damn sure I'd never heard that one before. Detective Lynch described his photo to me but that hadn't rung any bells either, which I'm sure came as a surprise to exactly no one. I had my talents but I was never going to make a great eye witness for the prosecution.

Despite no obvious connection to me, my books, or to Martin Reginald, the detectives seemed convinced that Scott Fisher person was the real killer. I didn't know what to make of that but a couple possibilities came to mind. The first was that my Clayton Babbit theory was hogwash and Martin was targeted for his own unknown indiscretions. That scenario would have done my troubled conscience a world of good, and I didn't buy it for a second.

The other possibility was the one that had me inwardly squirming like a virgin on sacrifice day. I knew Clayton Babbit was involved. He had to be because there was no way Martin had a secretive second life that somehow put him at odds with a murderer. It just wasn't conceivable, and I think Detectives Lynch and Zanetti agreed. Of course, it helped that Detective Zanetti had read my novels so he already knew of the serious crimes for which Babbit, or his fictional counterpart, was potentially being accused.

Eleven innocent people died when Deepwater Horizon exploded. How many more lives were disrupted or destroyed in the oil-soaked aftermath? There was no way of knowing because it was impossible to quantify devastation of that magnitude. Could you really put a price tag on an entire ecosystem? And what about Bryan and Debbie Royal? Bryan supposedly knew and feared what Babbit was up to. He confided in his sister. They were both gone now. It was possible their deaths were as accidental as police reports indicated. Or, they could have been murdered to shut them up. .

How far, I wondered, tucking my phone away as I unsteadily descended the stairs into the 3rd Street subway station, *would Clayton Babbit III go to keep the final chapters of his story from being told?*

The Deepwater disaster was almost a decade in the past. Even if he had been engaged in sabotage and was therefore responsible for the horrible outcome, how could anyone prove it now?

The causes of the explosion and blowout were well documented, as was the series of mistakes and oversights that served as detonator for the time bomb. I'd read a lot of the reports that were made available for public consumption. The real scientific stuff was lost on me so, when it came to my novels and describing the sabotage Bryan Royal believed had taken place, I deliberately fudged everything that didn't make sense to me.

I don't write technical thrillers so it was easy enough to gloss over any details I didn't understand. However, I do have a very good vocabulary. I like to think I'm smarter than the average bear too. And in all those official transcripts and reports, I never saw one hint, or suggestion, or implication that what happened in, on, or below that drilling rig might have been deliberate.

Are you following me here? If droves of investigators failed to turn up anything nefarious, what could Babbit possibly have to fear from a lowly fiction author, especially so long after the fact? I supposed the answer to that one was clear enough. The novels couldn't have been written without some level of inside information. He might suspect the source, the now deceased Royal siblings, but he couldn't know how many of his dirty little secrets had been passed on to others, namely me.

Given the drastic and even desperate nature of the actions he had, presumably anyway, already taken, I figured Babbit's most logical move was to stay the course and try to finish what he'd started. In other words, kill 'em all. He wasn't pulling any punches either. He learned Martin sometimes traveled under a different name, which maybe hadn't been that difficult, but then got details on his travel itinerary, and from his home somewhere in Louisiana, hired his own private hit man and sent him off on a Caribbean cruise to address the problem. That was some scary-ass shit, and it would have worked too had I not unwittingly set Martin up as a decoy. Spin that forward and I was probably next on the Clayton Babbit Scott Fisher hit parade.

All the cops seemed to know about Fisher was that he was a slick operator and his identity was phony. Oh, and two other minor details. He'd gotten on and off the Island Explorer in New York, and that really brought the whole thing home to me. The police obviously didn't have a valid address for him and there was no reason to assume he was one of the 8.5 million residents of the Big Apple. In my current frame of mind, though, he and I were neighbors. I'd probably walked past him on the street or stood in line with him at my favorite soft pretzel stand. He was every indistinguishable face in the crowd and that terrified me.

With uncooperative fingers, I extracted my MetroCard from my wallet and, after a few tries, finally managed to feed it into the reader at the turnstile. I felt like there were eyes on me the whole time, which isn't unfamiliar territory. I've got my own survival tactics if you will, and I depend on them whenever I'm out and about. I know they must look quirky to any onlookers, so I feel like I'm under the microscope whenever I stumble, misjudge a doorway, or pause for no apparent reason. The rational part of my brain insists no one is paying attention but rationality has never been my strong suit, and that was the case long before I learned there was a killer on the loose.

I flinched and let out an involuntary squeak as someone bumped into me from behind. A tall kid in a hoodie and bright yellow headphones mumbled an apology and elbowed his way past while I tried to catch my breath.

"Get a grip, Alex," I said, knowing I couldn't be heard over a three-way argument in loud Italian, the guy playing a kind of neat swing version of *Careless Whisper* on saxophone, or the general hubbub that's an integral part of New York public transit. "You're just being paranoid."

Of course, under the circumstances, I figured a certain amount of paranoia was in order. It's a reasonable response to learning that a complete stranger might want me dead.

That annoyingly rational voice spoke up again and argued I was in no immediate danger. *Martin,* it said, *has only been gone for about a week.*

I understood the insinuation. How could the killer, in so short a time, find out he got the wrong guy, discover that I actually authored the Deepwater novels, and then track me down?

He couldn't, I agreed, stepping onto the platform as the train neared. *Not yet.*

Even if Clayton Babbit, or his homicidal proxy, knew who to go after, there's no way he, or they, could have located me so soon. Hell, they might still think they'd already got their man, although I knew that was way too much to hope for

Martin always traveled with a small laptop, and that's what he used for most of his communications. According to the detectives, that computer had not been recovered with the rest of his belongings. Some other items were unaccounted for too, although they hadn't offered specifics. I got the impression the missing laptop was of most interest. It might have suffered the same fate as Martin and was now residing at the bottom of the Atlantic. Or, the killer took it because he was looking for information. That seemed like a more probable scenario. If the man was murdered because of his writing, it made sense to seize the object in which those writings were probably stored. That vault was empty, but would that be enough to convince Babbit he'd put a contract out on the wrong dude?

Yes, I thought. *He's desperate and scared, and he's not going to stop until he's sure the threat has been eliminated.*

The subway arrived, doors opened, and I made my way toward a section of empty seats near the front of the car. Nobody, so far as I could tell, took any special notice, but it's curious how vanity and mild paranoia could exhibit themselves in such similar ways. I didn't want to be the object of anyone's attention. I really didn't. I still couldn't help feeling observed and analyzed as I settled myself, pulled out my phone, plugged ear buds into the jack, and then inserted a bud into my right ear only, so my left was open to receive and process recorded announcements about approaching subway stops and any other potentially significant outside stimuli. Those actions were perfectly natural to me, but I supposed I must look like a weirdo to the huge black guy a few feet to my left, the three women across the aisle and the eight or ten utterly nondescript people at the opposite end of the car. From this distance, I couldn't even accurately identify their genders but I couldn't shake the feeling that they all knew a good deal more about me.

And you know what they say about paranoia. It doesn't mean they're not out to get you.

I parried that sentiment with a thrust of common sense. *It's the middle of the day. I'm in a public place. I have nothing to fear*—which worked until my myriad insecurities and neuroses started scratching their way back to the surface. I tried to ignore them: checking emails and texts, and then listening to a couple songs from the latest Kings of Leon album, all the while deliberately not making eye contact with anyone.

That, it turned out, was a mistake. Had I given a little more credence to my normally unfounded suspicions, had I not made every effort to ignore my early warning system, had I devoted even a few seconds to studying my surroundings, I might have noticed that, this time, someone really was watching, and apparently following me too. Thankfully, it sometimes is possible to rely on the kindness of strangers, and I was the unsuspecting beneficiary of someone else's vigilance.

-24-

The 59th Street station is generally busy even at midday and I fought the tide of passengers pushing their way into the subway car as I was trying to get out. I'm not crazy about crowds so I kept my head down, moved when I could, and the path eventually began to clear.

I rounded a corner and thought I felt somebody tug at my shirt sleeve but, when I turned to look, there was no one within arm's reach. I did see one guy striding in the opposite direction and toting a large camouflage backpack. Maybe it had brushed against me as he hurried past. I didn't really think anything of it. I still had my purse, phone and wallet so all was good. A piece of advice, though: if your goal is to avoid personal contact, if you don't want to be pushed, jostled, shoved and, on occasion, fondled, you might want to avoid New York City subways altogether because all that stuff is going to happen to you sooner or later.

I made my way toward the steps that would bring me up to street level, feeling marginally better now that I was that much closer to home. My plan for the rest of the afternoon was to engage in some serious thought. The press release was going out in the morning. A press conference would follow. Should I use that opportunity to *come out* for lack of a better term? Was that the time to pay the piper, face the music, put my cards on the table, or whatever other horribly clichéd metaphor you want to use?

The very idea of going public was both reassuring and horrifying. I knew I'd become instantly famous, something I still wanted no part of. In addition to the minor celebrity of authoring a bestselling book series, every media outlet in the world would be looking for my take on the Martin Reginald murder. Talk about scrutiny. I wouldn't just be under the microscope but on the dissecting tray. That made me think of Martin, and an autopsy, and how his now dead body would be subjected to the type of literal invasion I feared only in the figurative sense. I'm such a wuss.

As much as I dreaded the prospect of stepping into the spotlight, I knew that doing so would afford me a certain amount of protection. I'd be a public figure, at least for as long as the story remained in the headlines, and that meant I'd be recognizable everywhere I went. So, if Scott Fisher *or whoever* was really gunning for me, I'd hopefully be making his job more difficult. I had no personal experience in the field but figured it had to be harder to knock someone off if they were constantly surrounded by adoring fans and other random hangers on. They would be my salvation.

Okay, I knew I wasn't going to be so revered I could forever hide behind a wall of humanity but the thought was nice. At the moment, though, I had more important things on my mind. I had to ruminate and that would require suitable fortification. The wine rack was full, blessedly, but Mother Hubbard's cupboard was bare. What to do? What to do? Deli sandwich or a gyro? Hot pastrami or that amazing tzatkiki sauce? And why was I being tasked with such impossible choices? Life just wasn't fair sometimes.

I did a mental coin toss and the deli won out, mostly because I'd be walking right past the place. I could even call ahead and have my order ready when I got there. That would be convenient but it's not like I was in a big rush either. All I had waiting for me at home was eight hundred square feet of solitude and a decision I didn't want to have to make. I realized I could put that off a bit longer if I stayed and ate at one of the small wooden tables at the deli but they didn't sell alcohol and I had a feeling I'd need some.

I was still considering my options when a commotion broke out behind me. I heard a scuffle, some shouts of alarm, and when I turned around, a man was flat on the ground.

"What the fuck!" he protested, starting to pick himself up as a second man emerged from the crowd, lunged and grabbed me by the elbow.

"Come on!" he hissed, pulling me toward the stairs.

"Wait! Let go of me!" I tried to break free but his grip was too tight.

Years earlier, I'd taken a night class in basic self defense but I hadn't been very good at it, and, suddenly faced with a genuine crisis, I blanked on all the incapacitating and bad ass moves I'd been taught. I did remember one tip, though, and drew in a breath to scream at the top of my lungs.

My new escort must have sensed what I was about to do. "Don't!" he ordered, one hand still on my elbow and the other now planted solidly in the middle of my back and propelling me forward. "I'm not going to hurt you. I just want to get you out of here."

"Why?" I asked, stumbling as we started up the steps. "What's going on?"

"I was hoping you could tell me," he said, shooting a glance behind us. "You piss off a boyfriend or something?"

Fat chance. The closest thing I had to a serious relationship was in my nightstand drawer and in need of new batteries. "No," I said. "Why would you ask that?"

"I was already on the subway when you got on at 3rd Street," my new companion explained, quickening his pace and forcing me to do the same. "Another guy got on right behind you and he was staring at you the whole time."

Scott Fisher, I thought, as the stairs flattened out and then we started up the next flight.

"Pretty big dude," he went on. "Late twenties I'd guess. Thin nose, black hair in a military cut, jeans, leather jacket, and combat-style boots. He also had a nasty-looking scar from his right cheekbone down to his chin. Sound like anyone you know?"

"No," I insisted. "And could you please ease up? You're cutting off my circulation."

"Oh, sorry."

The pressure on my elbow lessened but only marginally. I could try to make a break for it but I knew it would be pointless. *Besides,* I thought. *What if he really is trying to help me?*

I glanced over, and although I couldn't make out any real detail, I noted a man of average height, brown hair, *maybe*, and clean- shaven. I couldn't even begin to guess his age. Based on the sound of his voice, I knew he was no kid. He wasn't elderly either. I figured that put him anywhere between twenty-two and sixty-two, give or take a decade.

Despite the hands that continued to guide me upwards, I didn't think his body language was threatening. He was determined but I didn't sense any immediate danger. He was just doing a good deed. Either that or I was a total sap. I supposed I'd soon find out.

"So that guy," I said, digging in my purse with my free hand and pulling out my sunglasses. "What was he doing?"

"On the subway, nothing more than what I told you. He was watching, staring really, and I thought he looked angry."

"That's odd."

"I thought so too, especially because it didn't seem like you even knew he was there."

"No," I said, distracted. "I didn't."

Could it really have been Fisher? That didn't seem possible, for all the reasons I'd already considered. And there was another one too. The person just described to me sounded nothing like the Scott Fisher Detective Lynch told me about. I was pretty sure she'd said he was brown-haired, and she definitely hadn't mentioned anything about a disfiguring scar. Then again, she had said he might have changed his appearance.

"So what happened when I got off?" I asked, keeping my voice calm even though my heart was racing in my chest.

"He followed you, and I thought I'd better see what he was up to."

"I guess I'm glad you did," I said, as this person who'd apparently saved my ass again turned to survey the stairs we'd just ascended. "Anything back there?"

"No," he answered, sounding like he didn't trust his own eyes.

Join the club, Buddy.

"Okay then." I turned to face him but not before putting my sunglasses on. "Whoever it was, he must be gone by now. I appreciate your help. I think I can take it from here." I stuck out my hand to shake, prompting him to release my elbow. "Thank you so much."

"If it's all the same," he replied, giving my hand a brief squeeze and then letting go. "I'd feel better if I stayed with you a while longer."

"What for? You said you couldn't see him anymore."

"That's true. And I'll say goodbye to you here if that's what you want, but I think I should tell you the rest of the story first."

I was pretty sure I didn't want to hear it but, short of covering my ears and running away, I didn't think I had much choice.

"Okay," I said. "Does it have anything to do with the shouting and that guy I saw on the ground?"

"Yeah. I think he may have been trying to help you too but it didn't work out so well for him."

Two guardian angels in the same day? I must be living right. "So what happened?" I asked.

"Do you mind if we walk and talk? I'm not comfortable just standing here."

That sounded ominous as all hell. I gave him a look and then turned toward my 63rd Street apartment building and we started that way.

"Like I said, he followed you when you left the subway. He kept getting closer and closer, and I had the feeling he was up to something."

"Like what?"

"I didn't know but he was giving off a seriously negative vibe. You know what I mean?"

He didn't wait for me to respond.

"I moved in right behind him and it's a good thing too. I saw him pull something out of an inside pocket of his coat. It was hard to tell from my angle but it looked like a blade. Other people must have seen it too. They started shouting. That one guy tried to grab him but he was pushed and fell down. The first guy put away his knife and took off in the other direction."

"He was gonna stab me?" I asked, voicing a question I didn't want the answer to.

"Maybe. I doubt you have anything to worry about now. He was probably a whacko or perv. Maybe hopped up on something too. I'm sure it's nothing personal."

"I'm sure," I said half to myself, and any other day I would have believed it.

"I'll tell you what. I think you're safe, but if you want, I'll walk with you until you get where you're going or you tire of my company, whichever comes first."

"That's very nice but I don't want to put you out."

"You're not. I was headed this way anyway. I've got an appointment on 75th."

"And you got off at 59th?"

He chuckled. "I hadn't planned that part. Thankfully, it's a nice day for a stroll."

"Well, I appreciate it and I apologize for the inconvenience. Can I pay you for your trouble?"

"It was no trouble and no you cannot. I'm just glad no one was hurt."

"And I'm glad to know chivalry isn't dead. I'd heard rumors."

"I think it's on the endangered species list. And before you get any funny ideas, I'm not carrying you over any puddles."

I was trying to come up with a witty response to that when I instead walked straight into another one of those fucking signboards, sending it crashing to the sidewalk and very nearly following it down.

"Are you okay?" he asked, grabbing my arm and helping me regain my balance. Too bad he couldn't do the same with my dignity.

"I'm fine," I said with a sign. "My shins are well callused by now."

He didn't say anything to that but I could feel his quizzical look.

"My eyesight stinks," I told him. "It's okay when I'm out in the open. Tougher when I'm in the shadows from all the buildings and awnings and what have you. My name is Alex by the way. You may have saved my life so we should probably be properly introduced."

"Okay. I'm John. It's nice to meet you."

We exchanged a more formal handshake while I waited for the inevitable question. It took half a block.

"So how much can you see? If you don't mind me asking."

"I don't," I said, and I meant it too. "But nothing I tell you is going to make sense."

"Try me. Are you color blind then?"

"Technically no," I said, smiling to myself because he'd immediately asked about one of the most confusing aspects of Best Disease. "I just can't distinguish most colors most of the time."

"Pardon my ignorance, but wouldn't that make you color blind?"

"No. I have the physical ability to see every color in the spectrum. I just need the proper lighting, background and contrast."

"I don't follow."

"I knew you wouldn't. I've been dealing with this for over twenty years and there are times I still don't understand."

"So you weren't born this way?"

I gave him a sideways look. "Are you calling me old?"

"Nope," he said, unapologetic. "But I think you've burned a few candles since your twentieth birthday."

"I resent that, even if it is a hundred percent accurate."

But really, I liked his direct approach and the fact that he didn't shy away from difficult or awkward questions. He seemed genuinely interested in my responses too, and not just making polite conversation.

"I'm closer to forty than twenty," I said. "And we'll leave it at that."

I found myself wondering about his age and wishing a person's voice was a more reliable barometer. He sounded like he could be about as old as me but I knew that didn't mean anything.

And why do you care, Alex? It's not like he's interested in hooking up and you shouldn't even be thinking about that.

"Okay," John said, placing a hand on my shoulder to guide me around a wet spot on the sidewalk where it looked and smelled like someone had puked. "So you can see colors but only when the stars are properly aligned. What about everything else?"

"Everything covers a lot of territory."

"Would you rather talk about the weather?"

"No," I said. "It's just tough to explain. People always want to know if my vision is blurry. I don't see well enough to know. It's more of a general lack of information."

He made a noncommittal noise and I was sure he had no idea what I was talking about. He scanned the street and then pointed. "Can you see that?"

"You mean the American flag in front of the bank?"

"Yeah. So you can see it?"

"Yes and no."

"I get it. You're trying to confuse me, right?"

"I'm just being honest. I can identify the American flag because I already know it's there. If I didn't know that was a bank, I could probably still see the flag but I almost definitely would not be able to make out the stars and stripes. It's kind of the same as what I said about colors. It all depends on lighting and contrast; proximity too. I could definitely see it if it was close enough."

"Interesting."

That and a total nuisance.

"So what about books and stuff?"

"Short answer. I can see that there's print on the page but not read what it says without magnification. I don't mean glasses either. Reading for me requires large electrical equipment."

"So what do you do for a living? And if that's too personal just say so," he added quickly. "I'm just curious."

"It's fine," I said, suddenly ready to bring our chat to an end.

He seemed like a nice guy but I had more important things to focus on right then and his last question reminded me I had an important decision to make too.

"I'm a writer."

He thankfully didn't ask for elaboration and I didn't offer any.

"Well," I said, pausing in front of the steps that led to my building. "This is my stop. I've got a deadline to meet so I should really get inside. It was nice meeting you and thanks again for your help."

"Alex. It was entirely my pleasure. Perhaps we will meet again someday."

He bent over then and actually kissed the back of my hand. I have to admit that made me a little weak-kneed. The dude had chivalry dripping out of his ass. I knew anything I said would sound idiotic so I waved, turned and headed for the door.

Brandon must have seen me approach because I heard the buzz and click of the lock disengaging before I'd managed to get my key card out of my pocket. I let myself in and was about to say "Hello," when the door behind me suddenly crashed against the wall. I spun and saw John standing there. He didn't say a word but his arm went up, I heard a sort of popping sound, and Brandon groaned, slumped over, and fell to the floor.

Holy Mother of God! I thought as some primitive part of my brain informed me that I had just witnessed a shooting. I felt like I needed time to process what had just happened but my central nervous system had other ideas and I was running for my life before I even realized it.

-25-

Mikhail Vasilek swore and tucked his custom Glock 9 back into his waistband. *Fucking Babbit!*

If he'd had his way the blind little bitch never would have made it out of the subway station. It would have been so easy too. Get into the middle of a crowd, restrain her briefly and casually slide the knife into her abdomen and up under her rib cage. She'd be down and bleeding out before anyone realized anything was amiss.

Sure, the hit would have taken place in full view of who knows how many cameras but so what? None of the images would give the security staff or the cops anything of significance.

Maybe, **maybe,** if they had a perfect angle, some top-notch facial recognition software and they got really lucky, they just might be able to connect the subway stabber with the recent Island Explorer passenger who traveled under the name of Scott Fisher. But again, so what? The Fisher identity was as clean as an operating room, not to mention that it didn't exist anymore. He had nothing and no one to fear.

The job should be over and Vasilek should be safely on his way back to Jamaica or wherever else he pleased. Instead, he was standing in an apartment building foyer, a dead doorman at his feet and literally in possession of the smoking gun. And why? Because Clayton Fucking Babbit was an unreasoning asshole.

He'd received the text as he was watching Rhodes on the subway and deciding exactly when, where, and how she would meet her maker. Babbit's written instructions were infuriatingly simple. *Call me NOW,* and Vasilek knew things were about to get complicated. What followed was a murmured conversation that left him so angry he wanted to strangle somebody, preferably Babbit himself.

When he first found out about Rhodes, Vasilek thought all he'd have to do was kill her. That seemed like a reasonable assumption since it's exactly what he'd been told. But all of a sudden, Babbit was increasing the scope of the assignment about a hundred-fold. He still wanted the author dead, but he also wanted every existing copy of everything she'd ever written, at least the stuff that had not yet been published. His concern was that the Reginald murder might speed up the publication timeline for the last book in the series. Barring that, the manuscript and any related content might be turned over to the authorities.

Vasilek didn't understand Babbit's motivations but the guy was scared. He must have done some bad shit, and Rhodes somehow found out and was writing about it in her novels. If he ever got the chance, Vasilek would have to read the damn things so he could find out what this was all about. In the meantime, he tried to talk Babbit out of what, to him, was a hopeless endeavor.

"No one keeps hard copies anymore," he argued, cupping the phone to his ear while discretely studying Alex Rhodes from the opposite end of the subway car. "Even if I can somehow get into her apartment, which isn't going to be easy by the way, I can grab her computer and any papers she has lying around, but she might also have external hard drives, thumb drives, CDs or DVDs. And what if she has a safe? I can pick most door locks but I'm no safe cracker. She might use cloud storage or an online drop box too. She probably does. I couldn't access that stuff even if I knew where to look."

"You let me worry about that," Babbit replied. "You just do what I told you and make it fast. I want everything you can get and then I want her gone. Are we clear?"

Babbit signed off with a fresh round of threats which all amounted to the same thing. Vasilek's continued liberty and anonymity depended on successful execution of his orders, however screwed up they might be.

He's insane, he thought, rising as the subway slid to a stop. *But I'll work with it. If I can't off her yet, I'll rescue her instead.*

Gaining Rhodes' trust proved almost as easy as the minor diversion he'd created at the 59th Street station. He tripped one guy, pushed another and chaos ensued. Because Vasilek didn't yet understand how much the woman could see, or not see, he wasn't sure how convincing his little drama needed to be. She bought his story, though, maybe as a result of already being nervous and suspicious. He smiled to himself as he took her arm and led her to the slaughter.

The four block walk to her apartment building had been interesting. Most of the time there'd been little indication she had any sort of impairment. Then, almost like she meant to do it, she walked smack into a wooden placard advertising a restaurant's soup and sandwich lunch special. Unless she was completely blind, and Vasilek knew that wasn't the case, he couldn't see how she'd missed it sitting right there in the middle of the sidewalk.

There was other stuff too. On the stairs up from the subway station, she seemed to not realize when they'd reached the top and tried to mount one more step than had actually been there. She also put on and removed her sunglasses with curious frequency. She'd sometimes take her glasses off only to then shield her eyes with her hand. Vasilek couldn't make any sense of that until she explained a little bit about her struggle with light and shadow. It still seemed odd, and had the circumstances been different, he might have felt sorry for her. That would present complications so he kept emotion out of it and focused only on the mission at hand.

The most expeditious way to accomplish his goals would be to somehow convince or subtly persuade her to invite him back to her apartment. The front door wasn't good enough. He needed to get inside. And when he extended a few flirtatious feelers, he didn't miss the brief involuntary smile or the sudden flush in her cheeks. He was getting to her, but he sensed it when she put the brakes on. The woman was too gullible but also possessed the automatic defenses of any single woman living alone. In other words, she wasn't stupid and wasn't about to open her door to someone she'd only just met.

That plan had its drawbacks anyway. Vasilek had been in the building a few hours earlier, and with a few minor deviations, his appearance wasn't much different now than it had been then. If that same slow-witted dolt was working the front desk he might recognize him, make a comment about his ill-fated delivery attempt, and that would be the end of it.

If this had been a normal operation Vasilek would have gone into fact-finding mode and spent the next few days monitoring the building as well as Rhodes herself. He'd find out how often the desk was manned and by whom, and search for any flaws or weaknesses in the security system. There had to be service entrances and maybe a loading area. Places like that weren't always as secure and doors were sometimes left unlocked if not open. He might be able to gain entry as a plumber, an electrician, an exterminator, a sanitation worker, or any of the blue collar, name-on-your-shirt types that typically don't warrant a second look. He'd still have to find a way to locate and then enter Rhodes' apartment but Vasilek saw those as minor details.

The best approach might be to go directly to the source. He and Rhodes had some chemistry. She thought so anyway. He could take advantage of that. It wouldn't be hard to arrange another *chance* meeting. He could talk her up some, invite her to lunch or dinner; before long, she'd be inviting him into her apartment and then her bed. It hadn't occurred to him before but maybe there were benefits to having a female target.

Unfortunately, both the personal approach and the covert required the one commodity that was in the shortest supply—time. He might be able to devote a few hours to impromptu surveillance but not the minimum three or four days he needed. Babbit wanted the job completed yesterday and that left Vasilek one option. He had to put his usual caution aside and hit Alex Rhodes like a tsunami.

Initially, it played out just as he'd hoped. She entered the building and he managed to sprint up and jam his foot in the door right before it closed. That was about the time things started to go south. The doorman saw him there and must have had at least an inkling of his intentions. His eyes got big as he leaned forward and reached for something under the desk. It could have been an emergency panic button, or a weapon, or nothing at all. Vasilek was in no position to take the chance. He shouldered the door hard and sent it crashing against the frame. Almost in the same motion, he drew his silenced Glock, sighted and fired.

The bullet hit its mark, a neat round hole appearing just above the man's left eye. His mouth flew open and his hands started flapping uncontrollably. A second later, he let out a moan that sounded like it came straight out of the grave. He collapsed then, his body going one way while his chair the other. They both ended up on the floor but Vasilek had already turned his attention to the woman.

His plan was straight forward. Grab the bitch, frog march her to her apartment, get what he needed, send her to that big library in the sky and get the hell out. He was confident no one had witnessed the shooting, and the now dead doorman's hand had never made it anywhere near the button that might have summoned help. The clock was still ticking and Vasilek figured he could safely allow himself about ten minutes inside. He could be persuasive when he needed to and he'd broken young strong men a lot quicker than that. He didn't anticipate a challenge from Rhodes. Because of her handicap, he believed she was already damaged goods. That was compounded by her gender, a handicap in itself.

Heroes, Vasilek knew, were a rare breed. You hear about fight or flight but there was a third response he'd encountered plenty. Most people, when facing real danger, simply froze. They might cry, beg or piss themselves but nothing more proactive or effective than that.

When the doorman went down Rhodes just stood there, her mouth agape as she stared at the spot where, moments before, the lump had been sitting. She didn't move to help him. She just looked at the now vacant desk and then at Vasilek, or the person she thought of as John or maybe Scott Fisher. Her lips started to form a question, and then her purse slipped from her grasp and fell to the carpet. She gave no notice and didn't even shrink away when Vasilek stepped toward her. He grinned, thinking his ten minute estimate had been too conservative. She'd break faster than his countrymen could tamper with an American election. He took another step, already knowing the battle was won. Then, quicker than he would have thought possible, she turned and disappeared around a corner.

"Damn!" he said, starting after her and then stopping short. He heard a thud and then a door slammed a short distance off. He headed in that direction but then stopped again.

"Damn," he repeated, this time mostly under his breath.

As much as he wanted to, he couldn't immediately give chase, not before securing the area. The front door had closed and locked of its own accord, and from the outside, he knew, nothing would look amiss. However, someone could enter at any time or the elevator doors could open and whoever got out would see a dead man and a small but spreading pool of blood. That would elicit a 911 call for sure. There was also the possibility someone in a nearby office had been monitoring security cameras, seen what happened, and made the call already. But based on the absolute quiet, Vasilek didn't think that was the case.

As fast as he could, he righted the doorman's chair and then part dragged, part shoved and part kicked the body under the desk. It wasn't a perfect fit, but with the chair positioned just so, there were no obvious signs of foul play--unless you somehow realized that the odd-shaped, darkening splotch on the beige carpet consisted of blood and cranial fluid. It would take a professional cleaning crew to get rid of that mess. Vasilek stared at the stain for a moment, then grabbed some papers off the desk and dropped them on top.

And now the dilemma. Because he didn't have the benefit of the information-gathering he liked to do prior to any operation, he knew next to nothing about the interior building layout and that put him at a serious disadvantage. Rhodes had gone around a corner to the right. He'd followed but only far enough so he could see down a short hallway and several closed doors. The one that stood out was at the far end, third down on the left-hand side. It was plain black steel with a silver push bar and kick plate, and a lighted exit sign overhead.

Son of a bitch, he thought. Did that account for the thud and slam he'd heard? Had Elvis left the building? Or was Rhodes holdup in a laundry room, mail room or stairwell? He didn't know, and didn't feel like he should waste time trying to find out. She might have flown the coop but she'd have to return sooner or later. He would just need to be ready, but first things first.

He returned to the lobby and picked up Alex Rhodes' abandoned purse. Her phone was on top. And from an outside pocket, he retrieved a small set of keys. The set included a fob, a couple keys sized for a mail box, safe, or safe deposit box, plus two larger ones. A squarish silver key showed the most signs of wear and he knew that's the one that would unlock her apartment door. Vasilek already knew the apartment number. He checked his watch, saw that he still had about eight and a half minutes, and headed for the elevator.

-26-

Oh my God!

He's dead.

Oh my God!

He's dead.

My brain kept sending and resending those two signals even though neither one was doing me a hell of a lot of good right then.

John, who obviously wasn't the Good Samaritan I'd believed him to be, had pulled a gun and killed another human being. I knew that even though I hadn't actually seen him do it, and the gunshot was much quieter than I would have thought. It was more of a snick than a pop or a crack, and the word "suppressor" suddenly came to mind.

I wished I could convince myself Brandon had only been injured and that help might still reach him in time. But that almost inhuman sound he made, and then the way he toppled out of his chair! It was like he'd lost complete control of his muscles and I knew he was gone. I wanted to scream, cry or throw up, but for several horrifying, debilitating moments, my body flat-out refused to respond to any of the panicked synapses pleading for physical action.

Move it, Stupid, or you're gonna be next.

I knew that and I truly believed I had just seconds to live. As ridiculous as it probably sounds, I was somehow too bewildered to even be scared. I just stood there like I was frozen to the tracks while the Grim Reaper Express continued to pick up steam.

At first, I guess I thought I was caught up in yet another senseless and random act of violence in a city full of them. However, once my mind started functioning at least in a limited capacity, I realized I'd totally misread the situation. John wasn't a nut job, or a drug-crazed addict or even a blood-thirsty killer. He was a pro. He was, in fact, the very person I'd been warned about not an hour before. I was less than fifteen feet from Scott Fisher, the man responsible for Martin's murder, and unless I did something fast the emergency responders that came for Brandon would need a second body bag in my size.

I started running before I knew where I was going or what in hell I'd do when I got there. I just needed to get away, and the first things that registered were the two elevators.

No good, I thought, reluctantly rushing past. Those big thick doors represented safety, or would if I'd been on the other side of them.

Somehow, though, even if I smiled, batted my eyelashes and showed some skin, I doubted Fisher would stand patiently by while I pressed the button and waited for an elevator car to come and whisk me away. And no elevator also meant no apartment which left… what exactly?

There were only two directions I could go, unless I turned around and made a desperate dash for the main entrance.

Blind Woman Attempts Frontal Assault on Man with Gun.

Catchy headline, I supposed, but suicide missions aren't my style. I headed toward the rear of the building, wondering vaguely if I'd hear the shot before the bullet tore into my flesh. Brandon was dead before he hit the floor. If it was my time to go I prayed it could be the quick for me too. I wasn't going to make it easy on him though, and I zigged one way and zagged the other, all the while expecting each step would be my last.

I didn't know what was down the hall to my left but had an idea it had to do with maintenance: boilers or air conditioning systems or whatever. I'd never had occasion to go that way and, as you already know, I tend not to do as well when the territory isn't familiar. For all I knew, those doors were kept locked anyway and I'd be walking—or running—right into a trap. I didn't like my odds with that so I veered right and rushed for the exit door.

I reached it in about ten strides and was about to hurl my full hundred and twenty-six pounds against the push bar when I suddenly reversed course. I knew what lay beyond—a small courtyard with a high fence and a gate. I'd been out there on occasion. You needed a key to enter the gate from the outside, but you didn't need a key to get out if you were already in. I could be on the street in seconds. Once there, I'd be free to hop a bus, call the cops, or find a suitable place to lay low. My salvation was that close, except for two things.

I'd apparently dropped my purse in the midst of my hasty retreat so I was without money, my MetroCard, my keys, my phone…. I didn't even have my sunglasses, and that would make it tough to get around in those most critical first few moments.

Yeah, I know you want to kill me but would you mind waiting until my pupils constrict so I can cross the street without getting run down? Gee, thanks.

And lacking pretty much all of my resources was only part of the problem. The real issue was the door itself. It was equipped with an alarm that notified the desk attendant anytime anybody went in or out. I didn't know if it was a buzzer or flashing light or what, but Fisher had been right next to Brandon's desk. Any signal would be immediately obvious to him. It would be like leaving a trail of bread crumbs. If I was going to provide him a map of my escape route I mighty as well sit down right where I was and wait for him to come find me. I couldn't outrun the man. My only hope was to buy time by doing something sufficiently unexpected. Solution? I hid in a dryer.

Yeah, yeah. I'm a fool. You can say it because I know it's true. My brilliant ploy was tantamount to trying to evade the executioner by standing in the middle of the gallows. There were only four dryers in the laundry room. If he opened one he'd open all of them and I'd be history, and my final moments among the living would be heralded by the unwelcome revelation that I was the biggest asshole on the face of the planet. I mean, a fucking dryer? Was that really the best I could do? I wish I could dispute the point but right then, curled into an uncomfortable ball, feeling claustrophobic and hoping the strong smell of fabric softener wouldn't make me sneeze, I knew I'd made a thoroughly boneheaded decision. If I had to pay the ultimate price I supposed I'd gotten what I deserved.

In my defense, I've never run from a killer before. And as hard as it may be to believe, my liberal arts degree from Molloy College hadn't properly prepared me for such an eventuality. I graduated Summa Cum Laude too, president's list every semester but one. I learned about theology, integrated algebra, philosophy, and the basics of early childhood development. Yes, I'm well-rounded thank you very much; yet not a single course syllabus said a word about how best to get away from a mad man with a gun. No wonder our educational system is in such bad shape. Math and science are great but a curriculum based on tactical evasion would be more practical.

At least I had the wherewithal not to run outside. I figure that should be worth something. After that, though? I don't know what happened. I turned around and all I could think was that he'd appear at any second. I was sure I'd surprised him by taking off but it's not like I had a big head start. I had to get out of sight fast. I think instinct took over then, and I'm referring to that same under-developed instinct that tells a three-year-old to escape his seekers by hiding behind the first piece of furniture he comes to and closing his eyes to ensure his invisibility.

I darted into the laundry room, not because I had a strategy but because I'd stopped next to the door and there was literally nowhere else to go. Inside, florescent motion sensor lights clicked on but only after I'd slammed a knee into the large double-basin slop sink against one wall.

"Shit!" I said, hoping the collision hadn't been as noisy as it seemed. I shot a worried glance at the door I'd just entered and then surveyed the rest of the room. It didn't take long. In addition to the sink and the four dryers, my new sanctuary was equipped with four glass-door front-loading washers, two metal folding tables, a white plastic trash can, and a couple contoured plastic chairs. That was the whole shebang. It was perfectly acceptable if I'd come in to do a load of delicates but good hiding spots were grossly lacking. I assessed the situation as follows. I could take my chances back out in the hall, try for the six foot high window that passed for an emergency exit, or squeeze my ass into one of those dryers. I regretted the decision as soon as I closed the door.

I'm guessing you've never spent any quality time inside an electric clothes dryer so allow me to enlighten you. The things are not designed with comfort in mind. They're spacious enough, considering, but the cylindrical thingy that spins the clothes has these thick, rigid bars or fins and, no matter how you adjust your body, you've always got one pressing into the top of your head, the back of your neck or the small of your back. Thankfully, you don't focus on that too much because it's so stuffy and dark, and you're bent over so far you get light-headed. That was my experience anyway. Maybe it will be different for you.

I don't know how long I stayed there. It's hard to keep track of time when you're convinced you're about to die. Oh, and here's another fun fact. Turns out dryers aren't as sound proof as you might think. I assumed closing that door would effectively shut me off from the world but I could still hear all the normal ambient sounds: the hiss of air through a vent, a steady drip from the slop sink, the hum of the fluorescents for however long they stayed on, and when the laundry room door clicked open I heard that too, followed by footsteps that seemed to draw ever closer.

This is it, I thought, crossing myself to the extent my confines and body position would allow. *They're going to bury me in a freaking Maytag.* I had a sudden vision of what the open casket would look like and I think I might have laughed had I not felt like all the breath had left my body. I tensed and waited for the inevitable. And nothing happened.

Sometime later, the laundry room door opened again. I heard more footsteps and the sound of something heavy hitting the floor. After some scuffling and a few electronic beeps and blips, water began to run.

Either Scott Fisher had come in to wash blood out of his clothing or it was safe for me to leave. I decided to go for it. I kicked the dryer door open, poked my head out, and nearly gave a poor Italian woman a heart attack.

-27-

“What now?” Detective Paul Zanetti asked, looking up from his computer monitor as Megan approached.

“I just came from Weiserman’s office,” she said and dropped a thick file folder on her desk as she sat down. “I briefed him on our conversation with Alex Rhodes and Vicki Goldstein.”

“Yeah? And what’d Wigs say?”

“He thinks it would have been nice if they’d enlightened us a few days sooner.”

“Well we sort of knew that already.”

“Of course,” Megan said, kicking off her right shoe and massaging her heel against the base of her chair. “He also thinks Rhodes’ story is credible and we should look into it.”

“Meaning?”

“Meaning you need to tell me everything you can about those books because I don’t have time to read them right now.”

“We could bring Ms. Rhodes in for further questioning.”

“Oh, we’ll definitely talk to her again, although it might be easier if we went to her.”

Zanetti nodded to show that he understood.

“For now, I want to get a better understanding of the storyline as it relates to Clayton Babbit III and any allegations of wrong-doing. We need to find out what we can about him too and try to determine if it’s even possible he did the things Rhodes claims in her books.”

“MythBusters NYC,” Zanetti said and grinned.

Megan looked at him but otherwise didn’t respond.

“All right, all right.” He leaned back and laced his fingers behind his head. “How much do you remember about the BP oil spill?”

“I know it made a big mess.”

“Is that all?” Zanetti asked, his expression suggesting he thought she could do better.

Megan frowned and pinched the bridge of her nose. “As I recall,” she said. “It started with a fire—something to do with a blow-out… something or other?”

“The blow-out preventer.”

“Sure. But I guess it didn’t prevent what it was supposed to and that led to the big mess I already mentioned.”

“True, but there was a bit more to it. Mind if I fill in a few gaps?”

"Nothing would bring me greater joy."

"It's been a long day," Zanetti said. "Let's shelve the sarcasm, shall we?"

"Sorry. Please go on Professor."

"Okay," he said. "So in February 2009, the BP corporation filed a fifty plus page environmental impact plan for the Mecando Well. It basically said there was no risk of a spill, and even if something unforeseen happened, there was no significant threat to anything or anyone because the drilling was so deep and so far offshore. Our government apparently agreed with that assessment and BP was exempt from a more in-depth study."

"Why?"

Zanetti shrugged. "The well was fitted with a blow out preventer and I guess they thought no other emergency measures were necessary. Unfortunately, that preventer was not equipped with some of the things that might have helped it operate as intended."

"Such as?"

"A remote trigger for one. There was a dead man's switch that should have cut the pipe and sealed the well when communication with the drilling rig was lost but that either wasn't activated or it just didn't happen. The preventer hadn't been inspected in five years. It regularly leaked fluids and it was actually damaged in an unreported accident a month before the explosion."

"Wait," Megan said, staring at him. "Unreported?"

"That's what I said. And it turns out that type of thing happened a lot. Workers were afraid they'd get fired if they raised concerns that might delay drilling. So even when there were clear safety issues or violations they kept their mouths shut."

"That's awful."

"Of course it is and it gets worse. Some employees falsified reports to get around different guidelines and restrictions. They made things appear safe and normal even when a lot of people knew that wasn't the case."

"And BP knew about this?"

"They knew enough. A U.S. District Court ruled that BP was mainly to blame for the accident because of what they termed *gross negligence and reckless conduct."*

"And it was all because of that blower whatever?"

"No," Zanetti said. "That was just the weakest link in a dangerously faulty chain."

"A disaster waiting to happen."

"It seems so. Eleven people died and seventeen more were injured. Then the real fun began. Attempts to seal the well failed, as I'm sure you know, and for the next five months it spewed oil at a rate of about thirty-three thousand barrels a day. All told, that's somewhere around two hundred million gallons but no one knows for sure."

"Incredible," Megan said, picking up a pen and clicking it open and closed. "And it was all because some BP execs wanted to make a few extra bucks?"

"Well, I don't know if you can put it all on them. That Deepwater Horizon rig was actually built and owned by a company called Transocean. In fact, at the time of the explosion, most of the more than one hundred people on board were Transocean employees. Only seven of the people there worked for BP.."

"Maybe the rest of them cleared out ahead of time because they knew what was coming."

"You could argue that they should have known but it's obvious no one paid close enough attention to the warning signs."

"Okay," Megan said, tossing her pen on the desk. "I've got another question."

"Shoot."

"Just how in blazes do you know all that?"

"I'm a detective," Zanetti said. "It's my job to know."

"Yeah, well, I am too and I can detect bullshit when I hear it."

"That hurts," Zanetti said, a hand to his heart.

"I'm sure. So fess up. You didn't get all that from reading a couple novels."

"Actually, Martin Reginald, or Alex Rhodes I suppose, did a good job explaining it."

"And you retained that information? And before you answer, keep in mind I've been around you long enough to know you have a hard time remembering your own shoe size."

"Geez," Zanetti said. "That's harsh."

"Am I lying?"

"No," he admitted, holding up a note pad covered with his chicken scratch. "While you were in with Captain Weiserman I spent some quality time with Captain Google. A lot of what I told you was in the books but, as you so delicately pointed out, I'd forgotten most of the specifics. I also wanted to make sure I could separate fact from fiction."

"Good thinking. So in terms of Clayton Babbit III...."

"The character's name is Charles Briggs."

"Whatever. So based on what you've learned, do you think a sabotage plot is conceivable?"

"Absolutely," Zanetti replied. "It's what I was saying before. There was so much pressure to maximize production that a lot of things were swept under the rug. Plenty of people had concerns but no one was willing to raise the red flag over fear of reprisal. With that sort of culture, I guess, a saboteur could act with impunity, because even if he were suspected, he could be relatively confident no one would say a word."

"So it is possible," Megan mused.

"I think so. When I get home tonight I want to skim through that first novel again to see how Rhodes described the sabotage itself. It seems like there was something to do with a bad metal casing on the preventer plus an additive in the cement that prohibited it from hardening. As far as I remember, though, she concentrates more on the why than the how."

"What do you mean?"

"Again, I want to double check but I think the books are more about motives than anything else. They're mysteries more than techno-thrillers."

"And as I understand it," Megan said. "Babbit's motives were the same as BP's, right?"

Zanetti thought about that. In a way I guess. BP wanted to keep drilling because of the money, and money was the reason Babbit wanted the drilling to stop."

Megan shook her head, thinking about all the news footage she'd seen of oil-soaked birds, turtles, and dolphins. It was disgusting and heartbreaking. What sort of person would bring that about intentionally, regardless of how many millions were at stake?

At first, she'd thought Rhodes' theory about the Martin Reginald murder was implausible at best, but now? Could someone really operate with such disregard for life just to line his own pockets? If so, it made sense that same person would go to extreme lengths to protect his secrets.

"Okay," Megan said with a shudder. "I'll give you a solid A on your Deepwater Horizon research. What have you learned about Clayton Babbit III?"

"Not much yet," Zanetti said. "I knew you'd ask, though, and I was just starting to dig into it when you came back from Wig's office."

"Anything interesting so far?"

"Depends on what you mean. He has a lot of business interests starting with Sand-Sational *"Environmental Restoration."* He made air quotes with his fingers. "Plus, he owns a handful of gas stations, a machine parts company, something involving industrial waste disposal, about twelve hundred acres of undeveloped real estate, and a portable toilet company called The Liberation Station."

Megan rolled her eyes but didn't comment.

Zanetti consulted his notes. "From what I can tell, and again, I've only just started, pretty much everything I've seen looks above board."

"Pretty much?" Megan questioned.

"You picked up on that, huh? It looks like the beach restoration thing has ruffled more than a few environmentally conscious feathers. It's not limited to Babbit's company either. The industry as a whole gets a lot of negative press. Plenty of people believe the restoration process, dredging sand from one place to dump it somewhere else, does more harm than good. I think we've got enough to worry about without getting involved in that debate."

"I think you're right," Megan said. "But his bad press—does any of it go beyond activism?"

"Meaning is Clayton Babbit III guilty of anything worse than being the owner of a controversial business? I'll have to get back to you. As I said, he's got his fingers in a lot of pies."

Megan considered. "Let's worry about the one pie for now. Find out everything you can about Sand-Sational. Specifically, I want to know about any possible connections between Babbit and any of the workers on that drilling rig. Bryan Royal knew his name, or ONE that sounded strikingly similar. He confided in his sister. If he talked to anyone else we need to know who.

Zanetti blinked. "Do you remember me saying there were over a hundred tight-lipped people on that rig when it blew? Eleven of them are dead now. The information you want may have died with them."

"I'm aware of that," Megan said, brushing a loose strand of hair away from her face. "I know it's a tall order but what else have we got? Scott Fisher is a vapor trail. That leaves us with Babbit. Let's start looking into his personal and professional dealings and see if any of them lead us anywhere near the Gulf of Mexico."

"Okay," Zanetti said, already sounding defeated. "Do me a favor and tell Wigs to cancel my vacation for the next three years."

"Look on the bright side," Megan said with a smile. "We'll be spending more time together."

"I always suspected I led a charmed life. Now I know for sure."

Just then, the phone on Megan's desk chirped.

"Detective Lynch," she answered, automatically reaching for her pen.

"WHAT?" she asked, rocking forward so fast she almost fell off her chair. Zanetti put out an arm to steady her but she waved him off.

"When did it happen?

"Right. And you said you already made the 911 call?

"That's good. Where are you now?

"Sure. I understand.

"No. Just stay put. We'll find you. Stay inside and we'll be there as soon as we can."

Megan kept her voice even for the benefit of her caller but the sudden rush of adrenalin was like an electric shock.

"Forget about Babbit," she said. "We've gotta move."

"Where," Zanetti asked, reaching for his jacket. "What's happened?"

"Fisher," Megan replied. "He isn't a vapor trail anymore."

-28-

Mikhail Vasilek paced the length of his hotel room, pausing occasionally to look at the items scattered across the bed. He'd spent exactly eleven minutes and fifteen seconds, a bit longer than he'd intended, inside Rhode's apartment and come away with an HP laptop computer, two unlabeled re-writeable compact disks, and five 16 GB flash drives he'd found in the top drawer of her desk.

He'd also discovered a microwave-sized safe bolted to the floor in her bedroom closet. It was still there. Vasilek didn't have the tools to remove it. And even if he could have, he figured it weighed the better part of a hundred pounds. No way to sneak that out of the building without attracting attention. The biometric lock would have made it a pointless endeavor anyway since he did not have Rhodes' finger prints at his disposal and had no idea how to bypass that type of system if such a thing was even possible.

So that aspect of her home security remained intact, and he decided he'd keep that piece of intel to himself rather than sharing it with Babbit. Rhodes didn't seem to own a printer anyway, which convinced Vasilek all the more that she did not keep hard copies of her writing. The safe probably contained her personal documents, cash, and maybe some jewelry, none of which interested him.

He was, however, very interested in a photo copy of a letter he'd found alongside a bizarre piece of electronic equipment on top of Rhodes' desk. The thing looked like a miniature camera, but the curious design made its use a mystery he didn't have the time to try to solve. The letter, on the other hand, provided the key to a different mystery altogether, and for the first time he finally had an inkling as to what was really going on.

Alex Rhodes obviously wasn't a reader, at least not in the traditional sense, yet she owned hardcover editions of all the Martin Reginald novels. They were lined up in chronological order on an ornate cherry wood bookshelf against one wall of her office. The two most recent books, based on the titles and cover designs, had some correlation to the big oil spill years earlier. Vasilek had known that part already. He just couldn't imagine how it had anything to do with Babbit, or how Reginald and then Rhodes ended up on his radar. Then he read the letter from someone named Deb and much of the cloudy picture snapped into vivid focus.

Vasilek wished he had more information about the document's source, mainly a last name and address, but a search of Rhodes' desk and office yielded nothing further. The letter was a copy so what happened to the original and the envelope in which it must have been delivered? He touched the gun holstered at the small of his back and thought again about the safe. Should he have made at least some effort to get it out of there? Was it worth going back for?

No, he thought, irritated he'd even entertained the possibility. *Go back? And for what?* The entire building would be crawling with cops by now. It would be suicidal to venture into their dragnet just to satisfy his curiosity. It wasn't worth it.

Besides, he rationalized. *I already know everything I need to.*

Whoever this Deb person was, her brother was evidently dead, and if Vasilek had learned anything about Clayton Babbit III it was that the man didn't like loose ends which suggested she was probably pushing up the daisies too. He wasn't scared of Babbit. Mikhail Vasilek wasn't scared of anyone. It was all about risk assessment, and for this job he knew he'd been risking too much already.

He sat on the edge of the bed, picked up the letter and ran it slowly through his fingers. If there was any truth to what was written there Babbit had plenty of compelling and personal reasons for signing the death warrant on Alex Rhodes. But what if the damage had already been done?

It was clear he didn't want the third Deepwater novel to see the light of day, but the previous one had been out half a year or more. Why had he waited so long to act? Had it taken him until now to realize he might be in danger? More important, how much of that final installment had already been written and shared? The answer to at least part of that was perhaps no more than three feet away, and Vasilek's eyes fell on the small silver laptop.

He had been instructed to collect whatever he could find in terms of computers and other storage devices. And like with Reginald, he was not supposed to inspect those devices but immediately turn them over. Vasilek followed that order without question the first time around because he was a man of his word. Babbit, however, was not. He'd changed the rules once and would do it again if it suited him. Vasilek knew that, and also knew the only way to get out of this mess was with the proper leverage. At long last, it seemed he had some.

He used his phone and snapped three high resolution pictures of the letter. He then had a decision to make. Should he follow his first inclination, tear the paper into bits and flush them down the toilet? Or, should it go in the FedEx mailer he'd already addressed and labeled? Both options had their merits. If he disposed of the letter he would know something Babbit presumably did not. On the other hand, if Babbit received the letter along with the laptop and the rest he would have to assume Vasilek had read it and understood the significance. That might level the playing field and even get the son of a bitch to back off some.

Vasilek considered, and then folded the letter lengthwise and dropped it into the box. The disks and four of the flash drives went in too. He held the fifth flash drive and bounced it a few times in his hand. He wouldn't try to delude himself into thinking his line of work was moral or ethical. He was a killer and nothing more. He had his honor code just the same, and he'd never been tempted to violate it. He'd never betrayed a client in any way and no client had betrayed him—not until Clayton Babbit came along.

Vasilek gazed unseeing at the hotel room windows, the heavy, characterless curtains tightly drawn. He was alone yet still felt unsettlingly exposed. He thought he knew why too. He was contemplating, perhaps had already decided to break that code. No one would see him do it, but no matter how long he lived, he'd never escape the unrelenting scrutiny of his own conscience. He made a disgusted sound, stood, and paced to the door. He knew his actions were justified. He also knew he had no real choice in the matter. Whether Rhodes was eliminated or not, Vasilek would not and could not be permitted to walk away. He was too close to the situation. To put that another way, he knew too much. Information was power but it could also be fatal under certain circumstances.

Solution? Babbit would have to neutralize him or try to anyway. Vasilek understood that and didn't resent it. That was the nature of the beast. More than once he'd been hired to kill the killer. He'd long assumed he'd meet his end that way sooner or later. This was too soon, though, and Babbit had made the mistake of making it personal. Vasilek couldn't tolerate that. He also believed he had every right to protect himself, to *cover his ass* as the Americans would say. Why, then, was he still feeling uneasy.

Nothing to be done about it, he thought, staring at the laptop still sitting there in the middle of the bed. It might be a treasure trove. It might also prove to be as empty and useless as the computer he'd taken from Martin Reginald. What would Babbit do if all Rhode's various devices yielded nothing more than a few innocuous emails? What if, like Reginald, she too was a stand-in for someone else?

Vasilek smiled grimly and took one step toward the bed but then changed course, retrieving a white ceramic mug from the coffee station atop the bureau and rinsing it in the bathroom sink. He then rummaged in his duffle until his hands fell on the bottle of Stolichnaya. He filled the cup to the brim and drank, luxuriating in the familiar burn from the vodka. He refilled his cup five minutes later. Only when it had been emptied for a second time did he finally grabbed the laptop, place it on the small work table tucked into one corner of his room and fire it up.

The first thing he saw was an enlarged icon depicting the image of an old-fashioned manual typewriter atop the single word *Me.* That was accompanied by a mouse pointer which looked about twenty times the normal size. He actually leaned backward like he was afraid it might jump off the screen at him. Some type of magnification program was obviously in use. Vasilek didn't know how it worked but he found navigation problematic to say the least.

He placed his finger on the mouse pad and moved it that way he normally would. In response, the monstrous pointer flew across the monitor and he briefly lost track of the login icon altogether. After a few fits and starts, he managed to locate it again and he double clicked.

Vasilek was afraid he would be prompted for a password but none was required. Everything went dark for a second and then he was looking at Rhodes' desktop and where the nightmarish magnifier, something called ZoomText according to the menu bar, took on a new form. Seventy-five percent of the screen was normal. The lower right hand quadrant, however, was blown up many times over. That's where the giant pointer took up residence and no matter where it moved the magnified window followed. It was bizarre, dizzying and infuriating.

Rhodes had several documents worthy of inspection and Vasilek knew he wanted a copy of her contact list too. It should have been a simple matter to plug in that last flash drive and drag over anything of interest. He just couldn't get that fucking mouse pointer to follow a straight line. Opening files was a chore too and reading something like a Word document was practically impossible because the magnified window kept getting in the way. How in the world did the woman do it?

"Shit!" he swore, pushing the laptop aside. He then pulled out his phone and did what he should have done ten minutes earlier. He searched *ZoomText Hot Keys* and learned the combination of Alt and Delete would deactivate the magnification function. He tried it and, low and behold, it actually worked. Vasilek smiled at he began transferring one file after another.

In truth, he was still miffed Rhodes had given him the slip. He'd under-estimated her physical abilities, limited as they might be. That was okay, though. He'd find her again now that he had the means and he knew she wouldn't be around long enough to see too many more sunrises.

He couldn't imagine what it must be like for her, walking into things like that sign board all the time and needing specialized equipment just to read or use a computer. What a nuisance. He'd be doing her a favor by killing her. It shouldn't present much of a problem either. He'd witnessed firsthand that she couldn't see for crap. If he happened to catch her on the street somewhere he could walk right up to her gun in hand and she wouldn't even notice until it was too late.

Dealing with Babbit, unfortunately, wouldn't be so simple. He needed serious ammunition for that and not the custom hollow point rounds with which his Glock was currently loaded. Thanks to Rhodes, thanks to Babbit's unreasonably risky orders, Vasilek believed he was now in possession of the type of real stopping power he required.

He spent several minutes scrolling through a 114,256 word, 411 page document titled *The Well from Hell,* and several more studying a second document labeled *WFH chapters synopsis.* The first file was the actual manuscript and it ended in the middle of a sentence four and a half pages into chapter 31. It was plainly still a work in progress. The second file contained notes, mostly in outline form, all the way through chapter 46. Vasilek could tell that's where the book would end.

He searched but didn't see the name Babbit anywhere. However, some dude named Briggs was in store for a very bad end. Rhodes hadn't gone into much detail but it seemed he'd be spending eternity as part of the foundation for one of his own construction projects. If only Clayton Babbit III could be disposed of the same way. What Vasilek wouldn't give to make the guy disappear. Really, though, he just wanted him out of his life. With a bit of luck, he'd be able to make that happen soon enough. He just needed to play his cards right.

Cover your ass, he thought, opening Chrome so he could look at Rhodes' browsing history. It was all unremarkable. She liked Google, Wikipedia, and Amazon's music streaming site, and she'd also made regular visits to USA Today, what he guessed was a writers forum, and something called Independent Living. He didn't click on any of those links because there was no need. He did go to onedrive.com as

Rhodes had done twelve times over the past two weeks, once a day every day except for Sundays.

The login screen requested Rhodes' email address which he had and her password which he didn't. He tried *Martin, Reginald, martinreginald, and* just for the hell of it, *raycharles*. Access was denied as he'd expected it would be. He wasn't bothered. OneDrive was a drop box, the type of online storage millions of people use to backup data. It was more secure even than a biometric home safe and Vasilek didn't need to try to crack the code because he had no use for duplicates of the same files he'd just saved to the flash drive. He had proof the account existed and that's really all he'd been after. Now, no matter what happened to the woman or any of the items he'd stolen from her, at least one copy of her manuscript would still be out there and forever out of Babbit's reach.

"Good," Vasilek said, reaching for the coffee mug and then remembering it was empty. He swore under his breath and glanced at the bottle of Stoli, still about two thirds full. It was tempting, but it had been hours since he'd eaten and he knew he should put something in his stomach before indulging any further. He'd have to talk to the red neck asshole soon enough too. Given the precariousness of his situation it was essential he keep a clear head.

Only one question remained. Had Alex Rhodes shared any portions of her current work with friends, her publisher, or anyone else? Did it even matter? She had, after all, shared with him, albeit unwillingly. That was the ace up his sleeve in the event it all went south.

Of course, he didn't want to give Babbit any indication of the strong hand he was holding. He scrolled through Rhodes' browsing history one last time and then cleared it all. He did the same with Internet Explorer even though it didn't look like she'd used that browser in months; still, better safe than sorry. To muddy the waters further, he again opened the *WFH chapters synopsis* file and deleted the notes from the last dozen chapters. He doubted it would serve any purpose but liked the feeling of control.

Vasilek contemplated other deletions and modifications. He found he was of a mind to make Babbit's life as difficult as possible. He also felt like he'd already broken too many of his own rules. He'd enjoyed it too and that was troubling. In the end, with some misgivings, he dropped the laptop into the FedEx box and sealed it with packing tape. He'd just finished when his cell phone buzzed.

-29-

"You sneaky son of a bitch," Clayton Babbit snarled, pressing the phone to his ear and listening to it ring two, three and four times. "Answer!" he demanded. "I know you're there." Then, to Louie, "Take my advice and never hire a foreigner. They can't be trusted."

In response, Louie, the only member of his large Italian family actually born in the United States, squinted at his computer monitor and continued to scroll through long lines of computer code he'd written to probe for weaknesses in various firewall programs. He didn't comment on his own ethnicity, or all the foreigners, mostly underpaid illegals, that Babbit depended on to do the heavy lifting on his beach restoration jobs and many of his other businesses.

In truth, it wasn't specifically Mikhail Vasilek Babbit was angry with, but the entire situation. It was all spinning out of control and he didn't think that was fair. It's not like the sabotage had been his idea. He'd just sort of expedited things. He'd benefited sure, but the safety standards on that rig were a joke and a disaster was bound to happen sooner or later. He had no way of knowing it would take five fucking months to finally seal that well. Nothing he'd been told suggested the explosion would be so large or deadly either. He did feel bad about that, but it was years ago. Wasn't it time to forget, forgive, and move on?

He'd prepared for any eventuality, or so Babbit had thought, but he'd barely put his plan in motion when he started hearing disturbing things about Bryan Royal. Most employees working that rig were afraid to say boo. Royal, however, bitched to anyone that would listen. It was strongly, even aggressively suggested it would be in his best interests to keep his mouth shut, but the complaints continued. Fed up with all of his noise, Babbit finally arranged to have Royal transferred off the rig. He thought that would be the end of it but then decided, given everything at stake, it made more sense to silence him once and for all.

Hiring someone to do the job proved far easier than Babbit ever imagined: practically, morally and financially. He'd consulted with Louie, and had a name and number less than an hour later. One phone call and one brief conversation, and Babbit's problem vanished, literally overnight. It was the best seventy-five hundred dollars he'd ever spent, or so he'd believed. It had all gone so smoothly he decided to spend another five grand plus the cost of a plane ticket to get rid of the sister too. There were no other relatives and he assumed that was the end of the trail. It had been too, for a little over six years.

Had it not been for his second wife, a southern belle turned bitch from hell named Bev, there was a decent chance Clayton Babbit never would have found out about the Reginald novels or their connection to him, at least not in time to do anything about it. He'd considered that a lucky happenstance but now he wasn't so sure.

Bev was a platinum blonde from West Virginia. A full decade younger than he, she'd been working as a hostess serving drinks and snacks in one of the VIP hospitality tents at a NASCAR event in North Carolina. He despised racing of any kind but was there as a guest to a corporate sponsor. She brought him a Jack Daniels and water and he was immediately taken with her smile, the sway of her hips and that soft southern drawl. They were engaged three months later. Bev liked to read, drink, and shop. Babbit had known all of that when he popped the question. It turned out she also liked having sex with men other than her husband. He'd found that part out the hard way.

They were together fourteen years. He gave her everything she wanted and then some, and went along with every ridiculous whim and fancy. The yoga room, vintage Jaguars, art studio, personal trainer and custom rose-shaped swimming pool were all for her.

It wasn't a perfect marriage. Babbit knew that. He worked too long and sometimes got angry too fast. Still, he'd done his best and never raised a hand to her. He kept her in the lap of luxury too and he thought that should have been worth something. She thanked him for his generosity by screwing the pool boy, another foreigner incidentally. He was a greasy Mexican named Manuel: gold teeth, multiple piercings, head-to-toe tattoos, and an addiction to crack cocaine.

Looking back, Babbit figured he should have known the woman was trouble the first time he saw the Dale Earnhardt tramp stamp. He was caught in her web, though, and turned a blind eye to that and a lot of other things that should have been obvious to him, starting with the fact that Manuel seemed to be at their house all the time. No pool was that dirty, but Babbit was focused on maintaining their high standard of living so didn't even think to question the wetback's frequent presence.

Then, one night, Bev and that crack-head fucking pool boy got high, split a bottle of tequila, discarded their clothing and went for a dip. It wasn't her first infidelity but did prove to be her last. Babbit came home to a darkened house and god-awful Merengue music thumping from the pool house speakers. He went to investigate and found them both floating face down in the shallow end. He was saddened, sort of, but at least their impulsiveness spared him the trouble of a costly and probably contentious divorce.

There was another silver lining too. According to autopsy results, the former Mrs. Clayton Babbit III engaged in anal intercourse shortly before her death. That activity normally repulsed her, so Babbit thought there was some measure of poetic justice there. Okay, so maybe he hadn't been entirely monogamous either but he believed his strong work ethic and the lavish lifestyle he'd provided entitled him to a few of his own harmless pleasures. What in hell was her excuse? For better or worse, he never got the chance to ask.

Babbit remembered the last time he'd seen his wife alive. It was that same afternoon. He'd stopped in to change into golf attire and found her in her usual spot, stretched out poolside with book in hand. Her skin was as dark as a walnut but she still devoted several hours a day to sunbathing, enhanced breasts spilling out of a practically non-existent bikini.

"You're a goddess," he said with genuine admiration.

She started and he could tell she hadn't known he'd been standing there. "Shee-it, Clay," she said, a hand to her heart. "Don't do that."

"Sorry, Babe. Just came home to change and grab my clubs. Dinner afterwards if you'd like to join me."

"Plaid pants and golf stories? I'll pass if it's all the same to you. Besides, I've got a headache."

"All right then," he said, already moving toward the house. "I'll see you tonight. Don't wait up," not that she would. He knew she'd turn down his invitation too and that was fine. The stories were boring but it was part of doing business and that was the price you had to pay.

"Hey," she said, flipping onto her back and giving him a view that made him briefly consider cancelling his golf outing altogether. "I'm reading this book. It's called," she turned it over to look at the cover, *Deepwater De-nahl.* There's another one too. I read it but I don't remember the name. Anyway, there's a guy in here that sounds like you."

"Yeah?" he said, not really interested. "How so?"

She frowned. "I don't know. He just does a lot of the stuff you do."

"Must be a great guy then." He smiled but she didn't.

"Not so much," she said, biting her lower lip. "Do you remember that BP thing a while back?"

Babbit froze and his smile suddenly felt heavy. "Sure," he said. "It was big news. Why?"

She glanced at the book again. "Did you make a lot of money from that with all the beach stuff you do?"

Babbit thought that was curious. In fourteen years his wife had never once asked about money, probably because he'd given her an unending supply. He didn't know what in hell she was reading but knew he didn't like it. He didn't appreciate her questions either and decided to downplay them as much as he could.

"I did okay," he said, a gross understatement for the millions he'd pocketed. "Of course, it was unfortunate my business benefitted so much from such a catastrophe. That's why I made significant donations to several different environmental agencies. I felt it was the least I could do." *They were also tax write-offs which didn't hurt.*

She looked at him but he couldn't read the expression behind her designer sun glasses.

Somewhat shaken, he finally turned and went into the house. He'd need to work on a better cover story in case she came back with more questions. Babbit also knew he had to get his hands on that fucking book too to see what it was all about. Bev didn't pay attention to real news. She read novels, the type of dime store crap you get off the rack at the airport gift shop. There was no way one of those pieces of trash could have anything to do with him. It was coincidence and nothing more. It had to be. Still….

He changed his clothes as quickly as he could and then got the hell out of there, Manuel pulling in with his White Aqua Boyz van just as Babbit was leaving. He acknowledged him by lifting one finger off the steering wheel of his F-150. Manuel responded with an enthusiastic wave and a gold-toothed smile, no doubt already thinking about the sex, drugs, and alcohol party that would soon commence. Had Babbit known what his wife had been up to and how it would all turn out, would he have done anything to prevent it? He'd thought about that many times over the years and was never able to come up with an answer.

Dealing with the funeral, distraught family members, the flood of cards, flowers and all the rest, he forgot all about Bev's strange questions until weeks later when he was gathering her belongings for disposal and found the book on a table in the pool house changing room. He actually read it and then read *Deepwater Deception* too. He didn't know if the Charles Briggs character was supposed to be him but there were way too many similarities and the story line hit way, way too close to home. Babbit found out what he could about Martin Reginald and then started researching the type of killer that would cost far more than a mere seventy-five hundred.

His impromptu trip down memory lane put him in an even worse mood than he had been and Babbit was ready to spit nails when, eight rings in, Vasilek finally answered his phone.

"Hello," he said, sounding out of breath.

"Did I catch you at a bad time?" Babbit asked. "Just coming in from a jog maybe?"

"No, I was just… in the shower."

Babbit was quiet for a moment. He somehow sensed Vasilek was lying but didn't know why or whether or not he should call him on it.

"I'm a reasonable man," he said, biting off the words like he was fighting his way through a three dollar steak. "I've paid you a lot of money with the promise of more. I flew you to New York first class and set you up with the best accommodations. You chose to snub my generosity and go elsewhere. I didn't object even though I should have. I think I've also given you considerable leeway in dealing with Ms. Rhodes. Wouldn't you agree?"

"Actually, no," Vasilek replied, clearing his throat. "If you must know I—"

"Damn right I must," Babbit interrupted. "I want to know what you think you're up to."

"Fine," Vasilek said. "Then I'll be blunt. I'm not used to someone looking over my shoulder. I don't like people knowing where I am or what I'm doing. I don't like being told how to do my job. I really don't like it when the timeline I'm given drastically increases the risk I'm taking. That all makes me uncomfortable."

"Tough titty." Babbit slammed a hand on his desk and Louie hunched a little lower in his chair. "You told me you found the woman. How much time do you need to get rid of her? I thought you were a pro."

"I am. And if you just wanted her dead it would have happened already. You altered the assignment. That's something else I don't like by the way."

"Listen, Mi-kha-il. I don't give two shits what you like or don't like. I'm in a spot here. I'm not going to explain myself to you but Alex Rhodes has information I need and time is of the essence. Am I making myself clear?"

"Quite. And as it happens, I have the items you requested."

Babbit stopped. "And when were you going to tell me that?" he asked, removing his old Stetson and running a hand through thinning hair. He wanted to tear the arrogant Ruski a new asshole but there were suddenly more pressing matters.

"Forget that," he said, putting his hat back on and adjusting the brim. "What'd you get?"

"Laptop, a couple computer disks, and a few flash drives."

"Did you look at any of it?"

"You were explicit in your instructions not to."

Babbit noticed that Vasilek hadn't answered the question. Even if the guy had seen something it probably wouldn't mean anything to him anyway. He'd also made it clear he wanted to get the job over and done with and Babbit was confident that was all he was worried about.

"What about paperwork?" he asked. "Did you find anything like that?"

"Not much," Vasilek replied. "The woman is practically blind so that wasn't surprising. I did find what looked like a copy of a personal letter. People don't usually make copies of stuff like that so I thought it might be important."

"Good," Babbit said, although he had no idea what that could mean. "So all that stuff is on the way?"

"Yes. I mean, it will be soon."

Babbit stopped again. "You haven't sent it yet?" He was too surprised even to yell. He just sat back and closed his eyes as if that could make the stupidity around him magically disappear. "What in God's name are you waiting for? I need that stuff and I need it now."

"I realize that."

"I don't think you do or you wouldn't be jerking me off like this."

"I just got in a few minutes ago," Vasilek said.

"But you apparently had time to freshen up. Did you visit the spa too?"

Vasilek gave an audible sigh. "I thought I should at least wash the blood off my hands."

That brought Babbit up short. "She's dead then? I thought you said—"

"There was some collateral damage," Vasilek replied. "It is not important."

Babbit was about to argue but realized the guy was right. What did he care if some bystander bought it if Rhodes was still out there? "So what happens next?" he asked.

There was a noticeable pause. "I need to reacquire the target."

"What?" Babbit asked, his voice rising again. "You told me you'd' found her."

"I know where she lives but I don't believe she will be going back there anytime soon."

"Care to explain that, Sport?"

"I am happy to," Vasilek said, sounding anything but. "You demanded things be done quickly and that forced my hand. I had no way to get Rhodes and the items you wanted at the same time. I had to make a decision. I thought it was best to go after the information first. I'm sorry if you do not agree. Perhaps you would like to come take care of the rest of this on your own."

"What I would like is for you to keep your fucking comments to yourself! I am paying you to do a job and I expect it to be done."

"And it will be. You just need to give me time."

"Sure thing, Sport. You've got forty-eight hours."

"Or else?" Vasilek asked without inflection.

"I know you think you're clever," Babbit said, picking up a cigar and biting off one end. "But believe me when I tell you I can find you anytime I want. I'm told there's a FedEx store right down the block from your hotel. You have a package for me and it needs to be on my desk by lunchtime tomorrow. As for Ms. Rhodes, forty-eight hours, Sport. Tick, tick."

-30-

Mikhail Vasilek was angrier than he'd been in a very, very long time. He stared at his reflection in the mirror over the bureau until his jaw finally unclenched and the hard stress lines around his eyes began to soften and fade. He wanted to jump a flight to Louisiana, find Mr. Clayton Babbit III, and spend the next forty-eight hours teaching him some manners. That, Vasilek knew, would be an emotional reaction and emotion had no place in his occupation. He instead paced the room from door to window and back again, until he was sure his rage subsided, and he was confident he could again think and act rationally.

With what Vasilek thought was incredible efficiency, he'd managed to find Alex Rhodes in a city of millions, and he'd done it despite working under trying circumstances including initially not knowing the target's proper gender. Then, he'd gained access to a secure apartment building, entered a locked apartment and gotten his hands on a pile of personal data, and all within a couple short hours of Babbit making the request. That was beyond impressive. It was amazing. Yet, rather than offering praise, all Babbit could do was find fault with his methods, his results,and his professionalism.

As Vasilek refilled his mug, only half way this time, he gazed at the FedEx box still sitting in the middle of the bed and reflected on what Babbit said shortly before hanging up on him.

I'm told there's a FedEx store right down the block from your hotel.

That, Vasilek realized, was the main reason his blood was boiling. Sure, Babbit's criticisms and lack of respect were infuriating. Mostly, though, he was mad at himself. He'd been careless. He'd let his guard down, and that allowed Babbit to pinpoint his location.

Stupid, Vasilek thought, taking a healthy sip and then placing the mug on the bedside table.

There were, he believed, really just two possibilities. The first and the likeliest was that Clayton Babbit, via computer hacks or phone inquiries, had somehow learned he was currently a guest of the Days Inn on West 94th Street in Manhattan. From there it wouldn't take anytime to run a Google search and determine there was a FedEx nearby. That had to be what happened and, if so, Vasilek had no real reason to worry. However, as remote as it seemed, he knew he had to at least consider the other thing Babbit had said and the possible implications.

Believe me when I tell you I can find you anytime I want.

That suggested an entirely different level of surveillance. Was it bullshit? Babbit made similar threats before and Vasilek had ignored them. He still believed it was so much hot air but what if he was wrong?

Babbit obviously made a monumental mistake when he arranged for the killing of the wrong person and that made him seem negligent if not incompetent. But at times he had also proven himself surprisingly resourceful. That's how Vasilek had gotten so close to Reginald in the first place. So how far was Babbit's reach? Could he really have watchers on every street corner? Had Vasilek been tracked from his hotel to Tower Brothers Publishing, and while he gallantly *rescued* Rhodes and escorted her back to her apartment building?

Not possible, he decided, picking up the mug again and draining the contents. New York City was too big and Babbit's operation was nowhere near big enough. Vasilek didn't know that part for sure, but given that he was working alone, he figured it was safe to assume Babbit didn't have a reserve of thugs on speed dial.

He paused then, his fingers straying automatically to the cell phone he'd tucked away in a rear pocket.

Speed dial….

He realized there might be a third possibility and it was far higher on the scale of probabilities. He started kicking himself for not considering it sooner. Babbit didn't need to call hotel after hotel. He didn't have to hack into countless databases either. If he was curious about Vasilek's whereabouts it was a simple matter of accessing the GPS tracker he'd been unwittingly carrying with him the whole time.

Vasilek pulled out his iPhone and glared at the offending item in disgust. He didn't understand how the whole GPS thing worked but was aware signals could be triangulated and people, usually members of law enforcement, could then use that information to not only locate someone but also determine where they'd been. That might not work so well in those wide open parts of the Midwest where cell phone towers were relatively few and far between. In a major metro area, though? They could probably isolate the signal down to a particular bathroom stall in Grand Central Station. And if cops could do it, Vasilek figured any semi-savvy tech guy could pull it off too. Clayton Babbit almost certainly had at least one such person in his employ.

Okay, Vasilek thought. *I know how he's doing it. I've got a good idea anyway. So what should I do next?*

His first inclination was to destroy the phone: remove the battery, flush it down the toilet, and grind everything else under his heel until it was nothing but dust. That might bring him a few moments of satisfaction but then what? Could he afford to so abruptly break off communication with one of the only men in the world who knew his true identity, and who had made it clear he'd use that information against him without pause? The answer was a reluctant but insistent No.

Vasilek considered the alternatives. What if he just turned his phone off for a while or disabled some of the tracking features? He did a quick web search and found out that simply powering down wasn't good enough. If he really wanted to *go black* the only real way to do it was by removing the battery.

He turned his phone over a few times in his hands and didn't see anything resembling a battery compartment. The device looked compact, smooth, tight, and inaccessible. But, Vasilek knew there was a battery in there so there had to be a way to get at it. He went to youtube, typed *how to remove iPhone battery* into the search window, and a thirteen-year-old Asian kid was suddenly demonstrating how it could be accomplished in less than two minutes. All he'd need was some special screwdriver he'd never heard of, a Phillips head screw driver, a suction cup, a razor blade, tweezers, and a hair dryer.

"Thanks a lot," Vasilek said, closing the video before the little twerp was halfway through. Even if he had the necessary equipment, which he didn't, it wasn't like he could find a place to plug in a fucking hair dryer each time he wanted to drop off the grid. *Great choices.* He could either ditch the phone or carry a signaling beacon around with him everywhere he went.

Or, Vasilek wondered. *Is there some way to use this to my advantage*? If he could realistically assume Babbit was tracking his movements, couldn't he also use his phone to deliberately throw him off the scent? The idea had potential, and he decided he'd need to keep it in mind.

He felt slightly better about things as he sealed the FedEx box, filled out the label, and used Babbit's credit card to pay for priority shipping. He then sent a text to let the bastard know the package was on the way.

The return text came almost immediately. *47:21. Tick, tick.* And Babbit had thoughtfully added an hourglass Emoji.

And fuck you too, Vasilek thought, unconcerned with the timeline. Even if Babbit followed through on his threat—doubtful in itself—the authorities would have a hard time finding him, let alone pinning anything on him. There was no solid evidence to connect him to anything he'd done. The one possible exception, Vasilek realized, was the murder he'd committed hours before. Blind or not, Rhodes had probably seen and heard enough to cause him some trouble. That meant he now had a personal reason for putting her down and it served as a far greater motivation than anything Clayton Babbit did or said.

If it came right down to it he was confident in his ability to disappear. Mikhail Vasilek could vanish as completely as Scott Fisher, Thaddeus Heart, William Todd, Douglas Ford, or any of the other aliases he'd used over the years. If he were so inclined he could rent a car and be across the Canadian border by midnight. From there he could go anywhere in the world, shedding his skin once or twice along the way to ensure his perpetual anonymity

Vasilek liked the idea of slipping away and leaving Babbit standing there with his dick in his hand. Rhodes would survive but what did he care? Even if he'd left some trace DNA evidence in the lobby with the dead doorman or inside her apartment, the cops would need to catch him for that to do them any good, and Vasilek was sure that wouldn't happen.

He thought about the two detectives he'd seen exiting Tower Brothers Publishing. They'd looked so determined as they hurried away, no doubt believing they were hot on Scott Fisher's trail. What would they say if they found out they'd practically been within arm's reach of him, yet never knew and never once glanced his way?

Well, Vasilek thought, striding towards the 96th Street station. *They've got more important things to worry about now.*

He no longer bore any resemblance to the delivery man who'd visited Rhodes' apartment building, or the hippy-type loitering outside Tower Brothers. The Lennon shades were gone, as were the wig, the work pants, the over-sized t-shirt and all the rest. He now wore a tailored navy suit, pale gray shirt, college tie—Georgetown of course—and freshly polished brown Oxfords. His close-cropped hair was dyed jet black, and he had a dark blue handkerchief square tucked into one pocket. He clutched a leather attaché in his left hand, and descended the subway stairs like he was late for a high level meeting. In reality, he was headed back to 63rd Street and Rhodes apartment.

Vasilek didn't expect to find her there. He doubted the police would allow her to return and she probably wouldn't want to anyway, at least not anytime soon. However, he needed to reacquire his target and had nothing else to go on. He didn't have a death wish and had no intention of attempting to enter the building. The place would be crawling with cops and it would be foolhardy to try to get too close. He'd just stay in the vicinity, stroll past once or twice and see what he could see.

He knew he looked every bit the uptown yuppie tight ass so he'd blend in as easily as if he were just another taxi driver, street peddler, or worthless homeless fuck. And, on the off chance Rhodes was around and happened to see him—unlikely in itself—there was no way anybody would be able to connect him with whatever poor description she'd been able to give. The woman seemed to get around okay, but then somehow failed to see a signboard the size of a garbage can. It was weird, and he figured he could probably stand beside her in the clothes he'd been wearing before and she still wouldn't recognize him. Better to take precautions, though. Better to be prepared too; and as the doors slid open and Vasilek stepped into the subway car, he touched the Glock again holstered at the small of his back.

-31-

Once I'd summoned enough courage to extricate myself from the clothes dryer, I'd bolted from the laundry room, made a bee line for the rear exit door, and let myself out through the courtyard gate. I'd never gone out that way before and was immediately lost. As I've said, I tend to stick to familiar streets and that wasn't one of them. I could, I knew, go around the block to the front of my apartment building where I could quickly regain my bearings. I could also catch a bullet in the head if Scott Fisher was still nearby. I was pretty sure he wanted me eliminated, and I had no desire to simplify his task by doing something so blatantly moronic.

So, despite mounting panic and confusion, I'd hurried in the opposite direction, crossing street after street, randomly going right at one block and left at the next. I had no plan and no sense of direction. I might have been going in circles for all I could tell. It was also possible Fisher had been on my heels every step of the way.

I kept turning to look behind me but I knew my vigilance was useless. To me, one face is pretty much the same as the next. I can distinguish black from white; usually male from female. Beyond that it's kind of a crapshoot. I mostly see impressions of things, and they are as much imagination as anything else. It's not that I'm especially fanciful. My brain just doesn't get enough information from my eyeballs so it sort of fills in the gaps with what it thinks I should be seeing. I suppose that's helpful at times but certainly not what you'd call reliable. Fisher could have been back there somewhere, staying within a few yards of me, and I wouldn't know it until his hands were around my throat.

At the risk of stating the obvious, I don't perform well under pressure. If you haven't picked up on that already you haven't been paying close enough attention.

Scott Fisher had just killed a man in cold blood. I'd stood there and watched him do it. Odds were good he'd murdered Martin too, and done so in a way that suggested he was both cool and clever. He wasn't about to hang around my apartment building, smoking gun in hand, and wait for the cops to arrive. He was in the wind. If I'd had a brain in my head I would have realized that and likewise realized my apartment was actually the safest place to go. I'd idiotically high-tailed it the other way, despite being without phone, money, sunglasses, or anything else that might have aided in my escape.

It's a struggle to make fast progress even when I know where I'm going. But on an unfamiliar street, the late afternoon sun casting long, dark shadows, I move with all the grace and efficiency of a tightrope walker with Parkinson's. I wanted to put as much distance as possible between me and my would-be pursuer, but I was constantly afraid I'd fall into a manhole, plummet down a flight of unseen stairs or step in front of a delivery truck. I progressed as best I could, alternately squinting or shading my eyes with my hand, and all the while feeling like a rat in a maze, except I didn't have the enticing aroma of cheese to help guide my way.

I kept telling myself to slow down and that I was in no danger. If Scott Fisher was back there he would have shot, stabbed or choked the life out of me blocks earlier. The fact that I was still breathing proved I was alone. That made sense but I kept going anyway, in part because I didn't know what else to do. I wasn't even sure I could find my way back to my apartment, not that I had any desire to go there. I had to go somewhere, though, and after a couple more blocks of stumbling indecision I finally stopped and took stock of my surroundings.

How should I put this? I recognized NOTHING. The sights, the sounds, even the smells were a world away from what I was used to. I could be reasonably confident I was still in New York City… somewhere. Beyond that, I had no earthly idea.

I stood in the middle of the sidewalk and people went by on both sides. It seemed they were all thin and dark-haired, and they flowed past like they didn't even know I was there. They definitely didn't include me in their conversations. The prevailing language was Asian, but whether or not they were all speaking the same tongue I couldn't even guess.

You're not in Kansas anymore, I thought, wondering if my whirlwind escape had somehow blown me all the way to the UN. I didn't waste time clicking my heels together but instead walked over to inspect a flag hanging next to the door of a nearby storefront. The background was white with a blue and red circle-ish thing in the middle, and small groupings of parallel lines around the outside. The lines might have been black but don't hold me to that one. I didn't know if I was looking at a national flag or an advertisement for the soup of the day. However, there was no way I could miss the intriguing scent wafting through the open door. It was spicy and pungent, yet oddly inviting.

I was about to move past, my destination still unknown, when the sudden peal of a church bell made me jump. I may have let out a shriek too, and my out-of-proportion reaction to something so commonplace made me realize I needed to get off the street, collect my thoughts, and figure out what in hell I was doing. I wished I had my phone and my helpful audio navigation app. Of course, wishes are about as useful as politicians and losing lottery tickets so I did my best to push that thought aside. I squinted up the street and was marginally proud of myself when I succeeded in identifying the source of the noise. Against the clear blue sky, I could just make out the distinct shape of a church steeple a couple blocks distant.

Sanctuary, I thought, considering heading that way. I then took another look at the odd flag, moved to the door, and after a few moments' hesitation, stepped inside.

I knew I was out of sight from the street, tucked into a small booth in the darkest corner of the restaurant. I still felt exposed as I tried to explain my troubles to the elderly proprietor. He made sympathetic sounds but I sensed he wasn't entirely catching my drift. To put that another way, he had no flipping idea what I was talking about, no doubt because he only spoke Chinese, or Vietnamese, or Thai, or something that definitely was not American English.

He sensed I was in danger—I think—but it was all I could do to make him understand I really, **really** needed to use the telephone. He finally brought it to me along with a piece of paper, a pencil and, for some reason, a few coins in a foreign currency. I couldn't even imagine what he thought I might do with those. He wanted to help, though, and I was grateful for that. I tried to tell him as much but he just stared at me and then shook his head and shuffled away.

The phone was curiously small and I couldn't read the buttons. After a few tries, I managed to locate the one that got me a dial tone. My first thought was to call Vicki, and it was only then I realized I didn't know her number, or the Tower Brothers number, or any of the numbers of any of my personal contacts.

Stupid technology.

All that information was stored securely in my iPhone, and maybe in the cloud somewhere, and neither did me any good. My phone, so far as I knew, was still in my purse which I'd foolishly dropped on the lobby floor. As for the cloud, I didn't even really understand what that was let alone how or where to find it. That lifeline was currently unavailable to me, and that left me feeling isolated and helpless all over again.

I got to thinking about Brandon and how his lifeline had been severed for good, and I had to choke back a sob. The tiny oriental man must have heard. He emerged from the kitchen, or somewhere, *and* delivered a handful of tissues along with a steaming pot of what I assume was tea, and then he drifted away again, his sympathetic murmurs accompanying his retreat.

For reasons I couldn't begin to fathom, that simple act of kindness had me blubbering in earnest. I blew my nose noisily, tears streaming down my face all the while.

Pull it together, Alex, I chastised. *It's not your fault and there's nothing you could have done.*

I tried but could really only believe part of that. There was no way I could have saved Brandon under any circumstances. I was lucky to have escaped with my own life. I knew that. But as for it not being my fault? There was no way to sugarcoat that. Unintentional or not, I was still the one who'd detonated the lethal crap bomb and no one would convince me otherwise.

Not knowing what else to do, I called 911, reported the shooting, and got the number for the 6th Precinct where I eventually got through to Detective Lynch. I don't know what I would have done if she'd been away from her desk, but on that one score at least, I'd been fortunate. I told her what happened as best I could and she, *God bless her,* didn't ask a barrage of questions but instead said she'd come to get me. The next trick was to try to describe my location which proved far more difficult than you might think.

"Okay," she said, and I heard a door slam followed by the echo of footsteps.

I guessed she'd entered a stairwell or perhaps a narrow, tiled corridor. I couldn't imagine how she'd go about finding me but she sounded confident enough.

"So you said you exited your apartment building from the rear. Which way did you go?"

"Left," I said after a pause, remembering I'd made that decision so I wouldn't have to walk into the setting sun.

"And then?"

I paused again, so long that it stretched into an awkward silence.

"Alex?" Detective Lynch prompted.

"I'm here. I just don't know what to tell you. I turned left like I said and went a couple blocks. I turned again at some point. After that it's all kind of a blur. I didn't know where I was or where I was going. I wanted to get away from my apartment and I chose where to turn based on the flow of pedestrian traffic and the angle of the sun. I know that sounds dumb but I have a hard time navigating outdoors when I don't have my sunglasses."

"And you don't have them now?"

"I don't have anything," I said, my voice a little too shrill. "When Brandon got shot, I just dropped my purse and ran. It was stupid I know, but I didn't know what else to do."

"You feared for your life," the detective said, sounding like she understood. "There is no reason to be ashamed or embarrassed by how you reacted in that situation. It's nothing you could have ever prepared for."

I had nothing to say to that. I appreciated her words of support but they didn't prevent me from feeling horribly inadequate. I sighed, wiped my eyes and blew my nose again. While I was doing so, I heard Detective Lynch cover the phone and say something to someone else.

"Detective Zanetti and I are on the way," she said, coming back on the line. "We will find you. What I need you to do is tell me everything you can about your current location."

"I don't know my current location!" I said, exasperated. "That's what I've been trying to tell you. I'm in an Asian restaurant. That's all I got."

"I understand and that's fine, but you may know more than you think. Let's work backwards and see where that gets us. After you left your apartment building, you said you turned left initially. Would you say you continued in that same general direction?"

I started to say no but then realized what she was really asking. "I guess I did," I said, looking toward the front of the restaurant as if my minor epiphany would elicit the detective's sudden and miraculous appearance. "I have a hard time going from light to shadow, and it's always toughest when the light source is directly in front of me. I didn't do it consciously but I kept the sun behind me or to my right the whole time I was walking."

"That's good. So you are somewhere to the south and east of your building."

"More east," I said, almost giddy with the knowledge I'd be found in no time. "I kept the sun at my back whenever I could."

"That's great, and how many blocks do you think you went total?"

The bubble of my giddiness burst as did my momentary sense of relief. "I have no idea," I said, hanging my head. "It was at least twenty but could have been twice that many. I just wasn't paying attention. I'm sorry."

"It's okay," detective Lynch reassured, clearly tuning into my feelings of despair. "What about the street you're on now? What can you tell me about that?"

"Nothing!"

"I'm sure that's not true. You obviously found the restaurant. You must have noticed some other things too."

"I noticed no one speaks English!"

"Okay. And is that all?"

"Well," I said, tiring of the exercise but realizing I was stuck there unless or until the detectives located me. "When I was out on the sidewalk, it seemed like everyone around was a foreigner. I mean everyone too. I'd say they were all Asian, or oriental, or whatever the PC term du jour is, but take that for what it's worth."

"And the street itself?"

"I don't know. It's just another street. You've got to understand, though. As a general rule, unless I walk into a place, I can't tell from the road if it's a butcher or a book store. If you're looking for identifying details, I'm not gonna be able to give them to you."

"That's fine. Just do your best."

What the fuck do you think I'm doing? But instead of lashing out, which I knew Detective Lynch didn't deserve, I closed my eyes and tried to concentrate.

"I think there are other restaurants nearby," I said, remembering. "The smell of food was everywhere. Some places had music playing too. Again, I'd say it was mostly oriental."

"How about visually?" Detective Lynch asked. "Can you give me anything?"

I was about to say no when I remembered the flag. I also had the impression other establishments had other flags on display and I told her as much.

"Can you describe any of them?"

"I think most were brightly colored," I said doubtfully. "I can't swear to that. The only one I saw up close is outside the restaurant I'm in."

"And do you have any idea what sort of restaurant it is, beside possibly being Asian?"

"I'd say it's not Chinese or Japanese because I'd recognize those smells. This is different."

"Okay, and how about the flag?"

"From what I could tell, it's white with a blue and red circle in the middle. I think it was blue and red anyway."

"White with a blue and red circle," she repeated.

"What?"

"Hold on Alex."

I heard a male voice in the background but I couldn't make out the words.

"Detective Zanetti wants to know if you noticed patterns of lines outside the circle."

"Yes!" I said, surprised.

More muffled conversation.

"I'm told that's the South Korean flag. Don't ask me how Zanetti knows that. But, if he's right, it should make it easier to find you. Sit tight and we'll be there as soon as we can. I need to caution you, though. Detective Zanetti says there are several dozen ethnic restaurants in that area so it may take us a while. Just be patient. Before I go, is there anything else you can think of that might help narrow the search?"

I was about to tell her nothing was ringing any bells when I suddenly stopped and smiled. "I'm about two blocks east of a church."

"How do you know that?"

"The bells were chiming right before I came in here. I'd guess that was about fifteen minutes ago."

"And you're positive it was a church?"

"Yep," I said, proud of myself. "I could see the steeple. It's due west of whatever road I'm on."

-32-

Megan Lynch stood in the doorway, taking in the dim interior, the dozen or so tables—most of which were empty--and the ornamental shaded lamps that hung over each. She thought she had the right place and was even more sure when a tiny, ancient-looking man appeared through a swinging door to her left and began hobbling her way.

He made slow progress, using chair backs and table edges for support whenever he could. His dark eyes were sharp though, and he seemed to know what and who she was there for. He stared at her, the concern plain on his face. Then, he bowed slightly and raised a thin, trembling hand toward the far corner of the restaurant. By then, Megan had already spotted Alex Rhodes, slumped against the wall and methodically wringing a cloth napkin in her hands. The detective nodded her thanks and headed that way.

"Ms. Rhodes?" she said, approaching the table. "How are you doing?"

"Fine," she replied without conviction, sitting a little straighter and running a hand over her hair. "I'm surprised you found me so fast."

From her utter lack of inflection, Megan could tell the woman had no earthly idea how much time had actually gone by. That was understandable given all she'd been through, and noting her ghostly pallor and the way she continued to grip the napkin, Megan wondered if she might need to be treated for shock. That would slow down the investigation, and she was anxious to follow up on any fresh leads while the opportunity was there. She debated, briefly, and decided she would proceed with caution until she felt she could accurately assess Rhodes' state of mind. Megan was no medical professional but, in her years on the force, she'd seen shock in many different forms and thought she knew what to look for.

"May I join you?" she asked, watching closely as she slid into the booth.

"Please."

Alex Rhodes looked up then, her gaze again seemingly focused on something just over Megan's left shoulder. It was still disconcerting but not as much as before.

"Is there anything I can get you, Ms. Rhodes?"

"Like a bowl of kimchi you mean?"

"Pardon me?"

"You said this place is Korean, right? I think that's their national dish. Fermented cabbage or something. Whatever it is, it smells like they fermented it in my gym shoes."

"Glad you've still got your sense of humor."

"Oh yeah. I'm a laugh a minute. Ever hear the one about the woman who nearly got herself killed by acting like a jerk?"

"Aren't you being hard on yourself, Ms Rhodes?"

"Geez, call me Alex already. Formalities make me nervous."

"Okay, Alex, and you can call me Megan, but I'm afraid some formalities are necessary. I'm going to take notes, and I'd like to record our conversation as well if that's all right."

"Do watcha gotta do." She blinked then, and it seemed to register with her for the first time that Megan was alone. "Where is Detective Zanetti?"

"He dropped me here and went to the scene. He'll be along shortly."

"The scene," Alex mused, shaking her head. "That sounds so… I don't even know." She shook her head again and then fell silent.

"I've got some questions," Megan said. "Do you feel up to talking? We can wait a while if that would be better."

"Waiting isn't going to make anything better. May as well get it out of the way now."

"If you're sure. Can I pour you some tea?" Megan indicated the small white pot and matching cup.

"No thanks," Alex said. "I'm afraid it will taste like whatever I've been smelling since I came in here."

Megan smiled. "How about some water then?"

"Water would be great. I just wasn't sure how to communicate that to Mr. Miyagi. And before you correct me, I know he wasn't Korean but it's the best I can do on short notice."

"I'll take care of it."

Megan turned and saw the man watching them from a table on the other side of the room. She caught his eye, gestured at a pitcher sitting atop a serving cart and made the universal sign for drinking. He tipped his head and got laboriously to his feet.

"Your order has been placed. While we're waiting, please tell me what happened today, starting from the time you left the Tower Brothers building. And again, I am recording. That will save you the trouble of going through this again once Detective Zanetti arrives."

Alex waved her hand as if that was the least of her problems, which, Megan supposed, it probably was.

"Should I just start talking then?" she asked.

"Whenever you're ready. You can give me a chronological account of your movements, or if it's easier, I can ask you specific questions."

Alex bit her lower lip. "That would probably be best," she said after a pause. "It's all kind of a jumble right now. I think I'll be less likely to leave something out if I'm responding to you instead of trying to remember everything on my own."

"Okay then." Megan activated her recorder and stated the date, time, and their location. "After Detective Zanetti and I left the Tower Brothers Publishing offices this morning—that was at eleven forty-seven—how much longer did you stay there?"

"I don't know exactly," Alex replied. "Through lunch. Vicki had sandwiches delivered but I couldn't eat anything."

"Why was that?"

"Upset stomach. My system's been off since Martin disappeared. I get ravenous and then I might go the better part of twenty-four hours without eating a thing."

"I understand. So can you give me an estimate at least?"

"A couple hours?" she said doubtfully. "I know it was quite a while."

"Why so long?"

She gave a sigh. "A lot to discuss. Martin's death will be big news. We need to have all our ducks in a row. That's what Bob kept saying anyway."

"That would be Bob Whetton?"

"Yes," Alex said, her sour expression making her opinion of the man clear. "I won't be getting a Christmas card from him."

"Do you think he blames you for what's happened?"

"You saw him this morning. He's definitely not a member of my fan club. I don't take that personally because from what I've seen, there isn't much he approves of."

"Okay," Megan said. "So you were discussing damage control?"

"That's about the size of it. We sat on the information too long. I don't need to tell you that."

"And what will happen now?"

"Well, we are publically acknowledging Martin's death. We don't have much choice anymore."

"And what about your role?" Megan asked.

Just then, the restaurant owner arrived with a pitcher of ice water and two tall glasses. He set everything down with some effort, and Megan noticed that Alex looked relieved at the interruption. She decided to give her a moment, so took a little longer than necessary to pour.

"Thanks," Alex said, picking up a glass and immediately draining half.

"You were about to tell me what the company position will be as it pertains to you."

"Yeah." She looked around the room but Megan could tell she wasn't focusing on or even seeing anything in particular.

"Alex?"

"As of tomorrow," she said. "I will be publically identified as the real author of all the Martin Reginald novels."

"You don't sound happy about that."

"I'm not. I believe it's necessary. At least I think I believe that; but I'm a clinically private person and this is going to be really, really hard on me. To be honest, I'm scared to death and what happened a little while ago didn't help."

"Let's talk about that then."

"Good. I wanted to change the subject anyway."

"That's fine, although we may need to come back to it later."

Alex didn't respond to that so Megan made a note on her legal pad and turned to a new page.

"So you think you were at Tower Brothers a couple hours. That would have you leaving around one-thirty or two. Does that sound right?

"I guess so."

"And did anything unusual happen?"

Alex stared at her like she couldn't have asked a stupider question if she'd tried.

"I know what happened at your apartment building. We'll get to that. But when you first left Tower Brothers, do you remember anything out of the ordinary?"

"Like what?"

"You tell me. Did you see anyone? Talk to anyone? Did anything disrupt your normal routine?"

"I don't have a routine," Alex said. "I mean, I don't make frequent visits to my publisher. I stay in the background. At least I did anyway."

"So nothing then?"

"Not until I got off the subway."

"And where was that?"

"59th Street. That's the closest stop to my apartment. I got off and was headed for the exit when a scuffle broke out behind me."

"Scuffle?"

"Yeah. It was weird. And looking back, I have to think it was staged, or I guess I should say orchestrated, for my benefit."

"Tell me about it."

For the next quarter hour Alex did just that, describing a bizarre encounter where a total stranger ostensibly rescued her from a stalker, mad man, or some other form of deviant, and then escorted her home.

"So you walked with him the whole way?"

"Yes," Alex said, sheepish. "He fed me a line and I chowed down like Garfield at an all-you-can-eat Lasagna buffet. I should have known better."

"He convinced you you were in danger and your situation made you more receptive to that."

"Very diplomatic, Detective. Ever consider running for public office? What you're really saying is that my blindness made me vulnerable and my paranoia made me a moron. That about cover it?"

"Try this instead," Megan said. "You were dealing with someone well-versed in the art of deception. You had no cause to suspect him. He knew that and took advantage."

"Do you think it was Fisher?" Alex asked, seemingly shrinking into herself.

"Maybe," Megan replied, noncommittal. In truth, though, she would have eaten her socks if it proved to be anyone else. "What can you tell me about him?"

"Physically?" Alex shrugged. "Not much. He's a few inches taller than me. Hair somewhere between light brown and gray I think. He didn't have glasses unless they were thin, clear frames. I probably wouldn't have noticed those. I couldn't even guess at eye color. I can't tell you what he was wearing either." She shrugged again. "I'm sorry."

"No problem," Megan replied, making a few quick notes. "I'm not real worried about a physical description."

"Then how will you find him?"

Megan smiled. "Do you have any idea how many cameras are in subways and subway stations, not to mention all along pretty much every New York City street?"

"Are you serious?"

"Absolutely. There were something like a hundred million new security cameras sold last year. They're everywhere. New York Transit, the NYPD, various federal alphabet agencies, business owners, private security companies—your image has probably been captured a hundred times since you got up this morning."

"That's creepy."

"You could say that. And some would argue it's a violation of your civil rights. We can have that debate some other time. But for today, you should be thankful the cameras are there. We'll be able to get a good look at our man in no time and probably also figure out when and where he started tailing you."

"Wow," Alex said, shaking her head.

"It's Big Brother's world. We're only living in it."

"I guess you're right."

"So," Megan said. "Take appearance out of it. What else can you tell me?"

But before Alex could answer, Detective Paul Zanetti arrived and Megan slid over to make room for him.

"I believe this is yours,' he said, placing a large purse on the table. "Now what have I missed?"

"Plenty. I'll fill you in later but we're going to have some surveillance video to look at."

While Megan was talking, Alex Rhodes was busy digging through the contents of her purse. She pulled out a phone, wallet and sun glasses, and then stopped.

"They're not here," she said.

"What?" Detectives Lynch and Zanetti asked in unison.

"My keys," Alex explained, checking each pocket in turn."

"Are you sure you had them with you?"

"Absolutely. And I always keep them in the same place. I'm kind of OCD with stuff like that."

"Do you have another set?'

"I have a second apartment key, but it's in the safe in my bedroom closet."

"That's okay," Detective Zanetti said. "We can get you in there. In fact, we're going to need you to check your apartment out anyway."

"Why? I don't want to go back there."

"I'm afraid it's necessary," Zanetti replied. "And if you plan on staying elsewhere for a while, this will give you an opportunity to collect some personal belongings."

"All right," Alex said, sounding dubious. "But why do I have to go there at all?"

The detectives looked at each other.

"I was going to ask you later," Megan said, "but I suppose this is as good a time as any. And I have a feeling it may solve the mystery of your missing keys."

"I don't think I'm gonna like this but go ahead."

Megan stared at her. "We are working on two assumptions. The first is that we're after Scott Fisher, or whatever his real name is. The second is that he wants you eliminated. If both those things are true, why did he take the time and trouble to walk you home?"

"I don't know I...." But then Alex stopped and most of the color drained from her face. "My God," she said, a hand to her throat. "I never thought of it before. He must want something he thinks I've got."

"I think that's right," Detective Zanetti said. "And I think there's a good chance he's been in your apartment. I'd like you to come take a look so you can see if anything is missing."

-33-

For the third time that day, Mikhail Vasilek exited the subway at 59th Street. The first was when he'd visited Rhodes' apartment building in the guise of a delivery man. Hours later, he'd accompanied her home. That hadn't worked out quite as well as he'd hoped. The woman was still breathing after all. But, he did get many of the items Babbit had been after and also learned a lot about his latest target.

And now?

Vasilek wasn't sure what he might gain by returning again; possibly nothing. However, he needed to pick up Rhodes' trail and there were only two places he knew of where she might go. Even if members of the Tower Brothers staff were working late to try to deal with the Martin Reginald crisis, a likely enough scenario, the regular work day was at an end, and he couldn't hang around their place of business without soon drawing attention to himself. The best way to stay under the radar was to keep moving, constantly shifting to the spots he'd be least likely to get noticed.

Given the time, just shy of six o'clock, he knew all the streets and sidewalks in the vicinity of Rhodes' building would be tightly packed with people headed home. Her residence was over thirty stories, and there were two equally large apartment buildings flanking it on either side. That made for a whole lot of work-a-day schleps anxious to get out of their suits and ties, or heels and hose, in favor of the comfortable couches where most would remain until bedtime. Vasilek had dressed the part and even spent a few moments mastering his world weary expression. He was just another overly-entitled American and he knew he'd have no trouble blending into that crowd.

As he made his way to the subway stairs, walking with purpose but no faster and with no more pushing and shoving than anyone else, he looked straight into every security camera he saw. It wasn't taunting *per se*. Why bother? He believed he was unrecognizable, even to those who might be looking for him. That the cops would look was a foregone conclusion. He'd known that at the same time he'd made the split-second decision to draw his weapon and put the doorman down. The police investigation would change direction to a degree. Accordingly, considerable resources would now be expended in an attempt to identify Alex Rhodes' mystery companion.

On the cruise ship, Vasilek, or Scott Fisher if you prefer, had good reason for hiding his face to the extent that was possible. He needed his thirty-six hour Reginald impersonation to pass a cursory inspection. But now? He knew the best defense was a good offense. He didn't want to be that guy who was always looking down or always looking away. That could be a tell. So he brazenly stared at each lens he saw and silently dared the watchers to come find him. He would have like to flip them all off but there was a fine line between confidence and stupidity, and he was determined not to cross it.

When he reached his destination, Vasilek discovered that the sidewalk directly in front of Rhodes' building was more congested than he'd expected. Crime scene tape had been stretched in front of the main entrance and other barricades were also in place. A large crowd was gathered, and Vasilek guessed it was a mix of residents and gawkers who just wanted to know what was going on. He heard shouts of both inquiry and annoyance, and he almost felt bad for the contingent of uniformed policeman responsible for keeping everyone under control.

What a pity, he thought, smiling inwardly as a balding man with a red face, a paunch clutching a grease-stained paper sack, got right in a cop's face and demanded immediate access to his apartment. *Sorry, pal. You'll have to wait a while for your television and takeout. You could afford to miss a meal or two anyway.*

At first, it looked like no one was being allowed in or out. Then Vasilek saw a thirtyish yuppie prick in designer running gear emerge from somewhere along the side of the building. He paused to plug in ear buds, do a few seconds of elaborate yet largely ineffective stretching, and then took off down the block. Vasilek shifted ten yards in that direction, not to get a better view of the jogger but so he could see where the guy had come from.

It was a plain, painted metal door, and several people were lined up on the sidewalk, waiting for their turn to be admitted. A stocky Latino patrolman with a clipboard and radio was asking questions while checking everyone's ID.

No getting in that way, Vasilek thought. Of course, he had no intention of trying. This evening's mission was about surveillance only and he could do that from a distance.

With that in mind, he walked to the end of the block, turned around and came back the other way. He studied every face, watching to see if anyone was watching him, but also on the lookout for a semi-attractive dirty blonde bumping into street signs and lamp posts.

"Where are you, Ms. Rhodes?" he murmured, crossing the street to join the throng behind one of the police barricades.

"What's going on, Officer?" he asked the closest man in blue, paying no attention to the deliberately vague response but instead focusing on the bits of coded chatter emitting from the man's handheld radio.

He heard someone call a 184, which was the code for homicide, but also a 207A which Vasilek believed was an attempted kidnapping.

Interesting, he thought, nodding his thanks as he backed away. The cops couldn't know what had happened yet, at least not all of it, but they apparently understood it was something more than a random shooting. Did that mean they'd spoken to Rhodes, or were they working other leads?

Good questions to which he had no answers.

Vasilek milled about, eavesdropping on conversations and entertaining himself by listening to speculation about what had happened. The consensus was domestic incident gone tragically awry, but he also heard theories about bad drug deals, unpaid gambling debts, and gang activity. It was obvious no one knew a thing, and he hoped the cops were equally in the dark.

Of course, onlookers also circulated rumors about the identity of the victim and the severity of his or her injuries. One of those questions was answered in stark fashion when the building's front door opened, and a sheet-draped body was wheeled out on a gurney. An ambulance was already there, but with no lights or sirens, and no one moving with any urgency. A temporary hush fell over the crowd and a few men even removed their hats as the body was loaded, doors slammed closed and the ambulance pulled away.

Give my regards to the morgue, Vasilek thought.

He hadn't wanted to kill the man. It had become necessary and that's all there was to it. Unfortunately, he'd scared off his quarry in the process and that part was too bad. He'd find her again. Of that Vasilek had no doubt. Whether or not he could do so in the limited time allotted remained to be seen. But he knew he was Babbit's best bet and that should afford him SOME leeway. Vasilek didn't want to count on that, and it wasn't because he was afraid of what Mr. Clayton Babbit III might do. He hadn't been comfortable with the job from the beginning and was increasingly anxious to get it over and done with.

About thirty minutes earlier, He thought he'd spied one of the two detectives he'd identified exiting the Tower Brothers building earlier that day. It was the older guy with the bad suit and haircut to match. He'd climbed into the driver's seat of a familiar-looking unmarked sedan and driven off. Vasilek couldn't swear it was the same car he'd seen before, or even the same detective. He thought so, but was too far away to be sure, and both cop and car disappeared before he could get any closer.

Vasilek thought it was curious detective number one was there, yet number two was apparently nowhere around. Or had he just not seen her? There was still a swarm of people in the apartment lobby, some in uniform and some not. It was possible she was a part of that press but had as yet escaped his notice. She could also be elsewhere in the building, maybe rooting out Alex Rhodes wherever she'd taken refuge.

He weighed the various probabilities and decided that was at the low end of the scale. The woman couldn't have been in hiding this whole time. She'd probably run away from him, hunkered down somewhere, waited for her opportunity and then scampered off. To where he had no idea, and that's why he continued to loiter outside her building. By now, he would have felt conspicuous had it not been for the dozens of other people waiting to get into their apartments or simply hanging around because they were nosy and had nothing better to do.

He wished he could get close enough to the lobby entrance to hear and see what the cops were up to, but he also knew their best investigator on his best day would find nothing in the way of concrete evidence. Vasilek had worn latex gloves for the few minutes he'd been inside Rhodes' apartment, and his closely-cropped hair had been secured beneath a wig. The hero movie detective, in a dramatic moment of epiphany, would make some amazing discovery that would send him to death row. These clowns weren't gonna get that lucky. They'd find nothing except for her ring of keys which he'd left in her bedroom and right on top of her pillow.

Vasilek had thought about taking them and had even slipped them into his pants pocket. Then he had a better idea. Locks would be changed. The keys would do him no good. Why take them when leaving them behind felt so much more *proprietary? Personal? Intimidating?* Whatever the proper word, he wanted to get in her head and thought that was a good way to do it. Trashing her place would have delivered a similar message and he had considered that too but ultimately opted for the more controlled response.

She would know he'd been there, and not just because of where he'd deposited her keys. He'd touched things. He'd moved things. He'd deliberately left things out of place, including rearranging some of the items in her color-coordinated closet. What would she think about that?

Would she feel violated when she realized he'd been through her underwear drawer, surveyed all her feminine hygiene products and even found her vibrator? That had been in a bedside drawer, and he'd moved it to a different drawer just to fuck with her a little more. As he did so, he'd smiled at the unintended pun.

Was any of that necessary? Would it serve any discernible purpose?

Vasilek asked himself those questions but had no answers. He likewise couldn't entirely account for why he'd taken her computer and other storage devices, yet chose to leave her purse, which he knew contained her phone. She'd told him she utilized various accessibility apps. He could have deprived her of those, temporarily anyway, and made her that much more helpless and vulnerable. So why hadn't he done it? It wasn't because he felt sorry for her. Mikhail Vasilek had never felt sorry for anyone. However, he wasn't about to so blatantly exploit a weakness either. It wouldn't be sporting. He didn't see her as a challenge anyway, and thought the least he could do was give her a semi-level playing field. He'd still prove victorious in the end. Once he found her of course.

Vasilek floated from one end of the block to the other, momentarily joining one crowd or one conversation and then moving on. He kept his eyes on the building throughout, but from his ever-changing vantage point, he had a hard time constantly monitoring the front entrance as well as the side door. Because he'd kept moving, he nearly missed it when detective number one reappeared on the scene, with number two and the previously unaccounted for Ms. Alex Rhodes closely in tow. They'd come from the rear of the building somewhere, which explained why he hadn't spotted them sooner. They approached the side entrance and, with a nod to the Latino, were waved inside.

Well, well, Vasilek thought. *The plot thickens.*

He was undecided as to what to do next. As he watched, crime scene tape was removed and barricades were pushed aside. It was clear they'd soon be getting back to business as usual and that meant sidewalks would empty, by New York City standards anyway. A businessman couldn't just stand around indefinitely. It was time for the chameleon to change his colors again.

-34-

"Okay, thanks. I'll see you in a while," I said, ending the call and slipping the phone into my jeans pocket. If I somehow lost my purse again I'd make damn sure my phone wasn't inside.

"It's all set. I can stay with Vicki tonight or as long as I need to. She also said she's happy to answer any questions you have."

"We appreciate that," Megan replied, leading the way to the elevator. "But one thing at a time. We're meeting the crime scene techs upstairs. You can look around, collect whatever personal items you need and we'll go from there."

"You really think he was in my apartment then?"

"I think we have to make that assumption since your keys were the only item missing from your purse. If he took them he must have had a reason."

"So what do you think he did?" I asked, as much to myself as either of them.

The detectives exchanged a glance.

"We can speculate," Megan said. "Or we can go see for ourselves."

I wasn't sure I was entirely thrilled with that idea. In truth, though, I was glad the detectives were there to take charge and sort of tell me what to do. I was starting to feel a little more like myself but I knew I still hadn't fully grasped everything that had happened. I kept thinking about poor Brandon, realizing he was dead, and also realizing how close I'd come to joining him. I felt relieved but also guilty as hell. I barely knew the guy and that somehow made his senseless murder and my improbable survival even harder to get my head around. I had some friends, no real family to speak of, and I knew my sudden demise wouldn't have had a huge impact on too many people. Brandon, on the other hand, might have been a husband, a father, a son or somebody's favorite uncle. I didn't even know which of course made me feel worse.

"Nineteenth floor, right?" Megan asked, blessedly interrupting my moment of emotional self-destruction.

I nodded and swallowed as she and Detective Zanetti ushered me into the elevator.

I held a spare key that had been given to me by the building super, a rail-thin, nervous man who licked his lips with such regularity and vigor I could usually hear him doing it. He'd always been too nosy for my taste, asking personal questions that tip-toed along the precipice of impropriety. He forever wanted to know what I was doing and who I was doing it with. When we knocked on his door I felt sure he'd try to wheedle some way into accompanying us upstairs, but he must have been as scared as me because he seemed only too eager to hand over the key and then retreat to the safety of his office. Maybe he thought there was a serial killer on the prowl and the guy was only targeting doormen and slimy apartment building employees. Regardless, I was relieved to be rid of him.

"So no one's been in there yet?" I asked, looking up as the elevator beeped and each floor indicator lit up in turn.

"We had reasonable cause," Megan said. "We could have legally entered your apartment without permission or a warrant."

Detective Zanetti cleared his throat. "We would have done it if we thought there was any chance our Mr. Fisher might still be in there."

"How do you know he's not?"

"Two witnesses reported seeing him leave the premises. We also have video of him exiting the building and heading west."

"Detective Zanetti and I will enter your apartment first," Megan said, seeming to sense my discomfort. "We'll secure the area and make sure it's safe, and then you can come in."

"Do I have to?" I asked, thinking I'd like it better if she could just grab some underwear and my toothbrush and send me on my way.

"I'm afraid so," she replied. "No one else knows your apartment. We're relying on you to tell us what, if anything, has been disturbed or removed."

Disturbed, I thought, not liking the sound of that. I had visions of slashed cushions, shattered glassware and overturned furniture.

I was the furthest thing from a hoarder and in terms of the tangible, I didn't own much of value. I had my parents' Waterford crystal bride and groom champagne flutes, an incomplete set of my grandmother's china, and two abstract paintings that an artist friend had done. They were in light pastels, and if you must know, I couldn't actually see them well enough to judge whether or not they were any good. I'd still be plenty pissed if some murderous jackoff sliced them to ribbons. But, in terms of priceless worldly possessions, that was about it. Most of the rest of my crap could be easily replaced at Wal-Mart, IKEA, or another *high-end* boutique.

And as for the intangible? I didn't print hard copies of any of my work. Why would I? In today's technologically driven world, why would anyone? Then again, I remembered hearing that Nelson DeMille still writes all his books longhand and in pencil. I've never met the man and have no idea if that's true. It sounds like torture to me and I wouldn't do it even if I could read my own handwriting. I'm a big fan of Cut, Copy, Paste, and especially Delete, and you can't do any of that with a Ticonderoga #2.

I had refined my writing and data storage practices somewhat over the years. I used to have one desktop computer, and that's where I saved my work at the end of each day. Then, about sixty thousand words into one of my earlier novels, I somehow ended up with the cyber equivalent of a sexually transmitted disease. Yep, my cheap whore of a PC picked up a virus resulting in a complete and total hard drive crash. I lost EVERYTHING!

Have you ever tried to recreate sixty thousand words from memory? It can't be done. In fact, after weeks of frustration, I scrapped that project altogether and started something new. While I was at it, I also came up with some new storage techniques. Now, when I finish a session, I save to my laptop, upload to a drop box, and because I'm paranoid, I backup my files weekly to an external hard drive I keep in my safe. It's overkill I know, but I learned my lesson.

I thought about my current *Well from Hell* manuscript which, unless I had another change of heart, would be completed and introduced to the world a few months hence. Unlike some writers I know, I never had a daily quota and never paid attention to word count. I started at the beginning and finished at the end, and that approach served me well. Still, based on the progress I'd made, I knew I had to be somewhere north of a hundred thousand words. That might sound like a lot, but in the greater scheme of things, it was one computer file probably no larger than five hundred kilobytes, considerably smaller than a single MP3 song file.

Was it possible Brandon had been gunned down merely because he stood in the way of something so insignificant? And if I could get that file back simply by opening my safe or entering the proper password? I shook my head, unable to deal with the brutal senselessness of it all.

Maybe, I thought, *I'm jumping to conclusions and Fisher, or whoever he is, had been after something more.* I couldn't imagine what that might be, but when my apartment door was opened, I almost hoped I'd find the place trashed beyond recognition just to give this nightmare some semblance of justification. However, when Detectives Lynch and Zanetti let themselves inside and then called me and two crime scene technicians in minutes later, my apartment looked, at first glance, exactly as it had when I'd left that morning.

"Try not to touch more than you have to," Megan said. "But I want you to go through room by room and give me your observations."

"Am I allowed to open cupboards and cabinets?'

"Yes, but don't use the handles if you can help it. Just pull them open from the bottoms or sides. Let me know if you need help."

I went into the kitchen first and, with a fingernail, pried open the cabinet to the left of the stove. The old cardboard box of Grandma's china was right where it was supposed to be. I saw the Waterford glasses too and breathed a sigh of relief. There were bigger concerns, obviously, and I had to take my comfort where I could.

I didn't notice anything out of place in the kitchen so I wandered into my office next, Megan a step or two behind. I saw my shelf and books, all right where they were supposed to be, or were they? I moved closer. From six feet away, I still couldn't read the spines but I could tell from sizes and colors that they were out of order. I must have made a sound then because Megan asked me what was wrong.

"Nothing," I said. "It's just... nothing."

I realized I didn't want to tell her because I thought she'd judge me for knowing what order the books had been in in the first place. And if he'd moved a couple, which I was sure he had, what possible difference could it make? They might be unorganized but they were all there. The letter from Deb, however, was not. I'd had an extra copy and left it on top of the desk. It was gone. Thankfully, the original was still....

With a sudden sinking in my stomach I spun, pushed past Megan, hurried into my bedroom and dropped to my knees in front of the closet.

"Alex?'

The safe looked undisturbed but the cops believed Scott Fisher was a pro. What if he'd somehow gotten inside? That letter, even unverified, was the closest thing I had to real proof of what Clayton Babbit had done. What would I do if he'd taken it and the copies too?"

"Alex?" Megan said again, walking up to stand behind me. "What's wrong?"

I ignored her, and in my panic, also forgot what she'd said about not touching things. The safe needed my fingerprint and I didn't hesitate to provide it, possibly smudging or destroying other prints in the process. At that moment, I didn't care.

I heard a thunk, turned the handle, and pulled the door open.

The letter was there, as were my passport, my social security card, a manila envelope containing a few hundred dollars in cash, the external hard drive, my mother's engagement ring and wedding band, which I'd forgotten I had, plus a couple folders of legal documents and other important papers. Nothing was missing and no one, I knew now, had laid his grubby paws on any of it.

I sat back, somehow overbalancing and landing on my butt.

"Are you all right?" Megan asked, crouching down and placing a hand on my shoulder.

"Yeah," I said, feeling foolish. "I'm good."

Megan leaned forward, withdrew a penlight from an inside pocket, and shone the beam on the floor all along the outside of the safe.

"What are you doing?'

She clicked off and put the light away. "There's no way he would have gotten in there without some heavy duty equipment. He didn't have the time even if he had the tools and the knowhow."

"So what were you looking for?" - "I was wondering if he'd made any attempt to take the safe with him. That would have been the easiest solution but I don't see any signs that he tried."

"I'm glad, but he unfortunately didn't leave empty handed."

"What's missing?"

I got to my feet, headed back towards my office and waved at her to follow. "Right there, I said, pointing at my desk. "I had a copy of the letter I gave you this morning."

"From your friend?" she asked unnecessarily.

What else could I have meant? "Yeah," I said. "He took it and, although it didn't click when I was in here before, it looks like he walked off with my laptop too."

"You're sure?"

I nodded, thinking this guy was really starting to tick me off.

"Any chance you've got tracking software on it?"

"Shit," I said in way of response. My laptop hadn't even been password protected. By now, the son of a bitch had probably taken all the files and then dumped the thing in the Hudson. It was my own fault but who really thinks about security inside their own house? Even when I bought the safe, it wasn't with burglars in mind. I was more worried about fire, flood or some other natural disaster.

Well, I thought, sighing and looking around. *I learned from my crashed hard drive. I guess I can learn from this too.*

For the next half hour, I roamed from room to room, peering at things and reporting my observations. Megan stayed with me while Detective Zanetti mostly watched the crime scene techs. They seemed like an odd pair: a bespectacled white male and a tall, dark-skinned woman with a musical accent I couldn't place. They moved around like ghosts or morticians, testing this, examining that, and depositing unseen items in small cellophane baggies. I couldn't imagine what they hoped to accomplish, and the infrequent bits of mumbled overheard conversations provided no clarification. However, I was pretty sure from their demeanor and Detective Zanetti's increasing impatience that they had not struck pay dirt. I couldn't get too bothered by that because I was busy being creeped out by the discoveries I'd made.

Next to the letters and computer, Fisher had taken almost nothing. I'd had a few thumb drives in an upper desk drawer and maybe some blank CDs too. I hadn't used any of them in so long I wasn't sure what, if anything, they contained. I'd never find out either because all that stuff was gone. But that, so far as I could tell, was about it. As burglaries went, I supposed I'd been lucky. I still wanted to throw up. My visitor may not have stolen things but he had handled them and he made sure I knew it.

The first thing was the books. The second was my keys--deposited right in the middle of my pillow. He'd even seemed to know which side of the bed I slept on. Talk about weirding me out. He'd been in my closet, my bathroom, even my bedside table. He hadn't left a mess but the signs of his presence were unmistakable and unnerving.

"I need to get out of here," I finally said, grabbing clothes and toiletries and stuffing them unceremoniously into a drawstring bag. "Can you take me to Vicki's?"

-35-

They were seated in the spacious sunken living room of an attractive brownstone in the heart of Brooklyn. Vicki Goldstein, dressed in a dark, flowing outfit that looked, at the same time, expensive but understated, brought in a steaming carafe and placed it on the coffee table in front of them. She returned to the kitchen and came back holding a tray of mugs in one hand and a second tray with cream, sugar and a small tin of cookies in the other.

"Can I get you anything else?" she asked, filling cups with a practiced hand.

"This is fine," Megan said, settling into what might have been the most comfortable couch she'd ever sat on. She thought about how nice it would feel to kick off her shoes, stretch out, and go to sleep for ten or twelve hours. She and Zanetti had been at it since early that morning and there seemed to be no end in sight. *How did that saying go? No rest for the weary?*

"Okay then," Vicki said, retreating to an overstuffed loveseat positioned between the couch and a large gas fireplace. "You can help yourselves to cream and sugar."

She was about to sit down but stopped and turned. "Alex," she said, crossing the room and briefly taking the woman's hand. "With the day you've had, I should have offered something stronger than coffee and cookies. I'm so sorry. Would you like a glass of wine?"

"Actually, I need to use the restroom if you'd please show me where it is. Then, if you don't mind, can I make a sandwich? I haven't had a bite since breakfast and I'm about ready to eat my arm."

"Of course," Vicki said. "Anything you need. I want you to make yourself at home. The bathroom's right…." She started to point down a darkened hallway but then looked at her guest and seemed to reconsider. "It's right this way," she said. "Follow me."

As they left the room, Megan heard them discussing cold cut options. She also noticed how Alex slightly misjudged the small step up from the living room, and how, from the moment they'd entered Ms. Goldstein's residence, she'd moved about more slowly and with far less confidence than she had when inside her own apartment. Zanetti had apparently picked up on that too.

"That's gotta be tough," he said, watching Rhodes and keeping his voice low. "I don't know how she does it."

"What's that?" Megan asked, confused.

"Her books I guess. They're full of detail yet she sometimes has trouble walking across a room. I don't know," he said with a shrug. "Those two things don't seem to go together."

Megan nodded, wondering if, when she did someday get around to reading Alex's novels, her perceptions would be different because of what she knew about the author's personal situation. She wished she had a better idea of what the woman could and couldn't see. She was at the center of their investigation, and there were plenty of questions that still needed to be asked and answered. That meant they'd all be spending quality time together. Megan hoped she'd come away from that with a clearer understanding. Somehow, though, she doubted it.

"And you know what I keep thinking about?" Zanetti asked, not pausing long enough for a response. "What it must have been like for her when she was out on the street, unable to make out her surroundings, and thinking Fisher might be closing in. That's a Stephen King plot if I've ever heard one."

Megan agreed and was about to say so when the two ladies re-entered the room.

"And I left a set of towels on the bed." Vicki was saying. "There are extra blankets and pillows in there too. Let me know if you need anything else."

"I don't even need that much. I'm low maintenance. You won't even know I'm here," Alex said, stumbling. "Assuming I don't break my neck on that stupid step."

"Can I help you?" Zanetti asked, beginning to rise.

"I'm fine," she said, sitting. "There's always a learning curve when I'm in a new place. By this time tomorrow, I'll be able to walk around with my eyes closed." She gave a rueful shrug. "I sometimes think I'd be better off that way anyway."

"Excuse me," Vicki said, standing in the kitchen doorway. "I'm fixing a sandwich for Alex. Can I get anything for either of you? It's no trouble."

"I appreciate the offer," Zanetti said. "But I'm fine."

"Me too," said Megan. "We'll do what we have to and then get out of your hair."

"Suit yourselves."

Vicki disappeared and Megan could hear cupboards and drawers opening and closing followed by the clatter of dishes and cutlery. She tried not to think about how good a nice, hearty sandwich would taste.

She hadn't realized how hungry she was until Alex mentioned it and then her own stomach immediately started to growl. She exchanged a look with Zanetti and knew he was thinking the same thing. They were a couple hours past their normal dinner break. Once they'd finished with Ms. Rhodes, Code 7 at the nearest diner would be the next stop.

In terms of police conduct, there were no specific rules preventing them from accepting food from a private citizen. One could argue that breaking bread with Alex would make her more at ease, and therefore more likely to be open and honest. However, Megan preferred to maintain a certain level of professionalism and when it came to questioning witnesses, accepting a cup of coffee was about as far as she was willing to go. She hadn't worked with Zanetti that long yet but knew he was of a similar mind.

"You've been through a tremendous ordeal today," she said, looking at Alex and automatically reaching for her pen, pad and recorder. "But if you're feeling up to it, we do have some additional questions. We'll try not to take up too much more of your time."

"I don't care how long you take," Alex replied. She glanced at the detectives but then looked away. "When I left my apartment this morning I had this theory, I guess, that Martin was murdered because of my books and his killer might now be after me too. I believed it, but it also didn't seem real if you know what I mean."

"And now it does," Megan said.

"Yeah, and it's scaring the shit out of me too. And to think he was that close to me and also spent time in my apartment." She shivered and hugged herself. "I'll answer your questions from now until Doomsday if that's what it takes. But if it's okay, I'd like to ask Detective Zanetti something first."

"Of course," he said, and as Megan watched, her partner sat up straighter and smoothed his tie.

"At Tower Brothers this morning," Alex said. "You asked about my eyesight."

"Yes," and Megan could sense his sudden discomfort. "I hope that didn't offend you."

She smiled. "I promise it did not. I was just wondering how you knew."

Megan had actually wondered that too. She'd thought something about the writer was a little out of the ordinary but a vision disorder hadn't occurred to her until Zanetti brought it up. She figured he'd say something detective-like about being a trained observer but his response took her by surprise.

"When I was a kid," he said, "I had an aunt with a vision issue. I don't know what it was. I didn't know her that well, and she passed away when I was still pretty young. However, something about your mannerisms and body language reminded me of her."

"How so?'

"I don't know exactly. It was a long time ago and, like I said, we weren't close. From what I remember, though, she didn't like to make eye contact with people and, when she did, it sort of looked like she was looking somewhere else."

"And I do the same thing," Alex said, her tone matter of fact.

"It seemed so," Zanetti replied, flushing. "I'm sorry. I don't think that came out very well and I apologize."

"No need. I asked the question. I appreciate your candor. And honestly, I'm most uncomfortable when people are unaware. I'd rather you ask than draw your own conclusions."

"And on that note," Megan cut in, sensing Zanetti was ready for a change of topic, "let's talk about Scott Fisher. Are you ready?"

"Oh sure," Alex said, looking up as Vicki returned from the kitchen and handed her a plate with a thick sandwich cut into two, some chips and a pile of red grapes.

"Thanks," she said, popping a chip into her mouth. "But you really shouldn't treat me this well. I might not want to leave."

Vicki sat down and picked up her coffee. "I already told you you can stay as long as you'd like. Besides, I'm just protecting my assets. A sandwich is a small price to pay." She turned and looked at Megan. "I hope I'm not interrupting. I can go into another room if you'd prefer."

"I don't think that's necessary," Megan said, placing her digital recorder on the table. "As far as I'm concerned, you're welcome to stay so long as Alex doesn't object."

"It's fine with me," she said through a mouthful of turkey and Swiss. She swallowed and cleared her throat. "Sorry. I definitely don't mind if Vicki's here. In some respects, this is about her too, or Tower Brothers anyway."

"Good enough," Megan said. "Then let's get to it."

-36-

Clayton Babbit III stared out his big bay window even though, with it being full dark outside and the desk lamp burning behind him, he couldn't make out much more than the reflection of his own brooding expression. He didn't want to see that, so swiveled around to face his empty office. Louie had taken off an hour ago and the rest of the staff were long gone too. Babbit felt alone in the world. He also felt like the walls, ceiling, and floor were all beginning to close in on him.

With a sigh, he picked up his phone and scrolled through his most recent text conversation with Mikhail Vasilek. It was now a little better than twenty-four hours into the forty-eight hour deadline and Vasilek hadn't yet done anything to suggest success was imminent. Babbit gave him credit for one thing. The night before, he had managed to re-locate Alex Rhodes when he spotted her entering her apartment building. That was nice, or would have been had the shithead not lost her again almost as quickly. According to Vasilek, she'd been with cops and left with them in their cop car. He'd been on foot and had no way to follow. Of course, he couldn't even guess where they might have gone. Babbit understood that, but his understanding had not prevented him from responding to the latest developments with a string of profanity-laced threats. That had been—he checked his watch—thirty-six minutes ago and Vasilek had not yet replied. And really, why would he bother?

Babbit opened his bottom desk drawer and removed a nearly full bottle of Jack Daniel's No. 27 Gold and a glass. He poured a couple fingers, and before taking a sip, capped the bottle and put it away. He was absolutely of a mind to tie one on and didn't want the temptation sitting right there in front of his face. Besides, he'd paid over eighty dollars for the stuff. If he decided to get plastered, he'd switch to rotgut first. He always had a supply of that on hand too.

"Here's to you," he said, thinking of Vasilek as he raised the glass and admired the rich, butterscotch-colored liquid inside.

He drained the contents and then just sat, relishing the lingering burn as he stared at nothing. For some reason, his cheating, good-for-nothing ex-wife chose that moment to pop unbidden into his head. What if she'd never mentioned the Martin Reginald books? What if he'd never read them and never learned they seemed to be about him?

What if? Babbit thought, his anger rising. *What if she'd never fucked the god damn pool boy and shit all over our wedding vows?*

Without realizing what he was doing, he cocked his arm back and flung the whisky glass across the room. It missed a brand new computer monitor by an inch, bounced off the wall and fell harmlessly to the carpeted floor. Babbit shook his head, not surprised he somehow couldn't even seem to break things properly.

"You're a piece of work," he said, getting to his feet.

He retrieved the glass, placed it back on the desk and then stood, absently running his hand along the polished wood surface. Everything in his well-appointed office was top quality and why not? He was in charge of a thriving company, several actually, and he'd worked his ass off for everything he had. Okay, so he'd cut some corners and taken advantage of some people and situations. He'd like to see a successful business person who hadn't done at least some of those same things. Babbit had, perhaps, gone a bit further than most but he'd accomplished more too. It was a high risk, high reward sort of world and he knew how the game was played.

Against his better judgment, he found himself thinking about Bev again, something that happened far too frequently in moments of solitude and contemplation. The woman was no good and he was better off without her. Of that he had no doubt. He might not have actually wished her dead but hadn't shed many tears at her passing. She made a choice and ended up paying the price. By his estimation, she got what she deserved. What was troubling him was the nagging suspicion that the same thing might now be happening to him.

Babbit walked a slow circle and then collapsed into his Italian leather chair. He looked with disgust at the open FedEx box in the middle of the desk. At least Vasilek had come through with that. Really, though, would it make a difference? He'd been told by Vasilek and by Louie too that Rhodes probably had multiple digital copies of her work and they would not be accessible to him under any *reasonable* circumstances. Babbit knew that was true but still forced the issue, mainly because he felt like he had no alternative unless, of course, he decided to be... *unreasonable.* What if, instead of killing Alex Rhodes, Vasilek found her, grabbed her, and forced her to turn over or delete everything from every cyber hiding spot? It sounded good, and was about as practical as paying a company like Sand-Sational to restore a fucking beach. He would have no way of ever being sure he'd actually recovered every file, or that those files had not been previously viewed or shared by others. Babbit was thoroughly disheartened, but he went through the motions anyway because he believed he no longer had a choice.

The flash drives Vasilek found in Rhodes' apartment contained nothing but some book cover image files plus a bunch of songs by a group called Beat Root Revival. Babbit had never heard of them and had no interest in expanding his musical horizons. He reformatted the drives and stuck them in a desk drawer. The CDs came next and they yielded even less. They'd either been wiped or never used, and Babbit tossed them into the trash without a second thought.

With Louie's assistance, he'd gone over the laptop next. They found several files related to her new book and one of them appeared to be the manuscript itself. Babbit didn't have time to read the whole thing and didn't want Louie reading it either. He'd printed the entire document for later consideration and then deleted the file. He'd done the same with a lengthy outline. Louie had known better than to ask questions and Babbit hadn't volunteered any information.

He didn't understand why he was always so guarded. Louie could be trusted. In the years they'd been together, he'd proven that time and again. Still, Babbit never confided anything unless he had to. Had that been a mistake? It seemed so now.

Where Babbit was often rash, Louie was more practical and level-headed. Had he known about the novels from the start, maybe he could have stepped in and prevented his boss from doing anything stupid. Spin it back a little further and Louie might have persuaded him to stay away from that Deepwater Horizon business altogether. Babbit knew better, though. For the kind of money he made, he'd do it all over again. He'd just make sure he handled things better the next time around.

And that brought him back to the final item Vasilek's box had contained. He'd almost missed it at first because it had lodged itself part-way underneath one of the inside cardboard flaps. Even when he spotted the single sheet of paper he'd assumed it was an invoice or some FedEx tracking bullshit. He couldn't have been more wrong. Babbit plucked it out and, suspecting nothing, unfolded it and scanned the lines of print. What he read hit him like a sledgehammer.

For the next several seconds, he literally couldn't breathe. All he could do was stand and stare, his free hand pressed against his chest. The letter, Babbit noted once he'd sufficiently recovered, had obviously been written by one Debora Royal and she, just as obviously, had been in contact with her brother.

A few things were made crystal clear. First, he now knew beyond any doubt where Rhodes had come by her information.

"Fucking high school classmates!" he'd spat, furious that something so damn trivial might be his undoing.

Second, he'd been sent a photo copy. That meant there were other copies out there and Rhodes, in all likelihood, had shared what she knew.

And third, if Mikhail Vasilek read the letter and wasn't a complete fool, he now understood not only who he was after but why. That was the part Babbit found most troubling. He liked it when he knew other people's business. He'd didn't like it when they knew his.

Had he gotten himself into a no-win situation? That was the question he kept asking and Babbit was becoming increasingly convinced the answer was yes. And what was really tearing him up inside was the knowledge that he had gotten away with it. What he'd done, or more specifically arranged to have done aboard that drilling rig had worked.

Despite the long, drawn out and exhaustive investigations, no one had ever suspected him or alleged in any way that he might have been involved. The same was true when it came to the deaths of Bryan and then Debora Royal. They were both ruled accidents. He had done it! He'd committed the perfect crimes. So why couldn't he have left well enough alone?

Babbit knew the answer. It was those fucking novels, which he wouldn't have even known about had it not been for his cheating, good-for-nothing wife.

Maybe, he thought, poking at the FedEx box with his middle finger, *the bitch somehow knew it was her last day on earth and wanted to make sure the two of them reunited in hell.*

He considered that, wondering if the devil would put lying whores in the same room with corrupt businessmen. He hoped not. If he was doomed to burn for all eternity he'd rather do it without looking at her and being forever reminded of all the misery she'd caused. To him, that would constitute cruel and unusual punishment and he figured Satan himself must have rules about that.

Had he been smart, when Bev mentioned the Martin Reginald novels, he would have dismissed her concerns, gone off to his golf game, and forgotten the whole thing. It's not like she was going to call the cops and risk losing her Platinum Amex and the other luxuries to which she'd become accustomed. More to the point, even if that had been her intention, she'd died before she had the chance. His secret was safe. And although thousands if not hundreds of thousands of other people had read the same books, no one else had raised any questions or come knocking on his door. That should have convinced him he was in the clear. It hadn't, because he was too busy getting spooked and then overreacting to imagined threats.

"Damn!" he said, finally beginning to grasp the sheer scope of the mistakes he'd made. He also understood it was too late to reverse the cycle. He had to press on.

Babbit stood and picked up the folder where he'd put the manuscript and outline. He hadn't read through it all yet. There hadn't been nearly enough time. However, he'd flipped through, and incomplete as it was, had still seen enough to get the picture. It wasn't pretty either. The rest of the story--his story--was right there in black and white. Like with the first two novels, certain details were lacking or just plain wrong. Even so, she made a good case, and if anyone chose to pursue it, he could have a difficult time proving his innocence.

That was the thing, though. Had he just kept his head down from the start, nobody would be pursuing anything because there'd been no reason to. Rhodes' tale, clever as it might be, was based on a dead woman's claims and a lot of conjecture. She hadn't provided anything substantive or actionable. He'd taken care of that part for her and, like an idiot, provided the hard evidence she'd been lacking. He'd gone to Louie, and Louie in turn found Mikhail Vasilek. Now, in addition to potentially incriminating text and phone records, Babbit could be linked to two dead bodies: Martin Reginald and the sap from Rhodes' apartment lobby.

"Damn!" he said again, shaking his head at the futility of it all.

He realized it was high time he got into damage-control mode. This was no longer about Alex Rhodes, or whether or not Vasilek killed her. Babbit hadn't rescinded the order, yet but was beyond believing that getting rid of the woman would do any good.

The story was getting too much attention. He'd seen the televised press conference that morning, and the whole world now new Rhodes was the real author of the Deepwater books. She was also, according to various reports, cooperating fully with police and their on-going investigation into the Martin Reginald murder. The cops addressed the media too and some bald-headed captain whose name Babbit didn't catch said they were *making significant progress* and *following numerous leads,* but he gave no real information. He had not mentioned either Clayton Babbit or the man they probably knew as Scott Fisher but those omissions provided little comfort. Sooner or later, he knew they'd come looking for him.

Babbit glanced toward the window, half expecting to see a string of cop cars pulling into his drive with lights ablaze. To his relief, everything remained quiet and dark. He wondered how much longer that would last. What if they'd stormed in at that moment, a box of Rhodes' stolen items sitting right there on his desk?

Fucking stupid, he thought, realizing that was one more connection they could make between him and Vasilek. Well, he could take care of that. The manuscript would go into a secret wall safe as soon as he got home. He wouldn't keep it forever but wanted to at least give it a more thorough read-through so he'd have a firmer idea of what he was dealing with.

And as for the laptop? He smiled grimly. One of the more accessible parts of the Atchafalaya River Swamp was conveniently no more than five miles away. He would bet his house and left nut the computer would never be seen again.

Babbit wasn't especially worried about talking to the police. He'd been in enough high-level business meetings and high-stakes poker games that he knew he'd never cave in to that sort of pressure. They'd get nothing from him. He wasn't worried about Louie either. The guy was solid and would remain loyal because Babbit had always treated him well, at least when it came to finances. And even if some especially gung-ho detective went at him with the thumb screws and rubber hose, what could Louie say? He had no firsthand knowledge of Vasilek's actions. He'd simply been the one to locate him. That had been through an intermediary and no names were ever exchanged. It was another dead end. That brought Babbit to Mikhail Vasilek himself. What would happen if the cops got him? Presumably, they'd get his cell phone too, and that's where things might come unraveled.

Activating the office security system, Babbit closed and locked the door and then headed for his pickup, the box and folder both tucked under an arm. As soon as he drove away, he pulled out his cell phone and called Louie, not at home but on his office line. It rolled over to voice mail after the fifth ring and, sounding upbeat and cheerful, he left a message about traveling to the coast for a few days to oversee the Oasis restoration project.

Louie would know that was bunk because they'd had no luck finding the huge quantity of sand required for the job. Unless that changed, which wasn't likely, there'd be nothing to oversee. In fact, Babbit was surprised they hadn't yet received the call informing them Oasis had hired someone else. His goal had simply been to let Louie Know he'd be off the grid for a while, and hoped his partner would have the sense to leave the message there in case anyone else came around with questions about his whereabouts.

Two hours later, with a full tank of gas and the bed of his truck loaded with gear, Clayton Babbit was on the highway headed north. According to his GPS, Grand Central Station was just over thirteen hundred miles away, about twenty hours if he drove straight through. That would give him ample opportunity to figure out the best way to find and dispose of Mikhail Vasilek. Babbit was accustomed to having others do his dirty work for him. At some point, though, you had to be ready to put your own boots on the ground. He knew that time had come.

-37-

It didn't take me long to get used to Vicki's place and, even though it was way, WAY nicer than mine, I kind of hated it, because after long hours of being cooped up, it started feeling like a prison, though one equipped with a fully stocked wine fridge, a big Jacuzzi bathtub, and the most beautiful kitchen I'd ever seen—everything bright and gleaming. It almost made me wish I knew how to cook. Almost. At least that would have given me something to occupy my mind and my time.

Yes, I am very much a home body. I readily admit that. I've happily gone days on end without once stepping outdoors. But I had the familiar comforts of my couch, my remote, my trusty microwave, and my computer. I didn't have any of that at Vicki's and it was driving me batty.

My normal routine is to get up early, eat breakfast, maybe exercise, maybe shower, and then fire up the laptop and get to work. Lately, I've been putting in a solid six hours of writing per day so I can finish the book on time. You might think that sounds a lot less demanding than your basic nine to five. For me though, six straight hours on one project is a marathon session and, by the end, my creative juices have been sucked as dry as Steven Wright's sense of humor if it were abandoned for three days in the middle of the Sahara.

I'd become a creature of habit and, until I was forced out of my regular schedule, I never realized how much I'd come to depend on it. I don't mean to sound ungracious. I genuinely appreciated Vicki's hospitality. She was, in essence, my boss and her willingness to take me in went above and beyond the call. I understood that. When this whole thing was finally over with, assuming I wasn't pushing up daisies, I planned on buying her the biggest bouquet of flowers I could find. For now, however, I just wanted my stuff.

I tried to explain how I felt and Vicki immediately offered me the use of her home office and computer. That was nice but she was missing the point. I didn't need *a computer*. It had to be mine. And no, I'm not trying to be difficult. For obvious reasons, she'd never installed the special screen magnification software that in my indistinct world is an absolute necessity. I was missing my other adaptive technology too but the laptop was the big one. I supposed there was a chance it would turn up somewhere and we'd be reunited. In my heart, though, I knew it was gone. I'd have to buy a new one and then deal with the hassle of customizing it to my satisfaction. It would be a major pain in the fanny but what else could I do?

The short answer was nothing. I had NOTHING to do. I couldn't work and had no other way to focus my energies. I did have some music and audio books on my phone but neither captured my attention for long. I wanted to accomplish something and I had no way to do it. I couldn't even wander the streets because I didn't know the neighborhood and I was afraid I'd get lost. And really, with a crazed killer out there, I wasn't of a mind to make an easy target of myself anyway. I knew my best bet was to stay indoors and out of sight, no matter how boring and frustrating it got.

There was one bit of excitement I could have done without. On Vicki's suggestion—*insistence really*—I was on hand for the big press conference when it was announced that Martin Reginald was dead, and I was the real author of the books. The scene was beyond surreal--the main conference room at Tower Brothers packed with reporters, all flashing pictures and shouting questions. I couldn't believe something I'd created was garnering so much attention.

Thankfully, I never had to take my turn at the makeshift podium. Vicki and Peter ran the show, and I thought they did a nice job keeping things under control, relatively speaking. Of course, everyone wanted to talk to me but they weren't given that opportunity. I was an integral part of an *ongoing police investigation*, and that made for a convenient out. I just sat, endured the chaos, and did my best not to look shell-shocked. When it was over, Megan Lynch, who'd also been there, whisked me away.

"That was interesting," she said, turning onto Vicki's block. "I had no idea so many people would show up."

"Me neither," I replied, relieved I'd cleared the first of what I knew would be many hurdles. "Like I told you before, I've kept myself in the background for years and avoided that side of the business. I guess those days are over."

"And are you okay with that?"

"No," I said, shaking my head while fidgeting with the seatbelt clasp. "I liked it how it was and I wish with every fiber of my being it could have stayed that way."

I figured she must think I was being overly dramatic but, if anything, I was probably understating my fears.

"I've got to do this," I explained, as much for my benefit as hers. "Martin was a friend and I feel like I owe it to him."

"I think I understand, and you're showing a lot of courage."

I appreciated the sentiment but didn't agree with it so quickly changed the subject. "Have you made any progress?" I asked, turning to face her.

"I believe so." Megan pulled to a stop, double parking in front of Vicki's building. "We've analyzed a lot of photos and video from the cruise ship, the subway, and from your apartment lobby. We don't have any additional information about Scott Fisher's actual identity, but we do know we are dealing with just one person."

"So what happens now?" I asked, groping for the door handle.

"More of the same," she said. "We continue digging until we catch a break. Detective Zanetti and I believe the murder of Mr. Barnes was spur of the moment."

"Does that matter?"

"Maybe so. Everything he did aboard the Island Explorer was carefully planned out and executed. What he's done since then seems more spontaneous. That often leads to mistakes. I expect he's made some already. We just need to find them and use them to our advantage."

"Did you find anything in my apartment? Did he leave finger prints or anything like that?"

Megan shook her head. "He wore latex gloves. We'd assumed as much. However, the way he moved and rearranged personal items—that could be telling."

"What do you think it means?" I asked, feeling violated all over again.

"Hard to say. It's one more part of his profile, though. The more we learn the better."

"But you don't know who he is, where he is, or what he'll do next. It doesn't sound like you have much to go on."

I hadn't meant to sound confrontational but I was feeling increasingly anxious and frustrated and having a hard time hiding it. If the detective noticed she gave no sign.

"I think we know what he wants to do next," she said pointedly. "It's why you're here and not in your own apartment."

"Yeah." I looked at the brownstone with distaste. "And I don't know how much more of this I can take."

"You don't like it here?" she asked.

"It's not that," I said, pushing my door open. "I just don't like feeling so vulnerable. Having to live with someone else, being interviewed by and also driven home by cops. It makes it all so real. You know what I mean?"

"I do," Megan said, "and I assure you I won't rest until I get this guy."

"Can you please do it soon?" I asked, trying to smile. "I'd like to go home."

"I'm going to meet with Detective Zanetti right now. It may not seem like it, Alex, but we are getting closer. Really."

"I know and I'm grateful. I'm sorry if I don't sound like it."

I started to get out of the car but she stopped me with a hand on my arm.

"Can I ask you something?" she said, and I could hear her reluctance. I thought I knew where it was coming from too. Instead of responding, I just looked at her and waited.

"During that press conference," she said, her hand sliding away. "Ms. Goldstein told those reporters you're legally blind. Did that bother you?"

"Why should it?"

She was quiet for a moment and I could almost feel her shrug.

"I've gotten to know you a little over the past couple days," she finally said. "You strike me as a private person. And if you don't mind me saying so, I think you're also self-conscious about your eyesight."

Self conscious? Try completely paranoid.

"I thought," Megan said, sounding less authoritative than usual, "that was a big part of the reason you had Mr. Reginald represent your books. I just wasn't sure how you felt about having something so personal brought up in such a setting."

I could tell the question made her uncomfortable. Ironically, it didn't bother me a bit.

"Believe it or not," I said, closing the car door again, "Vicki was acting on my instruction."

"You told her to say that?'

"Yes!"

"Mind if I ask why?"

"No, but you sort of answered the question already."

"Please explain," she said, and I wondered if she was tempted to pull out her recorder and notebook.

I sighed with the knowledge that whatever I told her would be insufficient and, despite my best efforts, she would never truly understand. You see someone with dark glasses, a cane, and a dog and you immediately know the deal. *That dude is blind.* No one would come to that conclusion when first looking at me. I look *normal*, for lack of a better word. And believe me, I'm profoundly grateful for the little bit of sight that I have. It's so much better than the alternative. That said, I sometimes wish my disability exhibited itself through some means other than the behaviors that those who don't know me must think are pretty odd.

Hey, did you see that woman walk into the advertising board over there? I bet she's drunk or stoned. Geez, and it isn't even noon yet. What a loser.

To be honest, I don't really know what anyone thinks of me or my various survival quirks. They seem awkward and oddball to me so I assume everyone else feels the same.

"The toughest thing," I said, choosing my words with care, "is when people don't know or don't understand. Think about what it was like when we met. Detective Zanetti figured out I had a vision problem. You just thought I was weird or whatever."

"I didn't--"

"You didn't what?" I asked, challenging her. "You knew something about me was different. You said so yourself"

"Okay, you're right," she admitted. "I didn't put it together as quickly as I should have. That doesn't mean I thought you were weird. And what does it have to do with the press conference?"

"Everything," I said. "Having Vicki explain things now makes it easier for me down the road."

"I'm not sure I follow," Megan said, gazing at me with an expression I naturally couldn't interpret. I didn't think I needed to, though. I'd sought to provide clarity and instead made her even more confused. I paused and tried again.

"Moving forward, I know I'll be getting a lot of attention from the media, especially in the short term. Vicki told me we'll control that as much as possible. In terms of interviews, I'd like to stick mostly to print and radio."

"Places you can't be seen," Megan said, and I knew she was starting to catch on.

"That's right," I said, nodding. "It's not that I care about what people think of me. I'm not that insecure, at least not in that sense. However, I know my sort of off-center gaze can be off-putting. I know how people react. They're not judging me. I don't think so anyway. They just don't understand."

"So it's easier for you if they know ahead of time that you have a visual impairment."

Yeah. It's easier for me and for them too. That's why I wanted Vicki to get the word out."

"That makes sense. Thanks for telling me."

"Hey," I said, climbing out of the car. "I might not be able to see the elephant in the room but I don't mind talking about him."

Megan laughed. "Do you need any help getting inside?"

"Thanks but I'm good. You've got my cell number. Please let me know if there are any developments."

"Will do," she said. "In the meantime, take care of yourself."

-38-

Peering over the top of the latest edition of the *Wall Street Journal*, Mikhail Vasilek adjusted his drug store reading glasses, cleared his throat, and noisily turned the page. He was occupying the same bench he had a couple mornings before, directly across the street from the offices of Tower Brothers Publishing. This time, however, he wore scuffed loafers, dark woolen slacks, and a tweed jacket with honest-to-goodness leather elbow patches. He had a pipe too, which he didn't light but did keep somewhat visible—the stem poking out of his shirt pocket. It was the details that mattered, and he had a lot of details stuffed into the brown rucksack at his feet. He glanced down briefly and wondered what someone might think were they to look inside his bag of tricks. He had a curious assortment of goodies to be sure, and he'd recently added a few accessories thanks to Clayton Babbit's generosity.

Vasilek would never use Babbit's credit card on anything that would reveal his whereabouts. When, for example, he checked into his new hotel, he provided a different card bearing a completely different name; a different gender too. And, unless Babbit and his flunkies started searching Manhattan hotel registries for Mrs. Olga Belenkaya and then somehow connected an old Russian woman with him, he knew he couldn't be traced. Still, Babbit was aware Vasilek was in the greater Manhattan area and would have to remain there until Alex Rhodes was properly dealt with. He, therefore, had no qualms about using Babbit's money when buying two new wigs, some eyeglasses, a checkered babushka, some art supplies, theater makeup and other odds and ends.

Vasilek hadn't been able to use plastic with the skinny, strung out, homeless-looking street punk that demanded far too much for a seriously abused 40 caliber Smith & Wesson, but he'd found an ATM close by and was able to complete the transaction. He'd owned a similar weapon before and didn't care for the sharp recoil, the hard trigger pull, or the way the slide release tended to hang up on the magazine. Vasilek thought he should have a backup piece, though, and was in no position to be choosy. He only hoped the thing would actually fire if he ever needed it to. And again, at least the four hundred bucks he'd handed over hadn't been his.

It was nearly four in the afternoon and Vasilek was starting to get impatient. Throughout the course of the day, he'd spent time as an elderly man with a sack of bread and a pigeon fetish, the aforementioned Olga Belenkaya, a sketch artist, and a mime. He knew he hadn't been very good at that but a few people shoved dollar bills into his pockets just the same.

Morons, he mused, turning another page.

He figured he could give it another hour in his current incarnation, somewhere between midlevel businessman and aging academic. If, however, by five o'clock he wasn't on the move, he'd have to undergo another transformation. It required time, effort, and vigilance, but Vasilek was confident it would pay off in the end. In some ways it already had.

He sat back and reflected on the new information he'd acquired. During the morning influx of people showing up for work, he'd only seen one person he recognized--the woman with the bracelets that had brought Rhodes her forgotten cell phone. There'd been a steady flow of arrivals from eight forty-five until about nine fifteen, followed by a lengthy lull. Vasilek had almost decided the day would be a bust. Then, at nine thirty-nine, Alex Rhodes appeared and she was accompanied by a tall, dark-haired woman Vasilek could only describe as handsome. She was more classy than sexy, and something about the way she carried herself was authoritative too. She might not be the boss but Vasilek would have bet she was near the top of the corporate food chain.

She and Rhodes walked with their heads close together and they were talking in earnest. More to the point, boss lady was talking and Rhodes was listening and occasionally nodding or shaking her head. To his chagrin, Vasilek was too far away to make out any of their conversation. That was okay, though. If they arrived together they might leave together too and that could present opportunities.

Thinking nothing more would happen for awhile, Vasilek had vacated his bench and walked down 5th Avenue until he found a diner busy enough that he could enter the rest room as one person, exit as another, and not attract any undue attention. He was back at his post and had just opened up his sketch pad and pencils when he saw another familiar face. It belonged to the female detective, and he wondered what she was doing back there and why this time she'd come without her stogy partner. He was still working that one through when he noticed traffic into the building had picked up considerably. They weren't the normal business types either. Most came in pairs, and several of those he saw carried television cameras or other equipment.

Strange, Vasilek thought, but he had a pretty good idea of what was happening.

He'd been following the news, and although the disappearance and suspected homicide of cruise passenger Martin Worth had been a front page story, he had yet to see any mention of Martin Reginald or Alex Rhodes. Likewise, no one had drawn any connections, publically anyway, between that incident and the murder of the idiot doorman. That, Vasilek had to assume, was all about to change. The presence of Rhodes, and the reporters, and the cop, surely meant the story would be blown wide open.

I can't wait to see how Babbit reacts to this, he thought, tilting his head, licking the tip of a pencil and trying to look contemplative. It wasn't hard because Clayton Babbit was very much on his mind.

Since the evening before, the man had been uncharacteristically quiet. He'd barely texted and hadn't called once. Vasilek didn't know what to make of that. It was refreshing not being constantly pestered, but the prolonged silence was making him nervous because it wasn't Babbit's norm. He'd sent an angry text full of crudity and poor grammar. He'd followed that with a curt apology totally lacking sincerity, and then nothing.

Why?

Vasilek had no answer but he was sure it had little to do with repentance. That wasn't the way guys like Babbit rolled. So, he must have something else up his sleeve. Vasilek just couldn't imagine what that might be.

I'll find out soon enough, he thought, concentrating on the office building door and wondering what was going on inside.

If there was a way to get in there…. But he didn't give the idea any credence. Many of the new arrivals had been reporters. He'd seen that much for himself. And if he wanted to know what was said all he really needed to do was wait for the next news cycle. In the age of technology and cyber journalism, that probably meant about five minutes. He had the feeling Scott Fisher was about to go worldwide.

"Too bad you're chasing a ghost*,"* Vasilek said into his sketch pad. "Let me know how that works out for you."

The press conference, or whatever it was, didn't last as long as he expected. Less than half an hour after they'd gotten there, the reporter-types streamed out again, many making calls or sending texts or tweets as they hurried away. Voices were raised in excitement and he overheard snatches of conversation. The names Martin Reginald and Alex Rhodes seemed to be on everyone's lips.

Should I check in? Vasilek wondered, thinking it might be time to break the silence and let Babbit know what was going on.

He considered the possibilities and even picked up his phone but that was as far as he got. The building door opened once more, and the chick cop emerged with Rhodes at her side.

What in bloody hell? he thought. *Is she a body guard now?*

Just like the *previous evening*, the two of them got into a car and drove off while he looked on impotently. He couldn't follow and likewise couldn't fathom where they were headed.

Seething, Vasilek pocketed his phone. He wasn't about to call Babbit now—not when the only news he could report was bad.

Yes Mr. Babbit sir. I did find her. She walked right past me and I couldn't do a thing. I'm sorry but I've lost her again. That would go over great.

Vasilek stood, stretched his legs, and walked a short way down the block. For once, he was at a loss as to what to do next. Alex Rhodes wouldn't conveniently keep popping up at the Tower Brothers offices. He'd been lucky to find her there at all. And after what he'd seen the night before, he knew she wouldn't be going home for a while either. She'd left with a large bag over one shoulder and that had to mean she was crashing somewhere else.

But where?

Pausing to watch a window washer work the highest floors of a building on the other side of the street, Vasilek remembered the striking woman with the dark hair. She and Rhodes had some sort of relationship that appeared to go beyond boss and client.

What was the story there? And even though Rhodes had already left, wasn't it possible the other woman could still lead him to her?

Feeling a twinge of optimism, Vasilek turned and headed back to his bench for a bit of re-evaluation.

When she and Rhodes arrived that morning, he recalled they'd been on foot. That didn't necessarily signify anything. Alex Rhodes didn't drive but there was a chance her companion did and had a car parked in the area. But they were in the heart of New York City, the congestion capitol of the east coast. No one drove if they didn't have to, and Vasilek believed the likeliest scenario was that they'd taken the subway like millions of other commuters. And if that was true, the mystery woman should be easy to tail on her return journey. That was his working theory and it proved correct a few hours later.

He'd given himself until five o'clock and it was about ten of when she finally made her appearance, pushing through the door at full stride, a leather handbag tucked tightly under one arm. She walked with purpose and never paused to look around. Had he been so inclined, he knew he could have stayed right behind her and not been detected. But, Vasilek was a pro and worked his craft even when there was no need. He drifted along, monitoring those around him, staying well back, and seemingly paying no mind as he followed the woman from sidewalk to station to subway car.

He was sure the middle-aged artist with the faraway look hadn't even registered in her brain when she marched past his bench. However, to be safe, he made slight modifications to himself as he trailed along in her wake. He didn't change wigs. That would be too obvious to anyone around him. His alterations were more subtle and gradual.

The first things to go were the eye glasses. He next ditched the tweed jacket, folding it and tucking it into his bag while simultaneously removing a green knit cap emblazoned with the New York Jets logo. He pulled that on, and a bit later a thin black sweater completed his new ensemble. Though contrived, his actions had been fluid, well spaced out and, to any onlookers, must have seemed perfectly natural.

Without appearing to stare, Vasilek's eyes never strayed from his target. For her part, she remained fixated on a text conversation or maybe a game on her phone, and was oblivious to the careful scrutiny she'd been under from the moment she left work. He was with her all the way to Prospect Heights, and watched from fifty yards off as she approached and entered a large brownstone.

Very nice, Vasilek thought, the size and location of her home reaffirming his initial impression that she must be one of the movers and shakers at the publishing house. He'd heard the book industry was dying, but based on her digs, at least a few people must still be doing okay.

Many townhouses, Vasilek knew, were nothing more than plain brick construction with a fancy masonry facade. He had no training in architecture yet somehow sensed he was looking at the real deal. He also suspected the price tag had to run into the millions. Even if she was renting it would cost a small fortune. He hadn't seen a wedding ring either—one more sign she was well off because there was no one with whom to share the expenses.

"Very, very nice," he said, whistling low, his rucksack over one shoulder.

He was aware he'd jumped to a few conclusions. The lack of a diamond didn't guarantee there was no husband. She could be divorced and collecting a hefty alimony. Hell, she could be a dike.

Did married lesbians wear rings? He had no idea.

Vasilek was curious but didn't let himself get bogged down trying to definitively determine her marital status or sexual preferences. He was more focused on the things that mattered.

Pausing as if reading a text message, he raised his phone and used the camera app to zoom in on the small gold plate affixed to the wall just to the right of the front door. The house number was 2017 which was barely worth noting. He'd find the place again if he needed to and it wouldn't require an address. He was, however, keenly interested in the other thing he'd seen. Just below the number, in fine black script, he read the first initial *V.* and the last name *Goldstein.*

Veronica? he mouthed, testing the name on his tongue. He thought she could be a Veronica, or a Vanessa, Vera, Victoria or Valerie. There was another possibility too. *V. Goldstein* could refer to a different person entirely because, as he'd lowered his phone, he'd caught a flash of movement through the big front window. Someone else was in there.

Unfortunately, he hadn't seen much. As was typical for the area, the brownstone's ground floor windows were protected by bars. They were made of wrought iron or steel, and designed to look ornate and decorative, which they did. That look was deceiving, though, and if he ever had to enter by force he'd need to find a different way to do it. Vasilek would worry about crossing that bridge if or when he came to it.

In addition to offering security, the bars obstructed his view, as did the sheer curtains that hung from the inside. Still, Vasilek hadn't missed the two plainly female silhouettes or the passing flash of dirty blonde hair.

"Hello Alex," he said, smiling. "We meet again." And then Mikhail Vasilek moved off down the street.

-39-

"You still here, Lynch?" Captain Weiserman asked, stopping and rapping his knuckles on the edge of her desk.

She glanced up and had to bite back a nasty retort about the stupidity of his question.

Of course I'm still here. You're standing there looking at me aren't you?

Megan knew he was only being polite and she could see the lines of concern on his face. She appreciated that, tamped down her mounting frustration, and surprised herself by producing an honest-to-goodness smile.

"Why stop now?" she asked, brushing loose strands of hair away from her eyes and hoping she didn't look quite as wrung out as she felt. "I haven't even been here twelve hours yet. I'm just getting warmed up."

"You're running yourself ragged. That's not gonna do anyone any good. Take a cue from your partner there," Wigs nodded at Zanetti's empty desk, "and knock off for the night. Get some sleep and come out swinging tomorrow."

"You really want me to pattern myself after that good-for-nothing bum? I don't understand why you stuck me with him anyway. You know he's a slacker."

Weiserman's jaw dropped and he took a step back. "I—" he began but didn't get the chance to say anything more.

"Are you talking about me again?'

Detective Paul Zanetti approached, holding a mug of coffee in each hand. He'd come from the direction of the break room where Lynch could see him but Weiserman could not. He was obviously aware of that, so played right along.

"I'd like to file a complaint," he said. "I have to put up with this kind of verbal abuse all day long."

"Yeah? And I've got to put up with your poor taste in clothes." Megan replied. "I think you got the better end of the deal."

Zanetti peered down at his rumpled shirt and stained tie. "I look great," he said. "You're just jealous."

Megan snorted. "You mean because my wardrobe didn't come from a consignment shop?"

Zanetti started protesting but Captain Weiserman cut him off.

"If you two are about done I'm late for a meeting and I'd like to get a status report before I leave."

Megan made a disgusted sound, accepted one of the mugs, thanked Zanetti, and took a tentative sip. "You've heard the expression no news is good news," she said, putting the coffee down. "Whoever came up with that was full of crap. We're getting nowhere and it's damned frustrating."

"The security videos haven't helped then?"

She shook her head. "Hard to believe, isn't it? We've been staring at that stuff all day. We have him from almost a dozen cameras so far, and about that many different angles and locations. There's no doubt it's the same guy we've been after all along but we knew that already."

"We just don't know who he is," Zanetti said. "The Scott Fisher trail is as cold as Lynch's love life."

She stuck out her tongue and he blew her a kiss.

"I'm not sure we're gonna get any further following that lead. Every well we've dug has come up dry. He doesn't seem to exist anywhere."

"That hasn't prevented him from killing two people," Weiserman said.

"Two that we know of," Megan added.

"How's that?"

She took another sip of her coffee and frowned with distaste. "Well," she said. "There's that letter that Alex Rhodes believes started all of this."

"From the high school friend, right?"

"Her name was Debora Royal. She died not long after contacting Alex. Her brother is dead too."

"And you think Fisher was responsible?"

"We think he could have been," Zanetti said. "Like everything else, though, it's speculation because that's all we've got. Both deaths were ruled accidental and there were no witnesses except for one unfortunate bus driver."

"Have you spoken to him?" Captain Weiserman asked.

"I did," Megan said. "About an hour ago. He couldn't tell me anything I hadn't already read in the police report. Dark night. Rainy. He didn't see her until it was too late. I asked if he thought she could have been pushed."

"And what did he say to that?"

"Not much. He retired within weeks of that incident and I got the impression he's spent the last several years trying to forget about it. I know he didn't appreciate being questioned again."

“All right,” Weiserman said, pulling up his shirt cuff to check his watch. “So let’s concentrate on what we might actually be able to prove. The person we currently know only as Scott Fisher murdered Martin Worth Reginald aboard the Island Explorer cruise ship. By the way, I got some additional information from the Broward County ME. There was no water in the lungs so he was definitely dead before he went over the railing.”

“Cause?”

“TBD. The body was in rough shape after all that time in the drink. I’ve got photos if you’d like to see them.”

“I’ll pass,” Megan said.

“Good choice. There were no bullet or knife wounds, and no signs of strangulation. We should have toxicology reports in another day or two and that will hopefully tell us something more. At any rate, a couple weeks after Mr. Reginald’s death, the same perpetrator, allegedly, shot and killed Mr. Brandon Barnes in an apartment building lobby. The motive, we’re assuming, has something to do with Alex Rhodes. Is that correct?”

“She believes so,” Megan said. “And so far we have no reason to dispute it.”

“And the only witness to this latest murder is Rhodes herself?”

“Yes, and she’s—”

“Blind as a bat,” Weiserman finished. “That’s just beautiful.” He ran a hand over his bald head. “Did we, by chance, get anything useful from forensics?”

“Define useful,” Zanetti said. “We know he used a jacketed hollow point round. The slug was recovered and it’s so deformed it looks like a wad of old chewing gum. Even if we had the weapon I doubt our best ballistics expert could definitively pair the two.”

“He had a Glock 9,” Megan said. “We could see that in the security video. The 40 caliber round we recovered could have come from that gun. We know it did, but proving it is another matter. The Scott Fisher on that cruise ship didn’t look anything like the guy that walked Alex Rhodes home from the subway before turning homicidal. We’re never going to get anywhere with this thing until we find out who the son of a bitch really is.” She looked at Zanetti and then stared down at her notepad as if the answer might be hidden there somewhere but Megan knew it wasn’t.

She felt like they should be so close to a major breakthrough. They had video from the subway station that showed Fisher creating a disturbance, approaching Rhodes, and then leading her away. In a second video--thirteen minutes later based on the time stamp--he burst into the apartment lobby, pulled a gun and shot a man dead. Rhodes fled and Fisher spent a few seconds tidying the scene and getting the body out of sight. He then plucked Rhode's keys from her purse and entered the elevator, not to appear again. He must have exited via the stairs and a side entrance, and Megan wondered if that had been before or after the police arrived.

She tore the top page from her pad, crumpled it into a ball and flung it across the room. "We've got nothing!" she said. "He commits a murder on video and with a witness and we're still no closer to catching the guy."

"And what about that forensics report?" Weiserman asked, retrieving the paper projectile and dropping it into a trash can. "I haven't had a chance to look at it yet."

"Don't waste your time," Megan said. "There's nothing to see."

"Smudged prints all over the lobby door handle and glass," Zanetti explained. "No surprise with so many people going in and out. He might have actually used his coat sleeve when he opened the door. Regardless, we didn't get anything useable."

"Bastard," Megan interjected.

"He shot Mr. Barnes and then put gloves on before proceeding."

"Something tells me he's done this before," Weiserman said.

"Seems so," Zanetti agreed. "He was in Ms. Rhodes' apartment long enough to search every room. He touched some things, removed others, but didn't leave any prints or DNA."

"We did get some hair fibers," Megan said without enthusiasm. "They came from a plain brown wig and are so common they're practically untraceable. That's the extent of our physical evidence."

"You guys should go home," Weiserman said. "But, because I know you're not going to listen to me, do this instead." He pulled out his wallet, extracted two twenties and dropped them on Megan's desk. "Order yourselves some pizza… on me. I know you're frustrated and I understand it. Keep digging and something will turn up. In the meantime, I've found that pizza makes everything better."

Later, long after Captain Weiserman departed and the empty, grease-stained pizza box had been shoved to the side, Zanetti stood, stretched, and walked to the window where he parted the blinds to gaze out at the city.

"He's out there you know. Probably trying to figure out how to finish what he started. So what are we going to do to stop him?"

"Hell if I know," Megan said, using three fingers to work the tightened muscles at the back of her neck. "The asshole is giving me an inferiority complex."

Zanetti returned to his desk and poked at the stack of papers and file folders. "So I'll ask again. How do we stop him? What's our next trick?"

Megan studied her partner. She knew he'd stay all night if that's what she wanted but she could see the dark smudges under his eyes. Her own eyes felt tired, red-rimmed, and bone dry. She also had a headache and realized it wouldn't be improved by putting any more time in that night. She needed a break; they both did, but Megan had a hard time walking away when there was so much left undone.

"What do we actually know about him?" she asked, pulling her blazer from the back of her chair and slipping it on.

Zanetti looked at her. "We going somewhere?"

"Yes, because I've made a discovery."

"Great. Are we ready to make an arrest?"

"Not quite. What I've discovered is that Wigs was wrong and pizza, though satisfying, doesn't make everything better. We're not getting anywhere and I think we need to step back for a while. I'm going home and I recommend you do the same."

"I'm all for that," Zanetti said, pushing the mess of paperwork on his desk into one untidy stack.

Megan watched him, amused. "Is that what your apartment looks like too? It's no wonder your wife walked out on you."

"I'm not sure she did. She might just be buried under one of the piles. I'll find her one of these days."

"Such a romantic," Megan said, moving toward the door. "But getting back to Fisher, what do we know about him?"

"You mean other than a whole bunch of nothing?"

"That's not true.'

"How so? It feels like we've been following a vapor trail since \we started."

"Well," Megan said. "We know he's a professional. That's something. And I think we agree there's a high probability he's working for someone else."

"Clayton Babbit?"

"Presumably."

"Are you suggesting we try to lean on him?"

"I'm pretty sure Louisiana is out of our jurisdiction. We could get help from another agency, possibly federal," Megan added with reluctance.

"But no one's gonna listen to us until we can present a stronger case. All we have now is conjecture and not enough of that to give us any bargaining power."

"I've got to make a confession," Zanetti said.

"Do I want to hear this?"

He paused as if not sure how to respond. "I might have called him today."

Megan stopped short. "You did what?"

"I called Babbit," Zanetti said.

"Are you crazy? We can't let him know we're onto him. That could ruin everything."

"Relax," Zanetti said, prodding her gently to get her moving again. "I'm no rookie. I didn't identify myself as law enforcement and I wasn't about to start throwing accusations at him. I just wanted to get some general information about beach restoration in case I needed to hire his company. Who knows where a conversation like that might lead?'

"That's good," Megan acknowledged. "I'm impressed."

"That's what she said," Zanetti quipped and Megan smacked his arm.

"And what did Mr. Babbit have to say?"

"As a matter of fact, nothing. He's out of town on business and the guy I spoke to, a Louie something or other, didn't seem to know where he was going or when he'd be back."

"When did he leave?"

"Sometime yesterday."

"Curious timing. The story of Martin Reginald's murder goes public and Clayton Babbit disappears?"

"That wasn't lost on me either. So now we've got speculation and coincidence. I'd say we're kickin' ass with both feet."

Megan bit her lip, something she often did when deep in thought. "It sounds like Babbit is a dead end for now."

"Agreed."

"So that means we're left with Scott Fisher. We think he's after Alex Rhodes, right?"

"Seems obvious enough."

"Yeah, so how did he even find out about her? Her identity as the author of those books was a carefully guarded secret. According to everyone we've spoken to, very few people knew anything about it. If that's true, how did Fisher find out who she is and what she looks like?"

"Are you suggesting he had inside help?"

"I don't know," Megan said, thinking about the meeting at Tower Brothers and how Vicki Goldstein and Peter Ireland seemed at odds. "Depending on how this plays out," she continued, "the publisher could take a big PR hit that might impact sales. Why would anyone there risk something like that?"

"Then what are you saying?" Zanetti asked.

"I'm not sure. Fisher first approached her in the subway but must have identified her sometime earlier. Maybe, if we can figure out how and when, that will give us something more to go on."

"Do you have any ideas?"

"I might," Megan said, biting her lip again. "Try to get a good night's sleep. I have a feeling we'll be looking at more video first thing tomorrow morning."

-40-

"I'll be fine!" I insisted, practically shoving Vicki to the door.

"Are you sure?" She had her coat on and purse in hand, but didn't seem committed to actually leaving. "I can stay longer. I don't have anything on my calendar until ten. That's just an interview and I could push it back until the afternoon."

"Why would you do that?"

"So you don't have to be here alone."

I gave her my best hairy eyeball. "I know it may not seem like it sometimes but I'm a big girl and perfectly capable of taking care of myself. The interview is about me and my novels, right? That's free publicity which means book sales. That's the priority here. I shouldn't have to tell you that."

I had her with that one. Since the press conference the morning before, sales of Martin Reginald books had spiked on Amazon by almost seven hundred percent. As the vice president of Tower Brothers Publishing, I knew Vicki would want to do everything in her power to ride that wave as long as possible because, sooner or later, it had to break.

"All right," she said, still hesitant. "If you want, I could send Jess over here today or you could come and work at the office now that you have a computer. That one will work for you, right?"

She was referring to the laptop she'd given me. Tower Brothers recently upgraded several of their laptops and they still had a few of the old ones lying around. One of those was now in my possession, and it was an upgrade for me too because their *old* computers were nicer, newer, and faster than the one I'd lost.

"It will be fine," I assured her. "Thank you for that and thanks for helping me get my magnifier software installed. I've got some customization to do but I can handle that on my own. You've been a huge help and I really do appreciate it."

Now go to work already.

"So what about Jess then?"

"What about her?" I asked, my gratitude morphing into exasperation. "You need an assistant; I don't, and I don't need a babysitter either. I've got a phone, a computer, and your Wi-Fi password. You brought home enough food for a month. And between the window bars, the security system, the deadbolt, and the security chain, I'm perfectly safe. There's no chance anyone's getting in. You need to go to work and I need to get to work so I can finish that novel. I'm assuming you still want me to do that?"

"Of course, Alex. But only if you're ready."

Ready? Her concern was touching, if not a little over the top. It wasn't like I'd escaped from weeks in captivity. I just had a mad man after me and by all accounts he wanted me dead.

Okay, I'll admit it. Even tucked away in Vicki's brownstone fortress, I was still freaked out about the whole thing. Part of me thought a constant companion sounded pretty good and part of me wanted to curl into a ball and start sucking my thumb.

I was fine most of the time—almost feeling like myself again. Then, out of nowhere, I'd start thinking about Brandon and how, in the blink of an eye, he was there and then he wasn't. No matter how long I lived, I knew I'd never forget the pungent odor of cordite or the pitiable, unearthly sound he made as he dropped to the floor.

I knew what would happen. If Vicki stayed home or sent Jess over to spend the next eight hours holding my hand, I'd keep reliving those terrible moments because there wouldn't be anything else to occupy my mind. I'd slipped down that rabbit hole a few times the day before and had no interest in a return visit. My new strategy was to get back in that proverbial saddle and try to get some real writing done. I figured it would be good therapy if nothing else. And if my muse was metaphorically holled up in a clothes dryer somewhere and unwilling to make an appearance, I already had my backup plan in place. Vicki's wine rack was full and I made sure I knew where to find the opener.

I finally got rid of the housemother with promises to check in periodically throughout the day. I also told her not to get concerned if she didn't hear from me for a while. It just meant I was in the zone and making solid progress on the manuscript. She wasn't thrilled with that, but understood it from all he years dealing with authors and our various whims and quirks. I liked to think I was one of the more normal ones. However, given my modern-day hermit lifestyle, I didn't have much basis for comparison. For all I knew, Vicki thought I was crazy as a bed bug on meth. She left me alone, though, and that's what I'd been after.

I made coffee and toast and then fired up my new computer, actually excited about what lay ahead. It had only been a couple days since my last writing session but I felt like I'd been away from it much, much longer. As a way of easing myself back in, I took my time getting the color settings, font size, and other accessibility options set to my satisfaction. I then downloaded the appropriate file, activated the document reader tool, and listened to the last two chapters I'd completed plus the one in progress. What followed was a prolonged period of quiet reflection. That's a nice way of saying I didn't accomplish squat. Monty the Muse was MIA, as usual, and it seemed remounting that saddle was going to be tougher than I supposed.

I had plenty of excuses for my lack of productivity. The new keyboard was unfamiliar and my fingers kept ending up out of place. Vicki had an entire grocery store in her kitchen yet didn't stock the hazelnut creamer I preferred. Worst of all, I couldn't figure out how to use her stereo. I needed music to concentrate, which meant I had to resort to the tinny computer speaker or the even tinnier speaker on my phone. It was painful. Out of desperation, I even tried using my headphones for a while but the stupid cord kept getting in the way. When I broke for lunch, a lot earlier than usual, I'd added one whole paragraph to my masterpiece and I knew it would be history as soon as I sat back down again.

The real problem, I realized, munching on a dill pickle spear, had absolutely nothing to do with creamers, keyboards, or stereos. Cold, hard reality had forced its way into my carefully-crafted fictional world. I always knew, or at least assumed, my Deepwater books contained some element of truth. It wasn't my truth, though, and that had allowed me to maintain a creative and personal distance. I never believed I was hurting anyone. I was just telling a story, and that was all well and good until Charles Briggs wasn't Charles Briggs anymore. He was Clayton Babbit III, and apparently pretty perturbed by what I'd done.

I'd reached the point in my three-novel narrative where, speaking proverbially again, the shit was about to hit the fan in a big way. Following the aftermath of the oil rig explosion, spill, and cleanup, all of which Briggs both had a hand in and greatly benefitted from, he did everything he could to shift the blame, making it appear that Olivia Gerhart, an overzealous environmentalist, had been responsible for the whole mess. Her motive, so claimed Briggs, was to demonstrate the evils of fossil fuels by causing historic devastation. Oil companies would suffer and her green energy interests would reap the rewards. It sounds farfetched I know, but it actually played out surprisingly well. I've always been big on character development. Create the right sort of character and he or she can believably be capable of just about anything.

That, I supposed, was why I'd had such a hard time with Charles Briggs. My characters usually sprang from whole cloth. I'd have to spend time getting to know them before I had any inkling of how they might respond to a given situation. I'd never dealt with real people or real events. I didn't know if Clayton Babbit was, in fact, the person Bryan Royal had told his sister about, or if the accusations he'd made were anything more than the products of paranoia and an overactive imagination. However, the Deepwater Horizon disaster was as real as it got, so anything I did had to fit the framework of that well-publicized incident. Maybe that was how, without meaning to, I'd evidently tip-toed a little too close to the truth. It seemed hindsight was 20/20 even for the visually impaired and I now realized I should have written just one book, demonized the imaginary Olivia Gerhart and left Clayton Babbit and his fictional counterpart out of it.

Woulda, shoulda, coulda, I thought, again plunking myself down at the computer.

Based on the sketchy outline I'd made for the last few chapters of the book, the police finally had enough evidence to link Charles Briggs to his crimes. He finds out the net is closing, makes a run for it, and dies in a blaze of glory shootout. I wasn't crazy about the various cliché aspects of the climax and hoped that, when I got to that point, something better would occur to me.

I looked at the single paragraph I'd painstakingly produced before lunch, re-read it a couple times and, as expected, sent it off to word processor heaven. I found that I couldn't write Charles Briggs without thinking Clayton Babbit, and Scott Fisher by extension, and that was really messing with my head. How could I bring Briggs any closer to meeting his maker without feeling the noose tightening around my own neck?

Maybe, I thought, after another thirty infertile minutes had gone by and my word count was right where it had been, *I could change the end of the book. Sure! It was all a misunderstanding. Charles Briggs was a victim of circumstances and guilty of nothing worse than benefitting financially from such an unfortunate event. Instead of suicide by cop, he could suffer tremendous remorse and my epic trilogy could end with a generous charitable donation.*

"Oh yeah," I said, standing to stretch my legs. "If my publisher didn't lynch me for that one my readers would." I had to smile at that, thinking my next book could be a how-to manual on destroying a literary career in three chapters or less.

Remembering I hadn't checked in with command central for a while, I called Vicki and assured her all was well. I figured she'd grill me on my progress, *or lack thereof,* but I'd caught her on the way to a meeting, about me I was sure, and she thankfully hadn't had time to press me for details. I hung up the phone with the same feeling of reprieve I used to get in grade school when a snow day saved me from a test I hadn't studied for. Of course, the teacher would be home four or five hours hence and I really wanted to give her something more than a host of apologies and excuses.

"Focus," I instructed. But instead of looking at the laptop, my eyes somehow strayed to the kitchen entrance, or more specifically, the tall wine rack positioned just to the left. Monty was fond of a nice pinot and I wondered if a small glass might coax him out of hiding. I was still debating the merits and potential pitfalls of indulging so early in the day when the ring of the doorbell brought me up short.

Who could that be? I thought, glancing that way but otherwise making no move.

I believed there were only four people who knew my current whereabouts. The first was Vicki and I'd just spoken to her. She wouldn't be ringing her own bell anyway. It likewise couldn't be Jess, because when I'd called Vicki's office, she was the one who'd answered the phone. That left Megan Lynch and Detective Zanetti.

A break in the case? I thought, starting to rise. *Maybe they've made an arrest and I can go home.* I considered that and there was a bounce in my step as I crossed the short distance to the foyer.

The glass in and around Vicki's front door was both contoured and frosted which made it nearly impossible to see out. Her security system was equipped with a camera and miniature monitor, but like everything else in her house, they were designed for people with vision a lot better than mine. I brought my face up close and squinted at the screen. What I could make out was a long coat, long blonde hair, and a person that couldn't seem to stand still. The woman—I assumed female from hair length and style—kept wringing her hands and looking back and forth between Vicki's front door and something on the street behind her.

My first instinct was to back away. I was sure I didn't know the person so what could she want of me? How could she know that I, or anyone for that matter, was even at home? However, something about her demeanor and her body language, told me something was wrong.

"Who is it?" I called out before realizing I'd made the decision to make my presence known.

"Oh, thank God!" she said, in a voice high and lilting.

Maybe Irish?

"Please help me?" She begged, coming a step closer to the door. "I don't know what to do. My baby is locked in the car. I stopped to mail a letter and.... I don't know what happened but I don't have my phone or a second key. I need to get her out of there. She's scared and starting to cry." The woman sounded like she was ready to burst into tears too.

"I'm sorry," I said, her mounting panic getting to me. I immediately flashed back to a time when I was three or four and my parents briefly abandoned me in an airport. I was alone for a couple minutes at most. But in my young and uncomprehending mind, I thought I'd been left forever. That fear stayed with me for years.

"Would you like me to call the police?" I asked. "I'm sure they can help."

"Yes, please!" she said, and I saw her brushing away tears. "Or, if you've got a phone I could use, I'll call my husband. He works nearby and he's got the spare key. That would be faster."

Call me gullible, or stupid, but it never occurred to me that the frantic woman on the stoop posed a threat. I was also aware I'd promised Vicki and Megan I'd be careful, stay on my guard, and not let anyone in under any circumstances. None of us, of course, had counted on this.

I could call the cops like I'd suggested. I was sure they'd respond quickly. The problem was that I didn't actually know what street Vicki lived on. I'd never thought to ask. So how was I supposed to give them a location? I couldn't. And it sounded like she preferred to call her husband anyway. If I unlocked the door but left the chain in place, would the gap be large enough to pass my cell phone through?

It doesn't matter, I realized. My phone's various accessibility settings, the VoiceOver tool in particular, would make it difficult for anyone else to use. The woman was worried about her baby. Could I really expect her to listen patiently while I tried to explain the finer nuances of customized tapping and swiping?

No, I knew, and without much hesitation, I unlocked and opened the door.

"Thank you!" she said, stepping inside. "You are a life saver. I'm so sorry to trouble you. If you'll show me to the phone I'll make my call and be on my way."

"It's okay," I assured her. "The phone's in the kitchen. Right this way."

I turned to indicate the direction and, as I did, the breeze that accompanied her in brought a strangely familiar scent to my nose. It took me a moment to place. It was sweet, spicy, and masculine, and I'd first encountered it days before when a gentleman stranger approached me in the 59th Street subway station.

It's him! I thought, and I knew I'd been duped again. This time, though, Scott Fisher's sudden appearance did not freeze me in my tracks. I bolted for the back of the house. He was already giving chase but it didn't matter because I had a head start and a perfect exit strategy. I'd run into the master bedroom, slam and lock the door, and then scoot out by way of the fire escape. I would have gotten away with it too if not for that fucking living room step. I tripped, fell on my face, and then all the breath left my body in a rush as two knees came down squarely in the middle of my back. I tried to scream but it came out somewhere between a gasp, a gag, and a choke.

"Fancy meeting you here," Fisher said, the feminine lilt replaced by something more familiar and more menacing.

This is it, I thought. *I'm gonna die.*

I heard a soft whistling sound and something struck the base of my skull. I saw a flash of color, bluish I think, and then nothing.

-41-

Mikhail Vasilek finished with his last zip tie and stepped back to admire his handiwork. The woman wouldn't be going anywhere for a while, but he knew she'd have one whiz-bang of a headache when she came to. He hoped that wouldn't take long, and chided himself on sapping her with so much enthusiasm.

He understood why he'd done it. He'd overreacted to letting her get the jump on him again. She had spunk. He had to give her that much. Fortunately, she was also blind and clumsy, and she'd gone down before he'd even touched her. He'd used the leather sap anyway, ostensibly to prevent her from crying out. Could she have really done so?

Probably not, he acknowledged, listening to her labored but steady breathing. He'd landed on her harder than necessary too, and knew he'd knocked the wind out of her.

Serves you right, Vasilek thought, returning to the foyer to relock the front door.

His plan to get inside the house had been a work of art. Who could turn away from a mother in distress? *Who indeed?*

Vasilek smiled grimly as he surveyed the brownstone's spacious interior. The owner had money as he'd already surmised. But what especially appealed to him were the thick walls, prevalence of frosted glass, and the blackout style drapes that hung in many rooms. Curious passersby wouldn't be able to see or hear what he was up to, and he'd be sure Rhodes would know that, once she was alert enough for conversation.

He was sure she wouldn't have gotten away even if she hadn't fallen on her face. Still, he wondered what tipped her off. There was no way she'd seen through his disguise. He knew that. But right before she'd run he'd looked into her eyes and seen that flash of recognition. She had known him. How? What was the trigger? Vasilek decided he'd add that to the list of things they could chat about, *if,* he amended, *she lives long enough.*

That part remained to be seen and it was why, although he was in control of the situation, he was also on edge. Vasilek was a killer plain and simple. He didn't involve himself in other people's problems or their business. He just did his job, collected his pay and moved on. It wasn't supposed to get complicated.

Because of the tight confines of the cruise ship, the Reginald hit had been more involved than some others. In the end, though, it was just another hit. He'd done his part and literally walked away undetected. Now, however, due to circumstances beyond anything he could have anticipated, Clayton Babbit had roped him back in. In addition to murder, with which Vasilek was all too familiar, he was engaged in… *what exactly?* The short list included burglary, illegal entry, felony assault, kidnapping, maybe abduction, and who knew what else?

From a legal standpoint, he didn't especially care what crimes he committed. Next to a possible murder charge none of the rest of it made much difference. And the thing about murder was that it was clean, safe, easy, and he could often do it from a distance. That was how he'd been able to operate in the shadows for years without any real fear of discovery. Babbit, through his demands and mistakes, had put all of that in jeopardy and drawn him into the light.

It was the latest set of instructions that had Vasilek pacing the room, muttering to himself and rhythmically clenching and unclenching his fists. "It won't work," he said, dreading the call he knew could come any second. "He's crazy."

Once again, had Babbit merely wanted the woman dead it would have already happened. Vasilek could have choked the life out of her the second she opened the door. He would have too had Babbit not realized Rhodes could do as much damage dead as alive. He still wanted her eliminated, but only after the bombshell she controlled had been located and defused. The items Vasilek found in her apartment were no longer good enough. Babbit was after the keys to the cyber castle. That, Vasilek believed, was an unattainable prize but he was being forced to go after it just the same.

He swung the sap slowly back and forth, his right hand tingling with the desire to crack Alex Rhodes one time in the side of the head. That's all it would take. He could tell Babbit she'd struggled and while trying to subdue her, he'd accidentally gone too far. The guy would be furious but what could he say?

Vasilek stopped, watching the rise and fall of her chest as he absently twisted the sap's smooth leather strap around one finger. The problem, he decided, was that he didn't have a real sense of what Clayton Babbit knew about him or what he might be capable of if provoked. He was also irritated with himself for ever suggesting Rhodes might have stored documents and other data online. Had he kept his mouth shut about that maybe Babbit wouldn't have thought of it and

Vasilek wouldn't be standing there, in a stranger's home, and with a trussed up woman at his feet.

"Shit!" he swore, swinging the sap hard but pulling back before it made contact.

He did still have one out. With his expertise, his *skill set,* he could drop off the grid. It would be a simple matter to adopt the Olga Belenkaya persona, or one of the many other identities available to him, and vanish. Babbit could expend all his vast resources searching for him and it would be to no avail. The only catch was that Vasilek would have to swallow some professional pride. He didn't know if he could do that because he'd never run from a fight nor failed to complete a mission.

Something else was giving him pause too. The Martin Reginald job had been the most lucrative of his career and successful completion of his latest assignment would pay even more. He could, if he chose, cash out and retire from the business or at least be a lot more selective as to the types of jobs he accepted. It was a simple choice. Walk away now and trade his pride for freedom; or hang around, get what Babbit wanted, and collect a monster payoff. That's assuming he wasn't caught in the process. *Did New York have the death penalty?* He wasn't sure.

Vasilek was still thinking about what he might request as his last meal when he heard the sudden snap of metal. He spun around, in one motion dropping the sap and pulling the Glock from the small of his back. He half expected to see a SWAT team drawing down on him but the only motion came from the mail slot in the front door as it clicked back into place. He then saw the small stack of letters that came to rest on the foyer floor.

"Fucking mailman," he said, getting to the security monitor in time to see an old fat guy descend the steps, stop to catch his breath, and then head off to the left.

"That's right, Grandpa. Nothing to see here."

Vasilek turned back around and saw that Alex Rhodes had woken up and was staring at him. Or, he thought she was. It was hard to tell with that weird-ass gaze floating somewhere over his shoulder, and one of her eyes was more off-center than the other. It was bizarre and he wondered how much detail she could really make out. Maybe they'd discuss that later but there were more important items on the agenda.

"Good morning," he said, his tone thick with sarcasm. "I trust you slept well."

Rhodes blinked but said nothing.

"That's okay," he continued, walking over to stand in front of her. "You didn't know the rules but we can fix that. Rule number one." He held up his index finger and waved it in front of her nose. "You can see that, right?"

She still didn't reply.

Vasilek looked at her and then, without warning, he backhanded her across the side of the face. She cried out and tears sprung to her eyes. He also saw a drop of blood at the corner of her mouth and a quickly darkening red mark on her right cheek.

"Rule number one is that you answer my questions. Understand?"

She still didn't reply, but after a moment gave a slow nod.

Something in her expression—*Was it defiance?*—irritated him and he was tempted to smack her again. He stopped himself with some effort. She had answered after all, and he didn't think he'd get anywhere if he started thumping her for no reason. The blow had been more to get her attention than anything else and he guessed his message had been delivered.

"Rule number two," Vasilek said, strolling around to take up a position directly behind her chair, "is that you don't cause any trouble. That means no shouting for help. It won't do you any good anyway. No one's around and no one would hear you." He bent over so his lips were mere inches from her ear. "Be a good girl and we'll get along fine. But, if you make a nuisance of yourself, if you make things difficult, I promise you will regret it. Do you understand that?"

"Yes," Rhodes said stiffly. She didn't move her head or try to crane around to see him but kept her body straight and rigid.

She's tough, Vasilek thought, impressed in spite of himself. *Let's see what we can do about that.*

"I have one more rule," he said, his voice calm and reasonable. "It's the simplest of all. Give me what I want or you're dead." He reached out and touched an area of bare skin at the nape of her neck. She spasmed like she'd just received a thousand volts straight up the ass.

"My, my," he purred. "We are jumpy today."

"What do you want?" she asked, leaning away from him as much as she could

"I guess I didn't make myself clear," Vasilek replied, moving to stand in front of her again. "I ask the questions. You answer them."

"Why should I?" she asked with a tremor. "You're Scott Fisher, right? You killed Martin and Brandon. You're not going to let me live whether I help you or not."

Damn, Vasilek thought, cocking his head as he considered her. *Tough and a little too smart for her own good.* She was right, of course. It wasn't like he would or could let her go. If she already knew that, how was he going to convince her to cooperate?

The problem was more complicated than it seemed. Vasilek was good at a lot of things but an interrogation expert he was not. He didn't, as the movies would say, *have ways of making her talk.* He'd perfected methods of killing people, not hurting them as a means of persuasion. When it came to that he was far out of his depth. And, to make matters worse, he was pressed for time. The home owner would return at some point and, when she did, he couldn't still be standing there, hedge clippers in hand and a growing collection of Rhodes' fingers and toes scattered on the floor.

He looked at her, and she glared back as if she really expected an answer to her question.

Fine. If that's how she wanted to play it, Vasilek decided he would be as blunt as the business end of his sap and try to use that to his advantage. He was about to explain that her eminent demise could be peaceful or extremely painful and the choice was hers, but before he could get into any of that the cell phone in his pocket chirped.

"This is your lucky day, he said, glancing at the screen. "I've got to take this. Depending on how it goes, maybe I'll be able to save us both a lot of trouble."

He gave her a wink and then realized she probably couldn't see it. "I'm not a fan of the Q & A session," he explained. "I think it's a waste of time. I'd rather slit your throat and be done with it but there are others involved."

Rhodes opened her mouth and then closed it again without a word.

"Here's the deal," Vasilek said, grabbing the sap off the floor for emphasis. "I don't need you listening to my conversation so I'm going into the next room. I'm leaving the door open and I WILL be checking on you. You are to remain quiet and still. You can test me if you want but it will be the last thing you ever do. Are we clear on that?"

Rhodes blinked and nodded her head, and Vasilek retreated into the kitchen.

"Yes," he answered, wondering what sort of messed up orders Babbit would give him this time.

"Hey Sport," he boomed, an echoey quality to his voice like he was on speaker phone. "You got her?"

"As a matter of fact I do. She's incapacitated at the moment but otherwise unharmed."

"And you're in a safe location?"

"For now."

"Good," Babbit said. "Glad to hear you did something right for a change. I hope you don't let her get away again."

"That will not happen," Vasilek replied, spying a dangerous looking boning knife on the butcher block and realizing there was one more throat he might like to cut.

"I'm sure that's true. Has she told you anything yet?"

"We were just getting to that." Vasilek poked his head around the corner and confirmed that Rhodes hadn't moved. "I assume my instructions are unchanged? I am to gain access to whatever online storage sites she uses and delete everything I find. Is that correct?"

"Yes and no," Babbit said, adding a four letter expletive but Vasilek could tell it hadn't been directed at him. "Stupid Yankee jackoff," Babbit said, his comment punctuated by a blast from a car horn.

"I'm sure I can convince—" Vasilek began but Babbit cut him off.

"Last time we spoke, didn't you say you'd be somewhere in Brooklyn?"

"Yes," Vasilek said, mentally kicking himself for divulging that information. Of course, if Babbit was tracking him then he'd already known his whereabouts, and what difference did it make anyway? He soon found out.

"I got some good news, Sport. I'm coming to see you."

"WHAT?" Vasilek asked, his voice rising with his blood pressure.

"Yep. I figure I'm about an hour out. Maybe a little more with this fucking traffic. How do people live in this place anyway?"

"You don't need to come here," Vasilek insisted, still too loudly. "I've got it under control."

He didn't catch Babbit's response, because for a second, he thought he'd heard Alex Rhodes talking. He looked but she was still just sitting there, her eyes closed and her lips moving slightly. Maybe she was saying prayers.

Good luck with that, he thought. *Divine intervention is your only hope.*

"I have this well in hand," Vasilek said into the phone. "You don't need—"

"What I don't need," Babbit interrupted, "is to take orders from you. That ain't the way this works. Give me the address so I can put it in the GPS."

"That isn't necessary. I—"

"Listen," Babbit said, his voice as cold as a cancer diagnosis. "Don't try to tell me what's necessary. It's my ass in a sling. I need to make sure this job is done right so I'm stepping in. While you're waiting for me, see if you can soften our girl up some. Screw her if you want. Just don't rough her up too bad. I want her awake and alert when I get there."

Again, Vasilek thought he heard Rhodes talking but he ignored it. It wasn't like she could talk her way out of the zip ties that secured her hands and ankles.

Seeing no other choice, he gave Babbit the address of the brownstone but again tried to plead his case. "This is a residential neighborhood," he argued. "People know each other. I went to great lengths to get in here without attracting attention."

"And I'm a dumb ass country bumpkin and I'd blow the whole thing, right?"

That was almost word for word what Vasilek had been thinking but he knew enough not to say that out loud. "I'm just afraid of this getting too complicated. Give me some time and I'll get you what you want."

"Too late, Sport. I'm on my way. See you in sixty."

-42-

This is not good, I thought, squinting down at the thin straps securing my wrists to the arms of the chair. The things were dark in color and felt like they were made of plastic. I had a bit of wiggle room. Given sufficient time and privacy, I imagined I might be able to work my way free. Unfortunately, both of those were in disturbingly short supply. Fisher, or whoever he was, kept appearing in the kitchen doorway and I knew he was checking on me. I didn't relish the thought of another smack in the head so I couldn't do much more than sit there, bite back my frustration, and wait for him to finish on the phone. From his heated tone, it was clear the conversation wasn't going his way and I hoped he wouldn't take that out on me.

Each time he withdrew I tried to test my limits without being obvious about it. Although I couldn't get a good look at my ankles, I assumed they were bound in similar fashion. My torso, however, was unrestrained. If pressed I thought I might be able to stand. The effort would be futile because I'd be bowed backwards and pinned to the chair at each extremity. That seemed like an awkward way to try to make my escape. The chair was heavy too. I knew that would prevent me from doing anything heroic. Like it or not, *and for the record I didn't,* I was about as stuck as stuck could be. I had one chance and I'd taken it with all the confidence General Custer must have felt the moment he realized he'd underestimated the size and strength of his enemy. Or, as Charlie Brown would probably say, I was doomed.

From what little I'd gathered, it sounded like we were preparing for company—*and there I was without a thing to wear.* So who could Fisher have been talking to? I thought I already knew. And somehow, the prospect of coming face to face with Clayton Babbit III was even more terrifying than my current predicament which already had me in the clutches of a murderer.

Fisher, I believed, had been hired to, well, I'll go literary here and say *cancel my subscription.* I thought about poor Brandon and imagined, naively perhaps, a similarly quick demise. With Babbit, however, there was a personal component. I'd attacked him through my novels and it was possible, once he got his hands on me, he'd take pleasure in prolonging the occasion just to make me suffer.

Since I had nothing better to do, I reflected on the epically brainless decision that got me into this predicament. I'd been tucked away at

Vicki's, safe and sound and completely out of reach. Then, like an idiot bimbo from a 1980's horror flick, I'd unwittingly opened the door to the man from whom I'd been trying to hide. One of the few things the cops actually knew about Scott Fisher was that he was a master of disguise. I'd been specifically warned about that and I like to think I've got a pretty good head on my shoulders most of the time. I guess I just didn't think there was any way the monster could have found me again, certainly not so soon. That's my only excuse for such a horrible lapse in judgment. As recompense, I feared I'd be paying my pound of flesh and then some.

Fisher hadn't made any demands yet but you didn't have to be an astrophysicist to know what he was after. Sadly, I couldn't even convince myself I'd be able to put up much of a fight. I'm aware of my weaknesses, and one of them is a low pain tolerance. If Fisher, or Clayton Babbit for that matter, started getting nasty—electrodes, thumb screws, ice picks, and the soundtrack from *Frozen*—I knew I'd cave faster than Kim Kardashian can snap a dozen selfies.

Curiously, it seemed Scott Fisher was feeling some trepidation too. I didn't know if he and Babbit had met before, but it was obvious he wasn't looking forward to seeing him now. He kept stalking back and forth, and muttering in a foreign language. It sounded Russian to me but could have been German, Polish, or almost anything else. I briefly wondered where he was from and then realized I didn't care. I just wanted him out of my life. And, with any luck, my mortality would stretch beyond the next few minutes.

Fisher stopped in front of the big living room window and looked through a slit in the drapes. Then, he moved to the foyer, stooped, and picked up something off the floor.

"Who is Victoria Goldstein," he asked, and my inner sleuth deduced that he'd grabbed a stack of mail. I then had to translate what he'd said.

Victoria? I don't know any…. Oh yeah.

"She goes by Vicki," I said. "She's the president and CEO of Tower Brothers Publishing." I wasn't sure those were her actual titles but figured it was close enough.

"Does anyone else live here?"

I hesitated as I considered fabricating a tale about Vicki's Army Ranger husband. He was six and a half feet tall, a weapons specialist, always got home in the middle of the afternoon and usually came in shooting. I was about to tell a scaled-down version of that story but then thought better of it. For Fisher to have found me he must already know something about Vicki and may have also spent some time watching her house. His question might be a test. And if I failed? I ran my tongue around the inside of my mouth where I could still taste blood.

"It's just her," I admitted, feeling like a wuss. "She's been letting me stay here the past couple days."

"And what time will she return?"

"I don't know. She didn't tell me."

Fisher stared at me and I shrank back as much as the chair would allow.

"I'm telling the truth," I said. "She got home at about six yesterday. I don't know what time she'll be back today. We didn't talk about it."

"Okay," he said, moving in close enough so I could get a decent look at his face.

He'd ditched the blonde wig but I could still see traces of lipstick and eye shadow. Or, I thought I could. I know that must sound crazy but it's sometimes hard to distinguish what's there in reality versus what my mind thinks should be there. Fisher had fooled me by pretending to be a woman and it was possible my detail-deprived brain hadn't completely given up on that charade.

"Here's what will happen," he said. "We have work to do and I need to know how long we've got to do it. So," he leaned in. "You will call Ms. Vicki Goldstein and find out when she'll be home."

"How—" I began, my throat constricted.

"I don't care how you do it, but get one thing straight." He grabbed my right elbow and squeezed, and the pain was spectacular. "If you say ANYTHING," his grip tightened and I could feel my arm going numb, "to try to tip her off, the next thing Tower Brothers publishes will be your obituary."

"You're gonna kill me anyway. Isn't that why you're here?" I glared at him even though every impulse told me to look away.

He held my gaze and I expected a slap or punch. Then, to my surprise and relief, he released my elbow and stepped back. I longed to massage the spots where his fingers dug in to my flesh but I couldn't do that. I instead sat, stared at my bindings, and tried not to cry.

"Honestly," Fisher said, his voice low, "and I am being honest. You'd have died in the subway if it were up to me."

Megan and I had discussed that and reached the same conclusion so I saw no need to comment. At that moment, I wasn't sure I possessed the power of speech anyway. *Did I really say I was more scared of Clayton Babbit? I take it back. Get this crazy bastard away from me.*

"I will give you a few moments to collect your thoughts," Fisher said, possibly sensing how close to the edge I really was. "Then, you will call and get the information I requested. There will be no tricks. Is that understood?"

I nodded dumbly.

"And as for your questions," he continued. "Mr. Babbit is on the way. Once he arrives he'll decide what we do with you. Until then, it's up to me."

Super, I thought. *Die now or die later. Thanks for the wonderful options."*

"I need a phone," I said, working to get my breathing under control. "I think there's one in the kitchen."

Fisher stared at me for what felt like a long time, as if he thought I was trying to get away with something.

I blinked my innocence. *Pay no attention to the man behind the curtain.*

He finally turned, disappeared momentarily, and came back with a small cordless telephone. It looked similar to the one I had at home. That was good. Maybe I could place the call without having to ask him which buttons were which. How demoralizing would that be? *Sorry to be a bother but would you mind helping me with this noose?*

"How do you want me to do this?" I asked, glancing at my still-bound wrists.

He didn't say anything but a shining blade appeared, seemingly out of thin air. One quick flick and my right hand was free.

Great, I thought. *A homicidal magician. This is getting better and better.*

"Make the call," Fisher growled. "I'll be listening so no funny business."

He handed me the phone and, for several nervous seconds, I blanked on Vicki's number. It came back to me, and my thumb searched for the tiny raised dot on the 5 so I could get my key pad bearings. I dialed, waited, and tried to tamp down my mounting anxiety.

Two rings and I was greeted with a cheerful, "Tower Brothers Publishing. This is Jess speaking. How can I help you?"

"Hey, Jess. It's Alex."

"Alex?" she asked, and I wished she hadn't sounded so surprised. "We just got—"

"Listen," I said. "I'm really sorry but I don't have time to talk. I've got a quick question for Vicki. Is she in?"

Fisher was bent over and he'd positioned his head so close to mine I could smell his breath. It wasn't bad, slightly minty actually, but the proximity still turned my stomach.

"She's here," Jess replied, "but she—"

"I know she's busy," I cut in. "I'm really sorry but this is important."

"Um, okay. Hold on a sec."

I heard a click and, after ten seconds or so, Vicki picked up.

"Alex?" she said. "Is everything all right? I just saw—"

"Everything's fine," I said, reassuring and interrupting her at the same time. "I'm sorry to bug you. I was just calling because, well, you've been so great taking me in and everything. I thought I'd make you a nice dinner tonight to say thanks. I need to know when you'll be home so I could have it all ready."

"But what about—"

"I really want to do this," I continued, looking at Fisher as he nodded his encouragement. "It's important to me."

There was a long pause and I was afraid she'd start asking questions. I bit my lip, and successfully managed not to vomit when Fisher pressed in so close our cheeks touched.

"Around six?" Vicki said finally. "Would that be okay?"

"Perfect," I replied, letting out a breath. "See you then." I disconnected before either of us could say anything more.

"Very good," Fisher said, demonstrating his gratitude by yanking the phone out of my hand, tossing it onto the floor and then re-securing my right wrist to the chair.

"Is that necessary?" I asked.

Fisher looked at me and appeared to consider. "Probably not," he said. "But I do not leave things to chance."

"Yeah, I sort of figured that."

He put his hands on his waist. "You seem like an intelligent woman. What else have you figured out?"

Shit, I thought. *Is this another test? Is he going to clobber me again if I say the wrong thing?* I hesitated, considered the odds I'd live long enough to listen to another episode of *Morning Edition*, and ultimately decided I didn't have a heck of a lot to lose.

"You're not really Scott Fisher," I said, hating the quaver that had crept into my voice. "The cops told me there's no such person, so what is your real name?"

"Does it matter?"

"I guess not. I was just curious."

"You know what they say about curiosity?"

I did, but decided to hold my tongue.

"You can call me Mikhail," he said after a beat.

"That's your real name?" I thought about the muttering I'd overheard. It had sounded Russian, and wasn't Mikhail Russian too?

"It will do," he said, the finality in his tone making it clear that subject was closed. I knew enough not to push.

"It's almost one-thirty now," he said, checking his watch and glancing towards the door. "Four and a half hours until Victoria Goldstein returns. That should give us more than enough time to do what we have to do."

I didn't think that sounded promising but wasn't given the opportunity to dwell on the unsettling implications.

"However," he continued, "Mr. Babbit will be here within the hour. He plans on taking over."

Fisher—*sorry, Mikhail*—walked a slow circle and then stopped, positioning himself right in front of me.

"I haven't met Mr. Babbit before but I think he is not a nice person.

Holy Christ! I thought. *This lunatic shoots innocent people without provocation yet tells me his partner doesn't work and play well with others? What could that mean? Never mind,* I decided. *I don't want to know.*

"My advice," Mikhail said, "is to be as cooperative as possible. Make things easy on yourself now so they don't get difficult later."

Yeah. And my advice to you is to go to hell and die.

"You broke into my apartment," I said, swallowing hard. "You stole my computer so you've already got my files. I don't have anything else."

He moved so fast I didn't have time to flinch. The slap was harder this time, leaving my cheek burning and both ears making a disconcerting, high-pitched buzzing noise. He may have loosened a tooth too.

"What was that for?" I asked before I could stop myself.

In response, the son of a bitch actually smiled. "I forgot to mention one of the rules," he said, rubbing his hand against the side of his leg. It probably stung. I hoped so, but I knew it couldn't hurt half as much as my face.

Coward, I thought. *Beat up a woman when she can't raise a hand to defend herself. My hero.*

"The last rule," he said, "is that you don't lie to me. I'll enforce that aggressively, as you now know."

While I blinked and tried to get my vision to clear, he walked over to the couch where my new laptop was open on an end table. He poked a key and then spent a few seconds staring at the mostly blank Word document. I hadn't authored anything incriminating that day. For once, it seemed my bout of writer's block had served me well. And thank God. I'd logged out of my OneDrive account. There was nothing there he hadn't already seen.

"Is this what you've been working on?" he asked with incredulity.

"Yes," I replied. *And fuck you very much for asking.*

"I assumed a famous author would be more prolific."

That hadn't been a question so I felt no need to respond. But, I don't mind telling you it was tough to sit there quietly while being judged by such an obvious example of human scum.

"At least you have a new computer," he said, coming back my way. "I did take the other one you know. You have a lovely home by the way—everything nice and organized. Even your night stand was very tidy."

My cheek was still burning but now more from anger and embarrassment than pain. He wanted to remind me of all the things he'd seen, and moved, and touched.

That's fine, I thought. *Just keep talking.*

"Here's my problem," he said. "I did take your computer and I saw the files you had stored there. It was all quite interesting. I understand why Mr. Babbit is upset with you. But he believes," he cooed, "and I have to agree, you must have backups stored elsewhere. What do you think about that? Before you answer, please remember my rule about lying."

I sat and stared at him, terrified and undecided. Of course, I had known we would get to this point eventually. I'd just been hoping it wouldn't happen so soon.

I wouldn't last long if he started really smacking me around. I didn't like admitting that, not even to myself, but I knew it was true. I mean, what chance did I have if I couldn't lift a finger in protection? *Okay, sure. My fingers were unrestrained. Technically I could still lift them but not much else.* I was in a completely vulnerable position. I had to sit there and take whatever he doled out.

On the other hand, if I did what he wished, if I gave in and provided my ID and password, what little bit of leverage I had would be gone. I might be gone just as fast. Would that be the best solution? It was the wimp's way out but I'd save myself a lot of pain and suffering. I looked at him, and my computer, and I wished I had more time to make up my mind.

"I do have a backup," I said, squeezing my eyes closed as if the admission itself was more agonizing than anything he might inflict.

"That's good!" He chuckled, proud of himself I was sure, and I felt like I needed to puke.

"I've got a OneDrive account."

"Thank you," he said, returning to my computer and beginning to type. It sounded like he was doing it with one finger. "Do you use any other online storage?"

"No," I said, wishing that was a lie.

"I don't know if I believe that," he told me, "but we'll leave it for now. And what about other copies of the files? Have you sent them to anyone? Your publisher for example?"

I had to think about that. The answer was no. No one ever saw any of my manuscripts until I had a clean draft. But what would happen if I made him believe otherwise? What would he and Clayton Babbit do if they thought the finished portions of the book were out of reach? Would they give up and go away? *No,* I thought, *because I'm not dealing with normal people. They'll just kill me and then try to figure out their next move.*

"I haven't shared it with anyone," I said. "And before you ask, there are no hard copies either."

"Okay," he said, pleased. "So let's have your sign in info and we'll get this over with."

Will I get a last cigarette at least? I'd like to shove it in your eyeball.

"My username is AlexR13, but I don't know if I remember the password."

He'd started typing but then stopped. "What do you mean you don't remember?"

"I change passwords all the time," I said, wondering if I'd really heard what I just thought I'd heard. I raised my voice and added a note of panic. "I keep them in a separate Word file but it was on my other computer. I think I know what the new one is but I can't promise it's right."

"You better not be fucking with me."

"No," I said, still louder. "I swear I'm telling the truth. I—"

The front door flew open then, slamming against the wall and smashing a large mirror to bits. Before my abductor could even stand up, Vicki's entryway was filled with cops in full assault gear. Megan walked in once the scene was secure, which seemed to only take a few seconds.

"Nice job," she said to me. "How'd you do it?"

-43-

"Captain Weiserman," Megan Lynch said. "I'd like you to meet Alex Rhodes and Vicki Goldstein."

"My pleasure," he replied, striding into one of the more comfortable 6th Precinct interview rooms and reaching across the table to shake their hands.

"Ms. Rhodes may have just broken our case for us."

"That's what I've been hearing." Weiserman said. He turned to Alex. "Detective Lynch has told me a lot about you. My wife is a big fan of your books. She'll be jealous when I tell her I met you in person.

Alex nodded and murmured her thanks.

"As of an hour ago," Megan said, "Ms. Rhodes was at the residence of Ms. Goldstein and being forcibly detained by the person we've been referring to as Scott Fisher. We now believe his first name is Mikhail. He hasn't volunteered anything more than that yet."

"Forcibly detained?" Weiserman inquired. "Ms. Rhodes, I hope you were not hurt."

"I'm fine," she said, looking at the Captain and then dropping her eyes.

"Minor injuries only," Megan elaborated. "He used zip ties to secure her arms and legs to a chair. She says he also hit her a couple times."

"I'm sorry to hear that. It must have been very frightening for you."

"She still managed to alert us," Detective Zanetti said, gazing at Alex with obvious admiration.

"That's what I understand," Captain Weiserman said. "Could you tell me how that was possible?" He was looking directly at Alex but she remained silent and Megan assumed she wasn't aware he'd asked the question of her.

"She texted me," Vicki said. "The message was garbled but I got the gist of it and contacted the police."

"I'm confused. She was bound but still able to text?" Weiserman spread his hands. "How?"

"Alex?" Megan said. "Would you mind going through it again? I think it would be helpful."

"The whole thing?" she asked, sounding tired but resigned.

"Not right now," said Megan. "I can update Captain Weiserman on how he got into the house. Just tell us what happened after that."

"Okay," she said, sighing. "He was made up like a woman but wearing a cologne or aftershave I recognized from the other day. That's how I knew who it was. I tried to run but I tripped, he jumped on me, used some leather thing to knock me out, and the next thing I knew I was tied to that chair."

"He sapped her," Megan explained. "Go on, Alex. What happened next?"

"Like I said before, he got a phone call. He told me it was Clayton Babbit. I don't know if that's true. Anyway, I was in the living room and he went into the kitchen to talk."

"Could you hear what was said?" Weiserman inquired.

"Not really, but he sounded agitated. While I was sitting there, wondering what he'd do to me, I realized I could feel my phone in my back pocket."

"You were still restrained?"

Alex nodded. "I was restrained the whole time, except for when he freed one hand so I could call Vicki. He wanted to know what time she would be home."

"I'd already received her text," Vicki interjected. "Then she called me and I almost blew the whole thing."

"That's why I kept cutting you off."

"I know that now."

"If we could please get back to the text," Weiserman said. "I still don't understand how you were able to send it."

"I'm blind," Alex said simply. "Legally anyway."

"Yes, Detective Lynch mentioned that. If you don't mind me asking, how much can you see?"

"I don't mind," Alex said with a trace of a smile, "but it's irrelevant at the moment. I only bring it up because I use a lot of adaptive technology. I have a special texting app. It's voice controlled and voice activated."

"That's amazing," Weiserman said.

"It's actually a pain, but better than nothing."

"Do a lot of people use these things?"

Alex looked at him. "I suppose that depends on what you mean by a lot. About 1.3 million Americans are classified as legally blind. I would guess most of them use adaptive technology of some sort."

"So the app you use," Weiserman said. "Is it like Siri?"

"There are similarities. One of the biggest is that it doesn't always hear and translate properly. I tell it to order a ham sandwich and it spits back something about a handsome witch."

"The text I received," Vicki said, and Megan watched as she pulled an iPhone out of her purse and began scrolling, "actually said *Fish is here. Call the cop scow. I'm going today if they don't give cheer soon.*"

Alex laughed. "I always knew you were a great editor," she said, shaking her head. "I had no idea your translation skills were so strong."

"You're giving me too much credit." Vicki handed her phone to Megan who glanced at the message and then passed the device along to Zanetti and Weiserman. "I couldn't make any sense of it at first. I knew a scow was a boat but I'd never heard of a cop scow and couldn't imagine what you meant by give cheer. I finally just focused on the first three words. It wasn't much of a stretch to get from *Fish is here* to *Fisher's here.* I knew I might have been wrong but also knew, under the circumstances, I couldn't take that chance.

"And I thank you."

Alex was still laughing but Megan could tell from her flushed cheeks and watery eyes that other emotions were bubbling to the surface.

"I'm just glad you got the text. Before you showed up," she waved a hand at the two detectives, "I didn't know if it really went through."

"Why was that?" Captain Weiserman asked.

Alex took a breath and wiped at her eyes.

"Are you okay?" Megan asked.

She nodded and fought to compose herself. "The app," she said, "uses audio prompts. It beeps and you record your message. It beeps again, reads the message back, and then asks if you're ready to send. I was sitting on my phone and couldn't hear any of that. I also had to keep my voice low so he wouldn't realize what I was up to."

"You're very clever," Weiserman said.

"I don't know about that. It's all I could think to do."

Vicki reached over and patted Alex's hand. "I'd already contacted Megan when you called my office. You sounded so strange. I didn't know what was going on but your behavior confirmed my suspicion that something was wrong."

"Thanks for acting so quickly. Another few seconds and I would have given him the login info he wanted. I had no choice." She turned to face Megan. "I'm very grateful you got there when you did."

"It's we who should be thanking you," Weiserman said. "Because of your courage and ingenuity, our primary suspect is now in custody."

"What will happen to him?" Vicki asked.

"That depends," Megan said. "We can put him away with the video from Ms. Rhodes' apartment building lobby. With some time and professional video analysis we'll be able to make a strong case connecting him to the Martin Reginald murder too. In addition, he's facing a slew of lesser charges."

"If any of this goes to trial," Captain Weiserman said. "The best case scenario for Mr. Mikhail is life in prison."

"IF it goes to trial?" Vicki asked, immediately zeroing in on what Megan already knew was the crux of the situation.

"We have one suspect," Weiserman said, "an important one to be sure. However, based on what Ms. Rhodes shared with us, a second suspect may not only be involved but might right now be somewhere nearby. We want him too."

"So, what?" Alex asked. "You're gonna try to get him to accept a plea deal?"

Captain Weiserman cleared his throat. "We can't discuss that at this time." He shot Megan a warning look but she knew not to say anything.

It wasn't that she didn't trust the two women. She did, and she believed they could keep a confidence if asked. But the situation was too sensitive and there was too much riding on whatever play they chose to make. That part had yet to be determined. They'd barely had a chance to speak with their new resident, currently cooling his heels in one of the interview rooms downstairs. Megan thought about him and wondered if Mikhail was his real name or just another smoke screen. She very much looked forward to finding out.

-44-

Seated in a cruelly contoured hard metal chair, and staring fixedly at the painted cinderblock wall, Mikhail Vasilek was still trying to figure out what went wrong. How had they gotten him? How had they even known he was there? Had Victoria Goldstein's home been under police surveillance since before he'd arrived? Had that whole scene been a trap set just for him?

No! he decided, forced to lean down to scratch his nose since both wrists were handcuffed to the tabletop. *It isn't possible.*

For one thing, he'd been in the neighborhood for two solid hours before finally making his approach. He'd been up and down the street, around the block, and for good measure, around the adjacent blocks. He was adept at picking out cops and hadn't seen a one. The only official vehicle in the area had been a Ford pickup belonging to the Department of Transportation. The sole occupant, an overweight woman in her late fifties or sixties, did not look like cop material. Could he have somehow missed something?

Sure, he grudgingly admitted. He considered the furniture delivery van and the two burly guys laboring to strap a huge stainless steel refrigerator to a hand cart. There'd also been a young woman walking an ugly, cow-headed dog, a group of three women in business attire, talking and laughing as they headed uptown, a flushed-faced man bent over the open hood of an SUV, a guy delivering papers, and another guy atop scaffolding and engaged in masonry repair.

Any of those people, Vasilek knew, could have been members of law enforcement, but he would have given ten to one odds that hadn't been the case. His confidence didn't stem from a misguided faith in his own powers of observation. He was a keen observer and generally trusted his instincts. However—and this was the reason he was so sure he was right—if there had been cops in the vicinity why had they waited so long to make their move? He'd been in the house for a good while and could have killed the Rhodes bitch at any time.

Maybe, Vasilek supposed, *she was wired.*

He toyed with that idea and quickly rejected it because it didn't add up. Even if there'd been cameras and microphones everywhere, allowing the cops to track his every word and motion, they wouldn't have stood idly by while he smacked the crap out of the woman they were theoretically there to protect.

They didn't know, he thought, leaning back as far as his cuffs would allow. *They somehow found out.* His trusted instincts told him that had everything to do with Alex Rhodes. He smiled in spite of himself and bit down on the inside of his cheek until he tasted blood.

Mikhail Vasilek knew he had made mistakes and not just today either. His first error in judgment was when he'd taken Babbit's phone call and let the man bully him into leaving his Jamaican paradise. Why had he come back to New York? Babbit had surprised him, maybe even rattled him some, but Vasilek had never truly believed he was vulnerable. So had he been motivated by a professional desire to finish what he'd started, or was he really nothing more than an easily manipulated and over-inflated loser? Given his current predicament, he had to at least entertain that possibility. And how might things have been different if he'd looked at his phone, seen who was calling and then tossed the blasted thing into the sea? He could, right now, be drinking ice cold vodka in a beachside cabana.

What was her name? Vasilek reflected. *Jade?* He thought that was it, and he could see the bar maid's mahogany skin and long, corn-rowed hair. He could also remember the captivating way she gyrated when she made one of those fancy umbrella drinks. He should have stayed on his bar stool, watched her work, and been happy and worry free.

It was a nice thought but had no basis in reality. Vasilek was restless by nature, dangerous, and not cut out for a life of leisure. Had Babbit not called on him he would have left Jamaica in another day or two anyway and gone in search of his next job. No time for regrets, though. He heard footsteps followed by a metallic thunk as the door lock disengaged.

"Sorry to keep you waiting," said the chick cop he'd first seen entering the Tower Brothers building a couple mornings before. She pulled out a chair and sat down. "My name is Detective Lynch and this is Detective Zanetti. We've got some questions for you."

I bet, but Vasilek said nothing. He was thinking that the lead detective—*maybe thirty-five?*--was kind of hot in a no-nonsense sort of way. Something about her partner, standing against the wall with arms folded over his chest, immediately annoyed him. It could have been the lousy hair cut, the way he slouched when he walked, or that his socks, an odd shade of blue Vasilek couldn't identify, didn't quite match his navy slacks. The jerk was also looking at him like he'd just sodomized an entire class of special needs preschoolers.

Well screw you too, Vasilek thought, and he believed he already knew how the scene would play out if they were going to try the good cop bad cop routine on him. The roles had been clearly specified. But then he got a surprise. The cute one placed a yellow legal pad on the table in front of her, looked him square in the eye and said, "You're fucked."

"I want to call my lawyer," was the only thing Vasilek could think to say.

"You can call anyone you want," the detective replied, "but first things first. Paul?"

She looked at the other guy, and he removed a card from his jacket pocket and began reciting lines Vasilek had previously only heard in movies and on television. "You have the right to remain silent. Anything you say can and will be used against you in a court of law. You have the right to an attorney. If you cannot afford an attorney..." *blah, blah, blah.*

"Here's the deal," Detective Lynch said once he'd finished. "We've got you dead to rights on a murder one. There are at least a dozen other charges that will follow. I'm being conservative, and many of those charges will be felonies. There isn't an attorney on this planet that can save you from spending the rest of your life behind bars."

"Sounds charming," Vasilek said. He managed to keep his voice calm but he could feel his pulse throbbing in his temples.

"I'm serious," the detective said, stone-faced. "We have video from Alex Rhodes' apartment lobby and it clearly shows you shoot and kill another man. Even if all the other evidence we have against you falls apart..."

"Which it won't," the second detective interjected.

"We have enough to put you away for good. You have no legal recourse."

"Then why are we sitting here? If you are so confident why don't you go ahead and—what's the expression?—lock me up and throw away the key?" Vasilek stared at each of them in turn, a challenge in his eyes. He believed he knew what was coming next and believed it represented a glimmer of hope.

"If you are cooperative," the pretty detective said. "You might be able to make things easier on yourself."

"And so there's no confusion," her asshole partner chimed in, moving a step closer to the table. "Cooperative means you waive your right to legal representation and answer every question we ask."

"I will not say anything to incriminate myself," Vasilek said, his hope already fading.

"Poor decision," Detective Lynch stated. "Your situation leaves you few options. You have nothing to gain by withholding information but a great deal to lose if you refuse to help us."

"Didn't you already say you're going to put me away for good? If that is true there is no reason to tell you anything. What's in it for me?"

The two detectives exchanged a look and Vasilek could sense something pass between them. The chick detective clicked her pen a few times. The other one just stood, holding up the wall and looking pissed. They obviously didn't like his question.

Well, Vasilek thought. *That's too bad. If you want something from me you're gonna have to give something first. I know how this game is played.*

Detective Lynch sat back, her head tilted to one side. "We don't have the authority to make any deals or any promises. What I—"

"Then get me someone who does," Vasilek interrupted.

"Let her finish," Detective Zanetti growled, coming off the wall and crowding into Vasilek's personal space. He wasn't a big guy but there was a coldness and toughness there that hadn't been evident at first. The two glared at each other until Detective Lynch cleared her throat. Zanetti gave him one more hard look before retreating.

"What I can do," Detective Lynch continued, "is offer our guarantee that we will try to help you as much as you help us."

"What does that mean?"

She gave a small shrug. "It's too early to tell. But," she gazed at him and Vasilek felt like she was staring right into his soul. "You need to make your decision now or we're not guaranteeing anything. You can call an attorney, we'll put you in a cell and we won't see you again until it's in front of a judge. Is that how you want this to go?"

Vasilek looked at the two detectives but then dropped his eyes to the table. As the one had so eloquently stated, he was fucked and he knew it. Did he really want to take his chances with a judge and jury? Was it possible the cops were lying? Maybe they didn't really have video of him killing that doorman but only said so to get him talking.

Vasilek tried to think back. He couldn't remember spotting any cameras in the apartment lobby. Then again, he'd been focused on other things and hadn't really looked. If, by chance, no such video existed, what else could they realistically pin on him? Sure, they had Rhodes as an eye witness to the murder but what was that worth? He seriously doubted her ability to see her own feet. She certainly wouldn't be able to pick him out of a lineup. Where exactly did that leave him? With his life and liberty at stake, did he really have the balls to call their bluff?

The detectives had promised him nothing. They'd been up front about that too. And really, what sort of deal could he expect? He was guilty of two murders: one they knew about for sure and a second they'd hang on him if given sufficient time. No matter what he did or said, that reality was inescapable.

Fucking Babbit, he thought, staring down at his shackles. *This is your fault!* He made a decision then. It wouldn't bring him salvation but, given his current circumstances, he figured a little satisfaction was the next best thing.

Vasilek listened to the click of the detective's pen, the metallic buzz from the overhead light, shuffling feet, the distant ring of a phone, and other muffled sounds from somewhere beyond the closed door. He took a few deep breaths, steeled himself and finally looked up. "Get these cuffs off me," he said. "Then I'll tell you anything you want to know."

-45-

Clayton Babbit III was operating on about three hours sleep. His nerves were scraped raw and strung as tight as guitar strings. He picked up his phone, stared at the darkened screen, swore, and then cast the thing aside. There was no point trying to call or text. He'd done both about a hundred times the afternoon and evening before and gotten no response. Eventually, out of frustration and a growing sense of foreboding, he'd contacted Louie and had his worst fears realized. Based on GPS information, Vasilek's phone was somewhere in New York's 6th Precinct or in that immediate vicinity.

"How?" Babbit wondered aloud, pounding the steering wheel of his pick up. *What in hell had happened?*

The last time he'd actually spoken to Vasilek, around one o'clock the previous day, everything was fine. He had Rhodes, again, and claimed the situation was under control. Babbit was already exhausted at that point because he'd driven straight through from Louisiana, stopping only for gas, food, and two rest area cat naps. He was running on pure adrenaline but that was enough. All he had to do was talk to the woman, make her spill her guts, and then he could leave Vasilek to handle the dirty work. Babbit's problems would be over.

That had been the plan anyway but it turned out his problems had only just begun. A tractor trailer loaded with potato chips somehow caught fire on the lower level of the George Washington Bridge. He was already committed to that route when he realized what was happening. Both lanes were effectively shut down and he crawled along, literally inches at a time, for the next hour and a half. Babbit reached his destination much later than expected and, although the lights were on, it was obvious no one was home.

He drove past the brownstone a dozen times and saw no signs of life. He called Vasilek repeatedly and got no answer. Finally, having no other recourse, he stopped his truck right in front of the residence, walked up, and rang the door bell. If anyone other than Vasilek answered he could say he was lost and looking for directions. No one did answer and Babbit returned to his truck, bewildered and uneasy. He found a diner and ordered food he couldn't eat, and then got a hotel room where he spent a mostly sleepless night alternately staring at the ceiling or flipping through channels on the television.

He knew what must have happened, but couldn't get his head around the horrible implications. As impossible as it seemed, Mikhail Vasilek had been arrested. Either that or he'd lost his phone and it somehow ended up in police custody. That was a comforting thought but not one he could put any stock in. His guy had been nabbed plain and simple, and all Babbit could do now was wonder what Vasilek was doing, what he was saying, and what would happen next.

He was tempted to pull a 180, point his Ford southwest and head back to the bayou. Depending on what transpired, maybe it would be better if he went all the way to Mexico. He had plenty of money stashed. Was his best bet to disappear? What might happen if he stuck around? Could Vasilek, a man he'd never met, be trusted to keep his secrets?

Babbit considered what he would do if their roles were reversed. That revelation didn't exactly fill him with optimism. If he stood to benefit he knew he'd screw over Mikhail Vasilek just as quickly as Vasilek, possibly at that very moment, was screwing him.

He had a second, potentially far greater concern too. Even if Alex Rhodes hadn't initially grasped his full objective, she surely did by now. She would have taken steps to protect herself and her interests, and that meant turning over all of her work—maybe to her publisher—or at least making additional copies and storing them someplace absolutely inaccessible: with a friend, a family member, or ferreted away in a safe deposit box.

One way or another, Babbit believed the horrible truth would be told. There was no longer anything he could do to prevent that. In terms of the Deepwater business, he still didn't think any of the fictionalized allegations or accusations could be proven. However, because he'd had Reginald killed and then gone after Rhodes, the entire world would soon know his name and learn those books had been about him. He'd be found guilty in the court of public opinion if nothing else. That could be enough to destroy his various business interests and his reputation too. His only chance now was to permanently remove the one solid link that directly connected him to those murders. That would have been hard enough before and now seemed virtually impossible. If Vasilek was really behind bars he was just as unreachable as everything else Babbit had been after.

Every impulse told him to flee, but he decided he'd stick it out until he had some idea of which way the wind was blowing. He'd been listening to news radio, and he'd picked up copies of the *New York Times* and *New York Post*. Both papers had write-ups on the police investigation and neither covered any new ground. He also read an article on Alex Rhodes, her writing career, her legal blindness, and how that led to the decision to introduce Martin Reginald as the author of her books. Babbit's name didn't come up. That was interesting but not reassuring. It was possible Rhodes hadn't told the cops the whole story. More likely, they didn't want to tip their hand by revealing too much to the media.

I bet I know why too, Babbit thought sourly. *They've got Vasilek and he's squealing like a baby pig.* That brought on a fresh wave of anger and uncertainty. He wanted to do something—act in some meaningful way, but he was at a loss. He didn't see any way out of his predicament and that both scared him and pissed him off.

"Yeah, it's me," Babbit said when Louie answered the phone. "Any changes?"

"Hold on. I'll check."

Babbit waited and he could hear the muted click of computer keys. Louie muttered something and Babbit could picture him working a wad of chewing gum as he peered at the monitor.

"Hasn't moved," he finally said. "It's still at—"

"That's fine," Babbit interrupted. Developments had made him paranoid and he wanted to keep their conversation as short and innocuous as possible. Thankfully, Louie seemed to understand that and didn't ask questions.

"Do me a favor," Babbit said. "Check that periodically—maybe every half hour or so. Shoot me a text if there's any activity."

"Will do. Any other instructions?"

"Not right now," Babbit said. "I'm still trying to tie up a few loose ends. Could be another couple-a days. Just hold down the fort 'til I get back."

"And your messages?" Louie asked. "You've had some calls."

Babbit paused. He thought there'd been something in Louie's tone. *A warning? Had any of those calls been official? Did it matter at this point?*

"Hold onto 'em," he finally replied, reaching for the ignition and starting his truck. "I'll be in touch."

Minutes later, Babbit again found himself in a part of Brooklyn called Prospect Heights, at least according to some Asian dude who'd tried to sell him a knockoff Rolex watch. He thought the name sounded as pretentious as all get out. However, as he turned down the now-familiar street, he was both surprised and impressed with the elegant brownstone homes and beautiful tree-lined streets he'd first noticed the afternoon before. He was not as impressed with New York City as a whole. He hadn't taken long to decide he hated it and dismissed it all as being too busy, too noisy, and the lack of sufficient parking was driving him nuts.

It was a little better in some of the more residential areas and he actually saw an available spot not far from his target brownstone. Babbit didn't consider stopping. He knew Vasilek wasn't there. Rhodes probably wasn't either. He'd only come because he didn't know what else to do. With Vasilek presumably out of action he no longer had a plan.

Babbit rounded the block and decided he'd make one more pass before returning to his hotel. He'd seen Rhodes' picture in the paper. If she was still in the area, unlikely as that might be, maybe he'd get lucky and catch her entering or exiting the building. He knew the odds of that were somewhere between slim and no fucking way. The endeavor was pointless, but futile activity was still somehow preferable to doing nothing at all. If he didn't spot the author, and he was sure he wouldn't, maybe he'd see someone else and that new contact would lead him… He couldn't imagine where but had to at least give it a shot.

His phone rang as he was driving past for the second time. Babbit was so startled he literally jumped in his seat.

Gotta be Louie, he thought, shocked when he looked down and saw Vasilek's name instead. Babbit stared, his already-taxed emotions bouncing erratically between relief and incredulity. *Has he escaped?* It wasn't possible.

The phone rang again. Babbit was so distracted he'd momentarily forgotten he was still behind the wheel. He looked up in time to hit the brakes a split second before his truck jumped the curb and plowed straight into one of the big trees he'd just been admiring.

"She-it," he swore, glad he'd only been going about twenty miles an hour.

He was anxious to answer the call but didn't think he should stop where he was, especially not after coming so close to causing an inexcusable one-car accident. If someone had seen and called the police he might be pulled over and subjected to a sobriety test. Babbit hadn't consumed a drop of alcohol in over forty-eight hours. He'd pass the test for sure but a report would be filed and his name would be on record. He needed to avoid that possibility.

While his phone rang a fourth, fifth, and sixth time, he drove to the end of the block, turned right, sped another block, made a quick left, and finally pulled to the curb behind an unoccupied black BMW. The vanity plate read PAMS-BMR. Babbit didn't give a rat's ass about Pam or her fancy ride. He was concerned only about Mikhail Vasilek and whatever was going on.

"Hello?" he answered, glancing around like he thought someone might be eavesdropping on their conversation. At first, there was no response and Babbit was afraid he hadn't picked up in time. Then, a familiar voice came on the line.

"Babbit?" Vasilek said, sounding breathless. "Is that you?"

"Of course." He ran a hand across his forehead. "Where are you and what's happened."

"I spent the night as a guest of New York's finest."

"You mean?"

"I mean I got busted," Vasilek snapped. "What do you think?"

"But how? The last time I talked to you—"

"The Rhodes bitch tricked me. She used some sort of blind bullshit and managed to alert the cops without me knowing. She would have been history days ago if you'd left this up to me. We're playing these stupid games and this is where it's gotten us."

You're probably right, Babbit thought but wasn't about to admit it. "So where are you now?" he asked, surprised Vasilek was willing to speak so freely. He pictured him in a cell or an interrogation room, the police listening in on every word. "Are you still—"

"Just got out," he said. "They didn't have enough to hold me."

"What?" Babbit asked, dumbfounded. Vasilek was already guilty of two murders and on his way to committing a third. How had he walked?

"There's nothing to connect me to that cruise ship. I'm good at my job, Babbit. You'd be wise not to forget that."

"Oh, I know," he replied. "But what about—"

"The doorman?" Vasilek laughed and the sound was chilling. "We caught a break there. The security camera in the apartment lobby was broken. Rhodes was the only witness. Suffice it to say her testimony was inconclusive."

"So you're free?" Babbit couldn't believe it. Maybe all was not lost after all.

"For now, yes. I posted bail for the few things they could charge me with. By the way, you owe me an additional fifteen hundred dollars."

"That's not a problem," Babbit said, beginning to regain his composure. "But what about the charges?"

"Inconsequential," Vasilek said. "Assault, battery, illegal entry, some other piddly stuff. They are all first offenses and I have no record. I was issued a public defender. I met with her last night and again this morning. She told me I'm most likely looking at fines but no jail time."

"So what happens next?"

Vasilek scoffed. "I'm due in court in a week. I plan on being long gone by then."

Babbit didn't understand the almost cavalier attitude. "But the murder investigation," he said. "They must know you did it even if they can't prove it. They'll keep digging. What if they come up with more evidence and more charges?"

"What if they do?" Vasilek asked. "I've been in this business a long time. Until you came along, no cop ever gave me a second look. I'm going to drop back under the radar and that's where I'll stay."

"What about Alex Rhodes?"

"Not my problem," Vasilek said, and Babbit could practically hear his shrug. "I'm gonna cut my losses and clear out."

"Aren't you forgetting something, Sport? I know things about you. If you leave me in the lurch I may have to turn that information over to the authorities."

"You know what, Sport?" Vasilek retorted. "I was arrested yesterday, or have you forgotten? I spent the night with *the authorities* and I doubt you know anything about me I haven't already shared."

"So you told them about Sam?" Babbit asked, dropping the one name he thought might actually have an impact. In truth, he knew nothing about the man who'd initially put him in contact with Vasilek. Babbit wasn't even sure it was a man. Sam, after all, could have been short for Samantha or the name could have been FALSE. Regardless, that was the only card left in his deck so he'd gone ahead and played it and hoped for the best.

His question was met with a prolonged silence, the tension palpable. Vasilek finally spoke. "You really don't want to go there," he said.

"You're right," Babbit replied, knowing there was nowhere he could go even if he wanted to. But, Vasilek hadn't called his bluff so he tried to press the advantage. "I still want Rhodes eliminated. I need your help. If you refuse..." He didn't complete the thought, believing a veiled threat would be most effective.

"I think I got it," Vasilek said. "I agree to pop her or you're gonna try to pop me."

Babbit didn't reply, holding his breath while waiting to see how Vasilek would react.

"It's pointless," he finally said. "You've got to realize that. Killing her now will do no good."

"I know," Babbit confessed. "But I can't quit. The woman has ruined me. She's gotta pay for that."

"So do it yourself," Vasilek said. "This isn't my fight."

"No, but I paid you to step into the ring. I'm asking you to deliver the knockout punch."

"And if I don't?"

"We've already covered that."

"You'll blow the whistle on me then?"

Babbit sighed as if bored. "I'll use the information I have if you leave me no choice."

"And what do you think I'll do if given no choice?" Vasilek asked. "I know more about you than you'll ever know about me. Maybe that doesn't concern you because you think you're going down anyway. Maybe a few years in a white collar prison doesn't sound so bad. Think about this, though," he said, his voice dropping. "What do you suppose will happen if I get to you before the cops do?"

"All right," Babbit said, sweat beading on the back of his neck. "So we both have something to lose. What do you propose?"

"A raise," Vasilek said. "You paid fifty grand for Reginald. This job has gotten a lot more risky. The new price is a quarter million."

Babbit thought about that but only for a second. "Done," he said, realizing he didn't care about the money anymore. He just wanted revenge.

"Two more things," said Vasilek. "This is just a hit. No more break-ins or any of that other garbage. I put her down and I'm gone."

"You have my word."

"And," he continued. "I want cash in advance."

"Half now," Babbit countered, his inner negotiator taking over. "The other half when it's done. I'll need a little while to get the money together."

"I'll call you at this time tomorrow. By then, I should know where Rhodes is hiding out. I'll expect you to have something for me as well."

Babbit started to respond but Mikhail Vasilek had already clicked off.

-46-

"So what do you think?" Megan Lynch asked once he'd hung up the phone.

Mikhail Vasilek sat back and studied her, his expression wavering between curiosity and indifference.

"I think," he said, hands flat on the table in front of him, "that Clayton Babbit is scared."

They were in the same interview room as before but this time the cuffs were gone.

"He should be scared," Zanetti said and Vasilek shot him a look.

The unvoiced hostility between the two of them had not yet abated. Megan supposed that was due, at least in part, to Zanetti's fondness for Alex Rhodes. The suspect had abused her physically, and put himself in position to do so by taking advantage of her poor eyesight. For whatever reason, Zanetti seemed to take that personally. In addition, although he had confessed to the murders of Martin Worth Reginald and Brandon Barnes, the apartment lobby doorman, Vasilek hadn't exhibited the merest hint of remorse. Zanetti's distaste for the man was evident and the feeling appeared to be mutual.

As Megan had already theorized, the first killing had been planned weeks ahead of time. Vasilek didn't know or hadn't yet admitted exactly how the information about Reginald's travel itinerary had been gleaned, or how it was that he had been conveniently booked into an adjoining cabin. His direct involvement, so he'd claimed, had begun when he stepped onto the cruise ship and no sooner.

Vasilek had told them he'd spent days observing his target and familiarizing himself with Reginald's routines. His only other challenge, so he'd said, had been to cover his tracks. He spoke with pride when he explained in detail how he'd entered Reginald's room by way of the balcony. And once his primary mission had been accomplished and Reginald had been dropped overboard, he went to great lengths to make it look like the man was still alive.

Megan already knew all of that, and listened with horror and fascination when he described his calculated movements in similar terms to those someone might use to discuss how they'd solved a difficult Sudoku puzzle. It was as though he were looking for praise for a job well done.

The Brandon Barnes killing had been nothing but impulse and reaction. Vasilek had an objective and the unwitting doorman literally stood in the way. He told the detectives he had considered aborting the mission. However, although Rhodes obviously hadn't gotten a good look at him, the doorman had. Vasilek had assumed, correctly as it turned out, there'd been cameras on him too. At that point, he'd thought he could still grab Rhodes and force her to let him into her apartment. All he had to do was remove that one obstruction. A single gunshot had done the trick.

Paul Zanetti pushed his chair back from the table with a loud scrape. "Let me ask you something," he said, his jaw clenched. "You were hired by Clayton Babbit to, as you put it, *eliminate* Ms. Rhodes. Is that what you're saying?"

"Precisely," he replied, Vasilek's gaze disturbingly intense.

"You were not hired to kill Mr. Barnes. You presumably didn't even know he would be there."

"I knew he'd be there," Vasilek said. "Or that someone would. I'd visited the building earlier in the day so I knew what to expect."

"And you didn't hesitate to take the life of an innocent man even though that wasn't part of your assignment?"

"He might have recognized me and I'm sure he realized I posed a threat." Vasilek shrugged. "If he'd contacted the authorities it would have made it harder to get to Ms. Rhodes. I did what I had to do."

"And it doesn't bother you that he had a wife and kids?"

"I don't think about those things," he answered, and Megan could tell from his matter of fact expression that he meant it.

"You're scum," Zanetti said. "Do you know that?'

"Paul." Megan cautioned, giving him a look. She understood how her partner felt and completely agreed with him. Mikhail Vasilek made her sick. How could someone have such disregard for human life? Did that come from years of killing or was he fundamentally and psychologically flawed? She figured the less she knew about that the better. However, as repugnant as it felt, they needed Vasilek's help and couldn't afford to provoke him.

"It's warm in here," she said, hoping to steer the conversation to safer territory. "Detective Zanetti, would you mind getting some refreshments? I'd like a Diet Coke. Mr. Vasilek? Anything for you?"

"Water would be fine."

He and Zanetti exchanged a few more silent insults then Paul left the room, muttering all the while. Megan knew his Italian blood was boiling and he needed time to cool down. He'd take the long way to the vending machines, kick a garbage can or two, bitch to whomever would listen, and hopefully be in a better frame of mind when he returned. He plainly didn't like negotiating with a piece of trash like Mikhail Vasilek but understood what was at stake. They'd made a good collar. Now, though, there were larger concerns.

"So," Megan said, once Zanetti was back and had taken his seat. "You told us Mr. Babbit was scared. What makes you say that?"

"Irrationality," Vasilek replied, twisting the top off the water bottle. "Despite my arrest, despite everything else that's happened, he still wants to proceed."

"Meaning?"

"You heard him. He wants Rhodes. I told him it would do no good. He agreed but still wants to move forward. I think he's unhinged."

Says the pot to the kettle, Megan thought and she knew Zanetti was thinking the same thing.

"Were you surprised he didn't object when you told him you wanted more money? Where did that come from anyway? It wasn't in the script."

Vasilek shrugged. "I didn't want him thinking too much about my release. That part of the story is weak. A dual murder suspect yet you let him go? Sounds fishy to me. If he thought about it, Babbit might come to that same conclusion so I gave him something else to focus on."

"And you weren't afraid he'd balk?"

"Balk?" Vasilek asked, looking at them. "What does this mean?"

"Sorry," Megan said. His English was so good—only the occasional trace of an accent—it hadn't occurred to her there might be words he didn't know. "You weren't afraid your demand would frighten him off?"

Vasilek shook his head and took a drink. "I was hired for Martin Reginald. I didn't want to go after Ms. Rhodes too but he gave me no choice. I didn't want to break into her apartment and steal her things either. But again, he forced my hand."

"Are we supposed to feel sorry for you?" Zanetti asked with sarcasm. "You were an innocent victim in all of this?"

Vasilek didn't even glance his way but directed his comments to Megan. "I made it clear I didn't approve of how things were being done. I objected to almost everything. When Clayton Babbit told me he still wanted Ms. Rhodes, it would have been out of character for me to just go along. I couldn't refuse, obviously, so I did the next best thing and raised the stakes."

"Well, that seems to have worked," Megan admitted. She popped the top on her soda but left the can sitting on the table. "That's fortunate because any arrangement we make with you is contingent upon Mr. Babbit being apprehended and arrested, and you testifying against him."

"I understand what I'm being asked to do. What I don't know yet is what you will do for me in return. I told you I don't want to serve time."

"That's great," Zanetti said. "And I bet Martin Reginald and Brandon Barnes didn't want to die but they weren't given a choice."

Megan cleared her throat. Even though she was the junior partner in terms of department seniority she could tell why Wigs gave her the lead on this one. Paul was too hot-headed and too emotional. His beverage run didn't seem to have helped either. Maybe she'd send him out for dinner next time.

"As Detective Zanetti and I told you, we are not the ones that handle negotiations in these matters. Captain Weiserman, our boss, is aware of your desire to avoid incarceration and he has relayed that to the District Attorney."

"And?"

"And," Megan said. "You murdered two American citizens."

"Two that we know of," Zanetti interjected.

Megan ignored him. "We're talking about an extremely high-profile situation, especially as it pertains to Mr. Reginald. It can't be swept under the carpet."

"Which means what?" Vasilek asked, and Megan saw the way the muscles tightened around his eyes and mouth.

Good, she thought with satisfaction. *I guess you're not as indifferent as you wanted us to think.*

"You will remain in federal custody until Clayton Babbit is tried and convicted."

Vasilek opened his mouth to speak but Megan didn't give him the chance.

"It's non-negotiable," she said. "I told you that would probably be the case. These things take time too. You're looking at a minimum of two years in prison."

"And after that?"

It was Megan's turn to shrug. "Some details still need to be ironed out. Here's what I can tell you right now. If your assistance leads to a conviction you will serve your time and then be on the first flight out of the country. You will be banned from re-entering the United States at any point in the future."

"That's not much of a deal," Vasilek said haltingly. He again picked up his water, his right hand trembling.

"I'm afraid it's the best you're going to get."

"And what assurances do I have?"

"Only one," Megan said, looking him square in the eye. "If your help proves insufficient I can promise you will spend the rest of your days in U.S. federal prison. We have enough to make that happen even without your confession."

"We're not blowing smoke here," Zanetti said, sounding like he finally had his anger in check. "Maybe you think a hotshot lawyer can get you off or work out a better deal. It's possible." He spread his hands wide. "We don't have much physical evidence to put you on that cruise ship. You know that already. But know this too. We will get Clayton Babbit, with or without your cooperation. When that time comes, will he be looking to do you favors or trying to save his own ass at any cost?"

Mikhail Vasilek's shoulders fell and something dark flickered in his eyes. Megan could tell Zanetti's comments—his suppositions—hit the mark. Maybe Vasilek had already been thinking along similar lines. After all, he was negotiating with the police, acting in his own best interests. He had to know Babbit would do the same thing.

"What we're offering you," Megan said, leaning forward, "is a level of immunity. Once we have an agreement, nothing Clayton Babbit says can alter that and you will be free of any further prosecution."

"Unless you sneak back into the country," Zanetti added. "If you are ever caught on American soil again then all bets are off and you will be prosecuted to the full extent of the law."

Vasilek sat, alternately staring at the table, the wall, the ceiling, and finally Lynch and Zanetti. "You leave me few options," he said, his voice quiet but steady. "I will continue to assist."

"I appreciate that," Megan said, "on behalf of the entire New York City Police Department. And now we'd better get busy. We have until tomorrow afternoon to come up with a plan."

"Babbit won't give us that long," Vasilek said.

Megan picked up her Coke and took a sip. "Why do you say that?"

"I told you. He's scared. He also likes to know what's happening all the time. There's no way he waits for my call. He will call or text me, and probably within the hour."

"Okay," Megan said, checking her watch. "Four thirty-five now," she muttered, thinking it was going to be a very long day. "So you talk to him if you have to, and stall until we know what we're doing. Can you do that?"

"Easily," Vasilek said. "He won't like it but he doesn't know where I am so he'll have to go along with what I tell him. One thing, though. I'm pretty sure he's been tracking me through my phone."

They all looked at Vasilek's smart phone which Megan had placed off to one side.

"What makes you think so?" Zanetti asked.

"Some things he's said and done. He booked me into the Grand Hyatt when I got back to New York City."

"Back?" Zanetti inquired. "We thought you'd been here the whole time."

Vasilek shook his head. "I spent a few days in Jamaica."

"You didn't tell us that."

"Because it's irrelevant. I was there on vacation. I would have stayed longer had Mr. Babbit not contacted me."

"Okay," Megan said. "Go on."

"I returned to New York but not to the Hyatt as he wished. I checked into a different hotel. He knew right away. I'd already had suspicions he was monitoring my movements and that confirmed it."

"And how do you know it was through your phone?"

"I guess I don't," Vasilek said. "But I have no other explanation."

Megan picked up her pen and twirled it in her fingers. "And if that's what he's doing," she said, thinking out loud. "He may look, see that the phone is still here, and reasonably assume you are too."

Vasilek didn't reply, and Megan studied his unreadable expression and tried to decide whether or not he was telling the truth. If Babbit really was checking, he might do so, see that the phone was still at the 6th Precinct, the same place it had been since the previous afternoon, and conclude he was being scammed. Their sting would be blown before they'd even had a chance to set and bait the trap.

On the other hand, the GPS story could be a ruse, something he'd made up so Megan would feel the need to get him and his phone out of the station as quickly as possible. Once that happened, who knew what he might attempt? He'd already demonstrated his intelligence, boldness, and daring. If given the opportunity would he try to make a run for it?

No, she concluded, *because there's a big difference between bold and suicidal.* She'd also seen his reaction at the prospect of life in prison and was sure—*fairly sure anyway*—he wouldn't be eager to roll the dice if he knew that's the price he'd pay for crapping out.

So it's come to this, Megan thought, getting to her feet. *We've maybe got one shot to nab this prick and I'm putting my faith in a soulless killer. I wonder if my old job is still open if this doesn't work out.*

"Get Alex Rhodes on the phone," she said to Zanetti. "We're gonna need to talk to her. And while you're doing that, I have to find Wigs so he can expedite the paperwork on getting Mr. Vasilek out of here for a while."

-47-

I sat cross-legged on the bed and wondered why Megan, who'd seemed so friendly before, was suddenly so willing to throw me to the wolves. "Am I missing something?" I asked, "or did you really just say you want to give those two maniacs another crack at me?"

"It isn't like that," she said, her assurances not holding much water.

I'd managed to get away from Mikhail Vasilek twice and I was in no hurry to test my luck a third time.

"You will be under police protection and heavy surveillance. It's completely safe."

"That's right," Detective Zanetti said. "We will make sure no harm comes to you."

He sounded confident but I just wasn't feeling it.

"Listen," Megan said, rolling her chair a little closer. "No one is going to force you to do this. If you're not comfortable we'll come up with another plan."

I knew she was sincere but I could also tell she had no idea what that *other plan* might be. I looked at her, sitting in the swivel chair in front of the desk, her legal pad resting on one knee. Detective Zanetti was standing with his back against the closed bedroom door. On the other side of that door, two uniformed cops whose names I'd already forgotten had taken up positions in the suite's small living area. Their presence gave my new hotel digs a cozy safe-house sort of quality emphasized by the disconcerting fact that I didn't actually know where I was.

I hadn't seen the hotel marquis and most likely wouldn't have been able to read it anyway. We'd bypassed the front desk too so I didn't have the benefit of hearing the standard, *Hello and welcome to Regency Witness Protection. I hope you enjoy your stay.* Check in arrangements had apparently been made ahead of time. Detectives Lynch and Zanetti escorted me through the lobby, ushered me into the elevator, and we were in the room moments later. I didn't know the name of the hotel, the floor we were on, or even my room number. I could have asked but vanity took over and I kept those questions to myself. It seemed like I was basically on house arrest anyway, so the exact location of that house was of little consequence.

"I just don't like it that he'll be on the loose again. That guy's as slippery as..." I immediately thought of something gross, sexual, inappropriate, and exceedingly unladylike. It was funny, though, and I held my tongue with reluctance. "All get out," I finally concluded, feeling like I'd missed an opportunity.

"We understand your concern," Detective Zanetti said. "I promise the suspect is not on the loose nor will he be at any time. He is currently confined to a nearby room in this hotel and he will be moved again soon."

"Why couldn't you leave him in jail?" I asked, even though that had already been explained. "I get the GPS thing, but couldn't you take his phone on a tour of New York and leave him where he was?" I knew I was speaking more out of anger than anything else

Hotel accommodations? I thought bitterly. *That's the punishment for killing someone in this city? That explains the high crime rate.* My stomach growled—a byproduct of stress no doubt—and I wondered if he and I would be ordering off the same room service menu. That didn't seem right.

Megan put her legal pad on the desk, stood, and then walked over to sit next to me on the bed. "I know this must seem unusual," she said. "It's not standard operating procedure for us either. We don't like to involve civilians in police business and avoid that whenever possible."

I could hear the *but* even though she hadn't said it yet.

"But," Megan continued, "these are extraordinary circumstances. Mr. Vasilek is cooperating with us and told us he thought Clayton Babbit would probably call him. He did, and we have reason to believe he'll call again. Assuming Mr. Vasilek's whereabouts are being tracked through his phone, it is crucial that he and his phone not be separated."

"You can't just disable it or turn the tracking off?"

"We could," Detective Zanetti confirmed. "But that might raise suspicion and we can't take that chance. We figure we're only gonna get one shot at this thing. And, if his movements are being monitored, we might be able to use that to our advantage."

I collapsed onto the bed, lay there for a while-—neither of my keepers saying a word—and then struggled back into a sitting position.

"I am NOT saying I'll do this," I warned them, brushing hair back from my face. "But just for the sake of argument, how would it work?"

"Well," Detective Zanetti came over and sat down in the chair Megan had vacated. He smelled like corn chips and Old Spice—not a horrible combination really.

"We think Mr. Babbit is in the area. If Mr. Vasilek is to be believed, he is determined to finish what he started."

"That's the politically correct way of saying he wants to punch my ticket."

"He might want to," Megan said. "But he won't get that chance."

"What we want to do," Detective Zanetti explained, "is create a situation where Mr. Babbit thinks he has an opportunity to make a move."

"A move?" I questioned. "Does that mean what I think it does?"

"As things stand," Megan said. "The only real evidence we have is against Mikhail Vasilek. We know what he did to you. We know he killed Brandon Barnes. We can prove that. We believe he killed Martin Reginald and, in time, we'll be able to prove that too. Unfortunately, Clayton Babbit's involvement is not as tangible. We have phone records that establish a connection between him and Mr. Vasilek. Beyond that..." I could sense her shrug. "We're gonna have a hard time making anything stick."

"Unless," I said, not wanting to finish the thought, "you can somehow catch him in the act."

"You got it." Megan reached over and patted my knee. "Just let him kill you and we'll be able to get him for sure."

"Screw you," I said automatically.

There was a beat of silence and then Detective Zanetti started laughing. "Hey, what do you think, Lynch?" he asked. "I'd say she's got your number. People usually have to get to know you better before they tell you off."

"I'm sorry," I said, my cheeks burning. "If it's all the same, though. I'd rather not die for the cause."

Megan smiled. "We'll try to prevent that."

"So how do you see this going down?" I asked, scared but strangely excited, and anxious to get it over with.

"Actually," she said, motioning for her legal pad which Detective Zanetti handed over along with a pen. "We're not sure yet. We have to think outside the box as they say. Maybe you could help."

"Me?" I objected. "I don't know anything about police work." I also wasn't thrilled with any plan that relied on my input. Maybe the detectives had already forgotten but it was my poor judgment that got us into this mess in the first place.

"We need to be creative," Megan said. "You're a writer. Doesn't that make you an expert on the subject?"

"I write novels," I said. "Fiction! It doesn't have anything to do with real life."

"Your last books did," she said, and I couldn't tell if she was being serious or not.

"My Deepwater books were structured around actual events, maybe. You could argue that they're historical fiction but they're still fiction. And what difference does it make?" I asked, exasperated. "I'm not qualified to do whatever it is you want from me."

"Are you about done?" Megan asked, calm and clearly amused.

"I'm just gettin' warmed up, Honey. But you can bet I'll soon be chilling cold storage at the morgue if you leave any of this up to me."

"Maybe Lynch didn't explain herself well," Detective Zanetti said. "She's like that."

"I'd tell you what Paul is like but we don't have enough time." Megan clicked her pen. "We already have what we'll call a work in progress. But, we're facing some unique challenges. That's what we were hoping you might be able to assist with."

"How?" I asked, still uncertain. "What's the problem?"

"If I may," Detective Zanetti said and I saw Megan give him a nod. "We need to catch Mr. Babbit doing or saying something incriminating. As Detective Lynch mentioned, we have the phone records connecting him to Mr. Vasilek. It's evidence but highly circumstantial. We need something concrete."

"And that's where I come in, right? You want him to try to get to me."

"That's right," Megan said. "Here's the problem. We need to create a scenario that's controlled but also appears open and unthreatening."

"Huh?" I asked, not sure I was following.

"Again," Detective Zanetti said. "Lynch struggles to properly express herself. We need to make it look like you're exposed without really exposing you. Do you understand?"

"I think so. This is the part where I don't die, right?"

"That's the objective."

We spent the next forty-five minutes discussing, proposing, adjusting, and ultimately rejecting one plan after another.

"What about a press conference?" I offered. "Vicki said she'd keep me out of the spotlight until all of this blows over but we could change that. If I addressed the media it would be easy to sneak some policemen in with the reporters."

"Where?" Megan asked.

"We usually do it right at the Tower Brothers offices."

"No good. It's too confined. He'd never take the chance."

"Okay." I nibbled a finger nail. "What about changing the location? We could do it on the sidewalk in front of the building."

Megan shook her head. "That would be too open. Besides, reporters mean television cameras. If Babbit goes after you he's not gonna want it on the six o'clock news."

"Well I don't know," I said. "You want to cover me with molasses and stake me to an ant hill?"

"Would you do that?" Megan asked. Her voice was teasing but I knew she was frustrated. We all were.

"Maybe," Detective Zanetti said, rising and walking to the window, "we could compromise and come up with something in between a remote ant hill and a busy city street."

"Such as?"

"I don't know," he admitted. "But with Mikhail Vasilek and Alex both assisting us, coming up with a viable plan shouldn't be this difficult. We already know Babbit's objective. How can we use that?"

"What if," I asked, regretting the words even as I was saying them, "he believed Vasilek had me again?"

"What do you mean?"

"Well, if he thought I'd been abducted—"

"No!" Megan said at once. "It's too risky."

"It wouldn't have to be," I argued, surprising myself with my own bravery *or stupidity as the case may be*. "Babbit has been tracking Vasilek through his phone, right?"

"We think so."

"Okay, so why can't you track him too? But use something he can't get away from. What about one of those ankle bracelet thingies?" I saw the detectives exchange a look which I, as usual, couldn't read.

"Too conspicuous," Detective Zanetti said. "It would—"

But Megan cut him off. "It doesn't matter if it's conspicuous or not. It's too damn dangerous. We need to come up with something else."

"All right," I said, thinking about Clayton Babbit and wondering how far he'd be willing to go. *Does he think I have proof about what happened on that drilling rig? Is that why he still wants me dead?* It seemed crazy. He'd presumably seen all the files on my stolen laptop. He must have seen Deb Royal's letter too. There was enough there for a novel but certainly not for an arrest. He had to know that. He'd been in the clear for almost a decade after all. *So why bother coming after me*? I supposed I might never know the answer to that one. He was coming, though. That was the idea anyway, and I had the beginnings of an idea as to how we just might catch him. I started to put that into words. That's when the smoke alarm went off and all hell broke loose.

-48-

Mikhail Vasilek leaned to one side and farted noisily. He made an apologetic face even though he'd made no effort to hold it in—quite to the contrary—and he was pleased the pungent aroma was as offensive as the sound .

"Excuse me," he said, groaning and pressing cuffed hands to his stomach. "Something I ate does not agree with me. I need to use the bathroom."

He was afraid one of his buzz cut, hard jawed, steroid-infused baby sitters would insist on going in with him and watching him take a dump but after a brief discussion and the insistent instruction to *not take too long* he elatedly found himself alone behind a closed bathroom door. The handcuffs had stayed on, which was a nuisance, but nothing he couldn't deal with.

He looked up and verified what he thought he'd seen when first led into the hotel room. There was a small circular heat lamp mounted in the center of the ceiling. It was controlled by a dial on the wall just to the right of the light switches and an electrical outlet.

Time for an experiment, he thought, kicking off his shoes so he could step onto the toilet seat in relative silence. He wished he had more farts at his disposal to mask whatever other noises he made but he figured he could do well enough with his mouth. He gave it a try, quietly at first, and the result seemed wet and disgusting enough to be convincing. He repeated the sound with more vigor and added a low moan for emphasis. *Not bad,* he decided, and Vasilek imagined his two cop guards looking at each other with distaste. He hoped his theatrics would buy him an extra minute or two. He couldn't count on that, though, so got right to work.

He started by plucking a handful of tissues from the dispenser underneath the sink. He then turned the heat lamp dial to the 10 minute max. It made a humming sound as it warmed but not one he thought could be heard through the door. He could feel the heat almost immediately and the heat lamp bulb--halogen he supposed--was already glowing orange.

Vasilek gave a constipated groan as he stepped onto the toilet, hands extended over his head. Unfortunately, although the heat source was in the middle of the room, the toilet was not. He had to stretch and reach. And, with his wrists cuffed together, balancing was trickier than he'd anticipated. He fell the first time and covered the sound with a loud cough.

"Damnit," he muttered, remounting his perch. This time, he braced himself by awkwardly hooking one foot around the back of the toilet tank. His hold was tenuous and temporary but lasted long enough for his purposes.

He was actually surprised by how fast the fire started. As a safety precaution, the heat lamp had been fitted with a wire grate, the holes too small to allow even a human finger to pass through. However, a twist of tissue slipped in with ease. He had smoke and then flame within seconds. He dropped the tissue to the floor, and added more tissues until the dispenser was empty. The unspooled roll of toilet paper went next, followed by a few towels and washcloths. He was careful not to smother the blaze. At the same time, he was more interested in the smoke than the fire.

Vasilek flushed the toilet. While it was gurgling away, he turned on the tap and dampened two hand towels. The first went over his face. The smoke wasn't bad yet but he didn't want to start coughing and hacking. *How much longer before the fire alarm went off?* He wasn't ready for that yet but would deal with it if it happened.

He dropped the second towel right on top of where his makeshift camp fire was burning the brightest. A cloud of gray-black smoke started filling the room and Vasilek knew it was time for the real show to begin. He grabbed the shower rod, gave a tug, and brought the whole thing crashing to the floor.

As he'd expected, the metal rod proved too long and unwieldy to use as an effective weapon, especially with the curtain and rings still attached. But his maneuver, meant mostly for distraction, yielded a bonus he hadn't counted on. When the plastic side of the curtain came in contact with his fire it quickly started to melt and burn, the resulting smoke cloud thick, dark and acrid. He was smiling as he again stepped onto the toilet, already planning his next move.

Without appearing to do so, Vasilek had been watching the two cops all afternoon. They were both white: one long and lean and the other, although not short, had a more compact build. They both seemed alert, serious and competent. But what had also struck him was their youth, early to mid twenties maybe. They probably hadn't been in too many scrapes, and he was banking on them never having trained for anything like the bizarre scene he'd constructed.

Their first mistake was standing too close together when they pushed the door open and rushed into the room. The stockier cop led the way. He had his gun drawn but pointed at the smoldering mess in the middle of the floor. He looked up but, by then, it was too late. Shoes back on, Mikhail Vasilek dropped him with a hard kick to the face. He fell backwards, nearly taking his partner to the ground in the process. The second cop was trying so hard to remain upright that he couldn't have used his firearm even if he'd wanted to. He was only off balance for a few seconds but that was all it took.

Like most hotel bathrooms, this one came equipped with an electric hair dryer. Holding it by its three-foot chord, Vasilek swung the thing like a manriki, the ancient Japanese weapon consisting of a weight at the end of a short chain. The dryer wasn't as heavy as he would have liked, but his aim was true and he caught the guy squarely in the side of the head. It was a stunning blow at best, and the cop instinctively raised his hands to protect himself. Vasilek was on him before he knew what was happening. He got him around the neck and, with help from the handcuff chain and some expertly placed pressure, soon sent him off to dreamland.

The first cop was barely conscious and making noises like he might be starting to come around. Vasilek put an end to that with one hard kick to the base of his skull. It hadn't killed him, probably, but he'd feel like shit for a while. Vasilek took a cuff key from one cop, a service weapon from the other, and then he left the room. By that time, the fire alarm had triggered and was blaring away at a hundred decibels.

Would the alarm be limited to one or two floors or going off hotel-wide? He didn't know but thought it would be prudent to create as much chaos and confusion as possible.

As he rapidly descended the stairs from the twelfth floor, he stopped every second or third floor to step into the hallway and pull another alarm. He'd ditched the cuffs, and with his new SIG Sauer semi-automatic hidden in his waistband, Vasilek knew he must look like any other hotel guest, the ones he encountered all exhibiting varying degrees of fear, uncertainty and irritation.

When he finally reached the lobby he was in the midst of a growing throng—groups of people milling about, talking in loud, agitated voices, and none of them seeming to know where to go or what to do. The reception desk phones were ringing incessantly, the alarm was still going off, and members of the hotel staff scurried about, no doubt trying to determine the exact nature of the emergency. He wanted chaos and he'd gotten it, and Vasilek liked the anonymity that provided. No one was even glancing his way, but how much longer could that last? He knew there were a lot more cops around than the two he'd so easily incapacitated upstairs. Did any of them know he'd escaped?

No, he surmised. *Not yet, or this whole place would be on lock-down.*

He looked with longing at the dozen or so people queued up, one by one pushing their way through the big revolving door to the outside. No one was stopping them. Could he really be that close to securing his freedom?

Vasilek took a step that way which altered his sight line slightly, and that's when he saw a policeman stationed on the far side of the revolving door. He was dark skinned and dark haired, and turned so he was facing the people exiting the building. Vasilek couldn't make out many other details from his angle, but he did see the large radio pressed to the man's ear. It appeared he was doing more listening than talking, *and had his body just tensed?*

He knew he was fighting the clock. Once the word got out, possibly any second now, every member of law enforcement within a ten block radius would be on the lookout for Mikhail Vasilek. Did he still have a small window of opportunity or was that net already beginning to close?

Although he was anxious, nervous energy coursing through his veins, Vasilek wouldn't second-guess his decision to try to make his escape. He knew the odds of getting away were slight. But, as far as he was concerned, the *deal* he'd signed with the cops amounted to a death warrant anyway. If given the option he'd rather die than spend his remaining days in a cell and in constant fear of being butt fucked every time he bent over.

Regardless of the chick detective's assurances, he didn't trust the cops and didn't believe they would fulfill their end of the bargain. They had his DNA now. They also had fingerprints, his mug shot, and who knew what else? He was in the system. They wouldn't ever set him free or allow him to leave the country, and that wouldn't change even if Clayton Babbit III was tried, convicted, castrated, and sent to death row. Their promise of immunity was bullshit. Vasilek's only real hope was to deal with Babbit on his own. And for that, he needed to be on the outside.

He concentrated on remaining calm even as he noticed that two more uniformed policemen had entered the lobby from somewhere on the far side. One held a radio. The other stood with his hand resting on his holstered side arm. They both spoke intently to a third man who, based on his name tag and hideous jacket, had to be a hotel manager. Vasilek saw that as a good sign. He guessed they were discussing the fire alarm and the best way to control the situation. If the cops had anything more serious on their minds the hotel dweeb wouldn't be part of the conversation. But again, even if they weren't after him yet, they would be soon.

He took another look toward the front door. Was it worth the risk? He'd be dangerously exposed for a few seconds. He'd have to pass within arm's reach of a cop. *But after that?* He could climb into a taxi, a bus, the subway, or just walk away. He didn't have money, identification, or any of the other items seized when he was arrested. He did have a gun and extraordinary survival skills. Vasilek believed that would more than make up for any other deficits. He'd about decided to go for it when, over the sound of the fire alarm, he heard another noise.

Sirens, he realized, but he couldn't see out as far as the street and didn't know if the approaching vehicles were fire trucks, cop cars, or an entire SWAT team. He wasn't going to wait around to find out either. He turned, hurried past the stairs and the bank of elevators, and headed in the direction of the swimming pool, the fitness room, and a welcoming sign that said EXIT. The hallway was deserted and he made it outside without incident. Another welcome surprise greeted him there.

-49-

"Call Duffy," Megan said, practically dragging me into the hallway. "Tell him to stay put 'til we know what's happening. This could just be a false alarm or a small kitchen fire. I don't want to worry about moving Vasilek until we know we have to."

"I agree," said Zanetti, his crackling police radio pressed tightly to his head. "There's just one problem. "I've been trying to get him and he's not responding."

"What about Fiorentino?"

"Same deal."

"Shit!" Megan said. "You don't think..." but she didn't finish the thought.

We'd reached the door to the stairs but Detective Zanetti stopped before opening it. "This is probably nothing," he said. "But we need to go up there and check."

I was standing right next to Megan and saw her nod but then she apparently had second thoughts.

"You go," she said. "If he's done something, I don't want to bring Alex anywhere near him."

"Come on," Detective Zanetti protested. "He doesn't even know she's here."

"I don't care." Megan's tone left no room for debate. "Go up and check things out. Call me when you get there. Get some backup too. We can't take chances with this guy."

"Okay. And what are you gonna do?"

I couldn't see Detective Zanetti's worry but I could hear it in his voice. He didn't believe we were dealing with a false alarm or anything of the sort. I could feel the tension between the two of them and I knew Megan didn't believe it either.

Their names hadn't been mentioned before in my presence but I assumed Duffy and the other dude were the cops responsible for guarding Mikhail Vasilek. Their silence in the midst of whatever the heck was happening was obviously cause for concern. Something serious was going down and you didn't have to be a bestselling mystery author or a master sleuth to figure out who was probably responsible.

"I'm getting her out," Megan said, a protective hand clutching my arm.

"You shouldn't do it alone. I'll go with you."

"No," Megan said, insistent. "You need to get upstairs and check on the red menace. If that maniac is somehow on the loose we need to know it as soon as possible."

"But—"

"We'll be fine," she said. "Our wheels are right out back. We'll be down the stairs, out, and gone. No worries."

"I'm sorry but I am worried. It isn't SOP."

"Yeah, well, procedure is sort of out the window on this one. I thought you knew that. Now go on, Paul. We'll touch base soon."

He hesitated and I could tell he wanted to say or do something more. In the end, though, he pushed open the door into the stairwell. We followed him onto the landing where he started up and we headed down.

"This can't really have anything to do with him, can it"" I asked, leaning close to Megan as if there were a need for secrecy.

There hadn't been many people around us at first, but their numbers seemed to increase with each half floor we descended. A chorus of raised voices and echoing footsteps reverberated off metal and concrete, escorting us downward and mixing with the constant bleeping and buzzing of the fire alarm. In the resulting din, I could have been practically shouting yet still inaudible or at least indistinguishable to anyone standing more than a few feet away. I wasn't even sure Megan had heard me. She didn't answer anyway but instead kept moving, turning every few steps to make sure I was still behind her.

"He had policemen with him, right?" I asked. "Isn't that what you and Detective Zanetti were saying? So he couldn't have gotten away."

I realized that last statement was more for my benefit than hers. Megan was obviously on edge and that made me nervous and increasingly paranoid.

Shit, I thought. *It is him and she knows it. But how?* That was a question neither of us had an answer to.

"You okay?" she asked, turning around again.

"I'm good," I said, and then I understood why she was asking and why she kept checking on me. She must have been worried I was having a hard time negotiating the stairwell. Her concern was touching and, for once, unnecessary. The lighting was bright, consistent—which was the most important factor—and all I had to do was follow along. There aren't many things more predictable than a commercial-grade flight of stairs: each step, each one hundred eighty degree turn, each length of hand rail exactly like the last and the next. For me, that was about as easy as it ever got.

"Here's the deal," Megan said, slowing and gripping my arm. "There's a loading dock at the rear of the hotel. It's right around the corner from the pool. There's a small parking lot for hotel management and that's where my car is. We'll pass an exit door when we leave the stairwell and many of these people," she gestured with the sweep of an arm, "will probably go out that way. We're not going to do that. I'll take you to the end of the hall and out through the kitchen. That will get us away from the crowd and, once we're outside, we'll be closer to that lot. Just so you know, it's out the kitchen door, down a small ramp, we'll turn left, go maybe fifty feet, and the lot and car are right there."

"Okay," I said. "But why do you want to get me away from everyone? If he's around wouldn't it make more sense to stay close to people. Wouldn't that be safer?"

"Maybe," she said. "We can't count on it, though, because we don't know what he might try to do. There's another reason too." She drew me closer and spoke directly into my ear. "I guess you haven't noticed yet but you're being recognized."

"What?" My mind sort of froze with that one because it wasn't making sense. Then, like someone flipped a switch, I got it.

"You're big news," Megan explained, verbalizing what I'd just figured out for myself. I mean, I knew it peripherally from conversations I'd had with Vicki. She told me Tower Brothers had been inundated with phone calls, inquiries, requests from the media, and everything else. I'd heard about that stuff but hadn't had to deal with it personally, and until now, I hadn't been out in the public eye."

"Your face has been on every newspaper, TV screen, and website for the past two days. Once you get that sort of attention you're not going to be able to escape it even when you want to."

"So these people..." I began but then trailed off. It all seemed so weird.

"Have been talking, pointing, and wondering if it's really you."

We'd reached the final landing and Megan pushed through the door and picked up her pace. She still had my arm so I had no choice but to stay by her side.

"If I take you out any of the regular exits it's going to turn into a mob scene. I don't think either of us wants that."

No doubt, I thought, and I remembered the way she'd kept turning around in the stairwell. I'd assumed she was checking on me, but maybe she'd really been keeping an eye on my observers. They'd apparently all been looking and I hadn't even noticed. That level of oblivion made me feel small and strangely vulnerable.

Is this my new reality? I wondered, and I missed Martin Reginald anew. He'd graciously, perhaps even gratefully occupied the spotlight for years so I didn't have to. I was front and center now and the light was brighter than ever. Believe me when I tell you, the last thing a self-conscious introvert wants is scrutiny. I wasn't sure I could handle it, and I made a mental note to invest in some wigs, ball caps, and maybe a Groucho nose and mustache. *Hey,* I thought. *And if I do run into that Vasilek bastard again I can ask for pointers on creating the perfect disguise.*

We made it to the bottom of the stairs and out into the hallway. I didn't understand how Megan planned on ditching what passed for my new paparazzi. She took care of that by hurrying a short ways and pushing me through a door with a placard in big red letters. I squinted and could just make out the A, U and T from the word AUTHORIZED and I was able to extrapolate the rest on my own.

"Okay," she said. "Let's go." She took my arm again and I heard some exclamations of protest as the door clicked shut but no one attempted to follow us.

I assumed the hotel kitchen would be quieter and less chaotic than the stairwell we'd just left. As is so often the case, I was wrong. In addition to the blaring fire alarm—just as loud in the back of the building—we walked in to a cacophony of clattering dishes, a ringing phone, a bubbling deep fryer, random buzzers I guessed were not related to the alarm, and male and female voices calling out in a variety of foreign languages. Nobody, so far as I could tell, sounded panicked or concerned. They might have been talking about the stock market, the Yankees, Beyoncé, or that night's dinner specials. They just went about their business, as unmoved by the fire alarm as they were by the presence of two strangers suddenly in their midst.

I followed closely in Megan's footsteps as she led me through the labyrinth. She'd either taken that exit route before or had an uncanny sense of direction. As we turned this way and that, I caught glimpses of a big slop sink, a huge hibachi style grill, large, flat work tables, pots and pans, a rolling cart loaded with plates, flatware and linens, industrial-looking equipment I couldn't begin to identify, white clad figures, and a vast array of stainless steel in every shape and size.

"You've got your purse, right?" Megan asked.

"Yes." But I didn't understand why it mattered.

"We're about to go outside," she said. "Make sure you have your sunglasses. We'll be moving fast. Just stay behind me."

I stared at her back and felt a wave of affection or appreciation or gratitude way out of proportion to what had just transpired. I knew I'd mentioned my light sensitivity to her. She remembered and was preparing me for what was coming. So what? Why was that simple expression of empathy bringing forth a whole tide of emotion? Why did I have the sudden urge to hug her and, at the same time, start crying?

Oh crap, I thought. *On top of everything else I must be getting my period.*

Megan stopped short and I almost plowed into her. I'd been so caught up in my hormonally-inspired idiocy I hadn't realized we'd reached the door.

"Are you ready?" she asked.

I swallowed and said yes. We were just going to the parking lot. Why was I nervous? Why did I feel like something evil awaited us just outside?

"Remember," Megan said, looking at me. "We go down the ramp and turn left. It's a straight shot from there."

"I got it," I replied. 'I'm good."

Given the time of day, I was afraid we'd be stepping out into the setting sun. I know it's counterintuitive. The way I sometimes have trouble getting around you would think sunlight streaming into my face would be beneficial—everything in front of me sharply illuminated. Instead, even wearing glasses, what I mostly end up seeing is glare. It can make the simple act of walking while avoiding obstructions a major ordeal.

Thankfully, although the sun had almost set, it was somewhere off to our right and effectively blocked by whatever giant structure was next to our hotel. I could see fine, at least by my standards, and I had a clear view of the black top ramp, large green dumpsters, stacked wooden pallets, a wide concrete sidewalk, and a line of shrubs that must have bordered the parking lot. I also saw the solitary figure that seemed to emerge from thin air. I couldn't make out any details but something in his posture or my own primitive survival instinct told me who it was.

"Get down!" Megan shouted, pushing me back toward the door as she reached for her gun.

Vasilek had a gun too. I couldn't see his arm move but I heard the report as well as an exhalation of surprise and pain as Megan staggered and fell to the ground.

“No!” I cried, rushing to her, but Vasilek was quicker and he got their first.

“Stop right there!” he ordered. “You can’t help her so don’t do anything foolish.”

I couldn’t believe he sounded so calm. He’d not only shot a cop but the lunatic just discharged a firearm right outside a New York City hotel. How could he just stand there? People would be coming on the run. *Or would they?*

I was staring at Megan, who didn’t seem to be moving, but other sensory information had again begun to filter in. Though it was muffled, I could still hear the alarm from inside the building. And from somewhere out front, it sounded like every siren from all five boroughs had been turned on at once. What was a single gunshot in the middle of all that?

Vasilek and I stared at each other, but then I looked down as Megan groaned and moved one leg, revealing a spreading pool of blood.

“Femoral,” he said with indifference. “Say goodbye to that one.”

Ignoring his prior warning, I dropped to my knees and took her hand. “She needs help,” I pleaded, as if, in a fit of conscience, he might summon an ambulance.

He gazed at us in silence. Then, off to the left and some ways away, I heard a shout. Vasilek looked in that direction. He then looked back at me and raised his gun again. I had just enough time to wonder which of us he was aiming at when the lights went out.

-50-

The next thing I remember was Mikhail Vasilek, no longer as calm or collected, shouting at me from the front seat of what I quickly determined must be Megan's car. I was face down in the back, nose pressed into the fabric, my hands painfully bound behind me. My head hurt too but, all things considered, that seemed to be near the bottom of my current list of problems.

Okay, I surmised. *I'm not dead. That's a plus.* But then I thought about Megan and how she'd looked when I last saw her.

Please, I prayed to Father, Son, Holy Ghost, and anyone else tuned into my frequency. *Please let her be all right. Let help get to her in time.* But that last appeal gave me pause. *Just how long have I been out?* I wondered. *Is Megan already....* That line of mental questioning was pointless and panic-inducing so I shifted gears and willed myself to focus on whatever the hell my abductor was squawking about.

"Are you hearing me?" he was saying. "Wake up now! I didn't hit you hard." He emphasized his incredible compassion by reaching over the seat and stabbing two stiff fingers into my ribs.

"Ow!" I tried to roll out of reach but there was literally nowhere to go.

"Sit up," he ordered, "and tell me how to work this damn phone."

Sit up? I thought. *Really?*

So here's a fun party game to try. First, lay face down on your sofa. Better make that a love seat, preferably one that was rescued from Public Works so you can get a good whiff of all the prior occupants. You won't have enough room to stretch out full length but get as comfy as you can. Next, ask a friend to yank your arms behind your back and pull until your eyes are ready to pop out of your skull. Bind your arms and wrists in that position. Now try to sit up. Fun, right?

Vasilek patiently let me thrash around for a good five or six seconds. Then he reached over the seat again, found the free end of the belt and gave it a vicious tug. I felt something in my right shoulder pop and then I was on the floor.

"Get up!" he demanded, as if I'd just been goofing off the whole time and he'd finally tired of my shenanigans.

Screw you, I wanted to say but feared he'd lash out once more. He was angry to the point of distraction and I sensed that had little to do with me. Perhaps he regretted shooting a cop and stealing her ride.

Then again, was the monster even capable of regret? I wasn't so sure about that one.

I wriggled around, used my knees and forehead for leverage, tasted a little floor, and eventually regained the seat in a more or less upright position. Because I was still bound I had to lean forward and slightly to one side. It was awkward and my shoulder burned but I didn't complain. I just positioned myself behind the driver's seat. If Vasilek was tempted to dole out more punishment he wouldn't be able to reach me quite so easily.

"What's with this phone," he snarled, holding an object up. "It keeps talking and I can't get it to stop."

I realized it must be my phone he had, and it was the VoiceOver feature that was giving him trouble. I knew it could be disconcerting, even frustrating to the uninitiated but I felt no sympathy. I just wanted to know why the jerk kept taking my stuff. Something else was bothering me too.

"How did you find me?" I asked. Hadn't Megan said he didn't know I was in the hotel? If that was true, how had he been lying in wait for us to come out?

"What are you talking about?" Vasilek asked, impatient. He wasn't in the mood for my questions but I pressed on.

"You were waiting for us," I said. "How did you know?"

He remained silent so long I didn't think he was going to respond. I was still curious, though, and was about to ask again when he finally spoke.

"I didn't," he said, sounding weirdly pleased. "I took a chance. As you can see, it paid off."

Maybe for you, I thought, and again wondered about Megan. He hadn't given her a chance. And what about the other cops he'd been with? I started to ask about that but he shut me down cold.

"No!" he said, shaking his head. "No more questions. Tell me how to work this thing. Now!"

I'd rather tell you to go to hell. "What are you trying to do?" I asked instead.

"What do you think? I need to place a call. Help me or I'll come back there to persuade you."

That would be a neat trick, I thought, glancing out the window. I couldn't make out any recognizable landmarks. What I did see was typical New York City: buildings, bustling streets, and bumper to bumper traffic as far as the eye could see. It wasn't like he could pull over and hop into the back seat. I was relatively safe as far as that went, but it was also clear that aggravating him would do me no good.

"It's an accessibility option," I explained. "I can't see the screen so it tells me what's there. I can make the call for you if you give me the number."

I wondered why he didn't just use his own phone and then remembered he'd been in police custody. They would have taken any personal items, *so where'd he get the gun he'd used to shoot Megan?* I thought again about the two cops that hadn't answered Detective Zanetti's radio calls and feared the worst.

"Nice try," Vasilek said. "Do you think I'm gonna put this phone in your hands after what you did to me last time? It's your fault I was arrested.

My fault? Interesting interpretation of the facts, but whatever. I couldn't have placed the call anyway, not with my hands secured behind me and he couldn't very well drive the car and set me free at the same time, not that he would have been willing to make that concession.

I'd been using VoiceOver from day one and I was fully aware it could be deactivated with a spoken command. However, his discomfort was about all I had going for me so I opted to keep that information to myself. "It's no different than any other phone," I said reasonably. "You just have to tap everything twice."

"Twice? What does this mean?" he asked, as if he thought I was trying to pull something over on him.

"If you want to make a call, touch the phone app and then tap that button two times."

He did but tentatively, and I could hear from the audio prompts that the app did not open. "This is not working," he yelled, waving the phone in one hand while punching the steering wheel with the other. "I know you are lying to me!"

Horns honked but that's a common occurrence in the big city. I doubted it had anything to do with us. Too bad, too. It would have been nice if some concerned motorist figured out what was happening and came to my rescue. Could I signal someone to my plight? *Better not try,* I decided reluctantly. *He's got a handgun and a bad temper.* I hated the idea of sitting there and doing nothing but I figured my best bet was to go along for now, do what he asked, try to keep him calm, and I'd hopefully get a chance to escape if and when we stopped.

"It's like a double click on a computer," I told him. "You have to do it quickly to get it to work."

He tried again and was successful. Entering the phone number was another struggle but, after a lot of muttering and cursing, he managed that too.

He kept the phone pressed to his ear so I couldn't hear so much as a murmur from the other end of the line. He was talking to Clayton Babbit. That much I knew. I also learned he was anxious to find a place to meet. It seemed Vasilek wasn't enjoying my company much. That's assuming I was the *troublesome bitch* he kept referring to.

"No," he said, his voice rising. "It's got to be now!"

A pause.

"I've got a bit of a situation here. I'm driving around in a stolen car and it belongs to the New York City Police."

Another pause.

"Because shit happens! The point is they'll be looking for me and they're probably already tracking this vehicle."

Like he thought he might be able to escape their prying eyes, Vasilek hit the accelerator as he made a hard left turn. I wasn't ready and almost fell off the seat again.

"This is your party," he said. "You either come now or I'm gonna leave this thing and just walk away. It makes no difference to me."

He listened for a while, sometimes nodding, sometimes shaking his head, and all the while making low grunts and other guttural sounds I couldn't interpret.

"Of course I have her," he finally said. "You think I'd be calling otherwise?

"I know. The troublesome bitch is a regular celebrity."

He listened again, and then raised his eyes and I could feel him studying me in the rearview mirror.

"That's a good point," he said. "I hadn't considered that." As Vasilek spoke he took a hand off the wheel and beckoned me forward. I thought he must have another question about the phone. Okay, I don't exactly know what I was thinking but, like a fool, I slid a little to my right and leaned toward the front seat. Quick as a snake he reached back, grabbed me by the neck, dug a finger in somewhere, and my lights were out before I even felt any pain.

. . .

"She give you any trouble then?"

The voice was unfamiliar, a little gravely but with a soft southern drawl. I opened my eyes and discovered that my new surroundings were unfamiliar too, my nose now pressed into black leather instead of beige fabric. I felt the rumble, heard the engine noise, and knew I must be in another back seat. I guessed pickup truck but wasn't quite ready to investigate further.

"Nothing I couldn't handle," Mikhail Vasilek replied. "Do you have my money?"

"As requested," said the guy that had to be Babbit. "You'll get it in due time. I need to have a chat with our friend back there first. I gotta know, though. How'd you nab her and how'd you end up in an unmarked cop car?"

"There was no other way. She had police protection. This woman detective was with her all the time. I know you are eager to conclude our business. I am too. An opportunity presented itself and I took advantage of it. I shot the cop, took her car, and used my belt to make sure Ms. Rhodes could not cause any more problems."

Babbit whistled. "Damn, Sport," he said. "You shot a cop? I'll tell you one thing. You got some cajones."

I thought that was a fair assessment. As I understood it, Vasilek had already worked out a plea deal with Detectives Lynch and Zanetti. Megan hadn't shared many details but I knew he'd get a lighter sentence in exchange for his cooperation. Vasilek apparently hadn't been satisfied with those terms so took matters into his own hands. It was ballsy too. But why was he withholding information? Now that he was out and free, why wasn't he telling Babbit what had actually taken place? *Curious,* I thought, and tucked that away for later consideration.

"I meant to ask before," Babbit said. "What happened to your phone? I didn't recognize the number when you called me. I almost didn't answer."

Vasilek was silent for a few seconds but then he spoke. "I had to move fast when the cop went down. I didn't realize it at the time but my phone must have fallen out of my pocket. There was luckily another one I could use."

"Hers?" Babbit asked.

"Yes. And that reminds me..."

I heard Vasilek shifting around, and then I both heard and felt the rush of air as his window was lowered.

"I won't be needing that anymore." He raised his window again. "She'll no longer have a use for it either."

Damn, I thought, realizing what he'd done. My phone was history, but that was small potatoes compared to what Vasilek had just said. I was a goner. I shivered involuntarily and immediately wished I hadn't.

My arms were still bound, maybe even tighter than before, and those extra movements sent fresh waves of pain through my shoulder, the tingling and burning so intense I had to bite the seat to keep from groaning out loud.

"So where are we going?" Vasilek asked, like we were on a Sunday drive.

Babbit cleared his throat. "Well, my hotel is out of the question. We'd have privacy in my room but getting to it would be tough, especially if she's still out and we had to carry her inside."

"Oh, she's awake," Vasilek said with certainty. "She has been for a while now."

I wondered how he knew that. I hadn't announced myself. I'd just been lying there quietly and kind of hoping they'd forget all about me. So much for that.

"Well then," Babbit said, raising his voice and sounding genuinely pleased. "Ms. Rhodes, I'm very happy to make your acquaintance. I'm looking forward to a more formal introduction later. We have a lot to talk about."

I didn't respond, choosing instead to stick with my possum routine even though it seemed no one was fooled.

"Did you drug her?" Babbit asked.

"No," Vasilek replied, "although I do have much experience in that area. I assumed you would want her fully alert. It was advisable to keep her out of sight, as you suggested, so I used a technique that is more short term and has no residual effects."

"That's... great," Babbit said, and I sensed I might not be the only one uncomfortable with the idea of riding around with a human killing machine. "Well," he added with a forced chuckle. "These windows are tinted all the way around so she can do whatever she wants back there and no one will be the wiser."

"She can walk into a hotel under her own power and I promise she will behave herself. Still," Vasilek continued, "she is highly recognizable and many people will be looking for her. It would be best to avoid any public places."

"My thoughts exactly, and that shouldn't be a problem. I was out this morning and drove past a service station under construction. It's not too far from here. You can't see much from the road with all the fencing but there didn't seem to be any activity. I saw what looked like a clinic on one side and a consignment shop on the other. They'll probably be closed by now. We'll have all the privacy we need."

"Probably isn't good enough," Vasilek insisted. "We have to be sure. We should stay away until it's full dark out and then drive by to see how it looks. Will you be able to park this truck out of sight?"

Babbit snorted. "There ain't nobody lookin' for my truck so far as I know, but yeah. We can keep it hidden all right."

I don't know how long we spent driving around. It felt like forever, and what kept going through my mind was this scene from the movie *Sneakers.* The Robert Redford character gets snatched and stuffed into the trunk of a car. He obviously can't see where he's taken. But later, with the help of a genius blind guy incidentally, he's able to identify the spot based on things he heard, specifically, the distinctive sound the tires made on a particular stretch of road.

For a while, from my prone position on the back seat, I kept track of each turn we made: two lefts, a right, another left. It was stupid I know. Since I hadn't the slightest inkling where we started, my information gathering was useless even if I could have somehow remembered it all. It kept me busy, though. And when I tired of that I tried zeroing in on my other senses. I couldn't see anything, and that wouldn't have improved much even if I sat up and looked around. That one sense I was accustomed to doing without. But as for the others?

I did a quick sensory inventory. I could hear my own heartbeat as well as the blood pounding in my ears. I smelled leather, testosterone, a pine air freshener, and my own sweat. Tactile sensation came next and that was a doozy. I could feel the belt biting into my wrists, while the pins and needles in my shoulder fought for attention with my suddenly full bladder. Finally, I could definitely taste fear and that was all mine too.

Vasilek and Babbit didn't say much to each other and they ignored me altogether. Somehow, that only added to my apprehension as long minutes stretched by in silence. Maybe it was just me but the tension seemed almost palpable. That was especially true when one of them, Babbit I assumed, turned on the radio news. It clicked off again almost immediately.

"Please," Vasilek said. "I must think and I need silence to do it."

"Whatever you say, Sport," Babbit replied with an exaggerated sigh and I could tell he was irritated.

How much more irritated would he become if I popped up and told him the real reason Vasilek didn't want the radio on? They would certainly be reporting on the incident at the hotel, the escape of a dangerous criminal *namely Mikhail Vasilek*, my abduction, and the condition of Megan and the other two policemen. I didn't understand what sort of game Vasilek was playing or why he and Babbit seemed to have different motives, but pitting them against each other right now might put me in the crosshairs and I decided that was a low-percentage play. Keeping quiet had kept me alive, so far anyway, and I figured I'd continue to roll with that strategy for the time being.

We drove a while longer, and I really started hoping we'd stop before I wet my pants. Had I known I was going to be kidnapped I would have planned better and used the facilities ahead of time. Live and learn.

"It's after seven o'clock," Vasilek said, as if responding to a question no one had asked. "Let's go check out your building site and see if it will serve our purposes."

"Oh, are you sure? I've still got a quarter tank of gas. We could keep at this bullshit for another hour if you want. I've got nothing better to do." Babbit's sarcasm was obvious but Vasilek didn't seem to pick up on it.

"You could question her right here," he said. "I told you that before. Taking her elsewhere is an unnecessary risk."

"Maybe so," Babbit allowed. "But I've been waiting for this chance for a while and I want to look her in the eye. And, no offense, Sport, but this is personal business and some of what I have to say I might not want you to hear."

Huh, I thought. *I guess they both have their secrets.*

"Your business is of no interest to me," Vasilek said. "Haven't I made that clear? Pay me what I'm owed and you can let me out right now."

How much? I wondered, straining to hear. As terrifying as it was to learn I'd had a price on my head it would be nice to know what they thought I was worth. That sort of information could be handy when it was time to negotiate my next book deal. I chose not to dwell on the odds any such negotiations would ever come to pass.

"Can't do it," Babbit said. "This is a delicate situation if you know what I mean. I gotta keep you around in case I need your special assistance. Don't worry, though. I don't think this will take long and then you can take your money and do whatever it is that you do."

Vasilek grunted but said nothing more. Moments later the truck slowed and made a sharp right turn. We bounced across a section of cracked or potholed pavement, turned again, and came to a stop.

-51-

"What'd I tell ya?" Babbit asked as the engine died. "Quiet as a tomb and we have all the privacy we need."

"Great," Vasilek said with obvious lack of enthusiasm. "So what happens now?"

"Get her out," Babbit ordered. "I want to take a look around."

Doors opened and I braced myself, thinking Vasilek would be as rough as before. I noticed my shoulder didn't hurt as much and mostly just felt numb. The fingers on my right hand tingled too. Neither of those things seemed like especially good signs. I flexed and tried to generate a little blood flow but it didn't help. The belt was still too tight.

To my immense relief, he didn't grab the free end and drag me out like a dog on a leash. He gave his instruction, his tone direct but unthreatening, and then stepped aside and waited for me to comply. I didn't want to push my luck so extricated myself as quickly as I could. Admittedly, though, that wasn't very fast because I was trying not to put any weight on my right arm or shoulder.

Once I was out and on my feet I examined my new digs, mostly so I didn't have to look at Mikhail Vasilek anymore. I'd had enough of him already.

Since our first encounter in the 59th Street subway station, he'd had several opportunities to terminate my literary career once and for all yet hadn't done so. Sure, he had gotten a little rough with me at Vicki's house but I thought he'd also demonstrated at least some level of restraint. That might have been encouraging except for the fact that I'd stood there and watched him kill Brandon for no good reason. He'd shot and possibly killed Megan too and I had no delusions about him having a soft spot in his heart for me. Babbit gave the orders and Vasilek followed them. That's all there was to it. He might have his own motives but I knew that protecting me was not among them. I would find no safety in that quarter.

With Vasilek's prompting I moved a few steps forward, hesitantly because I wasn't sure where I was supposed to go. Babbit had said he thought they were building a service station there but I don't know how he knew that. It looked like a lunar landscape to me: cratered ground, random piles of rock and gravel, and some unidentifiable, large, and big-wheeled piece of equipment parked at the far end. It seemed otherworldly, everything bathed in a yellowish glow from a single pole light directly overhead. It cast long, dark shadows and I felt like they were all reaching for me. Okay, so maybe I was letting my imagination take over and I tried, unsuccessfully mostly, to look at things with a more critical and less freaked-out eye.

I guessed the area we were in was about fifty feet across. My depth perception does kind of stink so consider a margin of error of a good twenty-five percent. Can I paint a mental picture or what?

Orange construction fencing lined the front, both sides, and maybe the back too although I couldn't see quite that far. To the right of where Babbit had parked I saw a couple of what looked like oblong concrete islands. Maybe they'd be gas pumps when they grew up. And to the left, I figured that would someday be a convenience store or mini mart. There was still a little work to do on that as it currently resembled something you might see in downtown Baghdad after the Taliban came calling—two partial walls and not much else.

Vasilek prodded me along but my feet suddenly got very heavy as Clayton Babbit came into view, materializing from behind one of those walls and starting our way. I hadn't gotten a look at him before and don't really know what I was expecting, maybe a Colonel Sanders type based on the few words I'd heard him speak. That image was shattered and I drew in an involuntary breath. The man was huge, seemingly twice my height unless that was a trick of the light combined with his big cowboy hat. There was definitely no mistaking his girth. I couldn't tell if it was muscle or fat but he lumbered along with the creepy, side-to-side gait of a grizzly bear. I half expected him to start growling. I doubt it would have made me anymore frightened than I already was.

"Well then," he drawled, rocking to halt right in front of me. "Ms. Rhodes, it is indeed a pleasure to finally make your acquaintance." He nodded and actually tipped his hat. I sensed he was smiling too but I couldn't really tell. "I'd shake your hand," he added, "but it appears you are otherwise engaged. Maybe we'll get around to that later.

"All right, Sport," he said, turning his attention to Vasilek. "Bring her inside so she and I can get comfortable."

Comfortable? Holy shit! I didn't like the sound of that and hoped it wasn't a euphemism for acts I didn't even want to consider. Was that the real reason Vasilek hadn't killed me already? Was that why Babbit said he wanted privacy? Was he planning to...? Restrained as I was, I wouldn't even be able to put up a fight.

Well, I thought. *If that's how this is gonna go down he'd better be careful. I'll kick him right in the gumbo if he gives me half a chance.*

Babbit led the way and Vasilek guided me around one corner of what I'll generously refer to as the building. Once inside, I realized it was slightly more complete than I'd thought. A third wall was underway and there were beginnings of a foundation or base for the forth. I didn't notice that until I tripped over it, and I probably would have fallen on my face had Vasilek not been there to steady me.

"Thanks," I said, momentarily forgetting who I was talking to. I then felt like an idiot for expressing any gratitude to him. The bastard didn't deserve it.

"Over here," Babbit said, gesturing at a knee-high pile of neatly-stacked cinder blocks. He must have arranged them just for me because the rest of the place was a jumbled mess of construction debris: big steel drums, lengths of pipe, pallets loaded with bags of something, a hand cart, some tools, and a bunch of other stuff too. There was no roof yet so at least I could kind of see what was around me and I took some comfort in that.

Vasilek held me by the shoulder—the left one fortunately—steered me to a spot Babbit indicated and forced me to sit. He then retreated, turning and taking up a position a little ways off.

"And just what the hell are you doing?" Babbit asked, staring at him.

Vasilek shifted and I could tell his posture stiffened. "I thought you said you wanted me here."

"No," Babbit replied. "What I said was that I might need your assistance. I also told you I wanted to talk to this little lady in private. That's why we came here, or have you forgotten that?"

"I don't forget anything," Vasilek said, something in his tone making the hair stand up on the back of my neck. I didn't know how those two had ever gotten together but they sure didn't seem to like each other much.

"Tell you what," Babbit said, magnanimous. "Just give us some space here. This won't take long once we get down to business. Ten minutes oughtta do it." "

Well, that's reassuring, I thought. *If he's on a schedule maybe my virtue will remain intact and he won't have time to question, rape, and kill me.* I wondered what I could do to avoid all those things but nothing came to mind. I couldn't call for help. My phone was gone and I was fresh out of Bat-Signals. What did that leave?

"Where do you want me to go?" Vasilek asked.

"I don't give a shit, Sport," Babbit said, his gaze now on me. "I just want you out of earshot for a while. You can wait in the truck. On second thought," he amended, "you might hotwire it and take off with all my money. We can't have that now can we. I think we're safe here but we want to make sure our position is secure. Maybe go out by the road to keep an eye on things. I'll signal when I'm ready for you."

Vasilek didn't say a word. He just stood, arms loose at his sides. I doubted he was used to being dismissed like that. I knew he had a gun tucked away someplace and I figured he was itching to use it. In the end, though, he turned and walked off, the crunch of his footsteps gradually fading until they could no longer be heard.

-52-

As he walked, Mikhail Vasilek's right hand strayed to his waist band. He touched the weapon there and fantasized about what it could do—what it wanted to do. There would, he knew, be time for that later. He just needed to be patient. Sighing inwardly, he dropped his hand back to his side and continued on, not even glancing at Babbit's pickup as he moved past.

The jackass had been right about one thing. Vasilek had briefly considered taking his truck and getting out of there. He wouldn't have had to hotwire it either. Why go to the trouble when it would be so much easier, *not to mention more satisfying*, to simply pop him and take his keys? What stopped him was the nagging suspicion that Clayton Babbit was a liar. Vasilek was sure he could search the truck from bumper to bumper and not find one dollar of his money. He'd have another dead body on his hands and nothing to show for it.

Of course, he didn't have to kill Babbit yet. There was another way to play it. He could overpower him, tie him up like a Christmas turkey, and deliver him to the cops in exchange for his freedom. The problem there was that he'd shot the lady cop and figured she was probably dead. He'd gotten the best of her ill-prepared cohorts too. They weren't about to forget that. True, he'd accepted their plea agreement but believed his recent actions made that null and void. The cops weren't gonna deal anymore. They wanted Babbit, but not so much that they'd ever be willing to let Vasilek go.

He knew he'd pulled off a minor miracle when he not only broke out of his room but actually made it all the way out of the hotel. He'd slipped out a rear door and that chick cop's car had been sitting right there as if waiting for him. He couldn't believe it—thought it must be a different car. After all, one unmarked looked much like another. But then he saw the dented rear quarter panel. It had to be hers . Should he have just taken it? He could have, and knew he would have been well away before anybody realized what he'd done. However, he'd still wanted Babbit. He wanted his money too, and that meant he needed Alex Rhodes. What Vasilek hadn't expected was for the woman to practically walk straight into his arms but that's what had happened.

"I must be living right," he muttered as he approached the street. From behind him, he heard the muted chirp of Babbit's truck horn. *So you don't trust me*, he thought, recognizing the sound of door locks being remotely engaged. *The feeling's mutual.*

In truth, Babbit had nothing to fear, not from that standpoint anyway. If Vasilek decided to cut and run, which was still a possibility, he'd be using a different set of wheels. He supposed the dark blue pickup was safe enough driving around Lower Manhattan, or wherever they were, but he wouldn't want to be in the vehicle to try to leave New York via any of the bridges or tunnels. By now, he assumed those exit routes would all be closely monitored.

Vasilek kicked at a loose stone and sent it bouncing across the macadam. "Fool," he said, remembering how sure Babbit had sounded when he claimed no one was looking for him. *No one was looking for me either,* he thought sourly. *Not until you came along. Now, thanks to your arrogance, the net is closing around both of us.*

He'd watched Babbit intently and seen the almost manic look in the man's eyes. He had a personal vendetta and, crazy as it seemed, appeared willing to risk everything just to get his hands on the blind author. *Why?* Vasilek didn't understand that and definitely did not share Babbit's fatalistic attitude. Yes, he still wanted the money he was owed. Failing that, though, he'd do whatever it took to get away unscathed.

Vasilek stood by the edge of the road, watching traffic stream past and wondering how he should proceed. Was his big payday already a lost cause? He thought so, and figured Clayton Babbit was too. It no longer mattered what Rhodes told him or how many secrets she revealed. It didn't matter if she lived or died. Babbit was going down either way, and Vasilek wasn't about to go down with him. It was time to retreat, regroup, and eventually resurface as someone else. The quarter million would have been nice but there'd be other jobs, other hits, and other opportunities.

Unfortunately, he couldn't look to the future until he addressed the present. He had to get out of there and didn't have any of the resources he was used to. His lack of funds wasn't a big deal. He could snatch a purse or roll a drunk if it came to that. However, along with everything else, the cops had confiscated his hotel key card. They might not have searched his room yet but they'd cut off his access to it, which likewise meant he couldn't get to his false IDs or any of the other essentials he'd stowed in the safe. For the time being, all he had was a cop's gun and the clothes on his back. Sam could help him with new IDs, new credit cards and whatever else he needed. That would take time, and Vasilek wasn't sure how much of that he had left.

His immediate concern was getting as far away from Clayton Babbit as possible. He could start walking but the ten minutes Babbit requested were about up and, if he realized Vasilek had split, the crazy redneck might actually come after him. That was a scene he didn't even want to imagine. He looked to the traffic light at the end of the block. As he watched, it changed from green, to yellow, to red. Vehicles slowed and stopped, and that gave Vasilek an idea. He never thought of himself as a carjacker before but, thanks to Babbit, he'd been adding all sorts of new things to his resume.

He wanted a single-occupant vehicle, preferably one driven by a female. Studying the limited pickings he rejected a silver Chevy Blazer with tinted windows, a Ford Focus with five people crammed into it, and a white, solid-panel delivery van he couldn't see into at all. The UPS truck was no good either. He had about decided to wait for the next red light and the chance of better prospects when, at the front of the line, he spied a red Camry. The long-haired driver had her visor down and appeared to be singing while applying makeup.

Perfect, Vasilek thought, striding that way. He had his hand at the small of his back and was about to make his move when an even better option presented itself. Approaching the cross street from the south, Vasilek saw the familiar illuminated beacon atop a New York City taxi.

"Count your blessings," he murmured, looking on as the light turned green and the Camry made a right turn and headed off, the oblivious driver bobbing her head and singing all the while. She'd never know how close she'd come to being his unwilling accomplice. Of course, she wouldn't have lived long enough to tell that tale anyway.

No matter how smooth and fast he'd been, Vasilek knew the carjacking would have been iffy, and might have been witnessed and reported. He didn't need that; but there was nothing more normal, more routine, more New York than climbing into the back of a cab. No one would give him a second glance. He didn't have the fare. That wouldn't be an issue until he'd reached his destination. By then, he might pay his tab in lead just to blow off some steam.

He waved to get the cabbie's attention and saw the driver, a tall man in a ball cap, nod and raise one finger. He then put on his signal and waited for a break in traffic so he could pull to the curb.

Vasilek had to figure out where he wanted to go—the airport was unfortunately out of the question—and how to quickly acquire a new identity. *If he'd only come through with my money,* he thought, knowing how a pile of cash would make things easier. But then he stopped. So maybe Babbit didn't have his two hundred and fifty thousand. He did have a wallet, credit cards, and a license.

It's a start, Vasilek thought, but then realized he could do better because Babbit had something even more valuable. He had Rhodes. What bargain would the police make for her safe return? Hell, Vasilek could give them Rhodes and Babbit too. Did he dare, with his means of escape sitting right there with the engine idling? *If I'm not gonna get paid,* he mused, *should I go for revenge instead?*

Still conflicted, he met the cabbie's eye for just a moment. He then shook his head, gave an apologetic shrug, turned and hurried away.

-53-

"I need to step outside," Babbit said. "Be a good girl and stay put. In fact, you move so much as an eyelid I'll come back and rip out your throat."

Okay, I thought as he left. *So that's the tone we're setting for this tete-a-tete*, and I started scanning the floor for a weapon or, failing that, something I could use to free my hands. Nothing was in reach—nothing I saw anyway—and I didn't dare get up because I didn't know how long he'd be gone.

Maybe, I thought. *He isn't gone but just spying on me to see what I'll do.* But then I heard his truck door open, and close again a few seconds later. That was followed by a muted double horn beep.

Huh. He had a key fob. I assumed so anyway. So why hadn't he locked up from here? *Did he put something inside? Take something out? Both?* Further speculation on that would have to wait.

"Alrighty then," Babbit said, reappearing and ambling over, thumbs hooked in the waistband of his jeans. "Our friend out there tells me you got some screwed up eyes or something." He stood in front of me looking down, and then raised a leg and rested one of his big boots on the cinder block between my knees. "So what's the story?" he asked, leaning in close and getting right in my face. "How much can you see?"

Not much, I thought, *but I perceive plenty. I know you're a bully even though I can't see your smug, superior expression. I bet you're a coward too and that's why Mikhail Vasilek is still here. You cover up your spinelessness by bullying him but I don't think he's fooled and I'm not either.*

"It's hard to explain," I said, not fooled but definitely scared. "I can't drive or read regular print. That's about it."

"Uh-huh." He lowered his foot and took a step back. "Well, the way you're all... cock-eyed and such, I bet it's a lot worse than that. Truth is I don't care. I'm just making conversation 'cause I'm a gentleman."

Gentleman? I couldn't come up with a civil response to that so said nothing.

"It don't matter anyway," he continued. "I've got more important questions and I suggest you give me better answers."

"What do you want to know?" I asked, swallowing against the tremor in my voice.

"Let's start simple. Just what in hell did I ever do to you?"

"What?" I asked, even though I already knew where this was headed. I also knew there was no way to stop it and that terrified me.

"I own a successful business," Babbit told me. "Several actually. I started with nothing but I worked hard and fought hard for every dime I have. People told me I couldn't do it but I did it anyway."

He paused then as if he expected me to offer congratulations for murdering his way to the top. I just looked at my feet.

"I had the world on a string. Then you came along with a pair of fucking scissors. I want to know why." Babbit moved in close again, bent down, and spoke directly into my ear. "Understand one thing," he said, his voice deceptively friendly. "I'm usually not a violent man. My wife, God rest her soul, cheated on me with a spic pool boy and I never once raised my hand in anger."

God rest her soul? I thought. *Holy crap!* I wanted to run but knew there was nowhere to go. So he didn't smack his wife around, or so he'd said. *That's great, but he still might have poisoned her, shot her, or pushed her in front of a bus just like….*

"How'd you know Deborah Royal?" Babbit asked, as if somehow aware of who I'd just been thinking of.

It took me a second to find my voice. "She was," I started, swallowed, and started again. "She was an old friend."

"Must have been a pretty good one."

"Not really," I said honestly. "We hadn't kept in touch."

"Yet she wrote to you," he accused, removing a folded sheet of paper from his back pocket and waving it under my nose. I knew it had to be one of the missing copies of Deb's note. He spat on it and threw it on the ground. "Tell the class what happened next."

I looked at him and then quickly looked away. There was nothing I could do to mollify him, and I had the disconcerting feeling anything I said would instantly set him off.

"Oh, come on now," he coaxed, reaching out and hooking my chin with a thick finger. I resisted and then my whole jaw was in his grip. "Listen girl," he said, squeezing. "I'm not playing games here and I don't have time to fuck around. I want you to look me in the eye and tell me why you decided to ruin my life." He squeezed harder and I could feel cartilage starting to pop.

I knew he could snap my neck as easily as if he were crushing a beer can. Fighting back tears, I tried to answer but his Vulcan death grip made that impossible. All that came out was a throaty gurgle.

"What's that?" he asked, blessedly letting go. "I couldn't hear you."

I ran my tongue around the inside of my mouth to see if anything was loose or broken. All seemed to be in working order but the lower half of my face felt like I'd just gone a few rounds with Kung Fu Panda. He wanted me to know he was serious and that message had been delivered. Unfortunately, my problem remained. There wasn't a thing I could say that wouldn't piss him off. My novels had fictionalized his story, sort of, and I'd done my best to crucify him based on the information I had. He knew that already, and forcing me to confess my sins wouldn't change a thing.

"You know he turned on you," I said, deciding deflection was my best and possibly only option.

"What?" Babbit asked, moving in again and looming over me, but I looked up and forced myself to hold his gaze.

"Mikhail Vasilek," I said. "The police never let him go. They arrested him, questioned him, and offered him a deal if he agreed to help them catch you."

"You're lying."

"No," I told him. "He was in their custody until this afternoon. He managed to escape. That's how the cop really got shot. I was there and I saw it happen."

"Bullshit!" Babbit said. "I doubt you can see your own toes."

That was true actually but irrelevant. "He told them he thought you were tracking him through his phone. He convinced them to move him out of the police station. He was being held at a hotel."

"Bullshit," Babbit said again, but this time mostly to himself. He started pacing, and I knew at least part of what I'd told him hit home. Maybe it was the bit about the tracking.

"In the car," I said, continuing to press. "Why do you think he turned the radio off so fast? He didn't want you to hear the news because you'd find out what really happened."

"Shut up."

"He didn't know I was in the same hotel. He got lucky. Had I not been there he probably would have taken off and left you hanging."

"Shut up!" Babbit ordered, spinning to face me.

"You're the one they really want," I said. "And Vasilek was helping them get you. You sent him away. He could be calling the police right now."

"**Shut up! SHUT UP!!**"

I realized in a flash I'd pushed it too far. Babbit stooped and picked up a short length of pipe or maybe a section of two by four. I couldn't tell in the dimness, but he came up swinging and aiming for my head. I tried to duck and roll at the same time, and was only partially successful. He didn't crush my skull as he'd surely intended but, as I dropped to the floor, his makeshift bludgeon made solid contact with my right shoulder. The pain was explosive, and I both heard and felt bones crack.

I screamed, collapsing in the dirt as I instinctively curled into a protective ball, my full bladder finally letting go.

"Stupid bitch!" he snarled, standing over me. He raised his club again and I knew he planned on finishing the job. I wished I could look away so I wouldn't see the death blow descending but I somehow lacked the muscle control even to close my eyes.

So this is it, I thought, thankful the end would come quickly. I'd been lucky in my apartment lobby when Vasilek decided to steal my stuff instead of coming after me. Fate smiled again when my S.O.S. text to Vicki was not only received but understood. This time, however, I knew it was all over. No one even knew where I was. They wouldn't be coming to my rescue and, trussed up and broken, there was no way I could rescue myself. It was hopeless. I was going to die in a puddle of my own stinking urine.

"Any last words?" Babbit asked, but then he froze as we both heard the sound of running feet. Seconds later Vasilek was there.

"What happened?" he asked, stepping into view. "I heard shouts."

"Ain't nothin' wrong here, Sport," Babbit said. "I was about to pop her like a birthday piñata. You're just in time for the show."

I struggled to lever myself out of reach, scrabbling ineffectually with my feet and unbroken left side and getting nowhere.

"Wait," Babbit said, turning to Vasilek and momentarily shifting his attention away from me. "You could hear that out at the road?"

That was encouraging. I'd find the strength to scream my guts out if there was any chance it might summon help, but Vasilek dashed that hope.

"I was already half way back," he said. "I still hardly heard you over the traffic noise. There isn't much around, no houses or people, but still lots of cars. You could probably run a jack hammer back here and no one would notice."

"That so?" Babbit asked, a disquieting note to his voice. "You know," he went on, switching his piñata popper to his left hand and dropping the other to his waist. "Our guest just told me something interesting. Maybe you'd like to comment."

"On what?" Vasilek asked, moving more into my field of vision.

"Well," said Babbit. "We know Ms. Rhodes here is a storyteller and she just told me a beauty. I'm sure it's a pack of lies but I'd like to know what you think. Mind telling me where you were when I called you this afternoon?"

Vasilek was quiet but only for a second. "I was in that police woman's car," he explained. "You know that. We—"

"Hold on, Sport," Babbit cut in, stepping back as Vasilek stepped forward. "I know about the car because I saw it. And I believe you actually did shoot the cop, but maybe you could enlighten me as to how and where that happened."

"What did she tell you?" Vasilek asked, and I felt his gaze shift to me.

"Sorry, Mi-kha-il, but I'm the one asking the questions now. Where were you?"

"At a hotel," he admitted. "Trying to save my life, and yours."

"Really? By lying to me? By being a snitch? Thanks a lot. I should use this thing to break your fucking neck."

Babbit had circled around so he was mostly behind me. I couldn't see what he was doing but pictured him swinging his so called popper over his head.

"I did what I had to do," Vasilek said, his voice ice cold. "I was facing a murder conviction at the least, and I would have spent the rest of my life in prison. They would have gotten you too. They had enough even without my assistance."

"So you decided to make their jobs easier."

"No!" Vasilek insisted, his denial convincing but I knew he was full of crap. I wondered what Babbit thought about it.

I heard scuffling feet. They'd both moved into the shadows by then and I couldn't see what either of them was up to. They didn't seem to be paying any attention to me. *Time to make a break for it,* I thought, imagining the futility of slinking along at a snail's pace, bucking and thrashing all the while. I doubted I'd make it two feet . *Pointless,* I concluded. So, rather than waste my energy, I waited, listened, and prayed.

"You don't know what I went through," Vasilek was saying, "the risks I took."

"To save your ass," Babbit retorted.

"To save us both! We're here right now because I gave us that chance."

"You expect me to believe that? You were doing me a favor?"

More scuffling and I could see Babbit again. He'd moved back into the pool of light but Vasilek was still mostly in darkness.

"I've been doing you favors all along," Vasilek said. "Trying to make up for one stupid mistake after another"

"Don't call me stupid, Son."

"No? Remember how this started? You hired a hit on the wrong person. You say you want information from Rhodes but look what you've done to her."

I willed myself to shrink into the dirt and disappear from view. No luck. I was sure they could still see me.

"She's not gonna tell you anything now," Vasilek went on. "Why should she? You're stupid and reckless."

"I said don't call me stupid!"

"You got another name for it? Things didn't have to get so far out of control but you didn't have the sense to back off. Your ego is bigger than your brain."

"That's enough," Babbit said. "I didn't hire you for your opinions and you'd best keep them to yourself." His tone was menacing but he moved backwards as he spoke, circling around to my left with Vasilek in measured pursuit.

"Then what did you hire me for?" he asked. "I don't know anymore because you keep changing the rules. One thing I do know is that I still haven't seen my money. So here's my rule. You pay me now or I'm taking Rhodes, and your truck, and we're getting out of here."

Um... what? I had no clue what game Vasilek was playing but knew I didn't want him to deal me in. I'd been on two rides with him already that day and didn't relish the idea of a third. Would it be preferable to having my egg cracked by Babbit? I honestly wasn't sure.

Their slow motion dance continued, stalking each other like two animals in a cage. Babbit still held his arm-breaker but in his left hand and down at his side. His movements were abrupt and jerky, and his body language gave off a vibe of indecision. He hadn't run, though, which I would have done in a heartbeat had I been in his shoes. Vasilek was flipping scary, seemingly floating along, tracking Babbit's progress without pause and with no wasted motion. His hands were empty, loose at his sides just as I'd seen them before. I knew or assumed he still had a gun tucked away somewhere. It didn't look like he planned on using it, and I knew he wouldn't need a fire arm to inflict quick, lethal damage. Babbit must have sensed that too because he kept retreating.

"Kill her and we have no leverage," Vasilek said. "I take her and maybe I still have a chance. Come to think of it, maybe I take you too. I know the police are anxious to meet you."

"That's too bad for them," Babbit said. "'Cause I don't plan on going down without a fight."

He pivoted then, swinging his pipe or board in a wide arc. The motion was awkward because he still held it in his left hand and I knew him to be right-handed. The weight of the bludgeon seemed to throw him further off balance. He compensated by lunging forward, turning his body as he did so. He had his back to me, and I saw a flash of light glistening off an object at the small of his back.

He's got a gun too, I realized, remembering how Babbit had gone out to his truck. *He must have retrieved it then.* And in that moment, I knew his clumsy charge was a ploy. I considered calling out a warning, but what was the point? Could protecting Mikhail Vasilek really increase my own odds of survival? I was still debating the various possibilities and implications when Vasilek stepped in close, grabbing Babbit's weapon in both hands and easily wrestling it away from him.

"Pretty good," Babbit said. "But I think it's time we renegotiate our contract." With that, he pulled his gun and shot Vasilek at point blank range. "You're fired," he said, as my former captor lurched and fell.

I shrieked, and that dissolved into a period of spasms and dry heaves. Babbit's body mostly blocked my view so I thankfully hadn't seen Vasilek go down. The sounds were bad enough, all wet and gurgly. I'd already had more than my share of violence and bloodshed, and I felt like I'd been pushed beyond my limits.

"Well, that's one problem I ain't gotta worry about no more," Babbit said, and then he turned to me. "Get up," he ordered, jabbing the toe of his boot into my stomach. "We gotta go."

Huh? I stared at him dumbly. I knew I'd heard right but it didn't compute. I was defenseless. Why didn't he just finish it already?

"That son of a bitch gave me an idea," he said. "No one will care that Mikhail Vasilek is dead but the whole world loves you because of those god-damn books. You know what that means?"

I thought so and it made me sick.

"It means I've got me a cute little hostage. We're gonna drive right on out of here. They'll come after us. I know that, but they'll back off when they realize I got company, especially once I make them understand I'll splatter you across the windshield if anyone gets too close, Should be clear sailing after that. They'll meet any demand I make. You ever been to Mexico? I hear it's nice this time of year."

You're insane, I thought, and surprised myself by saying it out loud.

"Maybe so," he replied, giggling and sounding like he'd gone completely around the bend. "But you're the only chance I've got. So," he waved the gun in my direction, "get on your feet and start walking."

"I can't," I said, trying and failing to even get into a sitting position. "You broke my arm."

"Bitch, I'm gonna break more than that if you don't do what I say."

I tried again but my right arm was useless and every move I made sent fresh jolts of pain up and down that side of my body. With tremendous effort I nearly made it to my knees and then collapsed back to the ground: trembling, sweating, crying, and not really caring what happened next.

"Damnit," Babbit shouted, hauling off and kicking me in the stomach and then the face. "You've got one more chance. Get up now or die right here."

I heard the click as he cocked his gun. Knowing it was all over, I closed my eyes and held my breath.

"Police! Drop your weapon and put your hands in the air!"

There were sounds of struggle along with a muffled curse, and by the time I dared open my eyes again, Babbit was on the ground, a cop in tactical gear cuffing his hands behind his back.

"Ms. Rhodes. Are you all right?"

I recognized the voice and turned to see Detective Zanetti coming my way. "Sorry we cut it so close," he said. "Let's get you out of here."

-54-

Six Weeks Later

"Sounds like you guys are feelin' pretty good tonight." Freddie Franco said as the spotlight tracked him from one side of the stage to the other. "I hope you've all been enjoying your time aboard Island Imagination."

The crowd cheered, and Megan leaned over and nudged me. "So what do you think so far?"

I stared at her and then looked down at my glass and the large pineapple spear poking out of the top. "That I still can't believe I'm here," I said. "It's been…" I shrugged then, suddenly overcome and at a loss.

"Wow." Megan smiled and toyed with the new strings of turquoise-colored beads in her hair. "I didn't mean for you to take that so seriously. I was only asking about Freddie. He's funny, right?"

"Oh, yeah," I said, flushing. "He's good." I meant it too. I'd liked him when we met him for dinner our first night onboard and I really was enjoying his show. I was just having a hard time staying focused.

A solid month and a half after the fact, nightmares about Clayton Babbit and Mikhail Vasilek were still a regular occurrence. They were troubling enough when I woke up in my own bed, sobbing and drenched in sweat. But somehow, this new setting of sunshine, sea air, and swim-up bars made me feel even more disconnected. Martin died on a cruise ship. It should have been me yet I was alive and well. Why? There were no answers, and I'd allowed Megan and Vicki to talk me into this vacation in part so I could begin to come to terms with that. It was working, I thought, but I knew I'd never be completely over the guilt or the hurt.

"Hey," Megan said, nudging me again. "He's talking about us."

"You might not be aware of this," Freddie Franco was saying, "but we've got a couple genuine celebrities here. I'm sure you've heard of this woman. Fresh off appearances on *The Today Show, FOX and Friends,* and *The Late Show with Stephen Colbert,* Ladies and Gentlemen, bestselling author Alex Rhodes is in the house!"

The showroom erupted in applause and I wanted to crawl under my seat. Instead, I smiled, waved, dropped my hand to my lap and discretely gave Freddie the finger.

"Did he see that?" I asked Megan.

"Well, he just winked at us so I would say yes."

"That's right," he continued once the noise subsided. "And one of the biggest reasons she's able to be with us is because of some heroic efforts by one of the NYPD's finest. Badly injured in the line of duty but here tonight, please make some noise for Detective Megan Lynch!"

The crowd cheered again and, to my amazement, Megan stood and, leaning on her cane, made an awkward bow and pirouette.

"I thought we'd agreed to keep a low profile," I said when she sat down again. "What's gotten into you?"

"Captain Morgan," she replied, picking up her glass and draining what little liquid remained. "I'm at his mercy. Now shut up and watch the show."

That seemed like good advice so I finished my own drink and settled in.

"We got any married folks here?" Freddie asked.

"Yeah? And how about honeymooners?

"Young love," he said, as some people hooted and whistled. "It's a beautiful thing. But old love sucks which is why I avoided it.

"That's right. I was married for a while. It didn't work out.

"Oh, don't give me that shit," he scoffed, responding to a chorus of sympathetic sounds. "It was for the best. And I'll tell you what it came down to. Irreconcilable differences. Anybody heard that phrase before?

"Yeah? You know what it means?

"I'm still trying to figure it out. It makes it sound like we both made mistakes and I suppose that's true enough. I never claimed to be perfect. I left the toilet seat up and squeezed the toothpaste tube in the middle. She screwed every guy in New York City so I guess it all balanced out.

"But hold on," he said, a hand raised. "I'm not being fair. She didn't screw everybody. She wouldn't have sex with me if she'd spent a year stranded on Aphrodisiac Island and I showed up with a hard on big enough to ride all the way home."

I heard Megan giggle. At some point, she must have signaled the waitress too because fresh drinks arrived at our table. "Thanks," I said but she shushed me.

"For the record," Freddie was saying. "I'm hung like a Pygmy gnat so I don't want any of you lovely ladies getting too excited.

"It's tough, though," he said, and I could see his indistinct figure pace the stage. "We've all got our quirks and sometimes it's hard to work things out. My wife used to like to play these fantasy games, and I'm sorry fellas, but I'm not talking about the ones involving fishnet stockings, thirty-weight motor oil, and a rubber chicken."

"Was he really married?" I whispered, nibbling an orange slice.

Megan shook her head. "When I interviewed him he told me there was an old flame he joked about but I think this routine is different. We can ask him later."

"I'm talkin' about the *what if* type fantasy games," Freddie went on. "Like what if you're stranded on a desert island and you can only take one person with you? Who would it be? No brainer, I'd tell her. I'll take anyone but you so I don't have to spend the rest of my life having these stupid conversations.

"And here's another one. What if you're stranded on an island and you can only have one store? That's easy too. Boats R Us. I'll buy me a one-seater kayak and paddle the hell away.

"But the one that really drove me crazy," Freddie said, stopping in the middle of the stage and sitting down right at the edge, no more than a dozen feet from Megan and me. "The stupidest what if of all? My wife loved this one and I'm sure, at some point, you've all been asked this same question. What if you're stranded on a desert island and... wait for it. " He hung his head like he couldn't believe what he was about to say. "You're stranded and you can only take ten albums with you. Which ones will they be?

"All right." He waved his arms in exasperation. "Stop right there. First of all, who plans ahead when it comes to being marooned? Knowing my luck, I'd wash up on some beach somewhere, I wouldn't have had the foresight to make the appropriate musical selections, and all I'd have with me would be Cheap Trick's greatest fucking hits.

"But I'm a good sport. I'll play along. Maybe things worked out my way. Right before I booked my doomed sunset cruise I went through my extensive music library and picked out the absolute perfect tunes for just such an occasion. Next question. Are they CDs? Can I use the reflective surfaces to signal for help or start a fire? Because otherwise they're pretty damn useless. This is a desert island, right? I don't see any random electrical outlets or stereo equipment laying around.

"Or, did I get really lucky?" Freddie asked. "Am I on Gilligan's Island and those poor bastards are still there?" He stood up and resumed pacing. "You remember that show, right? Worst thing ever on television? Seven people shipwrecked, including a professor. That genius invented a lie detector, a Geiger counter, shark repellant, a bicycle-powered washing machine, and nitroglycerine, yet somehow couldn't figure out how to tie some logs together to build a raft? Brilliant.

"Oh, I can picture it too. I'd be stuck there with those morons and one day the professor would come up to me. *Hey Freddie,* he'd say. *I've got some good news. I know you've been wanting to listen to your music. I made a CD player out of this coconut shell and some parrot intestine. The laser is constructed from a diamond I stole from one of Mrs. Howell's earrings. It's primitive but it should work. The next problem was a power supply. I designed a furnace. It's fueled by salt water and capable of generating the nearly eighteen hundred degrees necessary to melt sand. I used the resulting glass compound to make these solar panels. They should provide the sufficient electrical charge.*

"Wow," Freddie said, spreading his hands in apparent admiration. "That's amazing. So we're all still stranded in this God-forsaken place, probably forever, but we have tunes now. Is that what you're telling me?

"*Yes,* that dumbass professor would say. *And we still can't have sex with either of the hot women stuck here with us. Isn't that wonderful?"*

Freddie put a hand on his forehead. "That's probably about the time my ex-wife would show up because that's the sort of charmed life I lead. It's okay, though, because I've got a plan. First, I'd fire up that coconut shell CD player. Next, I'd pull out my cherished copy of U2's *How to Dismantle an Atomic Bomb*. Finally, I'd flip the solar panels over, reverse the flow of electricity, play the album backwards, learn how to make a bomb, and then I'd detonate that motherfucker and put us all out of our misery. It would be worth it so I'd never have to play that stupid game again.

"You guys have been awesome. My time is up. Enjoy the rest of your stay aboard the Island Imagination." Freddie took a bow and left the stage to cheers and enthusiastic applause.

"And here we go," he said, placing a plastic tray in the center of the table. "One Bahama Mama and one rum punch."

"And what's in your glass?" Megan asked.

"Iced tea."

"Really?"

"Yep. I'd gotten a little too fond of vodka. I may have mentioned something to that effect the first time we met."

"So, what?" Megan asked. "You've sworn off alcohol then?"

"I wouldn't go that far. I'm just working on that whole moderation thing." He turned to me. "So how'd you like the show?"

"It was great," I said. "Except for when you told everyone Megan and I were there. I could have done without that."

"Are you kidding? They loved you. And it could have been worse. I could have told them you were both single. Lots of hot dating prospects on a cruise ship."

"Oh, yeah," Megan said. "I don't know which one I found more attractive: the winner of yesterday morning's best chest hair contest, or the one last night that stuffed sixty-three cocktail olives into his mouth."

"That's what I'm sayin'. It's a bachelorette's paradise. By the way, when I suggested you go on a cruise someday I never thought you'd take me up on it, certainly not so soon."

"Me neither," Megan replied. "But I'm not cut out for desk work. Paper pushing gets very boring very fast. I decided to get away for a while. I talked to Alex and she said she could use a break from being America's sweetheart."

"I don't think that's how I put it."

"Whatever," Megan said. "Long story short, I looked you up and here we are."

"Well I think it's great," Freddie said. "I haven't been based out of Miami that long yet but I've gotten pretty familiar with the different ports of call. Let me know if you want a personal tour guide. I'd be happy to show you around."

"We may take you up on that," Megan said, looking at him but poking me under the table. I knew she thought he was interested but I wasn't. I didn't think he was my type, and I wasn't sure I was ready for anything like that anyway. Besides, I sort of had someone else in mind. Paul Zanetti had visited me twice in the hospital and, once I was home, he sent flowers and then called and asked if I'd like to go for coffee sometime. I hadn't committed but I'd certainly thought about it and was starting to come around to the idea. I wondered how Megan would feel about that, and I knew that was part of my hang-up.

"We've been discussing excursions," she told Freddie. "We haven't made any decisions yet, and obviously have some limitations. I'd say the zip line is definitely out."

"How's your leg?" Freddie asked. "I noticed you carry that cane more than you actually use it."

"I'm progressing. The doctors said I'm lucky to be alive. The bullet missed my femoral artery by three millimeters. I still lost a lot of blood but a tourniquet and quick response from a hotel guest saved my leg and probably my life."

"Any permanent damage?"

"My x-ray will never look the same again. The round carved a trench in my right femur on its way through. It still hurts and I've got the limp but all that will go away eventually. There shouldn't be any loss of mobility and, assuming I pass the physical, I can return to regular duty at the end of the month."

"That's good," he said, turning to me. "And how 'bout you? I thought I'd heard broken collarbone?"

"That and a separated shoulder."

He sucked in a breath. "That must have hurt like hell."

"Honestly," I said. "I don't really remember. I mean, there were a few very specific and very painful moments." I flashed on Clayton Babbit wielding what I now know was a solid steel bar with which he was fully prepared to bash my head in. "I'd rather not talk about those. Most of that night is a kind of blur. I was aware of everything that was happening. But now that it's over, it's like a series of weird snap shots in my mind and none of it seems real."

"It must have been an incredible ordeal. And that Vasilek guy was really killed right in front of you? Wait," Freddie slapped his forehead. "Don't answer that. You're on vacation, trying to get away from it all, and here I am asking all these horrible questions. I'm such an idiot."

"Hey, that's my line," I said, smiling. "And don't worry about it. Even when I try to forget, I get reminded whenever I go to use my right arm for anything."

"You're right-handed I assume?"

"Embarrassingly so. Put a toothbrush in my left hand and it becomes a deadly weapon. I almost took my own eye out this morning."

He chuckled. "That's pretty good. Ever think about going into comedy?"

"No thanks. I've never been one for the spotlight."

"You'd never know it the way you've been hitting the talk show circuit lately. You're really gettin' around."

"Now that's what a girl likes to hear. You're right, though. I'm like an STD."

"You really don't like it?"

"I'm learning to tolerate it. I think that's as good as it's going to get. I just want to write my books. You can keep the rest of the nonsense."

"Speaking of..." Freddie said, leaning forward. "When's the new one come out? I can't wait to read it."

"My publisher is pushing the release date up as much as possible. It will still be another couple months. It's done, though. Finally. I had to dictate the last few chapters because there was no way I could type with my arm in this damn sling. That was a strange experience. I never knew how scatter-brained I am until I tried to explain my thoughts to someone else. I'm used to writing something, deciding it stinks, and then reworking it until I get it the way I want. It never comes out right the first time. I guess I never realized how much revising I was doing until I had to do it through someone else. Never again. I'm steering clear of lunatics, maniacs, and killers from now on."

"Seems like a wise strategy," Freddie said. "How much longer before you can start using both arms again?

"Two more weeks and I can't wait."

"I bet. So am I allowed to ask a question about the new book?"

"No spoilers."

"No, no," he said. "I was just wondering if you made any changes based on what happened to you. You don't have to tell me if you don't want."

"There's nothing to tell. With the first two novels already out there, I was pretty well locked in to that storyline. I ended the third novel the same way I'd envisioned it all along. But, I did add an author's note and described where fact and fiction crossed paths. I didn't go into much detail on that. Vicki—she's my publisher—wants me to save it for the next book. I'm not so sure."

"I think she's right," Megan said. "That would be one hell of a story, especially if I was in it. Do me a favor, though. Make me a little taller."

"I don't take requests. I am spiteful, though. Tick me off and I'll turn you into a titless dwarf."

"Geez," Megan said. "That's cold. Give the girl some celebrity and the power goes right to her head."

"I'm sorry," I said, laughing in spite of myself. "I didn't mean that. These drinks must be stronger than I thought. I'm getting silly."

"Well, there's only one thing to do about that. We need another round."

"That's the problem with coming in here this time of night," Freddie said, looking around at the covered billiard table, the darkened bar and the half dozen empty tables. "We're not gonna get any service."

"That's okay," Megan said. "We said we wanted privacy and you picked a perfect spot. I don't mind walking a little ways. The fresh air will do me good." She stood and picked up the tray. "I'll be right back."

"Please, let me," Freddie said, beginning to rise.

"Nope. It's my turn. Well, I suppose we could send Alex but she'd never find her way back here."

"Says the titless dwarf," I muttered into my empty glass. "And no fruit this time. It's slowing me down."

"I've got another question," Freddie said when Megan was back and seated. "Just tell me to shut up if you don't want to talk about this stuff anymore."

I gave a one-shouldered shrug. "I don't think I'll ever be done talking about it. It's okay, though. It makes me appreciate how fortunate I am to be here."

"That's kind of what I was wondering," he said. "That Mikhail Vasilek guy died at that construction site, right?"

"Technically," said Megan, "he passed away at New York Presbyterian. In reality, he was dead before he hit the ground."

"Okay, so Alex and that other asshole were alone at that place." Freddie looked at me. "And weren't you tied up too?"

I nodded but didn't speak.

He turned back to Megan. "So how'd you rescue her? How'd you even know she was there?"

"We didn't," she said somberly. "We lost every trace of her trail as soon as Vasilek abandoned my car on the side of the road."

"Then how…?"

"I'd like to say it was brilliant police work. Really, we caught a break. He damn near killed me behind that hotel but his desperate acts led us to Alex later on."

"How?"

"He was recognized," Megan said. "We had an APB out. His picture and description were everywhere. A taxi driver spotted him a short ways from that work site. Vasilek had actually hailed the cab but then apparently changed his mind. The driver wasn't sure it was the right guy but thankfully called in a tip and we got there just in time."

"Amazing."

"It really was, and I'm so glad we already had units in the area."

"They'd been so concerned about me," I said, absently running a finger through the ring of moisture my glass left on the table top.

"What?" Freddie asked.

I looked up. "Babbit and Vasilek," I explained. "They were so worried someone would see and recognize me. They should have tried harder to stay out of sight too. Certainly Vasilek should have, and Babbit was the one that sent him out to the road. It was pretty dumb, considering. They didn't like each other and there was a lot going on. I guess they just got careless in the heat of the moment. Good thing too. Another few seconds and I would have been a goner. Thanks again, Megan." I raised my glass to her. "I owe you guys my life."

"You're paying for the cruise," she said. "I think that makes us even."

"So what will happen to Clayton Babbit?" Freddie wanted to know.

"That," Megan replied, "depends on the effectiveness of our judicial system. He killed Mikhail Vasilek. That part is cut and dry. As for the rest," she shrugged. "We have to see if we can compile enough circumstantial evidence to make a case. I'm told it's doubtful we'll ever be able to tie him directly to the Deepwater disaster. But, he did plenty of other bad stuff too. Vasilek obviously won't be testifying against him but we do have his confession and Babbit is implicated. He also had a business partner, a guy named Louie, and we're putting the screws to him. Once we apply enough pressure, he'll fold."

"You sound confident."

"I am," Megan said. "Clayton Babbit is a shit, and no one is going to go too far out of their way to protect him."

"So you are predicting a happy ending?"

She gazed at me. "I suppose that depends on your point of view. And now," she said, standing and swaying slightly. "I think I'll retire. Alex, do you know how to get back to the room?"

Freddie saved me the embarrassment of admitting that I wasn't sure. "This place is a maze," he said. "I'll get her where she needs to go."

Megan thanked him, picked up her glass and wandered off.

"Beautiful night," he said later, when he and I were on the ninth floor deck, leaning against the railing and staring out at the wide, dark expanse of the Caribbean.

"Mmmm." I agreed, reluctant to say more.

Once Megan had left us alone, I'd noticed Freddie's looks had gotten longer and more frequent. It seemed like he was building up to something. I couldn't read his face, and I hoped such a wonderful evening would not have to end with me giving him the brush-off.

We were both silent for a while and then he cleared his throat. *Here it comes,* I thought, stiffening.

"I don't mean to pry," he said, turning to me. "But there's something I've been thinking about. It's personal, but I hope you don't mind if I ask."

"And what's that?" I immediately relaxed, smiling to myself because I already knew.

"Well," he said, fiddling with the buttons on his shirt. "I was just wondering… um… how much can you actually see?"

I breathed a sigh of relief, and then I started to tell him.

Blind Switch is a work of fiction. Some well known organizations, agencies, offices, and institutions are mentioned but the characters and related incidents are products of the author's imagination. Any resemblance to actual events or persons, living or dead, is purely coincidental. The 2010 Deepwater Horizon disaster, however, was only too real. The sabotage scenario that preceded the explosion was invented for the sake of this novel and has no basis in fact.

Author's note:

As mentioned in the disclaimer, the characters in *Blind Switch* are entirely fictional with one notable exception. Alex Rhodes and I conspicuously have much in common, gender notwithstanding. I've been legally blind since the age of seven. I manage fine, but deal with a lot of the same practical issues described in this book. I can't read facial expressions even close up, and it's a good thing I don't drive because I'd lose my car keys every time I put them down. I'd also become a weapon of mass destruction if I ever actually got behind the wheel. Thankfully, I have never been on the run or had to evade a killer. I have, however, spent the past forty plus years trying to explain to friends, family members, and the occasional stranger just how much I can and cannot see. I'm sorry but I've never been terribly successful in that endeavor. By creating Alex Rhodes and attempting to show you the world through her eyes, I hope I've provided a bit more clarity to what can be a rather blurry subject matter. If you'd like more information on me and my novels please subscribe to my newsletter by visiting michaelsova.com, or drop me a line at michaelsovabooks@echoes.net.

About the Author:

Michael Sova is the author of the suspense novels *A Shot at Redemption* and *Parlor City Paradise,* and the football-themed cookbook *21 Sundays of Fantastic Football Food: Celebrating the Foods and Follies of Professional Football.* He lives in New York where he is currently at work on his next book.

Made in the USA
Columbia, SC
22 October 2021